Earth Against Earth

Peter Apps

Published in the United Kingdom
TAUP UK
Sheerness
Kent

enquiries@taup.uk

Demetrius' Tale (Prologue)

Demetrius walked contentedly along the track from his Master's workshop to his mansion. It was rare for a slave to be truly happy even when his masters were as kind and as gentle as his present ones. He was not beaten because of his many mistakes. He slept in a room fit for a king instead of on straw in the stable. He helped to prepare wonderful food and was even expected to sit with his masters and eat with them but it was all too new.

They were rich, powerful and able to do things that he thought only Gods could do while he felt like a little child unable to carry out the simplest task without being taught. The real problem was that although it was easy for them to say that he was no longer a slave, it was far harder for Demetrius to believe it when he was so dependent on them.

Mind you, there was so much to learn. A lot had changed in the two and a half thousand years since he was born. He understood that something called electricity ran this place, providing heat, light, and a host of other things he barely understood. It powered the translator he wore round his neck that allowed him to talk in foreign tongues and was slowly answering the questions whirling around his head.

For now there was time before he needed to start preparing the evening meal. Still fascinated by them he thought he would wander down to see if there were any four wheeled monsters - cars roaring past on the paved road. He drove a small one under his Master's - his friend's supervision and it was exhilarating to go careering around the field faster than a galloping horse. Now that he was no longer scared of them, he grinned sheepishly when someone noticed his fascination and called him a 'petrol-head', just beginning to understand what it meant. But at times they still seemed like monsters.

It was all so different to his previous home.

Demetrius barely remembered his parents though he did remember being hungry all the time. He had been exchanged for grain to feed his other brothers and sisters and set to work on his owner's farms. The work was hard but at least he was fed. He was strong, athletic and, for a time, the farmer's favourite especially when he accepted special training to develop his running skills. His owner saw him as a contender in the Olympic Games and indeed his fame was already spreading with his victories in local events. His owner would have freed him to compete, adding to his own status by association with a Hero of the Games.

Demetrius could have ended up rich, enjoying a comfortable life on his own farm if he had not fallen awkwardly and broken his leg. The bone healed well but he was left with a slight limp that would take years to go and it meant the end of his training. His owner lost interest in him and sent him to the market to be sold on.

There was another young man in the cage beside him. He was tall and well muscled yet there was also something soft about him, as if he came from a rich or noble family. There seemed to be something wrong with his left arm as he was constantly rubbing it, stretching it as if trying to relieve some ache and he was obviously mad. He muttered quietly at times. It was in a strange language and then he would nod as if he had received a reply.

The other youth seemed friendly, greeted Demetrius cordially enough and they talked quietly. The stranger looked nervously at the guards with their whips and swords but he had an air of confidence about him that only wealthy free men possessed. His skin was so fair that he must have come from some distant Northern place and he called himself Dave, a strange, foreign sounding name

Demetrius was hopeful that he was handsome enough and clever enough to be bought as a household slave but it was still a frightening time until he found out just how cruel or kind his new master would be. Dave on the other hand seemed impatient rather than nervous. He might be scared of the guards but there was often anger in his eyes rather than fear and Dave even seemed to hate being naked. While he submitted to the odd passer-by scrutinising him, there was no acceptance and oddly, neither was there rebellion. He reminded Demetrius of an actor in the theatre, playing a part but one that he did not like much. It was all very strange.

It became stranger still when two foreigners appeared and seemed to take an interest in both of them. It was unusual for customers to arrive so late in the day when stock was at it's lowest, and the market was at its hottest and smelliest.

Once again Dave seemed to be play acting as he put on a show to attract them. Even his arm seemed better but it was what he said that intrigued Demetrius.

"No promises but these are the people we want." he said, "Strut your stuff and you could be free in a month." Demetrius did not believe Dave but what harm could it do?

"Why bother?" Demetrius asked, "Does it matter who we're sold to or what we do?"

"Normally no, I suppose." Dave conceded, "And if we were chained up we couldn't do much but we're in this cage. Supposing you saw this beautiful woman looking for a bed slave. Wouldn't you try to attract her before the fat old slob holding a castration knife arrived?"

Demetrius grinned, "It would be the lady's family who'd have us castrated but I understand what you mean. You haven't been a slave for long, have you?"

"No," Dave admitted, "but let's see if we can be sold as a pair. I'll look after you."

Demetrius was a little curious to know what Dave was up to even if he did not believe his wild promise about being free. He was not even sure if he wanted to be. He possessed no money, nowhere to go so what would be the point. His previous owner had promised to teach him how to run a farm but the promise ended with his broken leg. Yet Demetrius did not doubt that Dave expected these two men and he even sensed Dave's satisfaction, as if a plan was coming together.

He stood beside Dave, flexing his muscles to show them off and even, a little cheekily for Demetrius, advising Dave how to stand a little better to show off his assets. They were both too old to attract men looking for boys to play with but Demetrius even considered it worthwhile to discreetly stroke himself to show off his eagerness. Dave looked shocked at the idea that he do the same. Nevertheless he reluctantly followed suit.

However when they got close, it was obvious that the men were more interested in muscle development than anything else. Demetrius was a little concerned when they pointed some object at them but since Dave did not mind, he relaxed.

"According to our scanner, you broke your leg recently." one of the foreigners said, "Does it trouble you much?"

"No Master." Demetrius replied, "I've got a slight limp but it's still getting better."

He wondered how the foreigner knew about his leg and what a scanner was but they turned their attention to Dave, "You have muscle strain." one said, "It will heal."

"Yes Master. Thank you." Dave said in an unusually meek tone of voice.

Another thing Demetrius noticed. Dave's madness was gone. Before he had almost been listening out for his imaginary voice but it seemed to have gone silent.

Demetrius watched as the two foreigners negotiated with the slave trader, then approached them again. They passed two collars through the cage.

"Put these on." one of them said, "Disobey us and they will cause terrible pain. They can even kill you. If you cooperate then we'll remove them when we get you safe."

Demetrius saw the same anger, resentment but for once, a little fear in Dave's eyes as he complied. Yet he did not seem surprised at how light they were or the peculiar locking device. With a curt instruction to follow their new Masters, they were let out of the cage. The two men were in no hurry as they strolled through the market examining the goods on the few stalls still open. While Dave was annoyed at being left standing beside the table while the men relaxed with a final glass of wine, Demetrius accepted that little luxuries like that were not for them.

Finally they left the town, trudging on for about an hour. Dave seemed to be tensing up more as if he was preparing for something.

"Are you thinking of running?" Demetrius asked, "They don't have bows and arrows or slings. They don't have horses and even with my limp, I don't think they can run fast enough to catch us."

"No!" Dave replied, "Not while we're wearing these collars. Believe them. These things can kill us."

"Are they wizards, then?" Demetrius asked.

Dave grinned, "Maybe but my friends and I know more tricks than them. We're just waiting until the job is done."

Every time Dave spoke he left more questions than he answered. Demetrius thought it best to stay silent for now.

The two men turned off the road and led the way towards some hills before stopping.

"Don't be alarmed but we're going to tie your hands and blindfold you." one of them said, "We're not going to harm you. It's just that you might see a few things that could frighten you until you know us better."

Demetrius nodded resignedly. Dave lowered his eyes and also nodded but Demetrius briefly saw the triumph. Talk about being free was one thing but Demetrius was sure that Dave was planning something and it was more than just running. He did not like the mystery. If something happened, it would mean trouble for other slaves whether they were directly involved or not.

Once they were secured, a short chain was connected between

their collars. Demetrius felt another fixed to the front of his collar and he was led forward. He was jerked back slightly until Dave meekly followed him and allowed a little slack in the chain.

The texture of the ground changed. Was he indoors? The floor was smooth and cold; like marble and judging by the distance they walked it must be a massive building yet he did not know of anything like it in the area. He could no longer feel the sun, there was no breeze and the air seemed different.

Suddenly the chain pulling him went slack and Demetrius felt a restraining hand on his chest. There was no warning so Dave walked into him. As Demetrius' hands brushed against him, Dave jerked back in alarm before relaxing.

It was only a small movement as if Dave remembered just in time that slaves did not worry about such things. Their masters would not have seen anything; only Demetrius who was getting used to Dave, had felt it.

The blindfold, handcuffs and collar were removed, He turned and watched as Dave's bonds were removed. Dave stepped into the room with a nudge from their captors then the door swung shut leaving them alone.

Demetrius looked around, impressed with the luxury. There were two comfortable looking beds stacked one on top of the other. There was a table and chairs with a second door at the back of the cell.

The main door of the cell opened and a boy of about fifteen entered. He beckoned them through the second door and proceeded to show them how to use the toilet and shower before leaving to return with bowls of delicious smelling soup.

Being a good slave, Demetrius accepted all that was happening without asking questions. On the other hand he could see Dave's irritation at being locked up and his amused contempt at being shown how to use the facilities in the other room.

Demetrius wanted to say something to calm Dave but did not know what. Instead he sat down to enjoy the meal. Even Dave was impressed when he tried it and he seemed much more cheerful as he ate. Just as they were finishing their meal, the cell juddered and they felt a slight vibration in the floor. When Demetrius saw Dave's quiet satisfaction return, his own fears vanished. The vibration continued and just became part of the background.

"Look at that lamp." Demetrius said, "It burns in that chamber but there's no oil, no wick and no smoke. They must be wizards."

"No they're not wizards." Dave replied, "You could learn how to make it work. They're just men who have learnt a lot."

Dave paused before coming to a decision.

"There's a lot to explain," Dave said, "but I must warn you, you'll have to make a choice. I can return you to where we met. You'll have money to buy your farm, all this will end and you will only be able to think of it as a dream.

"If you wish, you can stay with me. If you do stay with me then you can't imagine how your life will change, and believe me, it'll be an incredible adventure. Think about it."

"I'll stay with you." Demetrius said without any hesitation, "My last Master made me spend my time training me to run well and act as a servant. I know nothing about running a farm. I would like to serve you and maybe you can teach me what I need to know."

"If you come with me you'll come as a friend not as a slave." Dave said, "Understand this, if you stay with us then you'll always have food and shelter but you could have the farm you talked about when we were locked in that cage, instead."

"I met the great Socrates once." Demetrius said, "It was after I won a race in Athens. I told him that I wanted to compete in the Olympics and that my Master would free me if I was good enough to qualify. Socrates asked me whether I was free already if I was doing what I wanted. I think that I would like to follow you, so slave or friend I'd be doing what I wanted."

"Like I say, your life will change." Dave replied, "You can take your chances with those men if you choose. I won't stop you."

"It's all fine talk." Demetrius said, "We're both slaves because they have the whips, swords and magic collars. If you can defeat them then you can defeat me so I'll still be what you want me to be. I hope that you succeed because you seem different but maybe you're just a thief planning to rob our new masters."

"We helped some people and in return they told us a story." Dave began, "The trouble was the story was incomplete and we have to finish it for ourselves. Do you understand?"

"I think so." Demetrius answered.

"Good, you said that you were sold by your parents but many become slaves because they're captured by brigands and sold in the next city. Is that right?"

Demetrius nodded.

"It does happen." he said.

"Well you and I are part of a larger city that we call Earth.

Brigands are capturing our people and taking them to their own city and it's been going on for a long time."

"We were told that it was happening but we were not told where their city is. I agreed to be taken to help find the way there. We're in a ship. My friends can't follow it because they might be seen but they can follow me. My arm aches a bit because it has something that helps them and I can use it to talk with my friend, Stuart."

"And you're a more powerful wizard because the thing hides from them by making it seem like you've hurt your muscle."

"Partly. It's non metallic and operates on a higher frequency than they use. I did strain my muscle and the damage gives them something to find so they don't look further."

Demetrius stared at him with a puzzled look on his face.

"I didn't understand a word of what you said."

"You've got the general idea." Dave said, "The point is that we're plotting the ship's course and we think we know where it might be going."

"And then your army will attack this city, destroy it and rescue us."

"Not quite." Dave grinned, "A door will open and we'll have seconds to run through it."

Demetrius laughed.

"I was beginning to believe you." he said, "Even if you did find a secret way out of the city, their soldiers would track us down. I still don't want to be punished as a runaway."

"Trust me." Dave said, "No matter how frightening it might seem, if you see me running for a door then follow. Once you're through the door, you're safe."

"More wizardry?" Demetrius asked, "A magic door that'll make sure I'm not branded as a runaway?"

Dave nodded.

"That's right." he said, "We call our captors, aliens, not masters."

"Aliens?" Demetrius said, "If you were told about these… aliens, why weren't you told where their city was?"

"Ships leave trails like we leave footprints." Dave explained, "Sometimes it's called a wake but we call it a radiation signature. Our friends picked up the signature while visiting but did not follow it."

"Why not?"

"Because it did not affect their city and left us to deal with it."

"A noble could live in this room." Demetrius said, "Yet you're uncomfortable as if you're used to something even better. I don't understand you but if you're telling me the truth then I'll follow you, Master."

"Don't call me Master and act as if I'm just another slave. Remember that for now, I'm just that, locked up in this prison like you." Dave laughed, "God, I hope this trip's not too long. I tell you one thing, I'll never volunteer for anything again."

"Why do you complain?" Demetrius asked, "We've got food, water, shelter and beds. What more do you want.?"

"Clothes would do for a start. Knowing that the door's not going to open and some dirty old pervert is going to start groping me. I don't like being handled like a piece of meat."

"If I'm to be your slave then you can handle me as much as you like." Demetrius said, "What's the difference?"

Dave used a finger to draw an imaginary line around his own waist then two more halfway down his thighs.

"Once we're out of here, no one touches you inside those lines unless you invite them to. Outside of those lines you might get a friendly pat on the shoulders or a hug but if you make it clear that you don't like it then they should stop. Do you understand?"

"No Dave, I don't." Demetrius said sadly, "I'm just a crippled slave. I can't own a farm because I couldn't work it properly. I only know how to run and I can't do that any more. If I can't serve someone what else can I do?"

"Trust me." Dave said.

There was something in Dave's voice that Demetrius believed and he just nodded.

For Dave it was a trip of boredom and isolation. There was no sense of time, the cell was drab and bare with a hard, uncomfortable bunk.

For Demetrius the room was part of a palace belonging to a wizard. The electric light amazed him, the plumbing in the bathroom intrigued him. The bed was sheer luxury compared to the hard floor he was used to.

Dave found the meals dull and monotonous while Demetrius was delighted that his belly was full and he was not doing any work. It was like a holiday. He found Dave's boredom and lack of fear comforting while Dave's reaction to Demetrius' excitement at his surroundings, swung between irritation and amusement.

In his turn Demetrius was puzzled by Dave's secretiveness when he attended to his bodily functions. Dave was not bad looking and looked like a human but Demetrius began to wonder whether he was a demon or another kind of monster. Certainly no male he knew would he ashamed of displaying his pent up feelings let alone relieving them in another's company.

Dave certainly regarded himself a free man yet refused to take advantage of Demetrius. It left Demetrius confused. Should he be insulted because Dave found him so repulsive or flattered that Dave held him in such high esteem. Demetrius did not understand that Dave thought in terms of straight and gay, and that Dave was uncomfortable with Demetrius' assumption that Dave was entitled to use him.

It did not help that Demetrius continued to see himself as junior to Dave and therefore expected to be used and it was the one part of their relationship that could have caused real bad feeling. However, with little else to do they spent a lot of time talking about their lives and they came to see how different their backgrounds were.

The last time Stuart spoke with Dave via the translator embedded in his arm, he told him that their cell was not monitored in any way so Dave found himself talking freely about his life. Demetrius listened spellbound especially when Dave gave up trying to explain that Earth was not the whole of existence but a tiny speck in an immense universe.

Dave described the portal as a magical door that opened onto mystical lands. It was far easier than explaining that it could fold multi-dimensional space allowing them to travel immense distances through time, space and parallel universes. Instead of space stations, Resolution and Endeavour became forts defending his home against the savage hordes beyond, and his home, 21st century Earth, became a distant city across the sea.

Demetrius half believed the stories because it was so obvious that Dave believed them. If he did indeed come from such a mystical land then it would explain why there was something about Dave that was not quite right. In the meantime, it did not matter. They were still locked up and completely at the mercy of their new owners.

They were both startled when the slight vibration in the floor suddenly stopped. Dave became even more impatient until a strange looking object appeared and floated before them. Dave spoke in his madman's tongue and to Demetrius' surprise the thing replied in the same tongue. They seemed to be arguing before the thing flickered and a necklace now dangled from it. Dave took the necklace and handed it to Demetrius before turning back to the object and talking to it again.

To Demetrius' surprise, he found that he could understand them.

"It's a mistake," the thing was saying, "but I'd probably do the same, especially after sharing a cell with him for a couple of days. You're still in orbit and this seems to be some sort of base. They're very sloppy. The two crewmen have just left the ship on automatic and gone on shore leave in a shuttle. There's just a couple of kids to look after the prisoners. We picked up something about quarantine so we've got time to get you out of there. One thing. The ship's got ten cells and each one has got two people in it. We can't rescue them all."

"I know." Dave said, "It was a mistake telling Demetrius here but I couldn't just abandon him like his old Master."

"You're just a big old softy," the thing said. Whatever it was, it sounded kind and willing to accept him so Demetrius remained more puzzled than worried. So what was new, he had spent the last few days in that state, in fact, ever since he met Dave.

"There's no shuttle activity at the moment," the thing said, "and there's a large cargo bay where we can materialise a portal. The cell doors are not locked, just latched so James is going to do his heroic rescue thing. You're just going to vanish without a trace."

"What does it mean, vanish?" Demetrius asked nervously.

"In the eyes of our captors, one moment we're here, the next we're gone." Dave explained, "We'll be stepping through a door not vanishing in a puff of smoke so don't worry. Did you understand the rest?"

Demetrius giggled.

"Most of what you say still sounds like your story. Your friends are going to board this ship while the crew are ashore and open the door to this room for us. We then use your magical door to escape to a land that our owners can never find."

"Just follow me." Dave said, "I'm going to run away from danger, not towards it."

"Now that I can understand." Demetrius laughed, "I'll be a good slave and follow two steps behind you."

As the probe vanished the two prisoners settled back for another wait. Demetrius assumed that the magic show was over and they were waiting for their masters. He enjoyed the story that Dave was telling and did not doubt that he was a skilled magician who would be well treated while he entertained their owners. Maybe Demetrius could become his assistant.

It was a scary moment for Demetrius when the door finally opened and a stranger stood there. To his surprise, Dave gave a huge sigh of relief and sprang to his feet.

"At last." he snapped, "Come on Demetrius. Don't just stand there, James. Lead the way."

To Demetrius eyes, the stranger was dressed most strangely. His arms and legs were wrapped in some material, unlike the tunics the men he knew preferred. It was multi-coloured yet the colours were drab greens and browns. His black heavy footwear seemed most uncomfortable.

Unaware of the curiosity his fatigues were causing James turned and strode off with Dave eagerly following and a far more nervous Demetrius bringing up the rear. When he saw the portal he finally believed that Dave was telling the truth. They approached it from the rear and Demetrius could not see anything except a slight shimmer. The closest notion he could think of was the way the view shimmered as hot air rose from the ground. As they walked around it he saw a thin ring hovering above the deck and then from the front he saw a huge tunnel. It would take him some time to fully understand that the portal was pushed through a fold in space. It was the same principal as how a pin could be pushed through a folded piece of paper, joining two distant points on the surface. What did matter was that Demetrius did finally believe that he was going to follow Dave through a magic door.

Even so he hesitated before entering the portal airlock staring at the cramped little chamber he was entering, liking the sound of the hatch door closing behind them, even less. Dave led the way, James brought up the rear and as another hatch in front swung open Demetrius turned to look back but found the view blocked by James' bulk. He half listened to Dave's warning without it registering on his mind. As he turned back he saw that Dave was already through the hatch and not wanting to be separated from the one constant in this mad adventure charged through after him.

It took him moments to realise that he was no longer touching the floor before realising that he was spinning helplessly with no sense of up or down and completely out of control. He struck a wall and as he tried to struggle to his feet he drifted away at an angle.

It was not a complete accident that he drifted through the hatch into the central chamber. As the portal fully materialised, it displaced a volume of air and Demetrius was caught up in an air current through the hatch as the pressure equalised. Dave or Stuart would have been able to grab the hatch frame to stop themselves but Demetrius was completely out of control.

"Help!" he screamed.

"Calm down." Dave called back, "Spread your arms and legs as far apart as possible."

The spin slowed enough for Demetrius to start looking around. He saw that Dave and another youth were flying after him. They landed on the wall absorbing their momentum as they allowed their legs to buckle beneath them and anchoring their feet under a rail.

"Relax. Let yourself go limp." Dave called out, "Whatever you do, don't grab anything."

Demetrius tried to comply and as hands grabbed him so the spin stopped and he swung round so that he could see the surface just below his feet.

"Bend your knees." Dave ordered, "When I say, go limp again."

"Now." he yelled a few moments later.

Demetrius tried to obey but he could not succeed completely. His leg muscles recoiled and he started to lift away from the surface.

"That's OK." The other young man yelled, "You're moving a lot slower and you've got very little spin. We've got to get back to the other side anyway so we'll catch you there."

The journey back across the great cavern took far longer. Demetrius relaxed as he watched the stranger drift in a similar fashion beside him.

"I'm Stuart." he said, "Welcome to the space station Resolution. We're in an orbit around the sun at a similar distance to the planet Pluto but at right angles to the solar plane. Don't worry if you don't understand. You'll learn."

"Yes Master." Demetrius instinctively replied, "I mean, are you my Master now or is it still Dave or is it your father, James?"

Stuart laughed.

"James is a friend not my father just as Dave is," Stuart replied, "I'm in charge here but it doesn't stop them arguing with me. You're not a slave any more. You have same rights as everyone else and you can call me Stuart."

"You may think me foolish but I want to be somebody's slave." Demetrius said, "My father was free but he sold me because we were starving. A kind master makes sure I have a full belly."

They were approaching a bulkhead again and this time Stuart, and Dave who had pulled himself around the handrails, brought him to a standstill.

They helped Demetrius through the hatch into the portal

chamber as it de-materialised again.

Seeing Demetrius look of disappointment, Stuart said, "It's OK. We're not sending you back. We're taking you to our home. Do you want the ground to be under your feet again?"

"Oh yes please Master." Demetrius replied then seeing the frown on Stuart's face added, "Please give me time to understand your ways."

As he looked around the workshop, Demetrius finally thought that he was almost beginning to understand his surroundings. Dave changed into a T-shirt and jeans while Stuart chose a button up shirt. To Demetrius eyes the clothes were weird, and uncomfortable looking. Stuart helped him into a one piece garment, all arm and leg coverings but it was loose fitting and did not feel too bad. Dave and Stuart also covered their feet and looked apologetic when they realised that there was none for Demetrius.

"Don't worry, Master, I mean Dave." Demetrius answered, "I'm still dressed like you so I don't look like a slave."

Once outside a dirt track looked familiar. He recognised cattle grazing in the fields and there were more trees than he had ever seen before. Although not raining at the moment, it was a showery day making everything so green and the ground was soft beneath his feet. He was glad of a covering for there was a cool breeze. He could see that he was in a new land but at least they farmed like his people did, they travelled tracks like his people did so he was not completely lost.

Demetrius was beginning to learn a lesson that his new companions had already learnt; too many shocks and surprises have a numbing effect and the amazing starts to seem ordinary. If he had been told that he was now on Mount Olympus, home of the gods he would have accepted it. Indeed the explanation would make more sense than some others that Dave was trying to give him. He listened as Stuart teased Dave about the indignities he was subjected to during his confinement and put up with.

"So what do you think, Demetrius?" Stuart suddenly asked him, "Would Dave have made a good slave?"

Demetrius was aware of the fun in Stuart's question and tried to answer appropriately.

"A master would have fun breaking him of his airs and graces..." he paused, remembering not to call Stuart, Master before continuing, "I don't know if he would have lasted for long if he been set to work in the fields. He has muscles but they're soft from easy living."

"I work out three times a week," Dave retorted indignantly, "and I swim nearly every day. I'm fit."

"Ah yes, but like all wealthy freemen you complain when your muscles ache and try to rest. Slaves have to keep going."

"Humph." Dave snorted, "Maybe slaves should keep their mouths shut."

Demetrius looked at him anxiously, wondering if he was in trouble but his other two companions were laughing happily and as he watched Dave relented and joined in the laughter.

They arrived at an odd looking villa. It was different to any building that Demetrius had ever seen before but it definitely looked as if people lived there. Then he had second thoughts. The massive openings in the walls would make the place draughty and uncomfortable but then he saw that the openings were filled with something. Mica? Glass? He could not be sure.

He was idly thinking about what the great Socrates would make of his experiences when a thought, generated by the translator, told him that Socrates died many generations ago.

More magic, he thought to himself, *Old men talk about living in better times. I'm doing it.*

They entered and were greeted by more people. Demetrius stood meekly against a wall waiting to be acknowledged until Stuart took him into a room with more furniture than he had ever seen before and told to… no, he really was invited to sit down.

"OK!" said James, "Let me introduce everyone. Firstly, Stuart. He's in charge nowadays. We explore using the portal and he knows more about it than anyone. Then there's Dave who you've also met. If you're in a tough spot and need help then call on him.

"I'm James. I used to be a soldier. My job seems to be making sure that these young idiots don't kill themselves in some harebrained venture. I was born nearly seventy years ago but like you, I've made a jump in time so to me it was only thirty five years ago.

"You haven't met Brian." James continued, "Brian is Stuart's… er, companion. He should be back later."

"Are there no women in your household?" Demetrius asked then greatly daring added, "James."

We live in different places. I'll explain later but let me finish the introductions.

"I'm sorry for my rudeness, Master." Demetrius said softly.

"No, you weren't rude. You probably think that keeping house is woman's work. I used to believe that too but for your own safety, I suggest that you don't mention it in front of the women here."

Demetrius thought of the stories that were told about Sparta and how they did not marry until their thirties. Maybe these people had developed similar attitudes.

He was pulled back to the real world by James saying, "This is Gable. He was born on a distant planet. You can call it Great City for now but like you, he grew up on a farm. He'll probably be the best one to look after you and get you used to our world, city, whatever you want to call it for now.

"Finally, there's Richard. He's Stuart's father. He and Gable are historians. They help us when we need it. Going back to your previous question, he's happily married and his wife treats Gable like a second son. You'll meet Mavis on one of her shopping trips through the portal and she'll feed you up, as well. Any questions so far?"

"Did I go to sleep for over two thousand years, James?" Demetrius used James' name more confidently that time.

"No, but travelling through the portal can have the same effect."

"Who will be my overseer?"

"No one." James replied, "You've been warned that your first job is to decide if you still want to stay with us. If you do then you'll have a lot to learn. Gable found even the simplest of jobs needed relearning. It sounds as if the translator's already started feeding you information so you're off to a good start."

"The translator is the necklace you gave me, isn't it, Master?" Demetrius asked.

James nodded.

"I'm sorry for being so stupid but surely I'm expected to work so someone has to be giving me my orders. I still don't understand who it is."

"Dave." Stuart interrupted, "It's your first night back. What do you want to eat?"

"Curry washed down with lager." Dave replied, "Make it a vegetable one if you insist but I want it hot, spicy and not tasting of parsnips. I don't know what they served us with on that ship but that's what it tasted like and they served it for every fucking meal. On top of that we only had water to drink"

"Gable, show Demetrius how to order the takeaways will you, please?" Stuart said, "I'll cycle down to the shop and get some cans."

In spite of the translator, Stuart's instructions were gibberish. Demetrius watched as Gable picked up a box, prodded it then spoke into it. It reminded him of Dave's mad rantings in the cage but Gable was definitely giving it instructions and he thought he heard it answer back. Satisfied, Gable sat back down leaving Demetrius to wonder when they would start cooking the food David wanted.

Richard sat next to Demetrius, asking about farming implements, weapons and other day to day things. At least Demetrius understood the conversation even if he could not answer Richard's more technical questions though he could describe the blacksmith's shop well.

Stuart arrived back carrying bags and headed for the kitchen before returning with a can each. Demetrius watched as the others casually pulled the ring on the top and put it to their mouths. He copied them and found himself drinking a foul tasting liquid that almost seemed alive in his mouth.

At least it was foul tasting until he realised it contained alcohol like the wine he was more used to. He found the tickling in his mouth was refreshing and it was not tart or sour like the leftovers he and his fellow slaves were given. He was still uncomfortable sitting there while his Masters busied themselves in the kitchen and even served him with a plate of hot food.

Demetrius cautiously dipped his finger in it and tasted it before grabbing for his drink to cool the burning from the hot spices.

"This is Dave's treat." Stuart laughed, "Give it a go but I'll find you something else if you can't manage it. Now you were asking about work. Do you understand that your first job is to understand how we do things here or do you think that you could have organised this meal for Dave?"

Stuart had made his point and Demetrius began a bewildering few weeks adapting to his new life.

The translator helped him. They were alien devices developed on the planet Terzon, designed to tune in on the speech areas of the brain and learn the language. They could also pick up electronic transmissions and, on Earth, could connect themselves to the internet, trying to answer in manageable quantities of information the unspoken questions that flashed through Demetrius' mind. Stuart and the others found that they stimulated their minds as they were forced to process the data being supplied.

When he lived in Ancient Greece he wondered about philosophers notions that the Earth was round but did not understand how it was possible. Now he was beginning to grasp concepts of gravity and a Universe that seemed larger every time he thought about it. He also accepted that it spread out in directions that he did not yet understand, accepted he had travelled in time but he did not understand the concept of dimensions, yet.

Using a spoon to eat the curry on his first night took most of his concentration and like Gable, he struggled with a knife and fork. Wearing shoes caused him another problem. They always felt rigid and uncomfortable.

He remained scared of television until Stuart took a video of Dave and played it back to him, proving that Dave was not trapped in the box.

On one occasion he was taken through the portal to Terzon. Doctors looked at his leg and did things to it. Ultrasound was another concept that he understood existed but did not understand what it was. He only knew that his leg got steadily stronger especially when he did the exercises he was shown.

Some things he learned faster than Gable. He understood the concept of money and how shops operated. Gable's home world had neither, just storerooms administered by the elders but even Demetrius found the village shop an enormous, bewildering place.

The village where Stuart grew up and now based his operations had prospered for centuries as a stopping point on a drovers trail, as well being the focal point for local farms. It still hospitably accepted strangers passing through but with only one road connecting it to the outside world it was very insular. Even after twenty years in the post the village parson was still considered to be the new man and referred to locally as 'that new parson'. Inhabitants worked in neighbouring towns, holidayed abroad but there was still a strong community spirit.

There had been so many strange visitors and events involving Brian and his team, the locals no longer believed their cover story that they were investigating solar particles from the sun. Dave and Stuart used the local pub and, like many young men, they sometimes got a little drunk, letting things slip. Neither did their incredible ability to speak to any tourist, no matter what country they were from, come from solar particles.

Everyone knew that Stuart and Brian were gay. The consensus was that they did not flaunt it so what they did in private was their own affair and it did provide a rich source of gossip though it was better that James and Dave were decidedly straight. Despite everything, when Demetrius went into the village alone for the first time, nervous and unsure of himself, still terrified of the occasional car or tractor roaring past he was easily accepted even though he scandalised Bill the pub landlord.

Greatly daring he asked for a sweet wine like the rich drank back in his old home. That had been all right but he asked for water to dilute it as they did. Of course, in the twenty-first century it immediately classed him as an alien.

"That's exploration." Stuart laughed when Demetrius told him, "You can't take anything for granted. That's why Brian's given it up."

Brian had invented the portal driven by his scientific curiosity but as vague ideas became hard plans, he saw it as a way of finding a place where his sexuality and genius could be accepted. He came to the village because he needed somewhere where he could continue his experiments and it was how he met Stuart who rescued him after he nearly blew himself up. They became friends and finally lovers.

Together they built the portal then the space stations and found the advanced civilisation on Terzon, a planet in the Andromeda galaxy. For a time they had been on friendly terms with the Terzons but relations were cooler as Stuart found himself helping various people who had got into difficulties. Because of their own history the Terzons refused to interfere with other people's affairs. There was a conflict because they also disliked seeing civilisations destroyed and Stuart seemed to be forever confronting them with their dilemma.

Brian and Stuart had changed. Brian was accepted by the Terzons and preferred to explore using probes sent through the portals and observe rather than travel and get involved. Stuart on the hand seemed to be getting more and more adventurous, wanting to experience the places he discovered by visiting them directly. Although they still loved each other, their diverging lives was putting a strain on their relationship.

Demetrius had met boys who only liked boys before but his old master and many of the free men he knew were married. It did not stop them taking a slave of either sex if they felt like it and he did not understand the concept of gay and straight. Surely any man would do his duty, get married and provide a healthy son to continue his family.

It was the part of his new life that bothered him the most. Oddly it was what told him most clearly that he was no longer a slave but an important member of a freeman's household. He could no longer allow himself to be used for other's pleasure and he would have to wait until he met someone obviously inferior to him before he could take his own.

It puzzled him that girls about his age could wander around the village so freely. They could not all be prostitutes but they seemed as eager to find a man as men were to go to a brothel. It was peculiar behaviour for nobles. If he could pluck up the courage he would ask Dave's advice.

For now he was going to take Stuart's advice, observe his new home's customs, learn about the portal and find a way to make himself useful.

And there was something he could do. To build up his muscles, his owner made him work with the blacksmith who happened to be a skilled sword maker. He would not be able to make a sword fit for a soldier but he should be able to make a blade that demonstrated the general design. He noticed that no one carried a weapon, not even a dagger but maybe they carried weapons he did not understand.

It did not matter. Richard was interested in artefacts from his old home, so he would make a sword for him. What harm could it do and he could do something for one of his new friends. After all, he was in a village serving local farms so all he has to do was, find the blacksmith.

He was upset to discover that the garage was the closest thing to a forge and it possessed nothing that he even recognised let alone could use. While Demetrius grappled with another assumption, Stuart was beginning to worry about Demetrius. Would he ever be happy here in such an alien environment?

If he could not make Demetrius happy then what should he do about the others who had been kidnapped and were held on the ship. Would they thank him for rescuing them or curse him taking them to a life that they could not understand. He was really going to have to be careful and not go rushing in but at least the Terzons would sympathise with his predicament and that would be an achievement in itself.

"I'm learning your life, Master." Demetrius said, "But I don't feel as if I belong. I feel that you could send me away because I'm too much trouble. My parents sold me, my last Master promised to look after me as long as I could make him look good and it's the way I understand."

He paused hoping that he was not annoying Stuart.

"You and Brian need slaves to run your home while you're doing your important work. I'll do it. It would be an honour to serve such great men as yourselves. I know you're kind and you'll only beat me when you have to."

He grinned.

"I forgot. You won't even beat me when I do deserve it, will you? That's more freedom than I've ever had before. Let me get used to it before you give me more."

Later Stuart talked things over with others.

"I think that manual work was for slaves while citizens concentrated on less worldly things." Richard said, "Working on a space station may be something that a god would do but keeping house should definitely be beneath our dignity. It probably makes sense to him that James and Dave get someone from the village to keep house for them. He's probably proud of the fact that he's amongst the chosen few allowed to wander freely around Brian's estate but he needs to contribute something."

Brian nodded.

"I see but I wouldn't say that I've got an estate." he said, "Added to what Stuart said about expecting to be sent away, then I can see why he's uncomfortable here."

"In his eyes, you have." Richard continued, "And you're the Lord of the Manor. We're used to alien cultures. He's not and we have to respect his ways in the same way that we respect other cultures we come across."

"Stuart. What do you say?" James asked, "You're as willing to help an individual as a planet. Do you think we should respect his culture?"

"It would be fun to say yes." Stuart grinned, "I'd like an obedient slave in my bed when Brian insists on staying on Terzon. Both Dave and I were originally hired as handymen but we don't do much nowadays so maybe we could use Demetrius, as a handyman I mean. We'll arrange for a legal identity for him, employ him with a proper wage but put it all into a bank account for him. We've done it before and we can show him how to use it."

The others nodded in agreement, waiting for Stuart to continue.

"Gable was never a slave but he's still a little uncomfortable arguing with us, especially Mum or Dad. He could help Demetrius feel more at home with us aliens."

Demetrius arrived back from the village store as the others chuckled their agreement. Stuart explained what they were been discussing. Demetrius frowned.

"You have your duties to perform yet you become uncomfortable if I ask about mine. Am I so useless that there is nothing I can do?"

"No, you're not useless." Dave said quickly, "You have to get used to not being a slave then you can decide what you want to do."

"I want to be a house slave for Brian and Stuart." Demetrius said firmly, "You and James have women from the village so you don't need me. You are right. This is an alien world to me and I want to become part of it. That's why I try to behave the way you want when I'm out. Indoors I'd rather stand respectfully and serve you because that is what I know and so I can relax."

Demetrius looked around.

"The other slaves back home would think I'm mad for not taking a chance to be lazy so I am getting used to you. If I was back home I would be whipped for being so rude and ungrateful so again I know I'm not a slave. I see that everyone is listening to me, which makes me feel important. I just want to feel useful and not like a beggar living off scraps."

"I owe you an apology." Stuart said, "I've insulted you. Let's see how much you've learnt. Prepare us a meal and serve it the way you think it should be done."

~~~

Demetrius' father was a prosperous farmer but he suffered two misfortunes. Firstly his wife proved to be highly fertile producing too many children and secondly a couple of bad harvests left him struggling to provide for his family. With yet another child on the way and another bad year, he saw little alternative to selling his older children.

Demetrius' new master was not only a farmer but he was also a trader and very wealthy. As his talent for running became evident he was given time to train and, to build his muscles set to work helping the blacksmith. As his successes mounted he was used as entertainment for his master's guests, showing off his body almost as a living statue or demonstrating his skills as an athlete.

His parents taught him to read and write as well as Athenian history and so he was well aware of what a well run household needed. Taking charge of Brian's house was a chance to use all that he knew.

What Stuart had not understood was how being a slave was so deeply embedded in Demetrius' psyche. If he had been freed back home with some money then he would have at least understood his world and would have adapted to being a free man. Here, he was completely dependent on Stuart and his friends, which made it impossible for him to adapt.
~~~

From the moment that Stuart gave him that first order so Demetrius began to think of himself less and less a slave. It was a paradox because indoors he behaved more and more like one yet Stuart and Brian's home took on a definite Ancient Greek flavour.

Demetrius thought of Brian's study as the andron, a room where the head of the household could entertain other male guests. Their regular meetings became symposia where Brian, Stuart, Dave and the rest would discuss their work.

As a concession to the 21st century female visitors would be shown into the living room albeit as close to the kitchen as possible. Male visitors were shown to the other side near the French windows leading to the garden.

Demetrius would serve them as determined that he should call Stuart, master as Stuart was determined that he should not. For once, Stuart was defeated allowing Demetrius to be the dutiful slave yet it was Brian and Stuart's lives that became more ordered as they conformed to Demetrius' ways.

One small break from tradition was that Demetrius would act as symposiarch deciding how strong their drink should be. He usually decreed that fruit juices should replace beer and wine unless he was sure that there was no business to discuss.

An evening meal might consist of bean soup followed by cheeses with a wide selection of fruit followed by honey cakes. Watching television Demetrius discovered that male chefs were highly regarded so he felt happier with his duties yet his cooking kept to ancient Greek principles of simplicity and frugality.

In his turn, Demetrius discovered tea and coffee. No matter what he was doing he would try to have his midday meal at the pub. He combined a hot drink with a traditional ploughman's lunch, bread though not dipped in wine, cheese and pickles which substituted for figs or olives. He learned to use napkins to clean his hands instead of bread and happily washed it all down with his black tea or coffee. As he ate, he politely ignored his fellow diner's barbaric habits of drinking milk or undiluted wine, eating meat that had not been hunted or sacrificed and other practices best left to the Persians.

He decided that the nearest thing to a chiton was a t-shirt and shorts, as baggy and as loose fitting as possible. He wore them whenever the weather permitted though he learned to appreciate waterproof jackets and wind-proof coats when the weather was bad.

He continued to get up at dawn accepting that it was not Brian and Stuart's way. In fact it helped him. It gave him time to tidy up, prepare breakfast and pack their lunches as he would have done for the farmhands back home.

He worked hard looking after the house and garden until noon when he would go to the shop followed by his visit to the pub for his own lunch. Neither Dave nor Stuart ever looked after Brian's house and garden. They both became involved in exploration but Demetrius was content to explore the new world he was now living in.

It took time but he finally got the house cleaned and tidied to his satisfaction and the garden tamed ready for the range of fruit and vegetables he planned on planting.

About that time Bill the pub landlord approached him while he was eating lunch.

"I don't suppose you know languages like your friends." he asked, "Only I've got a couple of tourists who don't speak much English."

"I can try, sir." Demetrius replied, "I'm only just getting used to English and of course I speak my own language."

"Don't worry. Finish your meal and if you'd like to come over and see what you can do, I'd be grateful."

There was only a single road out of the village and the nearest bus route was two miles away so visitors arriving without cars but arriving from the lane where Brian lived were noticed.

Brian tried promoting tourism over the internet with considerable success to cover his own visitors. He also backed villagers who wanted to start small cottage industries, again paying for the set up costs, promotion and advertising. The project was so successful that now, it was one of the few villages where people came looking for jobs, rather than young people drifting away in search of work.

In return, the village ignored the peculiar goings on, simply enjoying the gossip about Brian and Stuart's lifestyle. If the younger members of the group got a little drunk in the pub and said something out of turn one of locals might mutter something about there being strangers present and to tone it down. If it was one Brian's visitors he would be looked after until Brian or someone could fetch him.

Strangers included incomers, people who just bought a holiday home but took little part in village affairs and were the most disliked. Demetrius was obviously one of Brian's people so he was accepted as a newcomer while the gossip stepped up a notch, wondering about the relationship between the three of them.

Even talking with the tourists helped support the village and

Demetrius coped very well with the German tourists that Bill had asked for help with.

"Thanks lad." Bill said, "If I need you again, is it all right if I ring you or do you work with the others?"

It was a simple enough question for anyone except Demetrius. First he was being called lad, the same as the free boys in the village. Second ringing him meant the telephone, not a ring through his nose so he could be led around like a bull and third it really was a request with an excuse built in to refuse.

"Please ring me, sir." he replied, "I have my duties keeping house but apart from that I'm happy to serve you as well."

"I think you mean help me, lad." Bill said in a kindly voice, "It's not like you to slip up with your English. Oh and Bill will do. "

Demetrius grinned, "I was brought up to be respectful. It's difficult to be so informal."

"You're definitely not from around here then." Bill laughed, "Don't worry about it, lad. Any friend of Brian or Stuart's welcome here."

Demetrius was a little worried whether Stuart would approve but all he said was, 'Go for it'.

In ancient Greece, a person should not work because he should spend his time becoming more virtuous and preparing to take part in government. Earning a wage was similar to slavery. Demetrius could appreciate the idea but he now felt it was taken to extremes in his old home. His new friends worked, but it was hardly menial. They appreciated his efforts to make them comfortable so again he did not feel as if his duties were menial either. However to be truly independent he needed to feel as if he could make his own way.

For a time he relaxed in the afternoons often just sitting in the pub, watching villagers go about their daily lives. As his confidence grew so he chatted more freely to Bill about the problems in his new life.

"Why don't you build yourself a forge." Bill said one day, "I'm sure Brian and Stuart would help you."

"Yes but where would I build it?" Demetrius asked.

"How about the bramble patch at the bottom of the pub garden?" Bill suggested, "You clear it and you can use it. Just fence it off. A village forge like that could be a new attraction. If you make something worth selling then we'll think about the planning regulations. In the meantime it'll be a feature to interest the tourists and you can carry on dealing with the foreigners."

Again Stuart encouraged him and Demetrius spent his afternoons working on the forge. It might have remained a hobby except that Demetrius stuck to the designs and methods he had been taught. He was far more skilled than he admitted to and impressed a passing rambler who just happened to be a professor of ancient history.

"Not bad for a kid." he said picking up a sword, "In fact, it's very good. Well done."

He had tried to be clever and spoke in ancient Greek but using an atrocious mix of modern Greek pronunciations and misconceptions about everyday usage.

Without thinking, Demetrius replied in a faultless Athenian dialect, "Thank you my lord. My Master will be glad to know that his kindness has not been wasted."

"Now that was impressive." the professor said, "What makes you think they used those tones and inflections in their speech?"

Demetrius thought quickly, glad that he still wore the translator, "I don't know but it seems to flow better."

"Possibly." the professor agreed, "How come you know so much about Ancient Greece?"

He noticed Demetrius' lunch, "Close but not quite right."

Demetrius grinned at him, "Bill doesn't like me adding water to his vintage wines. Chutney would have been popular if it had been around. I suppose I grew up being interested."

"Very well. So what oil are you using to prevent rust?"

Their conversation continued in Ancient Greek, becoming increasingly technical. The professor left impressed and Demetrius was left with a request to demonstrate his ideas to one of the professor's classes.

"I like the idea of a group of students spending an afternoon in my pub." Bill replied when Demetrius asked him, "They drink a lot."

"You'll be defending yourself against scholars almost in the same way as Socrates would debate his ideas." Brian said, "If you mention time travel or that you were born then, you'll lose all the respect you've earned because no one will believe you."

Realising that he was regarded as an expert, respected by scholars and philosophers did more to make Demetrius feel more like a citizen instead of a slave than anything else. So maybe it was not pure philosophy and debate but he lived in a different world now. More importantly he could regard himself as Stuart's friend instead of his slave.

Demetrius would never be interested in the portals or travelling. He was content to remain a servant, explore the village and prompted by his meeting with Professor Steadman. He was also curious about the history that he had passed through but he was content to just read about it.

Focussing

Stuart's body and mind had taken a battering during his previous adventures and he had been warned to rest. He was still surprised at how easily he could fall asleep or tire himself out from any sort of exercise so for a time it was great to have no responsibilities. While Demetrius was settling in, Stuart was recovering his strength and now he was becoming restless.

Not long after Demetrius' encounter with the professor, Stuart sat reviewing events so far.

The Dambons launched an attack on Earth believing it a threat but fortunately they were not in complete agreement. Having had portal technology for over two hundred years they understood Brian and Stuart's activities. They appeared to be peaceful and beneficial to the races that they came into contact with, however they saw the warlike uses the portal was being used for on alternative Earths and tried to stop them.

A faction decided to guide Stuart into dealing with the perceived threat. They succeeded but at some cost to Stuart's health.

By way of apology or possibly reward the Dambons had told him the story of the kidnappings. It was not urgent, it would give the inter-dimensional eddies a chance to settle down and it would intrigue Stuart enough to allow his mind to focus. The Dambons were aware of the dangers of changing history but in this case the kidnappings seemed to change so very little that again, the problem was curious rather than important.

The Dambons sent observers to study the development of Earth and they stumbled onto one of the earlier incidences. They did not recognise the kidnappers or their ship and were unable to trace them when they left Earth.

The first question to be decided was who was doing the kidnapping. Until they knew the answer to that they would not be able to find out why or how to stop them and they had very little information to go on.

"We've blundered through this time/alternate world thing, dancing to their tune and not knowing what we're doing." Dave said, "Are you telling me that they know all about these kidnappings and are playing games with us again?"

"No." Stuart replied, "They don't know all about it. Their explorers were studying Earth. They weren't equipped to chase mystery spacecraft. They'd have to set up their own project but instead they're telling us what they do know and letting us take it on."

"I suppose we could lodge the tip of a probe in their ship and track it back to their planet." James said.

"No," Stuart replied, "they use some sort of field drive similar to portal technology but it has harmonics that they're not aware of that would distort our fields. We'd never keep the probe locked to the ship unless we knew the exact course and speed at all times."

"Can't we install a tracker and follow from a distance?" Dave asked.

"That's the best plan," Stuart responded, "but there's another problem. They would discover any transmitter that operated without being affected by the drive and the drive would block any transmission that we could detect using our portal technology. There's one exception: the human brain. Some Terzon equipment is so sensitive that it can't be used within a hundred miles of a living thing. We could adapt it."

He paused.

"What I'm thinking is that we slip a miniature inertial guidance system under my skin. It can use translator technology to transfer the output to the speech centre of my brain, which in turn, would transmit to a beefed up translator attached to a probe. Instead of keeping the probe to within less than an inch in a highly manoeuvrable and fast ship, it could be anywhere up to a hundred miles away. We estimate that at the maximum acceleration the ship is capable of, we could stay within ten feet so we've got a massive safety margin. I could also plant beacons under my skin that I could activate if I got into trouble."

"Why not just put a beacon on their ship that could be activated automatically when it landed?" Dave asked.

"Because, like the probe it would need to use multi-dimensional warp technology and their drive could distort it." Stuart replied, "Also, although we could probably shut it down so energy transmissions were negligible, once it started transmitting they could easily find it. We'd get one shot at it so what happens if they stop off at a planet on their way home?"

If the tracker's hidden in a human body then any energy signatures could be masked by nerve and muscle signals."

"You seem to know a lot about their technology." Dave said.

"Only what the alien observers managed to find out when they found the ship," Stuart responded, "and that was two and a half thousand years ago. We can't risk even being interested in a modern ship because we don't know what detection devices they've developed."

"You'll have to come up with a different plan." James said firmly, "After those jumps between bodies you're in no fit state to do anything. You're certainly not well enough to smuggle yourself aboard an alien spaceship. Even if you were fit the plan is just too dangerous."

"I was going to get sold to them." Stuart said, "It should be easy to be in the right place at the right time. I think James should be my owner, selling his slave."

"And if it goes wrong?" James snapped, "You could find yourself doing forced labour in a mine."

"I'll do it." Dave said, "We've got the equipment to make it work and we can take as long as we need to set the scene just right."

"It's still too dangerous." James insisted, "They'll slit your throat without a second thought if they suspect anything. We'll have to think of something else."

"We were stopping an asteroid destroying all life on Earth. A shard cut through my space suit and cut my hand." Dave retorted, "How dangerous is that but we do our best to minimise the danger."

"And supposing they kill you as soon as you're on board their ship? Maybe your skull is a trophy to prove that they've reached Earth."

"Our alien friends telling us about all this have got technology similar to the translators." Stuart said, "They did not detect any sort of aggression like that. It seems that the kidnappers want their prey alive, fit and healthy. There's something in their mind about games and training but then it gets confused and the observers did not pursue it any further."

"Why not?" Gable asked.

"Because their brief was to study Earth. They earmarked these new people for further investigation later but they stuck to their original task. They've offered us the job as a peace offering. They seem to think that it'll be more fun than dangerous."

"These are the people that tried to destroy Earth." James retorted, "I'm not sure that I trust their idea of fun."

"Oh they're basically peaceful." Stuart replied, "Their real enemy was the alternate David Bradley. Once they understood other

Earthmen could use the portal without threatening them they let us deal with him."

"I still think that I should do it." Dave exclaimed, "Like James is always saying, Stuart's job is to run this outfit and he still understands it all better than any of us."

"What was that about a slave owner?" James asked suddenly, "Have you planned this out already?"

"The observers downloaded everything from their translators to ours but I hadn't realised it." Stuart replied, "I've been thinking about it and so I've been fed a lot of information. According to the translator the rich and wealthy arrive at the market in the morning before the day heats up and everything is more expensive. By late afternoon it can be stifling hot, and stinks. The best goods and stock has gone and it's left for the poor to scavenge the leftovers. So far as the slave traders are concerned they have a place to one side to buy stock for the next day. It's a good time to sell because the traders have got the days takings. The kidnappers seem to arrive about then, ignore the filth and the beggars and are willing to pay top prices."

Despite his objections, James could see that the plan could work and apart from one small problem it had worked as planned.

The problem came in two parts. Feeling foolish and awkward in a chiton, James set off at a brisk march towards the town and had arrived at the market earlier than planned.

Dave wore a short tunic with his hands tied in front of him. He had half trotted and half walked to keep up and the tunic which had been tied a little too loosely had slipped down. While James had arrived looking imposing and authoritative, Dave had arrived, slightly breathless, almost naked desperately trying to hold the tunic up and keep what was left of his dignity.

He was used to being naked on the Lizard Planet, the beaches of Terzon and sometimes on the space station Resolution. He also knew from the translators what to expect but experiencing it was something else.

They had slipped into character as they stepped through the portal in a copse of trees about half a mile from town. James was supposed to have strolled along like a gentleman without any cares in the world with Dave dutifully following his Master. They should have arrived at roughly the same time as the aliens with the idea that James could sell Dave direct to them. Instead they resorted to Plan B and Dave was sold to the trader.

Dave could have yelled stop at any moment and they would

have left as best they could. Stuart would want to try next time and Dave was determined not to fail where Stuart would probably succeed. It left Dave enduring the embarrassment of having the tunic ripped off him as the trader looked him over before examining his teeth then feeling his muscles. He even had to cough to show that he did not have a hernia and felt as if he was blushing bright red as James looked on.

Using the translator, James drove a hard bargain and the trader was annoyed that the price was a lot higher than it should have been as Dave was pushed into the cage and his hands untied.

Luckily for Dave, the trader knew the value of looking after his stock so the cage was clean. He was even given some water to tide him over.

He wrinkled his nose at the disgusting smell from a bucket in the corner with the flies swarming around it and retched at the sight of the animal remains beside the butchers stall a little way down the road. It was a relief to turn his face into a slight breeze and close his eyes.

He was not surprised when the cage was opened and, expecting to be taken out, he leapt up. It was a shock when Demetrius was put in with him. It was also worrying because there was no sign of the aliens.

None of them had considered the possibility that the aliens would want to go sightseeing and even spend time in a local tavern enjoying the wine. The butcher's stall had closed and some beggars were scavenging the remains for food when the aliens finally showed up.

Back on Resolution James breathed a sigh of relief which was echoed by Stuart.

At some point in their adventures they would have been seen by the Dambon observers creating some sort of temporal anomaly. However that was their problem and Stuart assumed that they knew how to deal with it.

Their own problem was that they had not bargained on Dave forming an attachment to the slave he should have replaced. James was annoyed about his own mistake, marching briskly and arriving early but as he pointed out, twentieth century military training did not put much emphasis on sword fighting. In his defence, he had been worried about protecting Dave and himself against bandits.

Understanding that a chiton was normal for the time and place he was operating in was one thing, actually wearing one was another.

Only Dave was unsympathetic but it was hardly surprising since he had been naked for most of the time.

However, the operation was a success and they had located the kidnapper's planet. The next task was to study the planet in the modern day.

Dr Tobias

Stuart was still not needed. It was routine to send probes, building up a picture of any new civilisation that they discovered. James and Dave could cope.

"Even the Terzons are becoming interested." Brian said one evening, "It's an intriguing mystery. It fascinates me as well though I wish you wouldn't go gallivanting off like you do."

"I'm innocent this time." Stuart laughed, "It's Dave who gets all the fun these days."

"Maybe but it won't last. Doctor Tobias keeps contacting you, doesn't he? He wants to thank you for those plans for the new brain scan. I'd like him to check you out and make sure you're OK."

"There's no point." Stuart replied, "He's more than a year from the MK1 model and it'll be another five before he can build one to show the sort of damage you're worrying about."

"I want you to take him to Terzon." Brian said, "I've spoken to their doctors and they agree. He's honoured our request to keep our part in the designs secret and we've no reason to distrust him. I'd feel happier if we had a human doctor on standby in case there was a serious accident."

"So now it's you who wants to let someone else in on the secret." Stuart said.

"I am worried about that. It's not ideal but we do need medical backup." Brian said, "How come everyone takes it all so calmly?"

"They don't." Stuart replied, "But we've got a couple of advantages."

"Go on." Brian said.

"Imagine taking Bill from the pub back a hundred years to buy a genuinely traditional guest ale."

"This is just imagination, isn't it?" Brian asked.

Stuart grinned as he nodded before continuing, "He knows the rumours about what we do though he doesn't know the details. He'll accept that something odd is going to happen but he'll be thinking more of covering it in his books, wondering if the barrel will tap OK and the rest. He'll be dealing with the side he knows and understands until he sees the portal."

Brian nodded.

"His attitudes will really start to change when he sees the portal de-materialise. We know that he'll spend ages studying it. Do you want to bet that he'll ask if it's blown up?"

It was Brian's turn to grin but he shook his head.

"OK." Stuart said, "That's when it starts becoming real because he can see something really weird. If he carries on then I warn him that he's going to be weightless. He'll nod his head but it won't register until he floats out into Resolution."

Stuart paused.

"I read something once, earthquake victims are particularly prone to post traumatic stress. The one constant in their lives is the solid ground below their feet. Suddenly it's not solid, it's betrayed them and that can be a terrific shock. It makes sense, babies fall over before they can talk and from then on, the ground is always there.

"Now going back to our theoretical trip. Suddenly Bill discovers that there's no ground, no up and no down and he's floating. He hasn't had years of training like an astronaut, there's been no blast of rockets to tell him that he's in space, just a warning from me."

"I've never thought about it like that before." Brian said, "Are you sure?"

"Ask James about his first trip." Stuart replied, "It fits in with a lot that I've noticed. Anyway he goes through another portal, feels delighted that weight is back to normal then realises that the scenery has changed. It doesn't matter whether we're in Howkbury, London, Terzon or ancient Rome, the significant point is that the quarry's gone. Bill would look around, check behind the portal and then start to accept that he's travelled."

"You call it the numbing effect." Brian said, "After a time, nothing can surprise you."

"That's right." Stuart agreed, "In Bill's case, the fact that we weren't in the quarry would be the shock and then he'd start taking in surroundings. If he panicked then I'd take him back but as we got closer to the brewery so his experiences would start kicking in. I don't know how it would work in detail. Possibly, he'd have a few tasters which should calm him. Then he'd have to deal with the fact a nine gallon barrel cost less than a pint and we'd have to figure out how to get it back to the portal. I don't know the pub trade so they're just examples but I'd imagine that there'd be a lot that's very familiar. It would all help to make early twentieth century Earth seem just another brewery that he had visited."

"It would be a bit more than that, surely." Brian said.

"Yes but don't forget Bill's world." Stuart said, "A lot would depend on how well that first barrel sold."

"You're saying that Bill or anyone else for that matter needs the familiar world to cope with ours."

"I think we need it as well." Stuart replied, "That's why we like this village so much but it's a problem that everyone half-believes in what we do. Joe Milne was talking about that ancient wreck of a tractor he's got. He asked me if my spacemen friends could make him some spare parts. The trouble was, he was only half joking."

"What did you say?"

"Some of our university connections may be able to help." Stuart replied, "Poking around in the last forty or fifty years seems harmless enough and studying recent history seems as legitimate as studying alien cultures."

"You use the portals as if it was a bicycle." Brian exclaimed, "You can't just pop into the seventies to do a bit of shopping."

"Why not?" Stuart asked, "Every trip contributes to the data. We create minor anomalies that can be observed, the natives are friendly and there's no drain on the resources. Attitudes have changed over the years and it's easy to say something wrong. It's good practice to observe without being noticed and there's no harm done if we are."

"I suppose that we do owe Joe a favour for the use of his barn." Brian conceded, "It's just that it seems so trivial. You know, like calling emergency services for a broken fingernail."

"Or dragging an innocent doctor off to a distant planet in case I'm ill."

"Good point. Visit him please. I still think we should have a doctor on call, just in case."

Stuart agreed that it was a sensible precaution so a few days later, he found himself in Dr. Tobias' office.

"I'm sorry but I'm amazed that someone as young as you could produce these plans." Dr. Tobias said, "I apologise. It sounds patronising but what are your degrees in?"

"I don't have any." Stuart replied, "It's never easy to explain without sounding completely mad. I'm an explorer. Putting it as simply as I can, my cousin had potentially fatal brain damage and your counterpart repaired it. We gave him the plans as payment and we sent you copies because of your links with him."

Stuart opened the laptop that he had brought with him. He booted it up and a three dimensional image of his brain hovered above the doctor's desk.

"This scan was done this morning." Stuart continued as he magnified it zooming in to the problem area, "My friends think it's healthy and I feel fine. However I've been through a time where my brain was put under considerable stress. They're insisting that I have a thorough check-up before I resume my work."

"Exploring." Dr. Tobias sought confirmation.

Stuart nodded.

"I've never heard of technology even approaching this scan." Dr. Tobias said, "I'd say there's nothing like it on Earth. Where do you explore?"

Stuart smiled, "I agree that's there's nothing like it on Earth."

Dr. Tobias stared at him then at the hologram then back at Stuart.

"Should I be thinking of radiation damage or anything?" he eventually asked.

"Not in this case." Stuart replied, "I've hit my head and cracked a rib but I could have gone to Accident & Emergency for those. A friend of mine cut his finger while working in a vacuum. He cut it on a rock shard that was well below zero. It froze the wound. It's the most serious injury that would have raised questions."

Stuart paused, "Until this check-up, of course."

"Of course. Is there anything else?" Dr. Tobias asked.

"We're looking for an Earth doctor who can handle the sort of emergencies we might encounter."

Dr. Tobias stared at him again.

"By Earth doctor, you don't mean some form of alternative medicine, do you?"

Stuart shook his head.

Dr. Tobias stared at Stuart again. He desperately wanted to ask Stuart if he meant working in outer space but he could not bring himself to. If Stuart had said straight out that he was a space traveller then Dr. Tobias would have laughed at him and the meeting would have ended. By leaving the question dangling, Dr Tobias was forced to confront it, producing the answer himself but for now he would deal with something that he did understand.

"I notice one or two signs of stress." he said, "Judging by that scan your brain seems perfectly healthy but I'd suggest a full physical and mental examination. It would help if I understood your working environment better. Would it be possible to visit?"

"Certainly, especially if you're interested in becoming our medical backup."

"Maybe. One thing at a time. How much notice do you need?"

"None. I'm on sick leave, remember. My time's my own and I can collect you whenever you like."

"Would you show my secretary the scan, please?"

As Stuart nodded he pressed a buzzer to summon her.

"I might be accepting a retainer to act as medical adviser to this gentleman's team and become involved in a new project, Sylvia. I also need to get away for a while to study this new type of scan. How quickly can you reschedule my appointments?"

"Dr. Urquhart said you were looking tired." Sylvia replied, "How do you feel about a bit of sick leave due to nervous exhaustion? In fact, I think you should go home now."

"That'll cover it." Dr. Tobias laughed then turning to Stuart asked, "How long do you need to arrange transport?"

"As soon as you're ready." Stuart replied, "I'm parked down in the woods at the far end of the grounds."

The doctor and his secretary looked at him quizzically but said nothing. Dave was manning the portal and could pick them up.

All Dr. Tobias had to do was phone his wife. It proved easy to convince her that he had to go away. The scanner that he was already building had Pound signs, Dollar Signs and Euro signs clocking up before her eyes. The idea that he might be involved in another prestigious and profitable project almost made them water. In most ways they were happily married but they both knew that she would prefer it if he was to exchange his considerable reputation for more money.

Stuart knew what Dr. Tobias was going to say next. The conversation was almost identical to the one that he had once had with an alternate Dr Tobias on a parallel Earth. So far as both Dr. Tobias's were concerned, the scanner would satisfy his wife's mercenary streak. He still worried that he was the victim of some student hoax but this new project could well give him chances to enhance his skills as a surgeon. He just had to take the risk.

Sylvia watched her boss leave with Stuart. She thought of the image she had seen and sighed. Something was going on but she did not know what. Over the years, her admiration for Dr. Tobias had turned into love. In his excitement at developing the first generation scanner, they had become closer. She hoped that the strange young man would provide a new project which would make them even closer. If it happened then who knows what else might happen. Although he did not know it, Stuart had an ally in Sylvia.

As for Dr. Tobias, he spent a bewildering few hours accepting he really was being hired by a bunch of space travellers. His reactions were much as Stuart had described. Like others before him, staring down at an incredibly bright star with the Earth lost in a myriad points of light, while floating helplessly in the observation chamber was an overwhelming experience. When he was taken to another of Stuart's bases on a planet of intelligent lizards who could talk to him through the translators, it seemed almost ordinary.

Tales of their exploits became so reasonable that he asked to examine Dave's hand.

"You say that this wound was exposed to a vacuum then cauterised because the rock that sliced through your spacesuit was about a hundred degrees below zero?" he asked.

Dave nodded, "It wasn't deep enough to need stitches and the scar's all that's left."

Dr. Tobias nodded, "And you, Stuart? You say that you've been injured."

"I bruised my ribs learning to move around weightless. I've cut my head a couple of times but it's been a period when Stuarts have been prone to head injuries."

"Stuarts." Dr Tobias said emphasising the plural, "We're back to parallel worlds."

Stuart nodded.

"Fair enough. And you'd like me on a retainer to deal with any emergencies that might occur. What about my other patients? Some would benefit from all the technology you have."

"We can't allow our activities to become general knowledge." Stuart said, "We can make it appear that you're developing new equipment, I don't mind interfering with Earth's development to that extent."

"Maybe I should leave surgery and concentrate on development. That way, I won't have a conflict."

"Maybe." Stuart agreed, "Let's see how things develop. We might be able to think in terms of a small clinic and a laboratory where you adapt the technology."

"OK tomorrow we do your examination. The day after you can fast and we'll run a complete blood screen. Maybe I should do everyone else. There'd be no problems would there?"

"Apart from Gable who's come from another planet and Demetrius who was born a couple of thousand years ago, it should all be straightforward." Stuart grinned.

Dr. Tobias took a deep breath as he considered the implications.

"OK I think that I should examine them every three months. I can pick up on changes to the norm and take things from there. Is there a medical database I could refer to?"

"You'll have to ask the Terzons." Stuart replied."

Fair enough. Is there anything else you want me for?"

Stuart frowned, "Maybe, we're looking into why people from Earth have been kidnapped. I guess I've been thinking about casualties and rehabilitation if we rescue them."

"I'm not specialised in a lot of the fields you want." Dr. Tobias said, "Apart from you, none of it is about a physical trauma to the brain. Physical check-ups are one thing but you sound as if you need a team of specialists."

"We can't breach security that far. Don't worry. We can get expert help for a lot of problems but we need a human doctor to oversee."

In his heart, Dr. Tobias knew that he was going to accept but his brain needed time to catch up. First it had to absorb what he was now involved with and his sharp incisive mind was raising questions that needed answering. Although he instinctively trusted Stuart, he was naturally cautious, constantly analysing his new surroundings.

He spent the following day giving Stuart's friends their check ups and found nothing seriously wrong.

"There are signs of stress in you." he said to Stuart, "But I've already said that. I know nothing about the mental jumps you experienced but I could imagine them being the cause. Mentally, you seem sharp and you're in excellent physical shape. Carry on as you are and you'll be fine."

He turned to Demetrius, "Given your background then you're fit and well. In anyone else, your lack of knowledge of current affairs could suggest short term memory loss or some sort of obsession with the past. Try to avoid Earth doctors if you can."

When he turned to Dave, also pronouncing him fit he added, "I could write a paper on your finger injury. Hard-vacuum, low-temperature traumas are very rare. The problem would be publishing it."

Gable surprised him. He was far more human than he expected.

"The Terzons are looking into it." Brian said, "Proteins and other organic molecules do exist in deep space. There could be a universal code more subtle than DNA that adapts to differing environments."

"And produces similar results in identical environments. How do you explain the Lizard planet then."

"I don't." Brian replied, "Maybe a mutation at the start of their evolution. Who knows?"

On the third day of his visit he joined everyone as they discussed their findings. Before they started, Richard raised another matter.

"It's Dave's parents." he said, "They're beginning to ask questions about what we're doing here. What with your Mum's accountancy business and your dad being a college professor they see themselves as a cut above the rest of us. The rest of the village tend to treat them like incomers and even you've encouraged that but I think that they're beginning to resent being cut out of the gossip."

Dave nodded, "Dad keeps asking what sort of work I do and what the prospects are. It's a step up from telling me that a handyman's job has got no future."

"I've always said that we shouldn't treat the portal like the family car." Brian said, "We've been lucky so far. All the official investigations so far have left the investigators looking a bit stupid. We're not going to maintain the secret for much longer."

"We are careful using the portals." Stuart exclaimed, "I know Mum uses it to trade fruit on the Lizard planet. Maybe Dave and I shouldn't play football on asteroids but we do collect data on those trips and it does help with the calibration. We could make it sound serious by planning exercises but it would be harder to incorporate a random element."

"I concede that you're careful." Brian said, "But it comes back to security and we never take it seriously. We're so relaxed we could be discussing a day at the office, not in space."

"Maybe that is a form of security." James said, "We make it sound ordinary so it is ordinary."

"I've always wanted to write a novel." Dr. Tobias said, "If I wrote one centred around your lives then you could claim to have been talking about that. I could say that I've known you for years and we've been corresponding."

"It wouldn't explain how we could speak so many languages or some of the other things." James said.

"No I suppose not."

"No, but I'll collaborate with you." Dave exclaimed, "It'll give me something to discuss with my parents."

"I could change the location and the equipment. Say my

characters use some sort of spaceship? I wonder if I could build a laboratory here to study language and the speech centres of the brain. It could be genuine, releasing papers based on Earth knowledge but of course I'd have some advantages in knowing where to look."

"If you're willing then I think it would be an excellent idea." Brian said, "I think the village likes the idea that it's at the heart of space exploration even if it can never admit it. If we can give them more down to earth explanations for events then they'll have something to openly gossip about."

"Welcome to the team." Richard said, "Do you intend moving here or commuting?"

"My secretary says that she's tired of a poky little flat in town." Dr. Tobias explained, "Maybe I could rent her a cottage in the village. It would depend on my retainer of course but she could oversee my research projects and depending on suitable sites I could move them all here."

"Don't worry about expenses." Stuart laughed, "We've got a diamond mine on Mars."

"Really?" Dr. Tobias queried.

"Well not on Mars but it's not far away or long ago."

Dr. Tobias still looked puzzled.

"It's easier to introduce cash in the past when security was much easier. We'll open you a bank account about fifty years ago, then transfer as many funds as you need."

Dr. Tobias grinned, "Is this another example of casual use?"

Stuart laughed with him, "Time travel is riskier but as long as we don't meet anyone we know and we keep a low profile then there's no problem."

Dr. Tobias became serious, "I'll leave time travel to you. I'm just happy for the chance to make a real contribution to medicine."

As he spoke, another thought occurred to him. His secretary Sylvia would be as thrilled as he was. She was an attractive woman and as he considered the possibilities, he wondered about some very personal ones. His mind was brought back to the gathering as they began discussing the mystery.

1925

"There's very little to tell." James explained, "The captives get taken to the surface by shuttles that enter a cavern then disappear. We've picked up readings that suggest a portal opens in there. I don't understand folding space enough to explain it clearly but we've definitely found ripples in the continuum."

"That's right." Dave added, "What we can't figure is why they use ships to get to that planet. Why not materialise on Earth? There's something else, the ship disappears too."

"Anything else?" Stuart asked.

"We can study the ship in flight." James continued, "We found one visiting Earth about ninety years ago. I'm pretty sure it's the same one that captured Dave and Demetrius."

Dave nodded, "It's got the same serving boy that looked after us. At least they could be twins."

"It sounds as if they're time travellers, too." Stuart said thoughtfully, "They use the planet's gravity well to navigate through time but they're not confident enough to add spatial displacements to their calculations. Their portals have to be much larger than ours to accommodate the ship. If there's a large temporal displacement then the fields could be too complex to allow for enough control."

"You mean travel a long way back in time." Dave exclaimed, "Keep it simple."

"They could be travelling from the past, the future or another dimension. It's not that simple."

"So what do we do now?" Dave asked.

"Keep a probe over the site." Stuart replied, "Wait until the ship returns then try to follow it. The trouble is, we don't know the interval between visits. It's the next thing to figure out."

"How?" Dave asked.

"We've got data about the ship from Demetrius' time and the last visit. The amount of deterioration might give us a clue. We could put a probe over the planet then programme it to drift back in time looking for field distortions."

"Why not work with the ninety year old one." Richard asked.

"We could slip back. What's the planet like?"

"It's fertile with carbon/oxygen life." James responded,

"Gravity is one and half times greater than Earth. Atmospheric pressure is correspondingly higher. Oxygen is at fifteen per cent compared to Earth's twenty per cent, with a greater mix of light gases such as helium. Not surprisingly animal life is small and sluggish. Plant life tends to spread outwards rather than upwards. It's not uncommon for a single plant to be a couple of kilometres across."

"Could we live there?"

"For a short time. Low oxygen levels tend to cancel out higher air pressure but the higher gravity would require higher levels of oxygen. Dr. Tobias would probably be able to explain more."

"Most research I've come across refers to high altitude or low air pressure." Dr. Tobias answered, "There's the diver's bends of course but that sort of diving is more extreme and short term. You're talking about long term exposure to less extreme pressures. Pilots experience several times gravity for brief periods but again you're talking a low level increase over a long time and I'm not even sure how research could be carried out on Earth. I would expect more heart strain and a tendency to light headedness or even fainting because of the effort of pumping blood to the brain."

"Why do you want to live there?" Brian asked.

"I was thinking of an observation post but even with time travel why take humans there? Are there any other inhabitable planets in their stellar system?"

"No, a few gas giants, a couple of asteroid belts."

"It's a big enough mystery to interest the Terzons. They may well offer technical help," Brian said, "But there's nothing I can do. Unless you find a real threat to Earth all you can do is wait and see."

"What did you mean, slip back?" James asked.

Stuart grinned, "The nineteen twenties should be safe enough. It might be a mistake to chat to Albert Einstein or someone who had made a big impact on the twentieth century. Apart from that, as long as we don't fall in love with our great, great grandparents we're not going to change much."

As the others hurried off about their own affairs, James and Dave gathered round Stuart.

"I didn't get myself captured just to wait and see." Dave exclaimed, "I want to get on."

"No, you didn't." Stuart agreed, "We're lucky the ship you were on didn't fly straight into a super portal. We'd have lost you so we need to be more careful. Let's deploy satellites to observe the system and the planet."

"Why not probes?" Dave asked then slapping his forehead in irritation, "I know. It leaves us able to create other warp fields."

"We can also study it over a longer period." Stuart said, "Focus on the inhabitable zone. I might go back and stop the last visit but I'll do it on Earth. Even here, I don't want to be spotted until I'm sure what we're dealing with so I don't want a portal close enough to be detected by them. With so much data on their ship we'll easily hide from them until we're ready."

What do you plan on doing? James asked, "Destroy their ship?"

"No, we'll go back and try to talk to them." Stuart said, "They've taken all these kids over the centuries so a bigger problem is, how do we rescue them? If we put them back in their own times then we risk changing history. We've been lucky that Demetrius has adapted so well but we can't bring them all back here."

"If they're happy where they are maybe we should leave them." James said.

"Of course." Stuart retorted, "I won't do anything without asking them. We'll be in twentieth century England, which makes it our territory more than theirs, so we'll have all the advantages. It'll be easy."

It would have been easy if Stuart had not been careless. He just saw a clearing in the woods when he planned his visit. It was secluded, hidden from the road and the nearest path. He may have noticed the boundary fence but assumed it had something to do with controlling wild animals. He was in rural England, and as usual he could not imagine any danger.

The gamekeeper appearing, holding a loaded shotgun was a rude awakening. The sensible thing to do was to cooperate though it was a little embarrassing to be treated like a criminal up to no good. They were taken to a large country house where the gamekeeper asked to speak to Sir Anthony.

As they were shown into a large study Stuart stepped forward offering his hand only to feel his shoulder grabbed to be pulled back.

"I admire your cheek," Sir Anthony said, "but I don't regard poachers as guests. I'm willing to give you a thrashing and send you on your way or I can send for the constable and you'll face me in court tomorrow. That's six strokes of the birch and maybe six months hard labour if you play up."

"We're vegetarians so we don't hunt meat." Stuart said, "We've got no guns or traps so we don't have the means to poach. We were walking openly along a path and talking to each other so we were hardly hiding or attracting game."

"Is that true, Archer?" Sir Anthony asked.

"I've never heard of anyone not eating meat but the rest is, Sir Anthony." Archer replied, "But what else would they be doing out in the woods? They're certainly not dressed as gentlemen."

"Good points." Sir Anthony said, "Do you have explanations?"

"The clothes are what we're used to, back home." Stuart said, "They're practical when using our transport. The rest of the explanation is more complicated. Our transport needs a landing site and we missed the boundary to your land when we planned our trip. That's why we were trying to find a gate to reach the road."

"Landing site?" Sir Anthony, "As in an aeroplane landing?" They use fields not woods or are you suggesting that you descended from a Zeppelin in an observation car?"

"I said it was complicated." Stuart said, "The point is, we were not poaching and unless you want to frame us you couldn't prove that we were in a court of law."

"Frame you?" Sir Anthony queried, "Oh yes, it's American slang isn't it? No, I would not ask Archer to perjure himself but I am the magistrate and in this case I would trust the evidence of my own eyes. What are you doing on my land."

"Like I said, we got lost and were trying to reach the road." Stuart said.

"That's not what you said before." Sir Anthony exclaimed, "How did you stray across the fence and what did you mean by landing site?"

The conversation was an impasse. Stuart knew that he was never as careful as he should be if he materialised in England. Even nearly ninety years in the past it was still home so how could it possibly be dangerous? He knew that his thinking was irrational but despite Sir Anthony's threats he did not feel as if he was in danger of his life though he could face a lot more embarrassment and discomfort. Sir Anthony would not believe the truth and Stuart could not think of a sensible cover story.

He was still trying to figure how to answer when a boy of about twelve entered carrying an odd looking gadget.

He looked at the three men standing in front of Sir Anthony's desk.

"I'm sorry, father." he said, "I didn't realise that you were still busy."

"That's all right. Come in, Freddie." Sir Anthony said, "These young men are trying to convince me that they aren't poachers but *landed* on our grounds by mistake."

"Oh!" Freddie exclaimed, "Are they poachers, Father?"

Stuart saw a chance to change the subject.

"Is that a crystal radio, Freddie?" Stuart asked, "I've never seen one before."

"I don't suppose your sort would know what to do with them." Archer snapped, "I'll not warn you again. Keep a civil tongue in your head."

"My sort thinks that they're an interesting little toy." Stuart retorted as the translator supplied him with a quick history lesson, "They work okay, but it's so easy to lose the tuning and go off station. I think valve radios are coming on the market now, which are much better, but those sets are a fascinating introduction into electronics."

"Is radio another American expression?" Sir Anthony asked, "Do you mean wireless sets and what are electronics?"

Stuart nodded, "I'm not sure where the words 'radio' and 'electronics' originate but I do mean wireless sets. Where I come from, wireless means something else."

"They say you can communicate with the departed." Freddie said, "I want to speak with my mother."

"His mother died in the influenza epidemic in 1919." Sir Anthony explained, "They do say that wireless waves travel on the same plane as the departed."

"Radio, I mean wireless can do many wonderful things," Stuart said, "but I'm afraid that we're not meant to contact the dead."

"They're departed, not dead." Sir Anthony said sharply.

Stuart knelt down gently taking Freddie by his arms.

"I'm sorry, Freddie." Stuart said, "Wireless waves are part of what's known as the electromagnetic spectrum. Wirelesses can detect the longer wavelengths while your eyes see shorter wavelengths as light and colour. Your mother may be alive in a spirit world but wireless is part of our world."

He turned to Sir Anthony, "There might be genuine spiritualists but there's an awful lot of con artists cashing in on people's grief."

Tears were filling Freddie's eyes.

"So this is useless." he screamed, throwing the crystal set against the wall and running out of the room.

Dave hurried over and picked up the pieces.

"There's nothing broken." he said, "It just fell apart."

He glanced out of the window, "You see that tree. If we ran a wire from there we'd have a fair sized aerial. Earth it through the plumbing system and it'll boost the signal even more."

"Yes but what's the point?" Sir Anthony asked.

"You have the BBC in this country." Stuart replied, "There're stations springing up all over the world. You'll be listening to live people but it can still be fascinating. There's also what I know as ham radio. It's where you have your own transmitter to have a two way conversation."

Sir Anthony stood up circled round his desk offering his hand to Stuart.

"I would still like to know what you're doing here but you're welcome." he said as they shook, "I'm Sir Anthony Darrington."

"I'm Stuart Johnson and this is Dave Hilford." Stuart responded.

Sir Anthony turned to the gamekeeper, "Thank you Archer. I don't need you any more. Go to the kitchen and have them feed you."

Archer raised his knuckle to his forehead and left as Sir Anthony ushered them to comfortable armchairs.

"Freddie's school says that he's just being a cissy and should pull himself together but I think it's more."

"He does seem obsessed." Stuart said, "What's he wearing? Are they called plus fours or knickerbockers? Either way they're not the best clothes for just mucking around in those woods of yours."

Sir Anthony frowned, "He is learning to be a gentleman. Clothes are important."

"How about appropriate clothes are important?" Stuart asked gently, "A boy who needs to think about this world needs to be able to climb a tree or wrestle in the mud with his friends."

"He does get up to all sorts of mischief when I'm in town but he's an only child and we're a bit too isolated to invite his school chums over."

"Isolated? Thorndown's just half a mile down the road." Stuart exclaimed then paused as a thought struck him, "I know, they're not the right sort of boys to mix with. At least they're alive."

As Sir Anthony tried to respond a tall woman entered. Stuart was aware of a scarf around her head with a cigarette in a long holder as Stuart and Dave followed Sir Anthony's lead and stood up.

"Anthony dear, what's got into you." she exclaimed, "Why on Earth have you allowed these ruffians to upset Freddie. His mother's very annoyed with you."

"She's dead." Stuart said bluntly, "And it seems that it's you who's upsetting him not Sir Anthony."

"No one gave you permission to speak so remember your place." the woman exclaimed, "I don't know who you are but I can tell from your aura that you're up to no good. Your sort keep your minds closed to the truth."

"This is my sister, Selena." Sir Anthony said, "And these are Mr. Stuart Johnson and Mr. Dave Hilford. Could we all remember our manners please?"

"I'm sorry." Stuart said, "We're intruding and should leave."

"Please stay, at least for tea. Let's all sit down." Sir Anthony said, "Would you be willing to tell us who you are and what you're doing here, Mr. Johnson?"

"Stuart please." he said before turning to Selena, "We're time travellers from the 21st century. We think that Thorndown in this time holds a key to a mystery that's been rumbling along since the days of Socrates."

There was a stunned silence.

"I knew it. You are a swindler." Selena exclaimed, "But how do you expect us to believe such a preposterous story?"

"I don't but I just wondered how my aura could say that I've got a closed mind." Stuart replied.

"Yes I see." Sir Anthony said, "It's a good question, Selena."

"So he told a nice little story." Selena pouted, "His mind's still closed to the astral spheres, just as yours is."

The three men stood as she flounced out of the room then settled back down.

"What I find strange is that I believe your story." Sir Anthony said, "I know it's ridiculous but there's one or two things that you've said and your friend's reaction to what you said. He was not amused or surprised that you could come up with such a tale but shocked as if you'd revealed some deep secret."

"Dave's a lousy poker player." Stuart laughed, "I promise you it's not part of some scam."

"Scam." Sir Anthony said, "I'm sure that's an American word as well but you have English accents. Yorkshire if I'm not mistaken but it's not very strong. You moved away to London perhaps."

"You sound like Sherlock Holmes." Stuart smiled.

Sir Anthony smiled in his turn, "I've had the pleasure of meeting Sir Arthur Conan Doyle. He and Selena correspond with each other. Selena lost her fiancé in the war. She was attracted to another young man who was also killed. Ever since she has become fascinated by spiritualism and still tries to convert me."

He paused, "With such logical thinkers as Conan Doyle believing, I have been undecided. It's why I've neglected to keep Freddie from their influences."

Stuart nodded, "We should be going. We have things to do and we're losing time. I'm sorry that I can't explain more and it's a bit of an imposition to ask if you mind us leaving on the path we arrived on."

"The landing site for your time machine." Sir Anthony said quite seriously, "Yes of course. I'll send word to Archer that he should stay away from there."

He saw Stuart's puzzled look.

"I also enjoy H. G. Wells." he continued, "Reason as well imagination dictates that I should accept your tale even if I don't necessarily believe it. You seem surprised."

"Yes I am." Stuart replied, "I can't imagine anyone accepting the idea so easily."

"Does ASDIC mean anything to you?" Sir Anthony asked.

"It's about pinging enemy submarines to get range and bearing." Stuart replied.

"Pinging?" Sir Anthony asked.

"You bounce a sound beam off the target and the echo sounds like a ping. Why?"

"During the war I worked for the Board of Invention and Research on anti submarine equipment. I was also on HMS Antrim during the 1920 experiments. The point is you talk about very new and highly secret apparatus as if it's every day knowledge."

He paused, "I've seen the development of the aeroplane and wireless. Who knows what could happen in the next hundred years?"

"I'm going to be in big trouble when I get home." Stuart said.

"Why?" Sir Anthony asked.

"I didn't research this operation properly." Stuart replied, "I shouldn't have turned up on private property and I should have checked on the people I might have bumped into."

"If you'll help me then I'll assist you in any way I can on your mission." Sir Anthony said, "And I do understand that it's highly secret and that you cannot reveal anything about it."

"And what do you want us to do?" Stuart asked.

"Rescue Freddie from his aunt." Sir Anthony replied, "I understand what you say about living in this world. I wish that I had understood before."

"If you believe me." Stuart said, "Then you'll understand that I'm not of this world either. I don't think that I'm best qualified to help. What do you think, Dave?"

"That James is going to have a heart attack and Brian's going to do his headmaster thing and make us look like stupid kids." Dave replied, "But you're going to help aren't you?"

"We can still meet up with the visitors but we could bring them here. A conference around the dining room table would be better than sitting in the snug bar of the pub. Setting up a link in an empty barn would be better than having anyone else stumbling in on us. Is it feasible?"

"We could take a look at the old stables and see if they would suit." Sir Anthony said, "And by all means arrange this conference of yours. Will you be staying?"

"I could stay for a while." Stuart said, "I can accommodate delays at the other end."

"Dave, I'd like you to go on a shopping trip. I want you to find the plans for a state-of-the-art 1925 wireless set then buy all the materials and tools needed to build it. You could go for a 1926 or even 1927 design providing most of the parts are available now."

Stuart paused, "I'm supposed to be resting and I can't think of a better place to do it. Let's see how things develop. Do you do things like dress for dinner?"

"We do." Sir Anthony replied, "Is there a problem?"

"I could add a dinner suit to the shopping list and anything else I needed but I can't always work to a timetable."

Sir Anthony rang for his butler.

"Phillips, Mr. Johnson is staying for a few days." Sir Anthony said, "While he's here we will not be dressing for dinner and meals maybe delayed. Will you inform cook and tell her to choose menus accordingly. Mr. Johnson will inform you of any other requirements."

"Yes Sir Anthony." Phillips replied.

"I would appreciate a candid reply." Sir Anthony continued, "Do you consider Miss Darrington a good influence on young Master Freddie?"

"Candidly sir?" Phillips replied, "No I do not. Miss Selena spends too much time with the dead."

"Where are they now?"

"According to Miss Selena they are conversing with young Master Frederic's mother. If I may still speak candidly, they are engaged in more of her hocus pocus."

"If you wanted to see Freddie then I think that you'd ask Phillips to fetch him." Stuart said, "I don't know if he can manage sarcasm but appropriate apologies to his mother for disturbing them might be in order."

"Phillips?" Sir Anthony asked.

The butler managed a rare smile, "I shall certainly try sir. Is there anything else?"

"Yes, I'd like some more comfortable clothes for Freddie." Stuart said, "I'd like him to come into the village with me without everyone knuckling their forehead and saying 'Good Morning Your Highness' or whatever. You might see this as a nanny's or a valet's work but I think that you'll understand what I'm doing better than them."

"Yes sir." Phillips replied, "I shall do what I can. If I may say so, I look forward to this becoming a Christian household again."

As the butler left, Stuart turned to Sir Anthony.

"I still can't believe that you accept me so easily." he said.

"I'm not sure what I believe." Sir Anthony said, "Do you happen to know a Dr. Tobias?"

He paused but before Stuart could answer, he continued, "I see from Mr. Hilford's reaction that you do."

He went to his desk, pulling out a drawer and taking out a small box. Inside the box was a coin which he handed to Stuart. It was a 21st century, fifty penny coin.

"Do you know how much that coin is worth in contemporary currency?" Sir Anthony asked.

"Ten shillings." Stuart replied, "Where did you get it?"

"It was about the time of the Diamond Jubilee. I was eleven." Sir Anthony replied, "I was playing down by the river. I do remember launching sticks into the water but I don't remember slipping on a wet stone and hurting my head. I came to in a strange room with strange devices around my bed and they were attached to me by wires."

Sir Anthony paused, "I say came to but it could have been a dream because there was a monkey sitting beside my bed and he hurried off when I woke up and groaned. He returned with this man who introduced himself as Dr. Tobias.

"He examined me then told me that I had concussion and needed to rest. He called it, MTBI at first but it didn't mean anything to me. At first my eyes wouldn't focus and I was very drowsy so I slept a lot that first day. I felt a lot better the next day and I was allowed to get up but I had strict instructions to get back into bed if I felt drowsy.

"Small things stuck in my mind. All I had to wear were cotton shorts and a shirt just like yours. It's not an under-shirt is it? I seem to remember someone calling it a T-shirt but I can't remember who. When I felt strong enough the monkeys wanted to play catch with me. Anything can happen in dreams but these damned monkeys even had a cricket bat and wanted me to play. Another thing, they seemed to know when I felt the least bit tired and guided me back to bed."

Sir Anthony paused again weighing up Stuart and Dave's reaction before continuing, "Two men came to see me the day before I came home. Looking back, I'm sure that they were you two. You gave me that coin, told me what it was worth and told me to keep it until you came back for it but I was never to show it to anyone or say where I got it. One of the men introduced himself as Stuart and said he was a time traveller.

"Not long after, Dr. Tobias gave me a pill and I fell asleep. When I woke up, I was fully dressed and lying on the bank above the river and it was the gamekeeper, Hodges it was then who was shaking me awake. He found a scar on the back of my neck, which puzzled him because it looked old, but I was very disorientated.

"I don't often think about the incident and if it hadn't been for that coin, I would have dismissed it as an intriguing dream. I thought I recognised you when you first arrived but it didn't seem possible. However I was prepared to give you the benefit of the doubt even if we weren't being completely honest with each other. As our conversation progressed through to the mention of time travel it seemed to trigger vague memories. With your off hand regard for the latest inventions and most importantly your concern for my son I reached the stage where I felt that I should confide in you. We'll talk again later but I think that I hear Selena's dulcet tones on the stairs. I think that Phillips may be capable of more than just sarcasm."

Sir Anthony was right for the door burst open.

"You'll have to dismiss Phillips." she yelled as she crossed the room, "He was insolent beyond all measure and has taken leave of his senses. I cannot imagine what Angela must be thinking."

"My wife is dead." Sir Anthony said, "And you're to stop involving Freddie in your mumbo jumbo."

"You don't mean that you're encouraging Phillips." Selena exclaimed angrily, "What's the hold that these people have over you?"

"None." Sir Anthony replied, "They've helped me clear my

head. Now, so that there is no doubt, you are not to mention Angela or any other dead soul to my son ever again. Neither will you hold any séance or spiritualist gathering in this house. If you cannot accept my instructions then you can move up to the town house."

Before Selena could reply Phillips ushered Freddie into the room. To Stuart and Dave's eyes he was oddly dressed. He wore a loose top with baggy sleeves to his elbows, grey flannel shorts that stretched to his knees, black knee length socks and leather lace up shoes.

Selena stared.

"You've all gone completely mad." she shouted as she flounced out of the room.

"That was quick work, Phillips." Sir Anthony remarked as he studied his son, "Where did you find the clothes?"

"It seems that young Master Freddie already had them."Phillips replied, "You may have seen the chauffeur's son about the estate, sir. It seems Geoffrey is only too pleased lend him young Reginald's hand me downs. The shoes are young Master Frederic's own. Geoffrey's son only has boots."

"I hope you don't mind, Father." Freddie said, "But I play with Reginald in the woods and these are more comfortable."

"Do you know what a spy is, Frederick?" Stuart asked before Sir Anthony could reply.

Freddie nodded uncertainly.

"Well I'm looking for some men who may be up to no good." Stuart continued, "Now the boys in the village may know more about them than the adults but they won't talk to me. They might talk to you more, especially if you relax and just be one of them. You don't have to lie or anything, just listen. Are you interested?"

Freddie's face screwed up as his imagination went into overdrive but it cleared and he grinned excitedly.

"Yes please, sir." he replied.

"OK You have two tasks to start with. I want you to recruit Geoffrey's son. Two of you, kicking a ball around should be a good ice breaker."

"What's an ice breaker, sir?" Freddie asked.

"Relations between groups of people can be difficult, icy. If you've got a ball and other boys want to play then…"

"It breaks the ice." Freddie finished brightly, "What's my second task?"

"Mr. Hilford, you can call him Dave by the way, will help you set up your crystal set. You will need to listen and decide which stations are just broadcasting like the BBC and, which may be sending secret messages. If you carry on after I've gone you'll have to learn Morse Code."

Freddie turned and ran for the door before hesitating, turning and asking, "Will you excuse me please, father?"

Sir Anthony smiled and nodded. As Freddie crashed through the door he turned to Phillips.

"I'm not sure what those two scamps might get up to but let Geoffrey know that it has my blessing."

"Yes Sir Anthony." Phillips replied, "Is there anything else?"

"No, that will be all." Sir Anthony answered, "Oh and Phillips, thank you."

He turned to Stuart, "I seem to remember from my dream that you prefer to be called by your Christian names. You look concerned."

"We haven't saved you yet." Stuart replied, "Events have happened out of sequence. I just hope that there won't be any problems."

"The perils of time travel." Sir Anthony chuckled, "Can Freddie really help you?"

"He'll be camouflage." Stuart replied, "I'll still stand out as a stranger but I'll be less suspicious if I'm buying a couple of kids ice creams."

"I understand." Sir Anthony said, "Let's see if the old stables will suit you."

The stables were just right for Stuart's needs and he was feeling much happier. He was sure that he could trust Sir Anthony and he was happier having a secure base. He just had to convince the others.

"It's ridiculous." Brian exclaimed angrily that evening, "Your priorities are all wrong. That family's trouble."

"I know I've got problems imagining that twentieth century Earth could be dangerous." Stuart said, "Sir Anthony's met me or an alternative me before. He's got a modern coin and can describe the Lizard Planet. That's a mystery in its own right."

"It's not all bad." Dave said, "We've got a secure base and some friendly natives on side."

"I agree with Dave." James said, "We were careful, arrived early to reconnoitre and we are dealing with the problems that arose. Maybe we took a chance with a boundary fence but the worst that could have happened was that we would have had to bail them out after they had been arrested."

"Yes and maybe I worry about Stuart too much." Brian said, "So you intend staying here until tomorrow then returning to half an hour after you left. You then plan on staying for the week. You'll adjust your time here so you're completely in sync and don't have jet lag problems."

Stuart nodded, "With luck we'll become accepted in the village. I don't want the aliens bolting because there's a couple of investigators waiting for them."

"You know I want to spend time on Terzon and I suspect you're just making it easy for me." Brian said, "I'll miss you though."

"You won't when you get there." Stuart laughed, "Interstellar gravimetrics are far more exciting than being in bed with me."

"And you're making James blush." Dave added, "Don't forget that it's illegal back then."

"I'm glad I'm not an English teacher," Brian said, "because we're certainly mangling the English language. Anyone else would say it *was* illegal back then but it's part of our present isn't it."

"I know I still get confused by it all." James said.

"Selena's probably been dead for fifty years." Stuart said, "Tomorrow evening I'll be having dinner with her and her brother. For them it's tonight and do you know what I'm dreading?"

The others waited expectantly.

"That she starts going on about how I've travelled a long distance and I've been on the Astral plane. I just hope she goes on thinking that I'm some sort of vagrant who's conning her brother in some way."

"I can see that." James said, "I take it that you don't want to add the astral plane to the realms you explore?"

"Not until I'm ninety-nine and losing my faculties." Stuart said, "I'll happily pop off and explore it then."

"That's a relief." Dave chuckled.

"OK, back to business." James said, "Your mission is to make contact with these aliens and see if they'll talk to us. We want to warn them off any future abductions and if possible prevent the 1925 one providing we don't cause any sort of anomaly."

Stuart nodded, "I've been thinking about this. We've said before that it would be easier to take kids off the streets in some large city. There's plenty sleeping rough and no one would notice if they disappeared so why choose a village like Thorndown?"

James nodded, "Go on."

"Thorndown's fairly prosperous." Stuart said, "Think of who's being kidnapped. Young men and girls in their late teens or early twenties. They're fit apart from minor ailments, possibly even taller than average. You might find recent runaways in a city, anxious to see the world but a lot are going to be starving, prone to T.B. and the like as well as not that used to authority."

He paused as the others nodded in agreement.

"Most of the cargo in Demetrius' shipment were slaves. They had been worked hard but were properly fed. Now think of the possible selections from Thorndown. They're not slaves but they've worked in the fields and are used to Sir Anthony being the Lord of the Manor. I'd be willing to bet that the aliens are going to have real problems with 21st century runs. Their targets are going to be a lot less cooperative."

"You're saying that the 1920s was the tail end of the feudal system." Brian said.

"Yeah." Stuart replied, "Archer the gamekeeper doffs, doffed his cap and touches, touched his forehead when he speaks, spoke to Sir Anthony."

"All right." Brian exclaimed, "You've made your point, the English language isn't ready to deal with time travel."

"I want to take a probe with me." Stuart said, "That means a power supply and computers as well. I'd like it boxed so that I can store it in the stable. It'll give me a way of contacting you or tracking them if I need to but there won't be any portal signatures when they arrive."

"You're saying that you want us to back off as well?" James asked.

"Unless you'd like to visit as well." Stuart replied.

"No." James replied, "I'll monitor Resolution. I'm getting interested in the various forms of radiation that Resolution absorbs. I'd like to do some reading and it'll be a good time while you're away."

"And if you glow in the dark when we get back, we'll know that you've tried an experiment that went wrong." Dave laughed.

"So you're coming too." Stuart said, "That's good but I wondered if you'd want to, this time."

"Why not?" Dave asked, "This trip's easy compared to Ancient Greece."

Dave was not so sure when he prepared for his shopping trip.

"I've never worn a suit so much in my life." he complained, "At least my modern one fits in fairly well. I'm not wearing one of those heavy things they had then but the trilby makes me look like a real prat."

"I don't know." Stuart chuckled, "Doesn't it make you a 'gay young thing'?"

"You would know." Dave growled then grinned, "I know it meant something different back then but I'll still clock anyone who calls me that."

"Careful, you don't lose the trilby James lent you." Stuart said, "It was the last one he bought in 1973 so he's quite nostalgic about it. Seriously are you sure about going alone?"

Dave nodded, "The translator will act as a tracker and send an alarm if anything happens. I just step out of the trees in that park, walk down the road to the shop and collect my order. I found it in a magazine and they even supply a ready drilled chassis."

Dave looked proud of himself, "I even wrote a letter to drop on their front door mat a week ago with a probe. It should be all ready for me."

"I don't remember you using a probe for that." Stuart said.

"I haven't yet. I'll do it just before I go." David laughed, "Brian's right, English can't cope with what we do. I have written the letter. I will use the probe. When I get to the shop it will have arrived a week before me. How come you don't want to come?"

"I wouldn't mind but I've got the feeling that you wanted to do this on your own. By the way, how did you find the magazine?"

"Remember, I did use a probe to check in the library." Dave explained, "I found a copy in there. I brought it back, had a good read and returned it."

"Way to go." Stuart said, "It's your project. Do you want to finish it without me breathing down your neck?"

"You don't do that." Dave said, "But I would like to go alone. If only to show that I can handle things."

"I know you can." Stuart said, "We're lucky. You don't have to cross the road, you don't have to talk to strangers and you can come straight back home when you're done in the shop."

"You make time travel seem so very grown up and adult." Dave laughed, "Couldn't you have warned me that I'll be in deep cover and not to engage the natives?"

"I could have done." Stuart chuckled, "I want you to think in terms of running for home if there's trouble, not reaching for your gun."

Dave had seen pictures of the twenties but what struck him as he walked down the street was the colour. He was used to the grey tones of old black and white photos. In the shop, the transaction went very much as normal until he handed over the money. The man behind the counter took it and along with the bill, passed them through a small hatch.

They waited patiently until the hatch slid open and the counter assistant handed Dave his change and receipt.

"You should have seen a department store about then." James said when Dave described his trip, "The ceilings were festooned with wires with little containers on wheels running along them. The money from all the counters went straight to the tellers who checked it and entered the sale in their day books. They fascinated me as a kid."

Freddie rushed up to greet them when they returned. Sir Anthony was just as welcoming.

"Cook has left us a cold buffet tonight." Sir Anthony said, "I think it'll be stews and casseroles other nights unless you can give us some idea of your plans."

"I want to spend as much time as possible in the village." Stuart said, "Thanks to your hospitality, meeting these visitors is going to be easier than I expected. They're due here in a week and I'm almost ready for them now. I'm sorry about not being properly dressed for dinner still."

"It's not a problem." Sir Anthony said, "I've taken the liberty of inviting Reginald. He's the chauffeur's son. I take it you don't object."

As Stuart shook his head Dave interrupted, "I always thought people like you panicked if everything wasn't in its proper place."

"We toffs, you mean." Sir Anthony retorted, "Some country houses don't see beyond being dressed for the next meal but I did serve in the navy. That dream I mentioned got me interested in science romances and that turned into a practical interest researching anti-submarine and anti-mine inventions.

"I spent a lot of time on small ships, which meant close quarters with the crew and with scientists who tended to be very informal. I just can't forget playing cricket with monkeys either. Putting it all together I'm glad of the opportunity to relax for a while. It also helps that Selena will be most put out."

"It would be rude of me to suggest that part of Selena's interest in the occult is because it's fashionable and gives her introductions to people, wouldn't it?" Stuart asked.

"Yes, it would be very rude of you," Sir Anthony replied, "but you would be perfectly correct."

Just then, Freddie and Reginald arrived. Reginald was about a year older than Freddie but similarly dressed. He stood nervously as he took in his novel situation.

"Phillips said that I shouldn't dress for dinner tonight, Father is that correct?" Freddie asked.

"That's quite correct." Sir Anthony said, "I think that Mr. Hilford wants to show you what wireless should be really used for. Of course we could dine as normal and you could begin tomorrow."

Freddie's face screwed up with the effort of considering the implications. He turned to Dave.

"May we begin now please sir." he asked excitedly.

Selena stared in horror at the resulting chaos. She complained that her spirit guide and sister-in-law would never appear in such a troubled atmosphere and retired to her room. Stuart noticed that she was not so distressed that she couldn't instruct Phillips to take a tray up to her.

As for Phillips himself, he busied himself finding cloths and trays to protect the dining room table. By the end of the evening he had removed his jacket, rolled up his sleeves and was assisting in assembling the new valve wireless.

Stuart and Sir Anthony sat comfortably in the library. They chatted but Stuart found himself dozing in the comfortable chair. No one could approach him with a new problem and the most technical device was the electric light. He could relax more completely than ever before.

That evening set the scene for the rest of the week. Selena became increasingly marginalised as the rest of the household became involved with the marvels of science. Even Sir Anthony sat with the rest as a voice appeared amongst the atmospheric crackles and pops.

Stuart and Dave made a point of strolling into the village each day and having a drink in the village inn. At first, conversation tended to stop when they were seen but when Freddie and Reginald arrived with a brand new football the village boys congregated around them.

With Stuart and Dave, providing a never ending supply of sweets and lemonade, the boys all forgot their inhibitions and at times they would sit in a group chatting happily.

In the evenings a growing group of children would gather in the dining room listening to the magical wireless voices. Selena complained that the noise disturbed the astral plane, cook delighted in so many hungry stomachs appreciating her efforts and Phillips cheerfully supervised the pandemonium.

With Freddie so much happier and the house so cheerful and

alive, Sir Anthony watched over it all with a benign smile. Most importantly the village mellowed and would greet Stuart and Dave whenever they strolled to the pub or the shops.

On the day that the aliens were due to arrive, Stuart and Dave took their usual walk. They knew when the visitors were due to arrive and the plan was to bump into them where the lanes converged at the village green.

It was Dave who was the most startled. He recognised the men who had bought him and Demetrius back in ancient Greece. For Dave it was bizarre as the men looked at him.

"Hi." Dave said as he recovered, "I haven't seen you for ages. Two and a half thousand years to be precise. What have you been doing all this time?"

"We wondered how you escaped." one of the men said, "You have a dimensional drill as well."

"I suppose the portal does drill through inter-dimensional space." Stuart said, "We need to talk. Would you like some lunch?"

"Why?"

"Because we're not very fond of you taking folk from our planet. We'd like you to stop doing it."

"It's our planet." one of the men said, "You're the interlopers. We only tolerate you because you'll make useful workers."

"How about that lunch so we can talk in private?" Stuart suggested, "Then you can return to your ship."

"No, you will come with us." the man said, "You're intelligent enough to realise that we're armed and can force you."

He paused, "When did you learn our language? Never mind, you can explain later."

"You might be armed but you can't force us." Stuart retorted, "There's people around and you don't want to be conspicuous."

"Peasants." the man sneered, "Who'd listen to them."

"The police, the newspapers would love a story about mysterious strangers killing people with futuristic ray guns."

"What are ray guns? Do they work like our stunners?" the man asked.

"If you look then you'll see some village boys coming over. Do you want to discuss this sort of thing in front of them."

"Then come with us." the man said, "Do not think that we will comply with instructions from the likes of you."

"I take it that your people don't understand the concept of an invitation." Stuart said, "You can go but understand that we'll block your future visits to Earth."

The second man spoke for the first time, "We do understand hospitality and we'll eat with you."

Stuart handed the approaching children some money.

"Do me a favour, will you," he said, "Share this amongst you but don't talk about my guests here."

"Thanks Mister Stuart." the boy replied, "We ain't seen nuffing."

"We're too close to London." Stuart laughed as they strolled along the lane back to the manor. That boy had a definite cockney twang."

"He spoke like a peasant so you should not have bribed him."

"So you only bribe nobles do you?" Stuart asked.

They walked on in a hostile silence.

Sir Anthony greeted them before personally showing them into the dining room then excusing himself. They found a buffet lunch and helped themselves before sitting around the table.

"My name is Stuart and my friend is Dave. Do you have names?"

"Of course. My name is Larik and my junior is Merrill. What do you know of this world? I mean it's early history."

"Not much. It's about five billion years old and life has existed on it for about half a billion years."

"Your ignorance is amazing. The Earth is nearer ten billion years old and though your cycle of life does indeed go back half a billion years so did ours."

"Your cycle?" Dave asked.

"Our next cycle will last considerably longer." Larik said.

"I think I see where this conversation is going." Stuart said, "Why don't you just spell it out for us though."

"Some two hundred years ago there was a nuclear war. Only the colonies on Mars survived. We knew that it would be impossible to return to Earth in the foreseeable future but we were discovering the full potential of the dimensional drill. We developed a plan to return to our home

"We reseeded the Earth once it had recovered sufficiently and allowed it to replenish itself naturally but guiding the life development. Once we created your kind, we collected samples to check our progress. Don't worry. Once we completed our examinations they were allowed to work with our own peasants. They are happy enough."

"Someone who met you mentioned sport." Dave said.

"Of course. By competing against the arrivals we develop our own bodies to cope with Earth's gravity when we return. We are completing our preparations and I can tell you that we can successfully interbreed."

"Just out of curiosity, what do you intend doing now?" Stuart asked.

"It would seem that you are arriving at a level of technology that would give us a level of comfort." Larik replied, "Once you have destroyed yourselves we can take what's left over."

"What makes you think that we're going to destroy ourselves." Dave asked.

"We programmed small changes to the DNA of this cycle. We had to be careful to make sure that we still ended up with humans but we increased aggression and greed. The beauty of it is that they only surface in times of plenty. During hard times the need to survive dominates."

"I don't understand." Dave said.

"That's why your kind will be the peasants." Larik sneered, "Look at the predator in the wild. When its belly is full, its prey knows that it prefers to rest and are not afraid. Your earliest ancestors were like that. You always have full bellies so you use your energy elsewhere. Greed sees to it that you fight each other."

"And you say that your people planned all this." Stuart said.

"Of course."

"But we now have nuclear weapons. If we destroy ourselves you'll be back to a radioactive world."

"You lie." Larik said, "There are no traces of radioactive materials. When we return again you'll have destroyed yourselves with simple explosives."

"Wrong." Stuart retorted, "We're from about ninety years in the future. The nuclear arsenal would pollute the Earth for a thousand years."

"So we must return now." Larik said, "Thank you for the warning."

"No you will not invade us. You will go home and you will not kidnap any more of our people." Stuart said.

"You did not listen. We created you so you belong to us." Larik snapped.

"You didn't create us." Stuart exclaimed, "You said yourself that all you did was to guide evolution. It's an intriguing plan to bring your people forward to when the Earth was ready for you again but it's not going to work."

"You can't stop it." Larik retorted, "I told you, you are programmed to destroy yourselves."

"And I'm telling you that we're going to release everyone that you've taken on this trip before you return home."

"How?" Larik laughed, "We still control and guide you."

Stuart pulled out the translator that hung around his neck.

"This device is a communicator." he said, "That's how I know that your ship's engines are being disabled as we speak. We'll return the parts and the spares when your prisoners have been released."

"You would not dare." Larik exclaimed angrily.

"Your shuttle hasn't been harmed so you can go and find out." Stuart replied, "But you can't leave orbit until we're done, and your plans stop now."

"Despite your fine talk, you prove yourself inferior." Larik said, "I told you; our plans are buried deep in your DNA. You cannot stop them."

"Maybe not but we can stop you from taking advantage of them. Don't forget, if you can make the changes then we've got millions of years to stop them. It was good of you to warn us."

Stuart did not need the look of fury on Larik's face to warn him as the visitor lunged forward but they were separated by the table. Instead he reached into his pocket and drew out his gun, aiming it at Stuart. Merrill also drew aiming at Dave.

"So, which is the violent race?" Stuart asked, "Just return your prisoners."

"Kneel down put your hands behind your back." Larik commanded.

"No." Stuart replied. He sounded calm but he was watching the gun a little nervously.

"They can kill." Merrill said, "And you're making Larik very angry."

"He's making me angry." Stuart said, "It's your last chance to leave peaceably. Now put your toys away like good boys and then you can go home."

In the moments as Larik's fury welled up to bursting point, Merrill wondered why Stuart was goading Larik. He did not have time to react though for Larik fired, holding his hand on the trigger. Instead of looking on in triumph as the insolent pup died, writhing in agony, he just stood becoming more bewildered. Stuart stood smiling, glancing down at the electrical discharges flickering across his chest, relaxed and completely unperturbed.

"Could you stop now, please?" Stuart asked, "It does tickle a bit and Sir Anthony's going to wonder about the smell of ozone in here."

It was Stuart's calmness that was unnerving and the complete failure of his most deadly weapon had left him so confused that he could not react to anything. It was Merrill who put away his weapon and gently rested his hand on Larik's arm. The gentle contact penetrated Larik's thoughts and he relaxed.

"An impressive demonstration." Merrill said, "Allow me to congratulate you."

"It was easy really." Stuart replied, "We have a material called kevlar. Layers of that to stop anything penetrating to the skin, layers of metal foil to dissipate the charge and we're nicely protected."

"We also have unlimited energy to recharge them." Merrill said, "I'll remember to aim at your face next time."

Stuart drew his own taser.

"We'd have changed tactics." he said, "And we can aim at your body can't we?"

"Are we your prisoners now?" Merrill asked.

"No, return to your shuttle." Stuart replied, "It was interesting seeing it manoeuvred into that barn but you shouldn't leave it for too long."

"You will pay for this insult to Kramon." Larik snarled, "Merrill, you'll be reported for your friendliness to the enemy."

"Our mission is a failure." Merrill retorted, "Maybe you need to make a report that we can agree on, not argue about. May we go?"

Stuart nodded and without another word, Larik and Merrill left.

"Let's see how James and the others are doing." Stuart said, "We can warn them that Larik and Merrill are a little upset and that they don't like being opposed."

Tiy and Ani

After his career in military intelligence, James should have been used to clandestine operations but nothing in his experience prepared him for sabotaging an alien spaceship. Neither did it prepare him for rescuing a group of disorientated or frightened youngsters. However, his first task had been to round up the servants who looked after the cells. As he entered their room he stopped, staring, appalled at the sight before him. A boy lay naked on a bed, obviously very ill. His skin, which was covered in blotches had a slight pink tinge, and he was bleeding from his nose, ears, gums and rectum. James was appalled, recognising the symptoms of advanced radiation sickness.

The other servant was dabbing water onto his forehead, trying to comfort him. James thought he recognised the short tunic the boy was wearing and without thinking spoke in Athenian.

"Let me look at him, son." he said as gently as he could.

The boy stood leapt up to stand against a wall as James swung his pack from his back and dropped it on the floor before extracting a radiation meter.

The boy could not imagine what James was doing or who he was but he could detect a sudden urgency in his manner and actions.

"Come with me." he snapped but the boy merely stood looking at him with a mixture of bewilderment and fear.

Not Greek then. James thought to himself, *Still that would have been too easy but I haven't got time to mess around.*

James dragged the boy out of the room before digging into his bag and handing him a translator.

As James led the way he kept glancing at the meter relaxing as the readings dropped almost immediately. Even though he marched briskly along he was patient enough to try to relax the boy by pointing out features such as the floor and ceiling, expecting the boy to repeat the words in English. Reaching the portal, he picked up the intercom.

"I've got two boys suffering from radiation poisoning." he announced, "The general surroundings are at safe levels so I'm wondering if the decks nearer the engine rooms are the source. If the really sick one was assigned to cleaning them that would explain it. Brian, will you use a probe to check the ship over and will you speak with the Terzons, please. They'll know what to do."

Turning to the boy he continued, "Your friend is very ill and I don't know if we can save him. You've got a little of the illness but you should be fine."

"It was our punishment." the boy said looking puzzled, "They said we could not produce babies so we were sentenced to doing the dirtier jobs. I was warned not to go near him but I couldn't let him suffer like that."

"No, of course you couldn't." James said, "I could kill the people who did that to him though."

Briefly James' anger petrified the boy but as the meaning in his words sunk in, the boy nodded and replied with a nervous, "So could I, Master. What language am I speaking?"

James aimed the radiation meter at the boy as he asked, "What's your name?"

"Ani, Master." the boy replied.

"Very well, Ani, my name is James, please call me that. I don't like being called Master. And you're speaking English with the help of the necklace I gave you."

"Yes Mas…" Ani trailed off nervously looking at James who smiled encouragingly.

"Let's get you looked at and then we'll sort the rest of the prisoners out."

"May I stay with Tiy please Master?" Ani asked.

Even as he spoke, he stared in horror at the monsters stepping out of the portal.

"Don't be scared, Ani." James chuckled, "They're just men in radiation suits. Think of it as armour protecting them from the illness that Tiy has."

"You called it radiation sickness, Master James." Ani said, "I've seen men wearing mail like it before. Will they kill Tiy quickly?"

"No." James exclaimed, "They'll try to make him comfortable."

Ani just nodded uncertainly.

"Let's get you sorted out." James said as kindly as he could.

While a Terzon doctor examined the boys, assisted by Dr. Tobias, James visited Brian.

"I think they're Egyptian." he said, "I keep picking up a name or rather the translators pick up on something about him reporting events to King Narmer and praying to Serket. I've got a date of around 3000 BCE."

"And what are we going to do with him?" Brian asked, "We only just get away with Demetrius though I'm sure Bill at the pub knows where he comes from. We'll never get away with another lad with a history fetish."

"I know." James agreed, "Let's hope he was just a field hand who couldn't read or write."

"Or keep house." James added, "Could you imagine Demetrius and him coming to blows over the housekeeping?"

"Don't even joke about it." Brian groaned, "You'd better get back. Let's get the other prisoners back home safely."

"I'm going to disable their shuttle as well, if I can." James said, "Don't worry, it won't be anything more drastic than hiding the equivalent of the ignition key but I need time."

James often thought of his time before he met Stuart. Although he was becoming disillusioned about the paranoia that surrounded his work in Military Intelligence, the work itself was interesting and varied.

Even so, it was nothing compared to what he was doing now and the idea that he had captured a spaceship to free the prisoners it carried, seemed bizarre almost surreal. Worse still, was that as he examined the engines that drove the shuttle he actually understood the components he was studying, thanks to the translator, and easily found a vital component that could not be replaced.

It was just after Stuart and Dave visited Sir Anthony that James began planning his part of the operation with the others.

"OK." James said when he was ready, "We're going to sort this out by location. We can track Larik and Merrill from when they arrived. They landed, captured a couple of youngsters then took them up to the mother ship then came back down to another site."

"Yet they landed the mother ship to pick up Dave and Demetrius" Richard said, "How come?"

"Possibly they were getting worried about detection. Don't forget Dave and Demetrius had a good hour's walk in deserted countryside."

Richard nodded as James continued, "We'll take them out of the cells in the order they were taken and simply return them to a minute or so after they left. There's only one problem. What happens if anyone doesn't want to go back? Some of them had pretty bleak lives."

"Larik and Merrill just stunned them if they argued about fitting the collar." Brian said, "I'd say we should do the same except that Stuart would never speak to us again. We're rescuing them in 1925 so we've got all the time we need at this end. Let's set up a camp on a deserted island, evacuate the ship to there and then see what they want to do."

"That sounds better." James replied, "It'll give me more time to talk to them. In many ways I can't forget Stuart's a kid but I agree with you Brian, I'd like him to approve of what we're doing."

In fact, it proved easy to get the prisoners off the ship especially the ones that had been imprisoned the longest for like Dave had been, they were bored.

Although he recognised American, Australian as well as British accents others did not speak English at all. One boy and girl spoke a language that not even the translator could recognise. It sounded French, with a strong Caribbean lilt but fortunately they had been put into different cells and their cell-mates helped guide them.

With Richard and Gable's assistance they were escorted to the island James had chosen for them, far from any shipping route so they were unlikely to be visited while they were there.

With James already feeling worried about Ani, Stuart did not want to get involved with any of the others so he kept his distance, contenting himself with ensuring the portal was activated at their site twice a day.

He was more interested in talking to Dr. Tobias and he found James at the hospital.

"I'm sorry." the doctor said, "There's not much we can do for Tiy. I don't know if I understand it right but he's got a very low sperm count so those bastards decided he was worthless. They used him like a remote control robot. He did maintenance on the engines under their supervision so he worked in irradiated areas for long periods where Larik and Merrill would only go for short periods and even then they'd be wearing radiation suits."

He paused, "If the translator's worked it out correctly then Tiy comes from Mesopotamia a couple of thousand years before Ani. His sperm count is low as well so they weren't worried about him either. My guess is that they stayed on the ship permanently but Ani stayed clean to look after the fresh stock. Once Tiy became too ill to work Ani would then take over Tiy's work and they'd replace Ani with a new boy.

"Ani's hovering on the edge of the maximum lifetime exposure, I'd think twice about giving him an X-ray and we can't let him near Tiy. I've discussed it with the Terzon doctors and we're agreed that we shouldn't offer treatment for his sperm count."

James looked at him quizzically.

"He could lead a normal long life," Dr. Tobias said, "but he could well be more prone to cancers and he could pass genetic damage onto his children. We'd try to treat him if he asked, it's not that high a risk but it would have to be his decision when he understands."

"Surely we spend more time in space." James said, "Aren't we at risk?"

"With the protection we've added, Resolution has a lower radiation level than on Earth. Stuart was worried that if we planted a probe on their ship then the signal would get lost in stray effects from the engines. He was right, hard radiation would have been a key factor and Tiy spent a significant amount of time outside the protected zone."

"Anything else?" James asked.

"Only that Tiy knows that he's dying. Poor kid just wants to go home but I've told him that the sun is prepared to receive his body and look after him."

"Go on." James prompted.

"It was something Brian said. He dropped some radioactive materials into the sun as the safest way of disposing of them and Tiy is happy to have the sun-god look after him."

"Brian's not going to be happy but I'm going to look after Ani." James said, "I might book some portal time and get him back to his people but either way, I'm going to see that he has a good home."

Dr. Tobias could feel James' fury as he stomped off to find Ani. James found him staring tearfully through the window of the isolation room that held Tiy.

He smiled in greeting at James.

"Tiy might pass his sickness onto me so I can't go to him." he announced sadly.

"But he's in good hands." James replied, "They're trying to make him better if they can."

Ani nodded.

"Are you gods?" Ani asked, "Tiy's so ill that his hair just fell out. How do have so much power over life and death?"

"You have people who know about herbs that cure fevers." James replied, "Our healers have learnt more."

"Am I your slave now?" Ani asked, "Or will you sell me?"

"Will you trust me for now?" James asked, "I'd like you to obey me as you'd obey your father and not as a slave obeys a Master. That means you say what you don't like and ask if you want something."

"I understand what you mean but you never met my father, did you?" Ani grinned.

"Hungry?" James asked.

"Yes." Ani replied, "I think that I should call you sir. You are a soldier and my father was a farmer so I should be respectful."

"You're learning a lot from that translator." James grinned.

"I know it's not a magical necklace, sir." Ani grinned in his turn, "It's like a scribe that reads and writes down all knowledge. It lives by eating tiny bits of lightning called electricity."

"And you'll live by grabbing a plateful of that vegetable stew and grabbing a plateful of fruit." James said gruffly despite the twinkle in his eye.

Ani caught James' mood and replied, "Yes Master, I'll obey to the best my ability."

As Ani sat back after his third plate he looked at James, "What are football and baseball, sir? The translator thinks that I should be trained to use them."

"They're games." James explained, "There's another one, cricket, that people play."

"A game, sir?" Ani looked puzzled, "But don't soldiers dress up in armour to attack the enemy?"

"It's a game so we don't want people to get hurt." James tried to explain, "But there's always a few who get carried away and take it too seriously."

Ani nodded wisely, "Ptah was like that. If something went wrong he'd work himself up into a temper then hit out at anything. He got a terrible whipping when he flung a scythe at a tree and blunted it."

He frowned, "Is this your thought? You don't whip people."

"No, or rather yes it's my thought." James replied, "And no, we don't whip people. We rescued another boy who was a slave and he's having trouble learning to think like a free boy again. The translator's picking up on me wondering how you'd fit into my world."

"If I think about the necklace, it tells me things." Ani said, "It tells me that you'd rather send me home. It also tells me that it could seem as if I'd only been gone during the flicker of the fire. If that is your command, sir then I will obey but I would rather stay with you. I would like to sleep through the reign of a thousand kings and see more of the marvels you have."

"You understand a lot of what has happened to you." James

said.

"I served on a spaceship, sir." Ani smiled, "Before that I only knew of the reed boats sailing on the River. If I hadn't tried to understand then I think I would have gone mad."

He paused and looked puzzled, "You started thinking about... ah, you call it sex and how your people have lots of rules. You started thinking that you had to explain it all and how you would not be interested in me, then you became embarrassed so the necklace switched off."

"I slept through the reigns of a couple of kings as you put it." James said, "I would say that I jumped forward in time by about forty years. Either way people's attitudes had changed and it was so easy to offend someone by saying something that was perfectly normal back home."

"I understand." Ani replied, "But I'm not a man am I? I cannot seed a woman."

"You are a man because of the way you're dealing with everything that's happening to you." James exclaimed, "I'm worried that you'll feel like an outcast while you adapt to our world."

"I could act like a king's slave. I could stand quietly waiting to be spoken to and not pushing forward." Ani said.

"OK!" James said, "Let's give it a go. From now on, I call you son and you call me, uncle and your name is Andy, not Ani. Get that translator to teach you about Memphis, Tennessee, and get you speaking in a Tennessee accent. You're my nephew visiting from the States because you're getting over a highly traumatic event."

"I understand, Uncle but shouldn't you call me nephew."

"You've only jumped five thousand years." James chuckled, "That's nowhere near long enough to fully understand the English language."

While James got to know Ani/Andy, Stuart watched Merrill and Larik hurry back to their ship.

"So what happens now?" Dave asked.

"I don't know." Stuart replied, "I'd like to verify their story but if I travelled back that far I'd want Brian monitoring the portal. "

"Why not use a probe?" Dave asked.

"Because I didn't think of it." Stuart laughed, "Of all the possible disasters I never thought of a war like this. I still reckon that we should take a look at these Martian colonies though."

"Then what?" Dave asked.

"I still don't know." Stuart replied, "Get copies of their genetic research and find someone who understands it. I'd be surprised if Mars has changed much in the last billion years so their colonists would have had as many problems as ours would."

"Damn these translators." Dave snapped, "I've got some memory surfacing of water activity on Mars only millions of years ago. Could that be anything to do with our friends?"

"Guess what I'm going to say." Stuart laughed, "I don't know. They were talking of a colony lasting a couple of hundred years, five hundred million years ago. How long did this water activity last?"

"That's what I meant, these translators give us information but it may not be relevant."

"What's more relevant, what did you make of them?" Stuart asked.

"Not much." David replied, "How about pompous twats?"

"That's what I think." Stuart said, "Technically they're slightly ahead of us but they didn't seem very bright."

"I know what you mean." Dave said, "Their attitude seem to be that nothing would dare touch them so they were sloppy."

"OK so we go slow and careful and beat them with our superior intellect." Stuart exclaimed, "It's a start. First thing is to give Sir Anthony his dining room back and the second is to rescue him."

Rescue

Still enjoying the peace and quiet of Sir Anthony's home, Stuart was in no rush to leave.

"You're welcome to stay for as long as you wish." Sir Anthony said, "I'm getting back some confused memories. One is of a tingle in the neck, which made me forget things, another is of a city but there something wrong with the sky or there wasn't one. I also felt very heavy."

He paused, "Then I was somewhere else and I was very light. I've got memories of jumping incredible distances. Does it mean anything to you?"

"Possibly." Stuart said, "It sounds as if you came with us on a trip but why would we take you?"

He paused, "I'm sorry, that sounded rude but I can't imagine a ten year old boy taking part in one of our ventures."

"I understood." Sir Anthony said, "I can't imagine it either."

Stuart chose to remain one more night, wanting to find out more about Sir Anthony's accident. Sir Anthony handed him a piece of paper.

"You asked me to write down the time place and date." Sir Anthony said, "I've spent my life convincing myself that it was all a dream. I couldn't account for the coin of course but it was easier to believe than the truth. Now I'm getting so many memories back I think I wanted to believe that it was real all the time. I could take you to the place if you like."

"That would be helpful." Stuart acknowledged, "We're leaving tomorrow."

Philips entered with a message for Sir Anthony.

"I hope we haven't given you too much extra work, Philips." Stuart added.

"No sir." Philips replied, "Now that I know what it's really for I find wireless fascinating. I wonder what they'll think of next."

"How about talking pictures." Stuart smiled, "Remember, Mrs Donaldson asked me to drop off the latest cinema magazines, or do you just fancy Mary Pickford?"

"Fancy Mrs Pickford?" Philips asked, "Oh no sir. I find the stories of all the stars most interesting. I should think talking pictures are some time off."

"Keep an eye on Al Jolson." Stuart said, "He might surprise you."

"Yes sir." Philips replied, "I'll do that and thank you sir."

"You've made Philips' day." Sir Anthony laughed, "I let Geoffrey take him into town when there's anything new at the Odeon cinema. I'm surprised that you didn't mention television and what was it called, internet streaming."

Stuart looked on aghast.

"How do know all this stuff?" he asked.

"I had an injection that should have cleared my short term memory but you'd loaned me a translator. Dr. Tobias was worried that it was stimulating my mind so that the drug wouldn't work so well and he was right. The adventures of Luke Skywalker were burned into my mind. I could never remember how I knew the story but my school chums loved it when I recounted the story. Seeing you again seems to have triggered my memory including what the translator taught me."

"Could that be a problem?" Stuart asked.

Sir Anthony looked as if he was about to faint. He stared desperately at Stuart muttering, "No not that."

Stuart leapt up to offer assistance but Sir Anthony raised his hand.

"I'm all right." he said though still clearly agitated, "Memories are still coming back. You and Brian are deviants yet no one in your home village cares. I don't think that I do either after what happens. Please give me a moment."

Stuart waited patiently as Sir Anthony marshalled his thoughts.

"It wasn't only Dr. Tobias who injected me and he only did so under the directions of another doctor who also used hypnotism and something else, auto-suggestion? I'm not sure. They explained that I would recover all my memories but I needed to block them while I grew up and chose my life. I understand now. I remember seeing an aeroplane for the first time and thinking how marvellous it was. If my memory hadn't been blocked I would have tried describing the jet engine to the pilot.

"I was so anxious to learn and had a translator that told me everything I asked. The conflicts between my knowledge and the rest of the world's knowledge could have sent me mad or at least, made everyone around me think that I was mad. Yes and I also now know the dangers of changing the time-line and what you call anomalies and forks.

"To sum up, the drugs are not breaking down they're fulfilling the promise that Dr. Tobias made. Various triggers have released memories in a way that I can cope. The first trigger was of a vegetarian poacher."

Stuart smiled then stopped as Sir Anthony added quietly, "The last memory to be released is that Reggie is developing leukaemia. Dr. Tobias noticed that he was lethargic and did some tests. Now can you imagine what will happen to Freddie if his first real friend dies? What are the chances of him falling back into Selena's clutches?"

"How does Reginald meet Dr. Tobias?" Stuart asked.

"It's quite simple really." Sir Anthony smiled, "I've always had the feeling that Freddie should be an inquisitive little boy and I've said too much."

It was the following evening and Stuart had left that morning. Sir Anthony settled in the library. Phillips entered to see if he needed anything.

"I'm expecting Geoffrey." Sir Anthony said, "I'm not sure what time he's coming and I feel like some company while I'm waiting. Would you care to join me in a drink?"

"The house does seem quiet, Sir Anthony." Phillips said, "I take it Master Freddie is playing with Reginald."

"Something like that." Sir Anthony grinned, "When he arrives Geoffrey will need a large drink. It may help him if he sees you enjoying one."

"I think I'm going to miss Mr. Stuart and Mr. David." Phillips said, "It's been an interesting week."

"Selena doesn't think so." Sir Anthony grinned.

"I'm relaxed enough to think that's a good thing." Phillips replied.

"So do I." Sir Anthony exclaimed.

He might have said more but he was interrupted by an urgent knocking. Philips went to bring him through. Aware that Geoffrey was agitated, puzzled at how Sir Anthony knew and following his orders he handed the drink to the chauffeur.

"Both of you, sit down please." Sir Anthony said waiting until they were settled, "Reggie's missing and you're worried because he's not well."

"He's here then." Geoffrey exclaimed sounding relieved, "I'm sorry if he's being a nuisance."

"Freddie and Reginald have sneaked off with Stuart." Sir Anthony said, "I know about it but I couldn't stop it. In fact, Freddie has my blessing. Now do you know how ill Reggie is?"

"Dr. Miller sent him for a blood test." Geoffrey replied, "He's saying there's nothing to worry about but he did say it needed to be done as quickly as possible. It's a little worrying."

"He has leukaemia." Sir Anthony said, "The blood test will confirm it, I'm afraid. However when he returns, he'll be cured."

"I don't understand." Geoffrey said.

"Will you trust me, please?" Sir Anthony said, "He's in good hands and he has my son as a companion."

"You shouldn't have let him go without consulting me." Geoffrey said angrily, "Phillips did you know?"

Phillips shook his head, "I assume Reginald and Master Freddie planned this together." he said.

"Yes but if you found out, why didn't you stop them, Sir Anthony?" Geoffrey exclaimed.

"The simple reason is that it was impossible." Sir Anthony said, "Another reason is that they're on an adventure that I've enjoyed and I couldn't deprive them of the fun I had. Would you have believed me if I'd said that Reggie's best chance of beating his leukaemia is with Stuart?"

Geoffrey was quiet for a time.

"You did secret work in the war." he said eventually, "Is this another top secret project?"

"It is." Sir Anthony replied, "But it goes beyond government secrets."

"Would you agree, Phillips?" Geoffrey asked.

"I think I do." Phillips replied, "I'm not sure who Mr. Stuart is but he's an exceptional young man."

"Very well." Geoffrey said, "We'll do as you suggest. Dr. Miller wants to see us urgently and we have an appointment tomorrow."

He glanced at his glass.

"I can't think what I'm going to tell Sarah."

As Phillips hastened to fill everyone's glass, he continued, "We are worried. It's so rare for Dr. Miller to say urgent."

They sat in a companionable silence each missing the boys in their own way. There were still loose ends. What to say to the boy's schools and what to tell Dr. Miller.

The schools were easy. They were off on a trip with Sir Anthony's cousin and a tutor had been provided. Geoffrey's appointment with Dr. Miller was more dramatic. Geoffrey had been briefed by Sir Anthony.

"I'm glad you didn't bring Reginald." Dr. Miller said, "I'm afraid I have some bad news."

"We already know." Geoffrey said, "He has leukaemia and although it's in its early stages, it'll get progressively worse. I expect you to give him six months."

Dr. Miller stared in amazement.

"How did you know?" he asked.

"I don't fully understand what this means." Geoffrey said, "His blood has damaged or immature white blood cells. He's gone somewhere where they can destroy the damaged cells."

"I don't know of any such place." Dr. Miller said uncertainly, "There are unscrupulous men who would prey on your fears and take your life savings."

"There's no money involved and it has Sir Anthony's approval." Geoffrey explained, "They've anticipated your diagnosis so I have to accept that the rest is genuine."

Dr. Miller nodded, "In that case, good luck to you. Let's hope for the best."

Meanwhile Stuart was dealing with Brian, relieved that he wasn't standing in front of his desk but sitting comfortably in the living room with Demetrius serving them coffee and biscuits.

"I accept that you couldn't predict a couple of stowaways." Brian exclaimed, "Nor could you predict meeting a child needing medical treatment but you got far too close to that family. If you had checked the site properly and landed on public ground none of this would have happened."

"You said much the same thing about Demetrius." James said, "Only it was David who got involved. They're not detached scientists or are you saying that Stuart set up this weird time loop with Sir Anthony?"

"I don't know what to think." Brian snapped, "And you're as bad. It's not only Andy. Why on Earth did you suggest taking Joe Milnes back in time to buy tractor parts?"

"I know. I just didn't think. I was in the pub reading an article on Higgs-Boson particles. He asked me whether we were having any luck finding his tractor parts and I wasn't concentrating. The thing is he didn't laugh at me or think I was crazy. He just asked whether he'd have to take cash."

"It sounds like your theory is in action, Stuart." Brian said, "He's accepting that we can do something but he's focussing on his part."

"We could use your bank account, James." Stuart said, "We opened it in 1973. He's been a good friend to us and concentrating or not, we'll offend him if we don't take him after we offered."

"Our security gets more and more ridiculous." Brian exclaimed angrily, "I'm beginning to think that we should leave the village."

"Security is pretty good." James said, "David's parents are starting to ask whether Dave could get a degree in astrophysics and they still believe that we're doing research into solar particles. Do you know why Demetrius started writing a story based on his early life?"

"Yes of course." Brian replied, "He was talking to that professor friend and mentioned how homesick he felt when his parents sold him. Luckily Bill was keeping an eye on him and warned him not to get lost in the book he was writing. That's what I mean, all the locals seem to know what we're doing."

"Some communities can be very close-knit but I never expected to find anything this extreme." James said, "And they do appreciate the money you invest in the village."

"So you don't think that we should send Freddie and Reggie straight back home, James?"

"It would be kinder to shoot Reggie than abandon him to a slow protracted death." James retorted, "I don't think that we can send them back while he's so ill. I wonder how Dave is enjoying himself, babysitting."

In fact Dave was quite happy. They were on the lizard planet and there was more than enough to keep two boisterous youngsters occupied. He was content to sit quietly watching as the two boys played some complicated tag game with the monkeys.

"You always have something new to show us." the lizard said, "Do your young ever rest, and is hitting my head really a sign of affection?"

"When it's gentle it's called patting but if you don't like it then ask them to stop."

"No, I feel their emotions. They're confused and intense but they add up to something warm and stimulating. I think that they want to talk to you so I'll leave you."

Reginald was tired. Freddie, concerned for his friend sat down beside him.

"I still don't understand what made you sneak into the stable in the first place." Dave said.

"We were playing and Reggie needed a rest. We'd watched you and Stuart going in and out and we wondered why. We were only going to have a quick look around then come and say good bye to you. We saw this round thing appear and wanted to have a closer look. The door opened and we took a peek inside."

He looked at Dave, "It was all so mysterious and a bit like Alice in Wonderland. I just had to explore. Then we started floating and drifted away from the door and couldn't get back. We reached a wall and held onto a rail and waited until you came through. Stuart saw us as you came out then suddenly the door thing got bigger and looked like a tube."

"Then we brought you here." Dave said.

"Because you've got to let events pan out." Freddie exclaimed triumphantly, "I heard you and Stuart talking and you think the portal should be monitored more and not left on automatic."

"We'll have to do something about toilet breaks." Dave grinned.

"You said that before." Freddie exclaimed, "I'm hungry. May I get something to eat."

"There's plenty of fruit and juices. Help yourself." David replied, "We'll have a curry takeaway later."

Freddie looked puzzled but turned as Dr. Tobias arrived. David spoke to Reginald and introduced him.

"This is Mr. Tobias." David said, "He's a doctor but he's called Mr. because he prefers cutting people open in an operating theatre. So just to remind him that he's just going to give you medicine, call him Dr. Tobias."

It was not much of a joke but Reginald smiled and looked at Dr. Tobias.

"Hello *Dr.* Tobias." he said.

"Will you come with me." Dr. Tobias said, "I'd like to do some tests. We won't be long."

"Will he be all right?" Freddie asked unhappily, "I've got friends at school but we need chums there, it's not like choosing someone because we want to. I like Reggie and I want to be his friend."

"I understand." David said, "Stuart and I were friends when we were younger. Then we drifted apart and I missed him. I had other friends but it wasn't the same. How would your best friend at school cope with this trip?"

"He'd call Reggie a lower class oik and expect him to be a servant. I'm not supposed to talk to the locals if I go into town. It's been fun going into the village with you and it's much nicer now that Father knows I play with Reggie."

"Do you understand that you're on another planet?" Dave asked.

Freddie nodded, "But I mustn't tell anyone at school, mustn't I?"

"No you mustn't." David said, "If I said that you'd travelled in time, would you believe me?"

"I've read H. G. Wells *Time Machine.*" Freddie replied, "Are there any Eloi or Morlocks?"

"No." Dave laughed, "At least not yet. Stuart and I have a job to do. If Stuart agrees, would you like to help?"

"Yes please." Freddie beamed.

"Wait here. I'll be back shortly."

For once it was Stuart who seemed annoyed.

"Brian's right, you know." he said, "We're getting ourselves into a real tangle. I'm not happy about Freddie meeting his dad when he's still a boy. There could be problems."

"I don't think that we can avoid it." David replied, "What would have happened to us if Sir Anthony hadn't started getting his memories back?"

"You mean that he might have been less willing to listen." Stuart said.

"There's something else." David added, "I know that we sent the Martians packing but I don't think that they'll give up that easily. We might need a secure base again."

"They're not Martians, they come from Earth." Stuart retorted.

"Well I'm going to call them Martians." David exclaimed, "What are you going to call them? First Time Around Earthmen?"

"Good point." Stuart laughed, "Let's go and find James. Let's see what he found out on the ship. Demetrius can go and fetch Freddie."

They found James in the pub chatting to Bill the landlord and Joe Milnes. Joe bought their drinks.

"James is saying that you can make some sort of trip to get those parts." he said, "It would be good to keep the old girl going for a few more years."

"You don't use it as a working tractor do you?" Stuart asked.

"Sometimes." Joe replied, "It's lighter than the new one and doesn't crush the ground as much. I like to do the rounds of the fairs and shows with it though. It wins the odd prize too."

"We've got a big project on at the moment." Stuart said, "If you can hang on for a bit we'll sort it."

"Fine, there's no rush." Joe replied, "The barn's yours for as long as you need it."

"Thanks. We don't use it all that much but it's nice to know it's available when we do need it." Stuart said, "And that we've got a backup in an emergency."

"Still keep it." Joe said, "You do a lot for the village and you keep an eye on them incomers. I've got to get back for the afternoon milking. "

Bill had moved onto other customers so they settled round a table to talk.

"Their ship is pretty basic." James said, "And like we've said before, their routines are pretty sloppy. It ties in with your opinion of them. They're so arrogant they don't believe that anything can touch them. The guys you met are the space travellers and are trained to have some knowledge of Earth. There's two servants Dave mentioned the one who maintains the cell area but between work duties they stay in their own quarters."

"Do we have any information on the colony?" Stuart asked.

"There were four. Two at each pole and were mostly underground."

"OK." Stuart said, "Let's take Joe up on his offer and install a couple of probes in the barn. Let's see how far back we can go in this gravity. I'm going to find Brian."

Stuart was obviously bothered about something so neither James nor Dave argued with him.

"It's Freddie and Anthony." Stuart said as he settled in the library, "I don't mind helping Reggie and since we know him I don't mind rescuing Anthony either. My problem is introducing two boys who could be brothers but are father and son. Do we keep them apart? Supposing Reggie has to stay for a few months, do we send him back to just after he left so that he's suddenly six months bigger or kidnap him. Even if he is treated, don't cancer patients have to be checked regularly?"

"Come in Freddie." Brian said softly. Stuart spun round to see Freddie and Demetrius standing at the door.

"Sorry, I didn't mean to eavesdrop." Freddie said, "I just wanted to say hello."

"Did you hear everything?" Stuart asked.

Freddie nodded, "Father mentioned slipping on some rocks. He told me about a dream he had where he played cricket with the monkeys. He was on the Lizard planet wasn't he and we're going to rescue him, aren't we.”

“If we do, how would you cope with knowing that a boy a bit younger than you is your father?” Brian asked.

“I don't know.” Freddie replied, “I promise that I'll do my best to look after him and I'm sorry that I'm such a nuisance.”

“You're not a nuisance.” Stuart said, “You are a problem in temporal mechanics though.”

Seeing Freddie's face screw up in puzzlement he added, “Time travel.”

“Can I help?” Freddie asked again.

“Only if you can convince me that I'm not fracturing the time-line beyond repair.” Stuart replied, “Demetrius, put a Star Wars DVD on for Freddie. His dad liked it so maybe he will.”

“Yes Master.” Demetrius replied.

Stuart was still uneasy. In theory he had all the time in the world but he was ignoring the real problem. Could a civilisation from half a billion years ago really be a threat: or was the real problem that Sir Anthony had been rescued by him in his memory but Stuart had not done it yet in his?

He went to bed early, slept restlessly and did not feel any happier in the morning. Still trying to clear his head, he planned on joining Demetrius for lunch and then helping him in the forge hoping that some hard work would clear his head.

As they were eating a man in his late thirties entered the bar. He reminded Stuart of someone but he could not decide who. The new arrival spoke to the landlord then approached Stuart.

“I'm sorry to interrupt your lunch,” he said, “But I believe that you're Stuart Johnson. I'm looking for a Stuart Johnson who may have known my great-grandfather. I was told that he'd be eating here with his Greek servant and that I shouldn't be put off by his age.”

“Please sit down.” Stuart replied, “This is Demetrius. He works for me but he's a friend more than servant. I'm sorry but I didn't catch your name.”

“Anthony Darrington.” he said holding out his hand, “Are you all right? You've gone quite white.”

Stuart nodded, “You remind me of someone I know but he's been probably been dead for some time. This may be a rude question but when were you born?”

“1975.” Anthony replied, “May I explain?”

“Please do.” Stuart exclaimed.

“My great-grandfather was Sir Frederick Darrington. As you

say, he died about twelve years ago but a few years before he sent for me. He took me into the library, sent everyone away and started off by saying that when he and his father were my age they became involved in the most incredible adventure. I wasn't sure how they were both involved at the same age but great-granddad went on to say that our family owed those at the centre of the story a great debt. He added that I was to help him fulfil a promise.

"It was then that he swore me to secrecy and made me promise to deliver it to you at just this time, date and place. I've always kept both promises. Do you recognise the box?"

"I believe it was once owned by Sir Anthony, I mean your great-great-grandfather." Stuart said, "He kept it in his desk at Thorndown Manor."

"I think it's the same desk." Anthony smiled, "Great-granddad did try to prepare me but this all feels so strange. I'm sorry. He told me some amazing stories as if they were true and had actually happened. Realising that he predicted just who would be sitting here nearly two decades earlier has made his stories seem even more real.

"He was extremely interested in astronomy and had an amazing knowledge of Mars. I remember we were talking about the possibility of there being life on Mars. He said that providing I turned up here as instructed, he'd take me and show me."

Stuart leapt up, heading for the bar, ordering a double scotch, he downed it in one swallow.

"Is something wrong?" Bill asked.

"I may have unravelled the entire space-time continuum that will destroy the universe." Stuart exclaimed.

"Oh! Let's hope you can fix it then." Bill smiled.

"I'll try." Stuart chuckled, "At least I'll try to make sense of it all."

"Demetrius." Stuart said when he returned to his table, "Look after our guest, please. Anthony, may I take the box and look at the contents in private."

"Certainly." Sir Anthony replied, "It's yours now."

Knowing that Freddie wanted to join Demetrius at the forge, Stuart headed for the lizard planet.

Meeting a contemporary Anthony was a shock and Stuart needed time to gather his thoughts. Once relaxed on a lounger he opened the box. Lying on top was an envelope marked 'Please Read This First'.

Stuart obliged and took out some sheets of typewritten paper.

Stuart began to read:

Dear Stuart,

This is the latest version of my account of our activities. Computers have finally got to Wordstar and floppy disks but you'll have to search second hand shops to find a machine that can read the disks I've included.

In your time, it was yesterday that I overheard you saying how worried you were and I promised to help. I was beginning to doubt that I could fulfil that promise but the latest Anthony seems to have more of the Darrington in him than either his father or grandfather or at least as I remember it. I have other offspring and descendants but Anthony is the one I chose.

First let me deal with Reggie. He made a full recovery. He spent time on Terzon but as soon as he was able he was sent home and Dr. Tobias visited every few months. He was lucky that there were no relapses and by the time he was sixteen he was pronounced clear.

Given the circumstances, Dad hired tutors, not only for both of us but any of the village boys who showed promise. Sometimes Thorndown Hall looked more like a school than anything. Reggie joined the RAF and sadly was shot down in 1942. He left a wife, a son and a daughter. He did try telling people about where he had been at first but his father said that the treatment had been severe and left him confused and delirious. He resented it for a time but he was keen to forget his illness so he settled down.

Seeing everyone laugh at Reggie's funny stories, I got the message and learned to keep quiet.

Aunt Selena bought herself a cottage just outside of the village and became a recluse. Rumours were rife that well into her fifties young men visited leaving with a considerable amount of money and a smile on their face. The Darringtons were still lords of the manor so it was all done very discreetly.

Phillips' interest in cinema increased though it was mainly devoted to the technical side. He became more of a family friend, sharing my interest in wireless. He remembered your advice about 'The Jazz Singer' and with his interest in what we called electronics he invested in a system that used a photo-cell to embed the speech directly onto the film. It made him a very wealthy man in his own right.

My point in mentioning them is that, yes, you did change history. However because of the nature of the people involved the changes were marginal.

After the mischief that I got up to with my father, albeit when he was ten, our relationship changed. In many ways we remained more friends than father and son. He continued managing our affairs until his death in the fifties when I took over. Before that I read mathematics at Oxford and wrote one or two obscure papers on switching in calculating machines. I was careful to match them to the technology then available but their significance was lost until war broke out and I was assigned to Bletchley Park where they broke the enemy codes.

I married and had three children. The two girls in their turn also married as did my son but where the girls made excellent lives for themselves, my son married a social climbing bitch. Fortunately they moved to America where she worked hard to be seen with all the right people. Their son was completely dominated by her and sent back to England to keep an eye on their inheritance. It allowed him to marry for love and I'm quite fond of his wife especially since they produced some delightful children.

The oldest who has brought the box to you reminds me so much of my father, especially when he was ten. I've lived long enough to keep the estate intact even if it is now a limited company. However I plan on leaving my shares to Anthony much to the fury of my daughter-in-law. We might have gone the way of so many old families in the thirties and after the war but you taught me how things were going to change. I approved of many of the social changes and I embraced them as well as adapting our affairs.

So again you changed history but I hope for the better.

This brings the story back to the promise I made. You must be careful but as events unfold they do turn out for the best. By now my eleven year old self should be talking to your visitor Anthony and learning that they both live at Thorndown. If you hurry then you may prevent Anthony from discovering that he's talking to his great, great-grandfather. If you don't hurry then he'll join you in rescuing my ten year old father. If you tighten up on security then you may stop Tony (that's my father at ten) and myself from getting too inquisitive and you having to find out just where and when we transported ourselves to.

They are your choices but I hope you go along with events as they stand.

One last thing. Dad had a folly built on your landing site. In fact it is a large room big enough to house a portal inside. There's also a path leading to a gate in the nearest point of the fence. The keys have changed over the years but there are copies in the box suitably dated. It's got a reputation for being haunted so maybe you did use it.

I could finish this letter with a conventional 'Yours Faithfully' or even with 'Best Wishes' but I think I'll make do with,

May the force be with you, Stuart.

Stuart read the letter twice before hurrying off to find Brian and the others and handing it around.

"I've been looking at the time-line for evidence of anomalies or forks." Brian said, "They show up as distortions at various dimensional levels and there isn't anything significant. That suggests that we're in the major time-line and events pan out as they should. Your problem, Stuart is keeping it that way. What really bothers me is that we've got this contemporary Anthony learning all about our secrets. That could give us problems in the future and he's as much an unknown to us as anyone else."

"The 1925 Sir Anthony's original story seems a little inconsistent." James said, "He said that he was alone except for the monkeys and Dr. Tobias."

"This was supposed to have been a simple problem while I recovered from those jumps." Stuart muttered irritably, "Now I'm just really worried about everything being out of sequence and causing one massive anomaly and I don't care if you haven't found it yet. It could still happen and I don't like the idea that events are already there and I'm just following a script."

"I think it's more like one of those computer games." James said, "You have to figure out the right path to get to the next level."

"And there might be more than one path to choose from." Brian added, "I agree it's disconcerting but I would never have expected Freddie to stow away either. What will you do next?"

"Rescue the 1897 Anthony." Stuart replied, "I think I've been putting it off because of all the complications and it's also why I didn't send them straight back. And yes I'll let Freddie and the present day Anthony come with me, if Anthony can accept what we're doing."

Just then the door opened and Freddie burst in towing an embarrassed Anthony after him.

"I'm Anthony's great-grandfather." he announced excitedly, "We've got the same bedroom at Thorndown. He found my secret store under a loose floorboard."

"Sit down, Anthony." Brian grinned, "You seem to be having an odd day."

"You could say that." Anthony laughed, "I don't know about this young lad being my great-grandfather but he certainly knows about Thorndown. I didn't know about the loose floorboard until great-grandfather told me about it and his box of mementoes hidden there and, how some of it had been passed on by his father. Among them was a flash drive and instructions to look after it. Remember this was in the eighties, I'd found it in a box supposedly from the twenties and it was another twenty years before a computer became available that could read it. It had been stored in a bag with one of those moisture-absorbing gel bags and it still worked after eighty years. There was a simple text file called 'Open First'. It warned me that it was all confidential, gave a list things I should bring today plus details of when and where I should buy certain items. The rest of the drive was a folder, full of pictures."

"What with Great-granddad's stories, the flash drive and one or two other oddities, I think I might be disappointed if you give me some straightforward explanation."

"It's mid afternoon." Stuart said, "Someone we know is in trouble and we have to help them. Do you want to come along and help?"

"Great-granddad told me that I'd be invited somewhere and insisted that I bring along a First Aid kit. He also said that it was a kind of test to be invited, to see if I'd freak out. At times he had an odd way of talking for an old country gentleman."

"And would you freak out if I said that we're off to rescue your great, great-grandfather in 1897?"

Anthony pulled out an envelope and opened it, reading the contents.

"I watched great-granddad write this in nineties." he said, "He sealed it and told me when to open it."

He handed the letter to Brian

"As you can see," he continued, "He's quoted Stuart's exact words. There's a phrase, 'suspension of belief'. I'm not willing to suspend belief that time travel is impossible but I'm willing to believe that Great-granddad believed that one day, I would travel to the past. I would find it easier to accept that I'm part of some great magical illusion and I am curious to see the next part of it but there's something else. I wanted to check with you first but I've got a package for a Joe Milnes in the car. I've also got a couple of bigger boxes stored in the folly that will need to be fetched by courier. Should I arrange it?"

Stuart stared, trying to clear his head.

"OK but first things first." Stuart said, "Let's clear up one paradox before we deal with another. We should only take an hour or so. You're welcome to stay tonight if you wish. That way we won't have to worry if we're held up."

"I was warned to prepare for an extended stay. I have my bags in the car but I didn't like to presume."

Stuart looked at Freddie, "Are you taking notes or do you just have a good memory?"

Freddie looked uncertain for a moment then grinned.

"I just don't think that I could forget any of this." he replied.

"Let's go then. James, Dave, I'd like you to come as far as Resolution. Anthony, Freddie and I will carry out the rescue while you act as back up. Brian will you operate the portal? You know, I'm suddenly happier having more people know about the portal, we've got more support if something goes wrong. I'll phone Dr. Tobias and make sure that he's nearby."

Compared to Bill's imaginary journey, Anthony had been prepared. However they allowed time for him to study the thin ring that he saw from the side one side and the metal tunnel that he could see from the front. Suddenly even for him, the prospect of travelling through time became more real.

The stories that his great-grandfather had told helped but as Stuart expected, being weightless provided a jolt that nothing else could. However, Anthony expected such a massive venture to be accompanied by countdowns, klaxons sounding alarms, and men in white coats monitoring screens while confirming that everything was 'go'. Instead, Stuart floated over to the console where Brian was entering the details then drifted across to the portal. Stuart's casual approach provided a surreal effect that left him a little disorientated.

"OK This portal's the same as the Earth connection." he said, "I'll go first, Anthony second and Freddie can bring up the rear."

He saw Freddie pout. The boy wanted to go first so Stuart added, "Freddie, you're more used to it. You know to make sure the rear hatch is secured."

Freddie smiled proudly and nodded. It was this casual approach that left Anthony disappointed not wanting to believe that an eleven year old boy could be entrusted with any part of it.

The stories that his great-grandfather had told could have been tales of the imagination but they and all the mysterious events in his life had led to this moment. He was still trying to take in what was happening as he followed Stuart out of the portal into dense woodland.

Freddie scrambled out looking around.

"It looks the same and it looks different at the same time." he exclaimed.

"I know what you mean." Stuart laughed, "I remember that big rock under the sycamore but the tree looks smaller, doesn't it."

"I know that rock." Anthony exclaimed, "I can't remember the tree but we should be standing in the folly. I don't recognise anything else though."

"Come on." Stuart commanded, "Let's get on before Hodges finds us."

"Who's Hodges?" Anthony asked.

"The gamekeeper." Stuart replied, "He was before Archer, Freddie."

Freddie nodded.

"I've heard of him." he said, "He didn't take kindly to trespassers. Come on, I know the way to the stream."

The young Anthony found them rather than the other way around as he staggered along the path towards them, collapsing into Stuart's arms.

"Quiet." Anthony hissed, "There's someone coming and he's trying to be quiet."

"It's either a poacher or Hodges." Freddie whispered, "I know what to do."

Before anyone could stop him, he darted off. Stuart rolled his eyes in despair and looked at Anthony.

"You've got good hearing. Army training?" he asked.

Anthony nodded but before he could answer they heard a loud crack and a yell. For a moment or so Stuart feared that Freddie had been shot but the sounds of someone crashing through the undergrowth eased his fears. He guessed that the crack had been breaking wood, relieved that Freddie seemed to know what he was doing.

"There's someone running off in the opposite direction." Anthony whispered as a voice yelled out 'stop'. They were startled by a shotgun blast, a yelp and even Stuart could hear the sounds of running disappearing into the distance.

"I reckon Hodges should be grateful to us." Anthony grinned, "He's caught a poacher."

"Yes but what about Freddie?" Stuart asked.

Despite the excitement, Anthony had examined the wound and as they relaxed then they all saw the gash in the back of his head and the blood soaking into his sailor suit.

"It needs stitches." he pronounced, "It's a nasty cut but I don't think anything is broken. The wound needs to be cleaned and he needs a tetanus booster."

He paused, "I'm thinking 21st century. When did tetanus shots come in?"

"I don't know." Stuart replied.

"OK." Anthony said, "That cut looks dirty so he's at risk. As far as I'm concerned, medical aid decides it. We'll take him to Dr. Tobias."

Stuart nodded, "We can send a probe to find Freddie."

Even Anthony was startled when Freddie charged out of the woods by the portal.

"Hodges is heading this way." he announced, "I don't know these woods, they're different, he may have heard me."

Anthony hurried into the portal carrying his patient as Freddie hurried off. Stuart stepped into the portal waiting to close the outer after Freddie. Again he was alarmed to hear breaking wood and high pitched yells then there was silence again.

Suddenly Freddie appeared again running as fast as he could and almost diving into the portal. Stuart got the message, slammed the portal doors shut and hurried through.

Immediately after they were back, James sent a probe to observe. Hodges arrived panting in the clearing just seconds after the portal de-materialised. The gamekeeper got his breath back looking around puzzled then hurried towards the stream.

"We'll have to get young Anthony back before he gets there." Stuart said, "Lucky we've got a time machine."

"Great-granddad used to talk about giving his father's gamekeeper hell." Anthony said while they waited for Dr. Tobias to examine the young Anthony, "Apparently he went poaching himself and learned not to get caught. I couldn't tell my parents or anything but he encouraged me to do the same. He said something about his dad encouraging him but that puts the timing out doesn't it?"

"It depends on what those drugs did or will do." Stuart said but said nothing more as Dr. Tobias straightened up.

"Freddie, what do you know about a tetanus injection. Have you ever had one?" Dr. Tobias asked.

Freddie shook his head.

"I don't know what it is." he replied.

"I think we need an immunisation programme for both boys. What about us and alien infections?" Dr. Tobias asked.

"Some races we encounter look just like us but their body temperature could be a degree or so higher or the make up of their blood cells could be slightly different, there's small things like that. Freddie and young Anthony are more at risk from us because we're the same species."

"There's nothing seriously wrong." the doctor said, "Young Tony slipped on a wet stone and gashed his head on a thorn or something. He's shocked but there's no concussion. I've stitched it and applied a dressing. All he needs now is a couple hours rest and he'll be fine."

"So you're not treating him for concussion?" Stuart asked.

"No." Dr. Tobias replied, "You said that all they found was an old scar. I couldn't find anything so that's the only one he'll have. I shaved a patch of hair around the wound so allowing time for that to grow back he's going to be here for a few weeks. I think I can guess how this is going to pan out, but does mentioning it risk changing the future?"

"I don't know, but I see how it's going as well. Let's hope that the concussion was a story to cover the drugs." Stuart said, "Freddie will want to stay until Reginald can go home so we'll have to see how it all works."

Stuart left Dr. Tobias to find James and Dave.

Research

Once James, Dave and Stuart were settled in the quarry workshop began their plans.

"How about sending a probe to see what's left of these colonies." he said, "Half a billion years is a long time but Mars is far more stable. Something might be left."

"Good idea." James said, "You still seem reluctant to commit yourself to anything. Are you all right?"

"Not really." Stuart replied, "I'm still worried about events being so badly out of sequence and this affair is becoming another war of the worlds. I guess I'm still tired."

"It's hardly surprising." James said, "This was just supposed to pique your curiosity to help you get over those mental jumps. Who could have guessed that the time-line could get so twisted."

"Let's think things through." Stuart said, "In theory they could launch their invasion at any point in time. If they did it before we warned them then we wouldn't exist so we wouldn't warn them. We'd have a paradox and Brian isn't detecting any.

"Second I think Larik and Merrill were lying. Maybe they could watch developments and ensure that we developed right but I've been checking. Their tampering with the DNA is too fragile to last and would be highly unpredictable. Besides there have been too many very stable civilisations for it to have worked."

"I wondered." James said, "Any thoughts?"

"There's a theory that all present day humans stem from a single woman who may have lived fifty thousand years ago and she had a mutant gene that changed the human race."

Stuart paused, "They mentioned that we could interbreed and they have time travel."

"Don't drag it out Stuart," Dave interjected, "You're saying that we could all be descended from this woman who went with Larik or Merrill. Yuck! That's disgusting."

"Yes it is. And at the moment they reckon that we're tying ourselves up in knots looking for this non-existent self-destruct gene. Now supposing ten years or so from our time, they introduce a virus into Earth's atmosphere. They let it shrink the population to a size that they can control then offer us the antidote. They'll effectively be in charge, have the means of controlling us and keep the industrial infrastructure that they say they want."

"Is that what they're going to do?" James asked, "Or are you guessing?"

"Guessing." Stuart replied, "Unless you're a religious fundamentalist, even the idea of the first woman is only a theory and not completely provable. It sounds kinky but the only way we could be sure would be to go back and watch but we couldn't interfere because it might change us."

"OK!" Dave chuckled, "I say that we stay in blissful ignorance of who our first granddaddy was but I reckon you could be on the right lines."

"They considered us the inferiors." Stuart said, "I don't think they cared whether they lied or told the truth. All that mattered was stopping us from causing trouble."

"Why do you think their plans will mature so close to our time?" James asked.

"Because I wonder if the technology they want is portal technology."

"But they've already got it." Dave exclaimed.

"They've got a working portal, a ship and shuttles." Stuart explained, "Maybe they can maintain it all and run it but supposing all the research and development was lost in the war."

"They're colonists." Dave added, "Maybe they don't have the resources to design and build new ones. We could go back, blow up their existing ship and that would be end of that."

"And leave them to die?" Stuart asked.

"Trust you to make it complicated." Dave grinned, "You wouldn't do that, would you?"

"Could you?"

"No, I suppose not." Dave conceded, "Any ideas on how to save them?"

"Apart from finding a world with no life and getting them started there."

"Would that work?" Dave asked.

"I don't know." Stuart snapped irritably, "Can we travel back to their time? Can we prevent the Darringtons from disrupting the time-line? Can we protect our world? Do we really know what they're planning? It's like last time. We didn't know what we were doing then and were just getting jerked around. Supposing they see us as a direct threat and focus their attacks on us? I don't know what to do for the best."

Stuart was getting hysterical and Dave was worried.

"You do OK." Dave said, "I know I joke about you making things complicated but you're usually right. They might have waited for a couple of hundred more years until someone else developed a portal but we're hurrying them up. You start looking at Mars and I'll wander around to the barn and see how far back I can go."

Stuart nodded but before he could speak Dave continued, "I can't imagine what those mind jumps were like but you're still shaken by them. Relax, let James practice his skills while you sit back and watch. I'll call you if I get into trouble but you say that those probes are expendable so I can't get into any real trouble, can I?"

"Do you want to bet?" Stuart grinned, "I'm going to go swimming on Terzon. We'll all meet up at Brian's tonight and compare notes. How does that sound?"

"Like you're the boss swanning off while your serfs do all the hard work." Dave laughed, "I tell you what, go for it."

It was a break that Stuart needed and even Brian could see that Stuart was brighter and more alert that evening.

Dave's day had been far more hectic, starting as he reached the barn and began checking his equipment.

One of the features of their equipment was that it could affect gravity. On occasions they had considered refining it and offering an artificial gravity environment for the International Space Station though it would need relatively high amounts of energy. However on Earth, plugged into the electricity supply, it easily adjusted the gravitational field around a chair. Dave had obtained a holographic display unit from Terzon and with the help of a Terzon computer specialist had wired everything into the readouts from an adapted probe. The result was equivalent to a flight simulator with the chair and screen reacting to the movements of the probe. Gravitational pulls were limited to 1g in any direction so he reckoned that it was safe enough but he had never used it beyond some cautious testing.

He chose Sydney, Australia as an observation point thinking that he could use the mass of the Earth to control the fields. The probe was high enough not to be seen from the ground and to pick out the harbour or rather the larger Port Jackson inlet but he was low enough to see the bridge.

The corrections for the Earth's mass worked and he was just in the right position to have the sun in the top right hand corner of his view.

He jumped back a hundred years. The chair remained steady and Sydney Harbour Bridge disappeared. He jumped back a thousand years. The software worked, the sun scarcely flickered and all signs of civilisation vanished. The next jump was a million years give or take a few days. The software selected the right moment so that the sun remained in a constant position. He was sure that Port Jackson was smaller and that the whole coastline had receded.

Intrigued he took the probe higher and tried a series of five million year jumps in quick succession and then, there was no doubt about it. Australia was sailing away. Dave had heard of continental drift but had never thought about it before. He just assumed that it happened over a much bigger time scale. He sent the probe even higher and continued the jumps and watched the Atlantic Ocean shrink as the Americas approached Europe and Africa.

The probe's fields still passed through Earth though not through the centre so Dave became a little concerned when his seat started bouncing and the sun in the image began jumping around.

He stopped the probe's backward drift but the bouncing continued and Dave was nearly thrown from the chair.

Intellectually he knew that he was sitting in a barn and perfectly safe but his senses particularly his sight and sense of weight told him that he was in an aircraft that was losing control.

He yelled in terror as suddenly he was nosediving towards the ground, for a moment he really did believe that he was crashing and he fought with the controls as desperately as a real life pilot.

He was completely disorientated, lost in the scene he had created, forgetting that all he had to was stand up. Dave did not realise it but he was trembling as, from his point of view, he came to rest at ground level. His deep sigh of relief was cut short as he glanced up to see a dinosaur charging towards him.

Once again Dave yelled in terror almost ready to leap out of his seat and run but he hesitated, trying to sort the confused information his brain was receiving. The camera was at ground level pointing upwards, which makes anything seem bigger especially since he had been hoping to see a giant dinosaur. However, the hologram's 3D effect allowed him to judge distance and size as if he was looking at the real world. His eyes were telling him that it was only a couple of metres away and for a giant dinosaur – it was tiny.

Dave was finished though, the conflicting information was just too confusing. He pressed the exit button and suddenly he was back in the barn.

He tried standing and nearly fell over so he sat back, focussing his eyes on a mark on the roof until he calmed down. No matter how shaken he had been, Dave would not accept defeat at the hands of an illusion.

He found some rope to act as a seatbelt, reset the probe for when he stopped and took another jump back. He made more use of Earth's mass to control the fields at the expense of not seeing much more than ocean and managed to slip back even further in time. Suddenly he was bouncing all over the place again and he was upside down.

He emitted yet another terrified yell as he fell from his seat and then briefly passed out as his organs crashed around his body. The illusion had become a bit too real. As the probe had flipped over so the generators had given his chair an inverted gravity, hence his sense of falling but the moment he left his seat so the display had cut including the field generators. He had gone from upside down to upright in an instant. Passengers in a car hurtling over a humpbacked bridge talk of leaving their stomachs behind. Dave experienced such a violent version of that he wondered whether he had injured himself.

He struggled not to be sick, had a shocking headache and was finally prepared to admit defeat. In fact he was ready to send for Dr. Tobias but he felt so bad but he did not have the energy to pull out his phone. His eyes closed and he fell asleep. He awoke about an hour later feeling weak and still a little confused but physically he seemed fine.

He was back to normal when he met up with Stuart and the others that evening.

"I actually saw a dinosaur." he exclaimed excitedly, "The probe was bouncing around all over the place but I did see stuff and the cameras pick up a lot more. Anyway I saw just one large continent. I tried scanning the planet and mostly all I could see was water."

He paused, "I think it was about one hundred and fifty million years ago. I've only looked at a few but some blocks of pictures I deleted because they just showed sea. Others were starscapes and empty sky. One was from about a thousand miles up and showed a sizeable chunk of the continent. I've got a print of it here."

Dave pointed to a shape.

"That looks like North and South America but it's so twisted and does that make this the Atlantic Ocean? It's only a couple of hundred miles wide."

"I've heard of this super continent." Brian said, "It's called

Pangaea. I'd say that you've confirmed the continental drift theory. Well done."

"Did you try out your new toy?" Stuart asked.

"At times I wish I hadn't though." David replied, "I nearly threw up."

"But you've managed to marry up all different technologies though." Brian asked, "That's well done as well."

I got a lot of help so I didn't do that much."

"Stuart always says things like that." James said, "It was your idea to put it together, did it work?"

Dave nodded.

"OK!" Brian said, "It was an interesting design exercise but they have similar rides at Disneyworld. Was it worth all the effort?"

"Yes I think it was." Dave replied, "You do need points of reference to judge size and distance but I reckon it could be really useful studying inaccessible places."

"So what about this dinosaur?" Stuart asked, "We've talked about going back to see them often enough."

"It only lasted for a few seconds." Dave replied, "But this creature came running towards me. Now my eyes told me that it was only about thirty centimetres tall, but dinosaurs were bigger than that, weren't they?"

"I think they came in all sizes." Brian replied, "Did you check the instruments?"

"They confirmed it."

"So while everyone else goes on about how big they were, you go and find the smallest." Stuart laughed, "It's different."

"OK. We travel by folding space." Stuart continued, "There are limits to what we can fold in one jump. Time travel relies on travelling along the gravity well, at least for navigation and the stronger the gravity, the more tightly it holds the folds."

He paused, "We could probably contain the folds by increasing the power but we'd have to build a new portal. In terms of power consumption it would be like an express train compared to a moped."

Brian nodded in agreement.

"I worked out some theoretical limits to what we could do when we first started." he said, "Straightforward space travel and it's probably ten times the distance to the Andromeda galaxy. I've done some work through our exploration and I'd say I was about right. I would have said that the theoretical limit for time travel was about a billion years, so possibly there's a solution to Dave's instability problem. Anyway it's James' turn. How did you get on today."

"I found one of the caves but it was destroyed by a nuclear bomb. The wall's like molten glass and the roof was blown away. It could be mistaken for a meteor crater from above but when you look closely you can see that it's all wrong. When I looked around I found a network of tunnels. Those closest to the explosion were destroyed but further away they're virtually intact. There was a body in one cave."

Everyone stared him. James grinned.

"It was in the damage zone and it looks as if a rock crushed his head. The rocks had absorbed the radiation and the heat, and the cave was shallow enough for most of the energy to go upwards. Anyway, it was still enough to give the cave a good shaking. At the right distance it seems to have pulverised the outer layer of rock filling the air with a fine powder.

"The body was covered by the dust but as the moisture was drawn out, the dust absorbed it and then set like concrete."

"Could there be anything left of the actual body?" Brian asked.

"It's been dried and frozen so who knows." James replied, "If the body absorbed dust over the millennia it could have fossilised."

"What were the caves for?" Stuart asked, "Surely bare rock would have been too cold and too much air could have seeped away."

"I don't know." James replied, "I've only been exploring them for an afternoon and the body got my attention. I did find piles of plastic in places, though. It was fragile and brittle but I'm guessing they lined the wall where there was a leak and air pressure held it in place. Over time the lining collapsed."

"So we're not going to find anything in the cave itself but we'll have to explore the tunnels." Stuart said, "Maybe it'll be something Dad could get interested in while you explore the other sites. At least Larik and Merrill could be telling the truth about where they came from. I've got a crazy idea."

"It wouldn't be you if you hadn't." Dave snorted, "Go on."

"We set up a base in one of those tunnels a few hundred million years ago." Stuart said, "You've seen them, James. Would they be big enough to operate a portal from?"

"Yes but I didn't think you liked operating underground like that." James replied.

"Normally I don't." Stuart agreed, "but we'd use this one purely for time travel back into Mars past. The Martians used a denser planet to navigate so maybe we should see if they knew something we don't."

"Why don't we find a place on Earth and try it?" Dave asked then grinned as he answered his own question, "Because the Earth's crust is far more unstable and everything shifts around."

"I was thinking that Mars was a dead planet so we wouldn't be able to change history," Stuart chuckled, "but yours is a good point too. James, you said that you'd found four caves. How did you find them?"

"Luck really." James replied, "I guess I'm more of a science fiction fan than I realised. You've always said that we should try our own projects so I've been planning my own colonisation of Mars. Mainly it was an exercise in using the equipment and learning more about the problems we face working in space.

"Anyway I'd started a geophysical survey and found an almost perfectly round feature near the south Martian pole and there was a canyon nearby. The canyon was short, the floor was flat and 'V' shaped sloping up to the ends of the canyon. All the lines seemed very straight, man made or at least artificial.

"Conventional Mars probes don't look for caves and the canyon is too small to show up on cameras but I had something to look for. That's how I found the second one diametrically opposite the first. I checked the North pole and found the remains of number three and finally the one I explored today."

"The remains of number three?" Brian queried.

James nodded, "I'd say the bomb hit the canyon and blasted in the side of the cavern. The wall was pushed in and part of the roof collapsed. Again, what was left was perfectly round and the software picked up on it."

"Why did you check a damaged cave first?" Dave asked.

James shrugged, "I don't know. I guess it was a bit of military training seeping through. Assess the enemy's military capability."

"OK tomorrow we'll look at an intact base." Stuart said, "Dave, how about using your set up?"

Curiosity got the better of them all and the following morning they all assembled at the lane to the barn. Anthony was invited along so Freddie and Tony also joined them.

Brian was unhappy at such a large group. As always he was worried about security and it was not helped when they passed Joe Milnes.

Joe was a typical countryman, he spoke slowly with a thick accent and his life seemed to revolve around his dairy herd and an evening pint in the pub. Like any countryman though, he was content to stop for a chat.

"Off on a picnic then?" he asked.

"No we're going to Mars." Freddie said brightly, "Would you like to come?"

Brian looked on aghast while the other adults were equally stunned.

"What's wrong?" Freddie asked, suddenly aware of the tension, "You said that Mr. Milnes knew a lot about the portal."

"It's OK." Stuart said, "Joe's a friend of ours. We just don't discuss what we do unless we have to."

"Like when Father thought you were poachers." Freddie exclaimed triumphantly.

Tony looked puzzled but Stuart gave a quick shake of his head.

"It's OK, Joe." Stuart said, "We're not going anywhere but we're going look at a live feed from Mars. You're welcome to watch as well."

"Well I'd planned on muck spreading in Lower Acre." Joe said, "But it's been quite a while since I've been to the pictures. I did see that War Of The Worlds on television though."

He paused, "I tell you what, I've got some parsnip wine that's coming along nicely, I'll fetch some along with a nice hock of ham and some Wensleydale cheese. The Missus said she was baking today so how about some rolls and pickle to go with it. Just let me set Zeb to the muck spreading. By the way, thanks for those parts, they're just what I need."

Brian glared at Stuart and Freddie.

"I know." Stuart said before Brian could say anything, "I didn't think he'd be interested. I didn't like him mentioning the War Of The Worlds though."

Brian shrugged then burst out laughing.

"Can you imagine what NASA mission control would make of it." he asked, "Imagine them watching their latest downloads from Mars while eating a ploughman's lunch washed down with home made wine?"

"I'm sorry." Freddie said, "I've messed things up again, haven't I?"

"No not really." Brian replied, "Stuart's right, Joe is a friend and he's good about letting us use his barn so it might help if he understood why."

Once they got to the barn Dave busied himself setting up the computers. In theory it only took a few minutes but like the rest of them Dave was cautious enough to check and try some dummy runs before switching on the hardware. As he was finishing they heard Joe's Land Rover draw up.

Stuart wandered out to greet him and stared at the reflecting telescope resting in the back.

"I was wondering if you could fix this up for me." Joe said, "It was Dad's. He hated being indoors and would spend hours looking through it. He taught me a bit but when I took over the farm I lost interest. I'm quite happy to sit indoors talking to my daughter in Toronto. That Internet thing lets me get pictures of my grandchildren and I can even talk to them. They like it when I video the animals for them."

He paused, "Knowing what you do has got me interested again. I was wondering whether I could fit a camera to it and show the grandchildren what I'm looking at."

"That's no problem." Stuart smiled, "Just don't tell them what we do."

Joe looked offended.

"That's village business." he snapped, "It won't leave here through me."

"Sorry." Stuart said, "Our security's got very lax and Brian worries about it."

"So would I." Joe chuckled, back to his usual cheerful self, "But you needn't worry about me all the time you keep an eye on them incomers like Bradley."

Freddie and Tony stared, fascinated by the old telescope.

"We'll have to get one of those when I get home." Freddie said. Tony nodded enthusiastically.

Joe was busily unfolding trestle tables and laying out the food and drink.

"I forgot about those." he said, "You don't want the village fête committee barging in to collect them. There's space in Home Barn. Tomorrow you can help me shift them and those boxes. Now where's the screen?"

"There isn't one." David explained, "It's a 3D set up."

Joe looked puzzled but said nothing more.

Everyone finally settled and Dave activated the probe. Joe looked startled as most of the barn seemed to disappear then watched amazed as the three dimensional image began to appear. In fact it was the first time that even Stuart had seen a 3D image on this scale. He watched just as fascinated as the rest while the reddish blur sharpened and cleared as finer and finer detail was added.

The image showed a ramp sloping away into a trench only to start climbing back up to surface in the distance.

"If I zoom out a little you'll see the cliff on the right and the plain to the left." Dave said, "When you're ready, we'll shift to the bottom of the ramp."

Joe stood up and walked to the ramp trying to take a step along it. He stumbled.

"I'm still standing on the barn floor, aren't I?" he asked trying to understand, "I tried walking down that slope but it's not real is it?"

"It is real," Stuart said, "but it's not here. It's on Mars. You're just seeing a photo of it."

"How can it be on Mars?" Joe asked, "Someone cut those ramps."

"That's why we're so interested." Stuart said, "Dave's going to shift to the bottom of the slope. You may get a bit disorientated if you're inside the image when it changes."

Joe sat down and the scene duly changed.

"Is that door as big as it looks?" Joe asked completely lost in what he was seeing, "It must be at least 12ft high."

"It is." Dave confirmed, "Magnetic resonance says it's thick enough to work as an airlock but it's no blast door."

"What about radiation protection?" Brian asked.

"From what?" Stuart asked, "I've really got to start thinking metric again. It's what I learnt at school and, most journals I read use it. It's only Brian that still uses the old system."

He glanced at Joe, "At least for this type of work."

"Anyway if the door is four metres high and the slopes take us twenty metres down then there's not a lot that can reach the door unless the source is at the bottom of the ramps."

"What's inside?" Freddie asked impatiently.

"Let's find out." Dave replied and immediately the image disappeared. He switched on a powerful searchlight and a circle of distant rock appeared, blurred, indistinct and according to their eyes, an incredible distance away.

As the searchlight beam shifted so the image grew as if a paintbrush was bringing a painting to life. Once the image was recorded in the computers then it remained and each movement of the light added to the data.

They were in a short tunnel that opened into a larger cavern.

The probe moved down the tunnel gradually revealing more of the cavern. It seemed as if everyone gasped at once as the steel joist bracing the rock roof came into sight.

Again it was Joe who walked into the image along what appeared to be a path. He knelt down and without thinking stretched out to touch something only to snatch his hand back as he remembered.

"Can you sharpen it up at all?" he asked.

Dave obliged and Joe watched fascinated as more and more detail appeared. Finally, satisfied he stood up and walked back to the others.

"Any idea what they were growing?" he asked.

"Growing?" Stuart asked.

Joe nodded, "If this was a normal field then I'd say that it had just been abandoned. There's still traces of the furrows between rows and there's a few shoots appearing but they're black. That's the cold getting to them. If there's any seed that hadn't started germinating then they might still grow. So how long ago was it left?"

"We think five hundred million Earth years." Stuart replied.

"I don't know of any plants that could be that hardy." Joe replied quite seriously, "If you're planning to go back, I'd like to talk one of their farmers."

He turned to Dave, "What's the matter lad? I've heard you in the pub when you've had one too many and young Demetrius knows about farming but he's got some very odd ideas about it. Did you think that I was so worried about getting the milking done, I couldn't take it in?"

"Er no." Dave replied, "At least…"

"At least you thought that I was one of Bradley's local yokels and not interested in anything beyond the village."

"Partly. I wouldn't make it an insult like David Bradley. I would have said it was the life you chose."

"It was but it doesn't mean that I don't want to see more of the world." Joe said, "Something led you here and you must think it's pretty important so what's going on?"

David looked uncertainly at Stuart who said, "OK Joe, it's a bit early for wine but how about a cup of coffee and some food. While we're eating, I'll tell you what we've used your barn for."

Joe listened intently but not saying anything until the story was finished. Stuart wondered whether he was taking it in.

"I'd say this place was big enough to feed two or three thousand people." he said still completely matter of fact, "There's four caves so that's ten thousand. What happened to them?"

"We don't know." Stuart replied, "Are you sure about those numbers?"

"Based on my farm, yes." Joe said, "There's obviously water and air, or at least there was water and air yet it looks as if the heating was turned off at the start of the growing season. That seems odd. Would they have the seed to plant again, somewhere new?"

"I don't know." Stuart replied irritably, "There's always more questions than answers."

"And you remembered those tractor parts." Joe said, "It doesn't seem very important now."

"It is though." Stuart said, "The village is as much part of my life as this. If we got soil samples and seeds would you be able to tell me anything about them?"

"Can you set me up a greenhouse?" Joe asked, "Up there I mean. Let's see if anything can remain dormant for all this time."

Stuart was not sure whether the information would help him but it was a relief to know that Joe was willing to join them rather go rushing off to the authorities.

While Stuart had been talking to Joe, Dave had been exploring the cavern. He had switched to a conventional but enormous VDU screen and the others had crowded round to watch.

"Take a look at this. I'll switch back to 3D." he called out to Stuart.

Stuart found himself in a tunnel, properly lined and with a proper floor. Not even dust had penetrated this far in and it looked new. The real surprise came as they slipped through a closed door and found themselves in a comfortable living quarters. There was a half finished meal on the table with what appeared to be six places. It was difficult to tell because there were no place settings, just a pile of what appeared to be desiccated fruit in the centre of the table and half eaten pieces around the edge.

"They look like children's building bricks on the floor." Stuart murmured half to himself.

Joe picked up on it though.

"Just looks like?" Joe asked, "What else could they be?"

"We don't take anything for granted." Stuart explained, "For all we know they had a weird idea about decorating hand grenades."

"This part of the complex is deep enough to protect them from solar radiation," James said, "but not deep enough to protect them from a nuclear bomb at ground level. I wonder if the alarm went off and they moved to a deeper shelter."

"Then why didn't they come back?" Anthony asked, "Why didn't they get the all clear?"

"OK, Let's destroy a probe." Stuart said, "James. Would you go back to the quarry, load a probe on the front of a portal then transport it to Mars. Maybe Anthony would help you. Brian's worked on some software modifications and we'll be operating in a tunnel with no spatial movement. We'll use a radio link to operate it from here and work back in fifty million year jumps. Let's see what happens."

"Can we help?" Freddie asked.

"Only if James agrees." Anthony said, "But no stowing away this time. You'll be dead in seconds."

"I know but can we go through the airlock and look through the window?" Freddie pleaded.

"I might have a quick look as well," James grinned, "but I think all the fun's going to be here."

"But I'm going to promise to take Anthony to Mars." Freddie exclaimed triumphantly, "I can keep that promise now, can't I?"

"What about the canals?" Tony suddenly said, "Can we have a look at them?"

It was the first time that Tony had contributed anything. He had been more shaken by his injury and subsequent events than anyone realised.

"I think that they were just part of someone's over active imagination." Brian said as gently as could then catching Tony's look of disappointment added, "We should fly over the surface though. Just to make sure."

Tony nodded contentedly, pleased that he was being taken seriously.

James headed off for the quarry accompanied by Tony and Freddie. Anthony accompanied them to supervise the boys.

Dave continued exploring the caves.

"I can't find any factories or workshops, just living quarters." he said, "There are some small parks or fields but I can't find heating or oxygen plants."

"Any bodies?" Brian asked.

Dave nodded, "I've seen quite a few on my monitor I didn't transfer those images to the main screen while the boys were here. Most were in their quarters, couples were in bed together, some had children laying between them. There was a group sitting around a table. It looked like bottles on the table and small containers. I say looked like bottles but they were more like ancient amphorae. Some lay in racks beside the table and were stoppered, open ones stood in little stands while what I assume were the empties had just been dropped on the floor.”

“I've got the picture but what did you make of it?” Stuart asked.

“That they had been left behind and had committed suicide.” Dave replied, “Most of the rooms were empty. Oh yes, most of the bodies were skeletons. I reckon the caves were habitable for a time and the bodies decayed naturally.”

“You're quite the performer, aren't you.” Brian laughed, “You always save an interesting bit until last.”

“We've got two caves destroyed by nuclear weapons.” Stuart said, “They were new because they were just cut out of the rock and they hadn't got around to lining them properly. We've got this one that appears to be inhabitable but was abandoned in a hurry and one we haven't looked at yet.”

“Any thoughts on it so far?” Brian asked.

“It's the precision I don't understand.” Stuart said, “They're all on the same circle around the planet. You know a line of longitude or great circle. The circle passes through the poles and each pair of colonies is equidistant from their relative pole. There're different geographical features, this one's under a cliff, none of the others are. Dave, how about a good look around the northern edge of the complex.”

“Sure, I concentrated on the main tunnels before. I can do a quick scan while James is setting up. What am I looking for?”

“A water purifying plant, a tunnel stretching out under the pole. Oh and a nuclear power station.” Stuart said before turning to Brian, “Larik referred to the portal as a dimensional drill. Could it be used for drilling and mining?”

Brian frowned, “I don't see how unless…”

Brian stood still frowning and obviously deep in thought, “There's two possibilities. You let a probe materialise inside the rock. At the right depth you could end up with nuclear fission that would vaporise the rock and cause a massive explosion, at a lower depth you'd get an ordinary explosion blasting the top layers outwards.

“The ends of our probes are hollow holding scientific equipment. If you had a solid tip pressed against the wall then you might dump the rock inside the field into multidimensional space."

"Found it." Dave yelled triumphantly, "At least I've found an open space beyond this wall. I can see a door now. It's almost as if they tried to hide the tunnel. OK I'm past the door and there's another one. It's more like a hatch and it looks like writing on it. I bet it says 'Keep Out – No Unauthorised Personnel'."

While he had been talking everyone else had turned to the image that was gradually appearing. They found themselves looking at another cavern, it's roof supported like the other one but full of machinery.

Brian pointed at an enormous steel ball.

"That could be the pressure vessel for a fusion reactor." he exclaimed, "Can you find any pipes coming in from above?"

"Not yet." Dave replied, "What are you thinking?"

"That they tapped the ice caps for water." he stopped thinking, "No it's too cold. They'd have to mine the ice. By mining up through the roof they would have nearly eight metres of ice above them, that's twenty five foot to us old timers. Either way that's a pretty good shield against radiation.

"Drop the ice into tanks and let the carbon dioxide evaporate. I wonder if the plants they grew could absorb that amount and produce oxygen."

"So that's why the colonies were at the ice caps." Dave said

He might have said more but his phone rang. He put it on speaker.

"Young Tony's operating the Earth-Mars portal." James said, "It seems that he might not say much but he's very observant. When he goes home we'll have to make sure that he doesn't try to smuggle a laptop back with him. We're all set up here so if Dave would like to establish the link from his end, we're ready."

Dave worked for a few moments before announcing that he now had full control of the probe.

"You can come back now James." he said, "We're working barn to quarry by micro-link, quarry to Mars by portal then Mars to ancient Mars by probe and all links are stable."

Visually the experiment was disappointing. They looked at a section of cave and every few seconds the view shimmered.

"Are they footprints?" Joe asked suddenly, "Is it my imagination or are they just appearing out of the dust?"

"You're right." Stuart exclaimed, "How far back are we?"

"We're at three hundred million years." Dave replied, "That

foot print is getting very sharp. The fields aren't starting to jump yet so I reckon that Stuart could be right. It's entirely underground and static so even the small mass of rock above this cave is holding the fields better."

"OK." Stuart said, "Let's go back in fifty million year jumps. The probe's got a gravity detector and will de-materialise if we try to embed it in solid rock, just keep a note of the dates we jump to."

"They're in the log." Dave said.

The footprints did not seem to change so much and there was no other feature to change. Suddenly the image vanished.

"It's de-materialised." Dave announced.

"OK send it back to the last temporal position and jump back in hundred thousand year intervals." Stuart commanded.

"Got you." Dave exclaimed, "We keep doing it in smaller and smaller jumps until we see signs of life."

In fact they did not see signs of life. The dust and the footprints disappeared and the tunnel was illuminated by the tunnel-lining glowing gently."

"We've done it." Stuart exclaimed, "Well done, Dave."

Dave de-materialised the probe.

"I picked up voices behind us." he explained, "I thought it better if we weren't spotted."

"Good thinking." James said.

"Let's have something to eat." Stuart suggested, "I reckon now's a good time to try Joe's parsnip wine. Then we'll take a look at the fourth colony and call it a day."

"Tomorrow Stuart and I should check the logs and see if we can stabilise the fields more." Brian said, "I'm wondering if it could be as simple as working to closer tolerances."

For Stuart the fourth colony was the most shocking. There were bodies everywhere, many huddled around what they now realised were air vents. In a smaller chamber they found the portal but it was badly damaged.

As Stuart had already pointed out it pays not to assume anything but the remote end looked as if it had melted. Icicles of molten metal dripped from it while the remains had collapsed under its own weight.

"The design is similar to ours." Brian said, "It looks as if the heat destroyed the generators and collapsed the field. Any thoughts, Stuart?"

"None of it gels." Stuart said, "I'd guess that they used that portal to get to the heavy planet, then something else to our time then the ship to us. If they were using that portal to get to the heavy planet, then someone else would have had to send a bomb to destroy it."

"Supposing there was a nuclear war on Earth but there were survivors existing in colonies like the Martian ones." Brian suggested, "Earth had settled down enough for them to start exploring. They found a missile complex and resumed hostilities."

"When it comes to blocs we tend to think East and West." Stuart said, "Maybe they thought North and South and they took that concept to Mars. I'm guessing but supposing that the South got here first by twenty years or more. That gave them time to establish a fairly sophisticated pair of colonies, then the North caught up, started their own colonies but before they could get fully established, they were nuked.

"The North retaliated on Earth, maybe both sides were sensible enough not to use nuclear weapons though judging by Larik and Merrill's arrogance I doubt it. Whatever the damage, it was survivable but it took a couple of hundred years to recover. The North discovered that the South still had Martian colonies and nuked the portal landing site. The last portal was smashed and that was the end of them all."

"So where do the trips to us come into it?" Brian asked.

"I forgot about them for a moment." Stuart admitted sheepishly, "It doesn't work does it?"

"It's a working hypothesis." Brian said, "We'll modify it as we find information. Maybe the North not only caught up but overtook the South. Our visitors are Northerners and their caves were just a staging post or something."

"It seems to me that they took their arguments to Mars and destroyed their last chance to survive." Joe said, "Are the details important?"

"Probably not," Stuart conceded, "but as Anthony says it might help if we understood the sequence of events. But I'm beginning to think that their attack on us just fizzled out without it ever being a threat."

"But you're going assume the worst, aren't you?" Dave chuckled, "I know you."

"Can we call it 'playing safe'." Stuart retorted, "It doesn't sound so negative."

"We've got one advantage over them." James said, "We've got all the portals and probes we need. Tomorrow, Dave and I can start checking the heavy planet while Stuart and Brian are checking today's data, and we'll see what we can find there."

For David and James the day proved enlightening.

"They store the ship in a cave on the planet's second moon." James explained, "It's there now, in about one quarter earth's gravity and in a vacuum. There was no sign of the shuttle though until we went back in time. That cave has only been around for a million years or so but there was another one nearby in their time zone and there was the shuttle. It was still there about a million years after the Mars colonies had died out."

"So there was no fighting on that planet." Stuart said, "Did you look inside the shuttle?"

"No." James replied, "We were thinking more about the overall picture. We can save the detailed investigations until later."

"You could be right." Stuart agreed, "And the ship?"

"It appears to be fully operational though highly radioactive." James replied, Again, it needs a thorough investigation.

"Good point." Stuart grinned, "It's time we got some answers and not more questions."

For the next couple of days they worked steadily exploring all four caves. While Brian became more and more exasperated by the way Joe Milnes and Mavis, Stuart's mother would 'pop in' to see how they were doing. Stuart found it amusing.

To everyone's surprise, James agreed with Stuart.

"If we put up barbed wire fences, issued security passes and hired security guards then people would know that we're doing something special." he said, "But what secret establishment let's people pop in for coffee and has kids playing around?"

"Yes I know we've had this conversation before but what about those kids. They're using a probe to look for canals."

James shrugged, "OK I'm a bit worried about it and to be fair Stuart is as well but there's this suggestion that they sneak back to the ancient Martian colonies. Stuart's trying to ensure they know what they're doing and don't get themselves killed this time around."

"This time around?" Brian queried.

James shrugged again, "They've already gone back in Anthony's memories and young Tony's if it comes to that. Stuart's trying to preserve those particular time lines otherwise he'd never let them near us."

Brian shook his head in despair, "I'm supposed to be the logical reasoning one but it seems all wrong to me and it scares me. The thing is, I'm so proud of Stuart. I thought he was a silly boy when I first met him. His Dad didn't even trust him with his car, now look at him. He's planning a base on Mars nearly half a billion years in the past and he's got two kids from the beginning of the twentieth century helping him. It sounds ridiculous even saying it."

"And we're back to why our security is so good." James said, "Unless you've experienced it then it's too fantastic to believe. The only guy I'm worried about is Anthony, he's a complete stranger."

In fact Anthony had his own worry. Two of his ancestors were about to put their lives in danger before they could have children. He had only just married and they were expecting their first child. More than anything he wanted to protect his unborn child. Supposing something happened to Freddie or Tony? Dave seemed to show his own emotions the most and it was to him that Anthony turned.

"What does happen to me if one of them is killed?" he asked, "I know, I should be worried about them but this is like nothing I could ever have imagined."

"Stuart says that his favourite words are 'I don't know'." Dave replied, "I think that they're mine as well. Supposing we sent them home and changed their memories? They'd be safe for now but they both live through a war. Supposing one of them leads just a slightly different life and ends up in the wrong place at the wrong time."

"That's not cheering me up." Anthony chuckled, "But I understand what you're saying. I'm just thinking of something Grandfather Freddie kept trying to drum into me though I'm not sure why it's relevant."

Dave waited patiently, and Anthony continued, "Governments can barely run things they understand. Heaven help us all if they had to handle something that they didn't understand."

Dave laughed, "I'd have liked to have met him. He seems to have been quite a character. And you're asking what would happen if they got a portal."

Anthony stared at him for a moment.

"You have met him." he said, "It's you and your friends who are turning him into that character. Are you sure about them using your equipment?"

"There are training locks in the system." Dave said, "They're learning to put the coordinates in properly and they're learning about Mars. We used a portal to put an inflatable dummy on the surface. They were quite shocked when it just exploded. We're impressing upon them not to even think about bypassing the safety protocols and I think we've got through to them."

"And you really are going to set up a base in one of their abandoned colonies. If they're all dead then there's no threat so is it worth the risk?"

"Stuart thinks so." Dave replied, "If he spotted trouble in a sardine can, I'd take him seriously. In this case I can just about keep up with him. They can still harm us when they were alive. We want to monitor all four bases while they were still inhabited to figure out precisely what they did do. If they tried to escape by coming forward in time to say ancient Rome, but they were taken and enslaved then it's all part of our history and it can stay that way. If there's some time-line where they took over the Empire then perhaps they should be stopped. If they see our portals as the key to developing their transport then they could be planning to attack us.

"It's all the different time-lines that are confusing. Your grandfather has told you about stuff that hasn't happened to me yet so you know my future. You're waiting for him to actually live through it so that he can tell you about it."

"I got the first bit." Anthony grinned, "The thing about Grandfather hasn't helped but let me see if I understand this bit. Your normal observation methods don't work because of the distances involved. I assume that you can talk of distance when time travelling. Either way you need a staging post to reduce the turbulence from too many long distance transportations to one spot."

"That even makes it clearer to me." Dave laughed, "Are you still in?"

"It's amazing what great-granddad knew." Anthony replied, "The family tried to persuade him to stand as an MP after the war. They saw the kudos and kickbacks, only thinking of the money he could make but he scandalised everyone by joining the Labour Party. He was too much of a capitalist for their liking so although the local branch welcomed him, appreciating what he had done for his employees and tenants he wasn't very popular at constituency level and above. He wasn't popular with the Conservatives either. They saw his reforms as sucking in their profits through taxes."

Anthony paused, "Going back to the Ancients, both their governments tried to control the portal without understanding its full potential. Each bloc tried pushing its use a little further until it spiralled out of control. Our lot aren't much better. They spout party dogma with little thought of what's really happening. I see where Great-granddad was coming from now. He tried to apply what he had learnt but no one was interested."

"Except on your estates." David said.

"The adult Freddie and Tony still got a lot of opposition from the family. They were capitalist enough to start running the estate as a business and not relying on the idea that gentlemen were entitled to own land. It got round the death duties and a lot of other taxation that the family approved of. Sending plebs to university, putting the doctor on salary so that the villagers didn't have to pay was too much like communism.

"Anyway I'm popping down to the pub. I need a break to digest everything we're doing."

Anthony wanted a quiet time calming his swirling thoughts by watching the world go by but he was unlucky. Dave's parents, Thomas and Brenda Hilford planned on eating out and arrived shortly after him.

"Sir Anthony Darrington isn't it?" Tom almost gushed, "I believe you know our son, David. It's a pleasure to meet you. How are you finding our sleepy little backwater? Can I get you a drink?"

"Thank you. It's more interesting than I could have imagined possible." Anthony responded.

"The thing is we're concerned about David." Brenda said, "He's such a talented boy and we're worried that he's wasting his time in a job way below his abilities. It's most embarrassing telling our friends that he's just a handyman."

"It wouldn't be so bad if Brian Chapman wasn't so obviously a madman with his wild ideas that go nowhere." Tom added, "You're not going to waste money by investing in his madcap business are you?"

For a moment Anthony was rattled by such a concerted assault. As always, even when he was not working, Bill the landlord was never far away from potential trouble.

Bill had worked in the pub trade all his life and it was the only thing he knew. In his time he had come across all sorts and while he vaguely disapproved of Brian and Stuart's lifestyle he could not see any harm in them. As Brian had donated more to village life so tourism had picked up which in turn had benefited the pub. He could not help overhearing conversations but he never repeated anything he heard and his regulars tended to relax in front of him.

With Demetrius' forge a developing attraction, an ability to accommodate visitors of all nationalities, courtesy of Stuart and his friends and a well established reputation for excellent food the pub was always busy. His wife might disappear into the kitchen rather than serve Stuart or Brian but Bill saw them as helping his own little world flourish.

When he saw the Hilfords tackling Anthony he knew that they were excluded from 'Brian's Real Job' as he thought of it. Rather than intervene he decided that the already pristine beer pumps near Anthony needed a further polish, just in case. He need not have worried.

"Brian's theories are a bit way out, I agree." Anthony said, "But they're based on sound scientific logic. My family has always seen scientific research as a long term investment. We were investing in cathode ray tube development in the 1920s while John Logie Baird was still working on mechanical systems for television and over the years we did very nicely out of it."

"Yes but David's still just a manual worker." Thomas said, "He's hardly going to share in any profits, is he?"

"Try to see him for what he is." Anthony retorted, "He's an intelligent young man who's being encouraged to develop his talents. He knows what he's doing."

"You wouldn't think so if you'd met the tramp he's shacked up with." Brenda exclaimed, "He can't take her anywhere that there's decent people."

"Oh so you don't want to be associated with me then." Anthony said quietly.

"Why on earth not?" Thomas asked.

"Because I've invited Dave and Sally to stay with me for Harvest Festival. It's a tradition that we hold a party for the village children and young Aidan is just old enough to appreciate it."

"Well that's very kind of you, Sir Anthony." Brenda simpered, "I'm sure David will be very grateful."

"Gratitude doesn't come into it." Anthony snapped, "And my father isn't dead yet. He holds the baronetcy. Now if you'll excuse me I came here to mull over a few problems I have."

Although Anthony did not realise it Bill saw his cue. He looked at Tom.

"There's a table if you're ready to eat." he said as he poured Anthony a drink.

Once the Hilfords were ensconced in the restaurant he handed Anthony the drink saying, "Sometimes they behave little better than incomers, sir. Young Dave's done wonders settling Sally down, she's a different person when he's around. They should be proud of him."

Anthony was mildly flattered to be included in the inner

sanctum of villagers. Thorndown, the village on his estate was far more open and nowadays, being close to a motorway the population was far more fluid so it accepted strangers far more readily.

If Anthony had to deal with Dave's parents then Stuart's problem was dealing with the Terzons. If they approved of a project then they willingly supplied equipment to ensure its completion but Stuart's projects were rarely straightforward research.

"We are only helping because you want to understand what is happening." Spock said

Spock was a Terzon whose real name was almost unpronounceable in human languages. He earned his nickname because his people were highly logical and disliked decisions based on emotion. Although Stuart's relationship with Terzon in general had cooled, Spock and he were still friends.

Spock was an anthropologist so Stuart understood that part of their friendship was based on Spock being able to study him. The Terzons were wary because there was a conflict developing between two Earth cultures and they would not take sides, so again, Stuart suspected that Spock had been sent to keep an eye on him. Even if Stuart helped the Martian colonists to save themselves the Terzons might consider it interfering and refuse to help.

However the Terzons were reluctant to see another civilisation destroyed if they could avoid it and they allowed themselves the emotion of curiosity. As a result, they were fascinated by Stuart's adventures and if it was not such an emotional response they would have been eager to help him.

The Terzons did not have time travel because it was so difficult to use without changing things. However, Stuart's present problem was one that they had never considered. He was pushing the boundaries of physics and, indeed the known universe in unheard of directions. As a result they were almost eager to observe his activities providing it did not provide them with an ethical conflict.

The result of this atypically emotional behaviour was for Stuart to establish a base on Mars in a very short time. Spock watched as Tony and Freddie excitedly leaping to well over head height and springing across the cave in long half flying steps.

"Our own teenagers would enjoy this." he said, "They have the same compulsion to explore physical boundaries."

"Pre-puberty youngsters." Stuart corrected, "You lot take a lot longer to grow up."

"Which means we have more time to get it right." Spock

replied, "Though I must admit, their energy is impressive. Is it wise to bring them here?"

"No." Stuart replied bluntly, "In any other circumstances I'd say that they were going to get themselves killed."

"But for you, the bigger risk is changing the time-line." Spock said, "It is a problem and you do seem to be trapped by events."

"Freddie appears to be the real mischief maker while Tony follows his lead." Stuart explained, "Freddie does take a promise very seriously. He promised not to go near the airlock and he even tries to shift their game if Tony gets too close to it. The odd thing is, when they're here I do have this weird feeling that everything is as it should be. It's hardly logical but we do have a saying about 'going with the flow'."

"And they are an interesting experiment." Spock said, "It's interesting to see how they're adapting to what for them is an impossible environment."

"Is that why you agreed to making spacesuits for them? It's all part of your experiment."

"Partly." Spock replied, "They don't complain about being used as subjects and the time-line is proceeding as it should. I am also curious to know how they settle down when they return home."

"Tony will have a few very selected memories and I have the feeling that Freddie will have this enormous secret that will make him feel terribly important." Stuart responded, "He's intelligent enough to realise that if he did try to say something, he'd become a laughingstock."

"And you've solved the problem of operating the fields through a planet."

"Not completely." Stuart replied, "By moving to this point in time we've generally reduced the field distortions we create. It not only makes it less likely to interfere with the Martian operations but it takes a lot of pressure off our equipment and we can make far finer adjustments. I've simplified it even further by using the beacons I developed when I was being jerked around alternate universes. They can be modulated to accept control data for the probes."

So you've put a probe in each of the colonies and they can be controlled from here."

"Exactly. Martian technology is far cruder than ours and won't be affected by our far weaker fields."

"And by Martians you mean colonists from the original Earth civilisation." Spock said.

Stuart grinned, "I haven't forgotten that to you this is a civil war between Earthmen."

For once Spock smiled back.

"It's a very curious one though." he said, "How would you define a victory?"

"Everyone living happily ever after." Stuart exclaimed, "I don't really know."

"The overall aim is a good one." Spock said seriously, "I'll be happy to help you put it into effect."

With typical Terzon efficiency their base was split into two time zones, the present day one and the research section set close in time to the original Martian colonies with the two parts connected by portal. As Stuart had said probes were exploring the four colonies while another was exploring the Earth of that time.

Gradually they formed a picture of the colony's history and of Earth. Brian finally surrendered to the situation and invited Joe Milnes to join them on Mars and in the earlier base so that James could explain everything.

Brian greeted Joe when he arrived. Joe was not exactly excited but he did take a few tentative jumps to test out the Martian gravity.

"Not your average day, is it?" Anthony asked.

"No," Joe replied, "But I've been thinking about those fields. How long were they being farmed."

"We think about two hundred years. Why?"

"My old Dad always said that you've got to put back what you take out." Joe said, "Fertilizers and the like do it, so does letting a field lie fallow, at least on Earth. But up here could the good soil seep away over time? What was the quality of their farm management like?"

"You're saying that they could have starved to death." Brian said.

"It's a possibility." Joe said, "There have been incidents on Earth where they've poisoned the soil through bad techniques. Here everything had to be tightly controlled and nature has a funny habit of objecting to that."

"Stuart's not going to be very happy with you." Brian laughed, "You've just given him some more questions and no answers."

"That's what he lives for." Joe said, as ever seriously, "Questions he can his teeth into."

They all settled down.

"OK." James began, "As you know we've been trying to

understand the history of these people We're having problems and not getting very far. There're all sorts of weird distortions that we can't explain and our usual methods aren't going to work."

"How come?" Stuart asked.

"If I didn't know that it was impossible then I'd say that they were blocking us." James replied.

Stuart turned to Brian, "Is it possible?"

"Anything's possible." Brian replied, "In this case I'm thinking of the feedback problems we had and vast amounts of energy. Possible but unlikely."

"OK but there was a war and afterwards the Martian colony survived by making the best use of what was left. There's a period between the war and Larik and Merrill's time that we can access then a brief time when we encounter the same blocking affect and sometime during that period the colonies fail."

"So you're suggesting that they saw portal technology as a weapon and created a defence against it."

"Possibly." James replied.

"So visiting the protected areas is out of the question." Dave said, "Stuart will be disappointed."

Stuart grinned and shrugged.

"I don't want to encourage him because it would be dangerous but he could do it." James began, "However, let's cover the basics first. Dave's already found Pangaea and this civilisation existed before that. The continents were distributed North and South as we guessed and there was an equatorial sea girdling the globe. It was warmer than now so the polar caps were smaller and they inhabited and farmed land much closer to the poles than we can. It was a harsh life in those regions and I think trouble makers tended to be exiled there.

"I know, it doesn't sound as if I'm answering Dave's question but I am. The bulk of their civilisation was in what we call the temperate zones. Cities and important centres were protected but it wasn't the sort of barrier that you can go up and touch. It fades over distance so there are gaps if you can find them and, at the polar regions I mentioned protection is at its weakest."

"That doesn't make sense." Stuart said, "Portals could just open up and troops pour through."

"I don't know." James answered, "The fields for that would have to operate through the planet, I doubt that they could compensate to avoid time travel and it could be why the Martian colonies were such a prime target."

"But we could visit these dissidents?" Stuart asked.

"The blocking field tends to vary so you might get trapped there for a time but we use higher dimensions than they do so we should be able to control the portal enough to get you out."

"That's comforting." Stuart chuckled.

"Right, explain why you want to visit." Brian commanded.

"We have to stop these kidnappings." Stuart replied, "To do that we'll change the lives of the colonists. In exchange for interfering then we should offer a better life and to do that we need to know more about them."

"I know that you need to talk to people." Brian said, "It's the only way that you get a feel for them but is it really necessary this time?"

Before Stuart could marshal his thoughts, Brian continued, "You need to know how they would mix with other peoples."

"Just be careful, please." Richard added.

Stuart grinned, "I'm having too much fun to want to kill myself."

"Hmm." Richard snorted, "That doesn't help."

Field Trips

Despite his flippancy, Stuart did plan everything he did very carefully, and this trip was no exception. The hardest part proved to be finding someone to visit. Many of the so called dissidents were what James described as hot-heads ready to shout from the rooftops but with little knowledge of their world. Others were quickly broken by the harsh conditions, some found themselves in places where conditions combined favourably and they thrived. There were a few suitable candidates amongst them but there no opportunities to talk undisturbed. They finally selected someone, an elderly man who lived a short distance from the village. He acted as a teacher in exchange for help in tending his field. As the threat of war increased so his students stayed with their parents and he was left alone.

Stuart chose about five days before the bombs were to be launched, giving him a wide margin of error but he would be able to relax and talk at length. If the old man proved to be hospitable the portal would de-materialise and Stuart would rely on a probe for communications. As usual Dave was more than ready to accompany him. Their venture started well as their potential host proved anxious for company to distract himself from his fear of the future.

"I'm Talik." he said, "Please come in and get warm. What brings you to these parts? Is the news any better? We just get the official government station up here."

"You need to prepare yourself for the worst." Stuart replied, "We're explorers and we want to learn about your world. Not military secrets you understand, but about you."

"I'm glad that you don't want military secrets because I don't have any." Talik chuckled, "However would you be happy with the public knowledge that we read about in books."

"Yes certainly." Stuart replied.

"Why?" Talik replied, "Where do you come from?"

His features softened.

"Will you tell me in exchange for what I tell you?"

"You might not believe me." Stuart responded, "We come from another world."

"Maybe I do believe you." Talik said, "I saw you arrive in a dimensional drill. What do you know of it?"

"That it can take you to different galaxies and it travels through time."

"Most would say that it's a weapon of great power and too dangerous to allow our enemy to have. I've met Kramons though and they say the same thing about us. Silly isn't it?"

Stuart might have replied but his radio crackled into life.

"Stuart, something's gone wrong. The blocking fields been stepped up and they're launching missiles."

From Brian down everyone relied on checking and double checking entries but for once James was distracted, worried about handling Andy. It was nothing serious, he was just unused to parenting.

In order to prevent a portal being activated accidentally, dedicated computers controlled them and data had to be entered. Once entered the data was stored and automatically updated. Normally a simulation showed up any errors, sometimes a probe proved to be a little out of position and it was all corrected before anyone stepped through a portal but maybe they had all become complacent. James was distracted so failed to notice errors in a peculiar combination of '3s', '5s' and '8s' and five days in a thousand years was still pretty accurate navigation. Whatever the reason, in hindsight, they agreed they should have been less concerned for the blocking fields and more careful checking their data.

~~~

Whatever the real cause Stuart and Dave faced a barrage of incoming missiles tipped with nuclear warheads.

"Missiles." Talik exclaimed, "Is it really happening?"

"There's a foul up somewhere," Stuart replied, "but we should take it seriously"

"I got a letter this morning. I'm a rocket engineer and I was being recalled." he shrugged, "At least I won't have to go. Follow me."

Talik led the way down into the cellar. One wall was lined with food and a massive water tank jutted out from another. The rest of the walls were lined with bookshelves full of books.

"It won't save us." he said, "But I wanted to save as much knowledge as I could. Learn what you can while you still live."

~~~

Meanwhile James had sent for the others.

"OK we can stretch things this end." Brian said as Richard looked on, "We should be used to that but it doesn't feel right this time, does it? It feels too urgent. What do you have?"

"There're thousands of rockets, both sides have launched everything they've got. Cities nearest the equator will be hit first then it'll be like a creeping barrage moving towards the polar regions."

"Can you figure out the targets?" Richard asked, "Is there anything near Stuart's location?"

"Our computers are doing the best they can, but they're being swamped." James replied, "They're learning though. Look, the ones we can ignore are being greyed out and there's those two flashing. There's a city two hundred and fifty kilometres to the south of Stuart's position. They're the threats."

"Can we stop them?" Richard asked.

"Yes but it might be better if we don't." James replied, "It's probably got a blocking generator that will be destroyed. Then we can deploy the portal. Hot air rises at the equator and blows towards the poles where it sinks and blows back towards the equator at ground level. Radiation should be blown southwards and these polar communities should be the last to get it. That would be the best time to fetch them."

"Are you sure?" Richard asked, "I don't like it."

"Neither do I." James agreed, "I've just said that it'll be better to let millions of people be incinerated in that city and it doesn't help to say that a quick death is better than a slow one by radiation poisoning. So far as Dave and Stuart are concerned, I can try to power through the blocking field, get them out into the open and risk leaving them exposed because the blocking field destabilises the portal."

"Just make sure that they're under cover." Richard said and Brian nodded.

James used the radios to contact Stuart, relieved when Stuart sounded unconcerned.

"You'll have to come with us." Stuart said to Talik.

"My life's nearly over anyway." Talik said, "I was exiled because I kept warning of this day. I have medical supplies, I shall spend what time I have left tending the village, unless you can take them as well."

He looked at Stuart, "Don't worry I can see the answer in your face. If you can save me, you could save the village, if you can save the village then you can save the town but you can't. I understand."

"I'm sorry." Stuart said.

"Why did you launch the…"

Talik was interrupted as the cellar lit up and then was dark again.

"I always meant to fill the gaps between the floorboards." he said as the cellar lit up again, "Did you notice? I'd painted the outside white. That reflected most of it but let's hope that the furniture didn't catch fire. We'll see what's happening after the shock-wave."

"You don't seem worried." Stuart said.

"I'm scared of how I'm going to die." Talik said, "I could plan to survive the day that the bombs arrive but not the days after when the radiation settles. You saw when you first arrived, all the shutters were closed. The blast and the shock-wave will do damage but we should survive at this distance."

"Should survive?" Dave queried.

"It hasn't arrived yet, the longer it takes, the further away it was and weaker it will be when it gets here."

"Does James really want us to sit it out?" Dave asked.

Stuart nodded but Dave was badly frightened. Never particularly patient he was unprepared for trusting his life to a bomb shelter. Stuart was just as scared but he was confident that James or someone was monitoring the situation. It gave him something to hold on to.

As the shaking began Dave looked upwards waiting for the ceiling to come crashing down but it remained solid. The second shaking was far worse and Dave heard loud cracks as if timber was snapping but again it passed. They looked at each other searching for relief but they were all shocked. Stuart and Dave turned to Talik.

"I believe that the war is over." Talik said, "But let's hear what your friends think. I was not sure whether to believe them about the start of the war but it was better to be safe. You wanted to see my library so it seemed like a good time to oblige. We should wait for them and you should use the time to choose the books that you want to take."

"Thank you." Stuart said, "If I can, I'll come back for you and the village."

Talik's home was little more than a log cabin. It had extra rooms but Stuart had the idea that they were tacked on as and when Talik could find the time or the inclination. It still cracked and creaked alarmingly as it settled again though nothing happened.

"Hello." a voice called and both Stuart and Dave breathed a deep sigh of relief but they both turned to Talik."

"Go," he said, "I believe that your promise to try means more than someone else's promise to do."

Stuart and Dave still hesitated.

"Go." Talik repeated, "And don't forget your books."

Still shocked but now feeling safe, Stuart paused to examine the outside of the cabin.

"Move it." James snapped, "Stuart, front and centre."

Stuart did not understand what James meant but he caught the urgency in James' voice.

"What's wrong." he asked as he hurried across.

James was staring at the twin mushroom clouds looming over the horizon.

"Let's just get out of here." James said, "Please."

Where Dave and Stuart were now thoroughly deflated, James was trembling when they returned.

"It all happened on my watch." he muttered.

"Yes it did." Richard said angrily.

"OK enough." Stuart said, "What was the urgency?"

"The weather." Brian explained, "Sorry that sounded trite. It's bad luck. Sorry that sounds wrong as well."

Brian was as shaken as the others as he tried to explain.

"It didn't seem important at first." he said, "But there's a deep depression between your landing site and that city. Wind speeds are up to a hundred kilometres an hour and it's dragging fallout in this direction. It'll be here in an hour."

"But that won't be enough time to rescue anyone." Stuart said, "Hang on, radiation will build up slowly we'll have time."

"No." Brian said, "It'll take experts ages to work out the mechanics but the storm's sucking in superheated air and fallout from the firestorm. It may also have been destabilised by gravimetric shifts from the blocking fields. Tornadoes are forming, one's an F5 and it's moving towards your site."

Stuart nodded, tears in his eyes and hurried off. For once he did not seek out his friends but headed back to Earth, hurrying to the pub and ordering a triple whisky. He knocked it back in one go and ordered another.

"Are you sure." Bill asked.

"Yes." Stuart snapped, "And you can start pouring the next."

"And that's your lot." Bill said, "This isn't like you lad. Come up to this end of the bar and tell me what's wrong."

"I had to take shelter from a nuclear bomb and leave someone to die of radiation poisoning." Stuart sobbed.

"I'm fetching Demetrius." Bill said, "I don't understand how that's possible but something bad has happened. As long as Demetrius looks after you, get as drunk as you like."

Dave thought about following Stuart but decided he needed time alone. Instead he looked at Richard, James and Brian, "Which conversation are you going to have?" he asked.

"How do you mean?" Brian asked.

"There's the one where you say it's too dangerous and we should stop. Maybe you should go for the one where you say that we've got to tighten up on procedures and we have to be more careful. Stuart doesn't need either one at the moment and he'll be knocking himself out because he nearly got me killed. I thought it was a mistake not to send a probe first but nothing had gone wrong before so I thought we'd get away with it just the once. Did anyone think differently?"

"You're saying that we should put it down to experience." Brian said, "And you're right that's the way I did think."

"You cleared everyone from the earlier base for this trip. So you've got some peace and quiet here. Read these books and see if you can find anything useful. I'm going to find Stuart."

No medical pundit will ever believe that getting falling down drunk is a cure for anything but when he found Stuart already staggering unevenly around the bar and his speech slurred, it seemed like a good idea to Dave. Luckily he never caught up with Stuart and was able to stagger home while Demetrius just about managed to half carry and half support Stuart on their way home.

"Good old Demetrius. Always there when we need him." Stuart managed to slur before passing out on the bed.

No one saw much of either Stuart or Dave the next day. It was not so much a hangover or shock at their own lucky escape, they both felt that they had abused Talik's hospitality. They visited a man who was about to die, taken what they needed and left him to his fate.

Also they had got so used to manipulating time so that it was a shock realise to discover that there were still limits to what they could do.

They talked it over when they did meet but were not prepared to discuss it with anyone else.

The day after that they met up to discuss James' finding.

"How do you feel?" James asked.

"OK, I suppose." Stuart replied, "I'd still like to help Talik's village but I don't think that there'd be time."

"How about leaving it until we've got somewhere to take them and then try." James suggested.

"I forget time travel." Stuart said, "It just feels so immediate and urgent. Let's get on."

"First, post-war history. We checked about fifty years after. Radiation was still too high to sustain life, the ozone layer was only just beginning to recover but the Earth's surface was still receiving lethal quantities of radiation from the sun, especially in the ultra-violet band."

"I thought that the old cold war propaganda said that we had to stay under cover for a fortnight." Brian asked, "How does that relate to their war?"

"That's what I thought." James said, "First they could deliver far larger bombs. Second, very little life had adequate protection during that fortnight. I could go into detail but nothing left out in the open survived, wealthy folk who could afford protection were the unluckiest. They got slightly smaller doses of radiation and took longer to die."

"I thought that you could make your home radiation proof." Anthony persisted.

"Even if we take the two weeks everyone talks about the problems are horrific." James explained, "You have to filter the air, and make sure you have enough water. If you live in an ordinary house that is undamaged but built of ordinary materials then you need a room at least four metres from the nearest outer wall. Most rooms are designed to have a window in them so you've got problems. Depending on the severity of the war, your chances of avoiding radiation poisoning are pretty slim and theirs was the severest.

The elite survived six months in well constructed fall out shelters. They emerged to a world freezing cold because of the thick clouds of dust. When they cleared after a couple of years the sunlight seared their skin. Plants had been badly damaged by radiation and had even less resistance to the ultra violet burning. Enough trace radiation remained to cause a catastrophic number of birth defects and life continued to dwindle over the next few years. Even if you do survive in your bomb shelter for a fortnight, how do you find water that hasn't been contaminated with plutonium, caesium or strontium?"

"I'm not sure if Tony and Freddie should be listening to this."

Anthony said.

"That's all right." Freddie said brightly, "I know it's horrible that lot's of people died like that. We've got to make sure that we don't do the same thing haven't we?"

"Fair enough." James said,

"I've seen it on other planets." Stuart said, "Can we move on anyway. I don't see that it's helping us here."

"OK." James agreed, "Whatever happened, we were left with the Southern colonies on Mars. Mars was home and Earth the hostile planet to be re-colonised. The Martian colonies lasted for about two hundred years but were in steady decline. Joe Milnes may be able to explain why because technologically they performed marvels. They had teams scavenging Earth to bring back what they needed. This continued until Larik and Merrill and then it all stopped, a blocking field was introduced and they died out."

"Did they do biological research at any time." Stuart asked.

"No. They did no development, they just scavenged equipment."

"This sounds easy." Stuart said, "We can't change events before Larik and Merrill visited us because then it wouldn't happen and that would create a paradox. If we do help them then it must be at the right time."

"Sorry Dave but this time it's me who's going to make it complicated." James said, "You see we've found a Northern colony but it's on Earth."

"Where we agree that life can't exist." Dave said.

"We've been doing surveys of Earth and Terzon sensors actually picked up intelligent thought or at least very faint but characteristic signals. We tracked it, and found the colony."

"Surely it would be spotted by satellites or something." Anthony said, "Then it would be a prime target."

"The clever bit was that it was in full view and open to the public." James said, "A spy just needed to buy a ticket to visit and it was there for fifty years before the war. I think it rated a few high explosives to smash the dome and that was that."

"Go on." Stuart said, "This is news to me."

"The public attraction was a biosphere, you know, a closed environment where they tried to simulate Earth's conditions. It probably provided data for designing the Martian colonies."

"Which the South stole." Freddie interrupted.

"Probably."

"You do say things like 'it seemed', 'probably', 'it may have' a lot." Freddie said.

"That's because I'm not certain." James said, "A lot is guesswork that fits the facts but there's still a lot we're not sure about. Anyway, the biosphere was just the entrance built in a quarry. Before the war the quarry walls were extensively mined and the real, underground, biosphere was gradually expanded."

He glanced at Freddie, "We think that the scientific caste even hid it from their leaders but we're not sure."

Freddie grinned as James continued, "Considering what they achieved on Mars imagine what they could have done on Earth when stuff could have been shipped in by truck. Stuart, do you have anything to add?"

"Not much." Stuart replied, "I've found an Earth where the Black Death was far more virulent and the death rate was over seventy five per cent or more. It pushed Asia and Europe over the edge and they never recovered. America is largely unaffected and it's the nations like the Aztec in South America or nations like the Apache in the North that thrive. The Ancients have got a portal, and have a ship which is now in our time and it seems that they had plenty of shuttles. Can we be clear on how they work, please."

"Actually they're an interesting design in that they use a form of portal technology." James explained, "Navigation is a problem because a ship doesn't have a fixed point to work from. They solved it by making a series of small jumps. As the front end materialised so the rear end used radar to locate it before de-materialising. They needed about five jumps to get from Earth to Mars. Shuttles are the one thing they've got plenty of. It seems that they were trying to colonise Phobos and Deimos as well. They might be the Martian satellites but I would have said that they were too small."

"Apart from their time travelling is this heavy planet relevant?"

"As it turns out, no, it was just a highway between time-zones." James replied

"Tomorrow, I'd like to explore this Earth colony at that point in time and focus on it for a bit." Stuart said, "What's the outside like?"

"Radiation levels are still above what we consider safe. I wouldn't recommend being there more than three or four hours at night. During the day and any bare skin would be burned within seconds."

"OK, one last question." Stuart said, "Could there have been a second war, this time between the Earth colony and the Martian one?"

"Possibly." James replied, "It's possible one may have discovered the other."

"Another last question." Stuart grinned, "Where or rather when would Larik and Merrill be in terms of this second war?"

"Just before it happened." James replied, "It's roughly where we trace ship signatures to."

"A lot of this is already in the files so I'm labouring points." Stuart said, "I don't know about anyone else but it's easy to ask where's so and so. It gets awkward when you have to be clear when you mean and whether it's relative to his time-line or mine."

"I agree." James said, "We've got to learn to think in a completely new way."

The meeting broke up not long after. They were all tired and headed home.

The following day, Stuart and Dave met up with James.

"We've all looked at it and none of us can find a way of travelling that far back in time on Earth because of continental drift and other instabilities." Stuart said, "However, our portal technology is more sophisticated than the Ancient's so we can use Mars instead of a high gravity planet.

"I spoke to Brian last night. Those portals we mothballed when we upgraded to the new ones, I want to send a couple to our early Mars base and install them on the surface in a dome."

"I thought we replaced them because the new ones offer better protection against radiation." Dave exclaimed.

"They do." Stuart replied, "We've been using portals for a couple of years now and we're going to carry on using them for many more years. The new portals will cut our total exposure over that time. If we use the old ones over a couple of months we won't increase our overall exposure by anything significant."

"So portal from Resolution to Mars, use a Mars one to portal back to our earlier base then use surface based portals to explore Earth of the period." Dave said.

"I like the idea of portalling." Stuart chuckled, "But how do you feel about doing it."

"Fine. After all we're checking to see if there's a threat to our Earth." Dave said, "You're not going to try to rescue the survivors or something, are you?"

"Not yet." Stuart replied, "Let's see what's going on first."

"The base is safe enough." James said, "We could stay there for a couple of nights. It would cut down on portal activity and reduce any multi-dimensional distortions in a small space."

As they worked on setting up the earlier base it became known as the outpost. It made sense because it was beyond anything that they would have considered doing or exploring and they all liked a name that avoided the muddled time lines they were dealing with. For the same reason, almost without realising it they made the outpost as comfortable as possible, trying to eliminate any sense of being on an alien world long in the past.

It took longer than they intended but as Stuart said, 'When you're dealing with time travel, urgent means something completely different'.

Of course they could not hide the lower gravity but they quickly got used to the 'spring in their step' as Joe Milnes put it. Much to everyone's surprise he became a regular visitor. Maybe Stuart should not have offered to set up a greenhouse for him but he did. Joe readily accepted and planted seeds that they recovered from the other colonies as well planting some of his own seed that he fetched from Earth.

"I hope you're not growing some alien monster that's going to attack Earth." Dave chuckled.

"It's unlikely." Joe replied as seriously as ever, "Brian's taken me to that place, Terzon. They've already done this sort of experiment and they've introduced one or two seeds to their own world for food. I tell you what though. If there's time I want to grow a marrow for the village fête. Seth Brady's won once too often and I reckon this low gravity malarkey will let one grow to a fair old size."

The caves they chose were large enough to allow for a comfortable living space, individual bedrooms, a portal chamber and laboratories to make them liveable. However, it was Joe, worrying about the village fête, supplying fresh food and home made wine that made it seem like home. And, more than anything it was Freddie, Tony and occasionally Reginald that reminded them that they were on Mars as they charged around in long ballet like leaps enjoying the novelty of low gravity.

Anthony was also a regular visitor. Like Richard, he was interested in history, accompanying him to a dig or practising his Greek while helping Demetrius in the forge.

"OK." Stuart said as the outpost was completed, "The way we're set up here, we're safer here than on Resolution. We've got a fusion reactor for power, oxygen, water and emergency rations for six months. We've also got two portals and a dozen probes. No one knows we're here and even if they do spot us watching them they'd still have to find us.

"Joe, we've more or less transferred operations from your barn to here. I'd like to hang on to it though, if that's OK."

"I've said before, I don't know why Granddad built it there." Joe said, "It's no use to me so help yourself."

He glanced around, "Besides, I reckon that this makes us quits."

"OK." Stuart said, "Tomorrow we visit Earth. I'd like James to be in control of the control room or should I have said take command of it. Let's see if we can't find out what's going on."

The sunlight had a harsh steely blue tone to it. Nothing had survived. The few stumps of trees still standing were bare, long dead. Anthony thought of it as a desert of death.

"Let's get those soil samples for Joe." Stuart's voice crackled over the intercom, "I don't want to stay too long."

"You were right, Stuart." Dave said, "It was pointless coming here ourselves. These suits separate us from the world too much. We should have used a probe."

"I don't know." Stuart replied, "It's a weird feeling knowing we're on Earth but we can't even take our gauntlets off."

"I always thought knights of old threw down gauntlets to challenge you to a duel." Dave said.

"Maybe but these come way up above our wrists." Stuart said, "It makes them more than gloves."

Stuart knelt down scooping soil into a container before standing again.

"You know we're about fifty years after the colonists died out." he said, "It doesn't seem possible that life will ever return."

"I know what you mean." Dave agreed, "Let's get back and stick with places where there is life."

"Not a bad morning's work though." Stuart said, "We'll take a look at the colony this afternoon. I'm hungry, let's get back."

The Trouble with Kids

"Where's Freddie and Tony?" Anthony asked as Stuart finished his meal.

Stuart glanced around before hurrying to the control room.

"It's started." he said quietly, "They've materialised a portal and set the coordinates for the Ancient's Earth Colony. This feels like such a massive mistake."

"Don't knock yourself out." Anthony said, "And you are right, you must avoid paradoxes. You also did the right thing teaching them how to do it properly. I suppose if it is a mistake letting them go, I'll just quietly disappear."

"You're right, it does seem wrong." Brian said, "But we're used to kids being kids into their late teens. Don't forget that during the Napoleonic wars, boys became midshipmen at twelve and could be in charge of seamen working on sails one hundred and fifty feet in the air. And they did have those memories before we started. We've got to follow it through. What do you intend doing, Stuart?"

"The natural thing." Stuart replied, "Go after them and bring them back. They've got all the memories that they should have so it's time to send them home."

"You mean you'll feel happier if they're home where they belong." Anthony said.

"There's still a memory missing." Dave said, "They were on the heavy planet."

Stuart's grinned looking smug.

"They're on it." he said, "We've got to follow events as we know them but they've spent nearly a week on Mars. Suddenly they're back in Earth's gravity. Why do you think I agreed whenever they begged for one more night up here."

"Oh that was so sly." Dave chuckled, "Can you beat history by cheating like that?"

"Let's hope so." Stuart said, "Otherwise we'll have to take them to see the spacecraft and who knows what they might get up to then. If you're coming then cover yourself in factor sixty sun blocker. I'm not planning on going outside but there's no harm in being ready."

As James took control of the portal, Stuart and Dave hurried through to find themselves in a tunnel. For a second or two, Stuart felt disorientated. Gravity told him that he was on Earth so why was he in an underground tunnel?

The moment passed and he took in his surroundings. The roof was unsupported, outcrops of harder rock had been left and altogether it had an abandoned feel to it.

"What now?" Dave asked.

"I think they learnt well." Stuart replied, "I'm hoping they chose somewhere where they could look out so let's see where that connecting tunnel leads."

"They did learn well." Dave said, "See the chalk arrow on the wall. Let's go that way."

Stuart glanced back into the tunnel that they had arrived in. It was dark, there were no lights on the portal that was hidden in the shadows. Almost at once they spotted Freddie and Tony crouched behind a low wall across the tunnel.

Freddie turned looking worried as he recognised Stuart and Dave.

"All that history stuff said that we were going to do this, didn't it?" he said, "So we're not in trouble, are we."

"We'll talk about it later." Stuart said, "Why did you choose here and now?"

Tony smiled proudly.

"It was my idea." he said, "It's a lookout post. You can see the main cavern from here and I've seen men with funny guns sitting here. We chose today because everyone seems to get very excited so we thought that we'd watch."

"Maybe it's you that they get excited about." Stuart said, "We'd better go, just in case."

Tony looked worried while Freddie shrugged.

"We know nothing happens. Let's stay." he exclaimed.

"Move." Stuart snapped. Even Dave jumped, unused to Stuart speaking so forcefully. Tony leapt up to obey while Freddie prepared to argue but seeing the other's reaction headed sullenly down the tunnel.

Tony was already in the side tunnel when they heard voices and the sound of running footsteps. Freddie hesitated, glancing at Stuart.

"Run!" Stuart whispered urgently, "Get back through the portal."

To Stuart's relief, Freddie nodded and obeyed. Stuart and Dave followed as if shepherding him. The tunnel they were in was a spur from another tunnel a few metres away. Men charged round the corner, raising their weapons as they spotted Stuart and Dave.

Stuart put out his hand to stop Dave before calling out in English, "Close the portal when Freddie's through."

He raised his arms in surrender and Dave followed suit.

"James will monitor us." Stuart whispered, "He'll get us out later."

Dave was unconvinced but nodded. He could see that if they had tried running they would have been shot before they got through the portal. Dave also had the feeling that Stuart saw it as a chance to talk to his captors.

Through the translators they heard the orders to step out of the tunnel and step back towards the balcony. They complied while two of the guards investigated the tunnel where the portal had materialised.

They returned while all five guards stood staring at Stuart and Dave.

"Do we shoot them now?" one asked and for once Stuart tensed, looking scared.

"No, there's something funny about them. Look at their clothes."

While Stuart and Dave were dressed in standard twenty-first century shirt, trainers and jeans, their guards were dressed in short tunics, sandals and a headdress. Stuart thought that they had an ancient Egyptian look to them and knew from their studies that head-wear denoted rank. Theirs were a plain white, placing them one rank above untrained workers but very low down in the hierarchy. Stuart knew that if a superior gave the order then he and Dave would be gunned down without hesitation but he doubted that they would do anything on their own initiative. Stuart was right for they were not even searched as they were led away. Dave always insisted on wearing a baseball cap and Stuart was sure that it was puzzling their captors, uncertain about Dave's rank. For once Dave was the boss and Stuart his servant.

The uncertainty about Dave's rank had one pleasant consequence. They were taken to a chamber not unlike the living quarters they found in the Martian colonies.

The senior guard looked at Dave.

"I hope that these quarters are satisfactory, sir." he said, "Our orders were to find out who was in a forbidden area and detain them."

"Very good." Dave said, "Do you know why it's called a forbidden zone?"

"Yes sir. Only our lords decide when the great cave should be observed."

"Thank you." Dave said, "These quarters will do."

The guard bowed and left.

"If these are the descendants of scientists then I'm not very impressed. They haven't searched us or separated us. Is this all part of the time-line?"

"I don't know." Stuart replied, "I don't remember any record of us being here so it's a new part of our personal time-lines. In other words our futures are completely unknown. I seem to remember that even small levels of radiation can cause brain damage over time. Even down here, radiation is higher than on Earth in our time. We'd be OK for a year or so but what happens to new born kids when their brains are the most delicate?"

"You're saying that their IQ could be dropping."

Stuart nodded, "I hadn't thought of it before but it could explain a lot."

"And I'm a prisoner again." Dave exclaimed, "I'm beginning to feel like a fugitive.

"I'm glad my Mum doesn't know how much time I spend in jail or under arrest." Stuart chuckled, "Still, I've been lucky, most have been quite comfortable."

As often happened when they were using the translator they tended to speak in the local language.

Making sure he spoke in English, Dave said, "Careful what you say in their language, Stu. They're probably listening to us, trying to see what we'll give away."

Moments later, the door opened and two beefy guards ordered Stuart out of the cell and led him to a room where he found himself standing in front of a desk flanked by the guards.

It was only minutes but it seemed an age to Stuart before the door opened again and a third man entered and sat behind the desk.

"We have a simple way of dealing with trouble makers." he said, "We let them go outside for a walk. We'll probably send your master out anyway but if you cooperate then we might put you to work in the fields."

"I'm Stuart and my *master* is called Dave." Stuart replied, "We use portal technology to travel through time."

"Portal?" his interrogator queried.

"I've introduced myself." Stuart said, "How about returning the compliment."

The man inclined his head with a slight smile.

"Insolence won't help you but to you I am Lord Trey." he said, "What is a portal?"

"The device we use to explore multidimensional space." Stuart replied, "You call it a dimensional drill and it's a pity your programme degenerated to a race to colonise Mars and the moon."

"You may be right about that," Trey conceded, "but at least the Kramons paid the price and no longer exist. One day, we will reclaim the Earth."

"You know that this colony is in decline." Stuart said, "You don't have the resources to maintain all your equipment and even the soil is getting more and more tired."

"The Lords of Traste know that." Trey said, "How does a peasant like you know?"

"At least they don't deny it." Stuart said, "Why keep it a secret?"

"Someone of noble birth would understand that we need to keep the peasants happy."

"You're as arrogant as that lot on Mars." Stuart exclaimed, "I thought that you were supposed to be scientists. At least you were descended from them."

"What lot on Mars?" Trey asked, "Our colonies were destroyed."

"The Kramons' survived." Stuart said, "They also have a spaceship."

"And you know where they are." Trey exclaimed, "We'll start preparing the attack."

Stuart realised that he had made a mistake telling Trey about the Martian colonies.

"I should stay quiet if I were you." Stuart said, "They could destroy you whenever they felt like it."

"Don't threaten us." Trey snapped, "You need to be convincing me that you should live."

"Try this." Stuart said as calmly as he could, "My master can rescue your people and find them a world where they can start again."

"Why? This is our world." Trey exclaimed, "We will stay and reclaim it."

"The ozone layer has improved. It's now about one per cent of the minimum safe level you need." Stuart explained, "You might be able to start farming outside in about three hundred years but allow another five hundred before you can wander around freely. How long will this colony last?"

"But you're saying the Kramons will win and live on Earth while we run and hide somewhere else."

"Forget this winning and losing crap." Stuart almost shouted, "Do you want your people to live?"

"We cannot betray the sacrifices our ancestors made." Trey exclaimed, "In spite of your knowledge, you're obviously not noble because you do not understand the concept of honour."

"Then I can't help you." Stuart said, "Will you return me to my master please?"

"I want the locations of your colonies on Mars." Trey said, "Help us and you'll live. Your sort is always happier with a simple life as a field hand."

"Dave and I would rather just walk through the airlock." Stuart replied, "We'll not help you make war."

Trey shrugged and turned to one of the guards.

"Fetch the other one." he commanded.

He turned back to Stuart, "It's getting dark and it gets very cold so you can keep your clothes. They won't help you when the sun rises tomorrow. Think about it and if you feel like talking, use the intercom."

Stuart was taken to a cell near the airlock leading outside. Sometime later, Dave joined him.

"He went on about the location of the Mars colonies." Dave explained, "Then he asked about the strange language we spoke but I don't think he really cared. He was more interested in the Mars colonies so why is he giving up on us so easily? I was expecting him to torture us or something. I'm not complaining though."

"Watch them when anyone mentions being outside." Stuart said, "They seem terrified. I bet they've all seen someone who's been left out there. The torture is that we'll have all night to think about how we're going to die. Even before it gets light our skin will begin to burn. That's because short wavelength scatters and bounces around the atmosphere. Sooner or later we'll panic and beg to be allowed back inside."

"And you want us to go out." Dave said, "Despite all that."

"Even if the ultra violet does scatter then we'll still be OK." Stuart said, "You did put on the factor 60 sun cream didn't you?"

"All over, you said." Dave smiled, "I do sometimes wonder when you're being kinky. I've got those contact lenses as well but I don't like wearing them. How did you know that we'd be captured?"

"I didn't, I was just being cautious." Stuart replied, "And our surveys had picked up on troublemakers being sent outside."

"You planned something with James didn't you." Dave said.

Stuart shrugged, "He's getting good at hiding a probe so I guess he's been watching us all the time. Once we have plenty of space all around us he'll send a portal. I hope he's quick though."

Dave nervously looked at Stuart but just then the door was opened and they were hustled out to stand by the airlock. Trey looked Dave.

"You can have your quarters back if you cooperate." Trey said, "Otherwise you can return as a field hand when you tell us where your colonies on Mars are."

Dave looked a little puzzled but still remained quiet.

Trey shrugged, "Such a shame, still, you've got all night to change your mind."

Stuart and Dave eyed the prods and the stun guns as they were pushed through the airlock. They heard the metal doors clang shut behind them as they stood getting their bearings.

They looked around. It was a moonless night but even the stars seemed to glow brighter with the same steely glare as the sunlight. The eerie starlight picked out cliff walls curving around in an arc while what could be the remains of a bomb crater, a broken ring of rock surrounding a dip in the ground lay a little distance away. Even without their knowledge of the hazards threatening them they found themselves in an inhospitable desert, bereft of life.

"From what that guard was telling me, I was expecting to be scrunching on piles of skeletons." Dave said, "Where are they?"

"Those that hang around are recycled as fertiliser." Stuart replied, "There's a couple of natural caves and some try to shelter in them until they need water. A few wander off looking for some and are caught out in the open at dawn. It's a nasty way to kill people. James was upset when he saw what happened. He put it in the files but he won't discuss it. Let's move. We reckon most of their CCTV failed years ago but I want to be out of sight before James picks us up."

"I might have Aidan but I want kids of my own." Dave said, "I don't want to spend too long in a radioactive desert."

"A couple of hours here will give you a year's safe dosage." Stuart said, "Did you really ask the Terzons for lead lined underwear?"

Dave shrugged, "Better safe than sorry but unless Sally gets counselling it won't matter much."

"OK, we're on a burned out Earth, hoping that James is on his way so let's talk about your bedtime problems."

Dave grinned, "At least we're alone. Her brother's doing three years for drug dealing. He was a nasty piece of work when he was little but as he got into drugs so they mashed whatever brain he had. I don't even want to guess at the stuff he did to her.

"I don't think she's got any long term injuries but mentally she's a wreck. You've seen her when she's out. She's either a timid little mouse who hides from everyone or ready to open her legs for anyone. Indoors she seems perfectly OK and the world centres around Aidan. Sometimes she cuddles up to me and we talk about the future but other times, if I so much as put my hand on her arm she tenses up and backs away."

"Why do you stay with her?" Stuart asked.

"Aidan." Dave replied, "I know he's not mine biologically but he's a great kid and he calls me Daddy. You often say the translators make us sensitive to peoples moods. Well sometimes I can see something in Sally and I'd do anything to bring it out."

They looked up as a soft scraping sound disturbed the silence. Relieved that James had arrived they hurried to the portal.

Lord Trey waited for the panicked beating on the outer door. He remembered with a shudder the times he had been sent out as a teenager to supervise the collection of bodies or to service the outer door. When they saw the body, it convinced impressionable youngsters that the outside was a place of unspeakable horrors. It provided them with a stark warning to conform and like all the inhabitants of the biosphere Lord Trey felt nervous even getting close to the exit tunnel.

While he could see that the guards were just as nervous, the two prisoners were relaxed, even unconcerned at being sent out. It was most odd.

A thought occurred to him. Maybe he should have thought more about where they came from. But why should he? He did not know every peasant in the world but what about their clothes? He could order a search for relics from the past. Find a stash of clothes and he would know which family they had come from. They would explain it all.

But they were not scared of the outside. Lord Trey gave up. The effort of trying to understand was too much. Besides once they start panicking they would explain everything. Lord Trey might have gone back to organising a work party to clean the sunlight diffusers the following night but it still niggled that they did not seem scared of the outside and that he was missing something. He waited in vain though, briefly admiring a couple who could face an agonising death so bravely but then he turned to more urgent matters.

Brian and Richard had been worried enough to gather around as Stuart and Dave hurried off on their rescue mission. When the guard was preparing to shoot them, James was ready to materialise a probe in the line of fire. He breathed a sigh of relief when the crisis passed but handed over to Brian while he changed into battle fatigues.

"I've done three years." Anthony said, "Do you need a hand? Great-granddad told me to bring suitable gear along."

"So that's why you keep that great big pack nearby." James chuckled, "The more the merrier. Stuart will see it as a chance to talk to them but let's be ready in case they start getting rough."

They all relaxed as they waited, watching as Dave and Stuart were interrogated.

"Is it really safe for them outside?" Richard asked.

"As long as we're ready to pick them up." Brian replied, "I'm worried that they could still get a touch of sunburn from the ultra-violet that's scattered around the atmosphere. It's not a problem anyone's been able to measure before."

"What about radioactivity?" Richard continued.

"They know not to drink the water. We'd have to think carefully if they needed an X-ray in the next couple of years but that's about it."

"You're thinking lifetime exposure then." Richard asked.

"That's right." Brian agreed, "But cracks about people glowing in the dark have stopped being funny."

For some reason, both Dave and Stuart felt the need to take a long shower and change into fresh clothes. Stuart even bundled up his old clothes to be sent back to Earth and burned. It had nothing to do with decontamination but they both had an overwhelming feeling that they had been somewhere dirty.

Freddie and Tony were nervously waiting for Stuart, wondering how much trouble they were in.

"OK." Stuart said, "You're not in trouble because we all knew it was going to happen but I think that your part is completed so it's time you went home. No promises but after all this settled I'll visit and maybe take you on another trip. How does that sound."

Freddie nodded thoughtfully, "I've got so much to tell Father." he said, "He loves a good adventure story and..."

He trailed off confused then continued, "But he's Tony and he already knows, I mean he knows now... My grown up father, I mean… I think. I wish I could take those DVDs back with me though."

"I've got the idea." Stuart chuckled, "There's one job left. Keep an eye on Phillips and see that he buys into the right sort technology. Let your dad handle it but the information will be fresher with you."

Freddie nodded happily, hugging Stuart goodbye when Dr. Tobias collected them.

It was not quite the end of the boy's visit. Stuart set up a second camp site on the Lizard planet where Freddie and Reginald could meet up. It was only a tent and there for less than a day but there was a time difference between when Reginald's treatment finished and Freddie returned from Mars

Stuart escorted them home and was surprised to find Sir Anthony, Phillips and Geoffrey, Reginald's, father huddled around the wireless set.

The boys rushed over to greet their respective parents.

"Reg, you look so well." Geoffrey exclaimed, "How do you feel?"

"Great. I don't get tired any more. The chemotherapy's worked." Reginald replied then added proudly, "I'm the first boy on Earth to have it."

Geoffrey grabbed Stuart's hand and shook it warmly.

"Thank you so much, sir." he said, "I don't know how we'll ever repay you. It's wonderful to see him so well and in just a week. Surely you're going to tell everyone about your treatment."

"If I said that there was an explosion in the laboratory so that all the research material was destroyed, would you believe me?"

"Sir Anthony warned me that it was all top secret, sir." Geoffrey said, "I don't think I do believe it but I'll accept it out of respect for what you've done for Reg. Thank you so much."

"If you'll excuse us I wish to talk to Stuart alone." Sir Anthony said.

"I remember missing Freddie when he returned." he continued, "How about you? Are you still confused by the sequence of events?"

Stuart nodded.

"You didn't say as much but I got the feeling that the Earth colony is doomed." Sir Anthony continued, "They won't admit the truth and can't see much beyond defeating their enemy."

Stuart nodded again and smiled, "It was disconcerting having you around, you didn't say much but you took everything in."

"And I have a confession to make." Sir Anthony said, "I

figured out how to get around the blocks in the translator. I know the history of the next few decades and I intend to use the knowledge to keep this family together. According to the other Anthony Darrington, I'll succeed, which is good to know."

"I wondered how you worked out what to do." Stuart said, "We tried to hide your future."

"Luckily you succeeded in my personal time-line otherwise I would have discovered when I would die and that would be a terrible burden to bear. I was able to look up general history though. I didn't understand a lot of it but I could memorise it and now I remember it as if I'm reading it all over again.

"I hope we meet again but if you'll excuse me I have a lot of catching up to do with Freddie."

Stuart returned to the Lizard planet to find Tony.

"Dr. Tobias says that I've got to forget this for a while. I don't want to though."

"I wouldn't want to either." Stuart said, "But it is only for a time. You grow up at a wonderful time with all sorts of wonderful inventions. You'll be able to share the excitement with your friends and then one day share this with Freddie again."

Tony grinned, "And I'll be an adult and his father. I'll have to tell him off for all the things he did."

"As long as you tell yourself off as well. You were happy enough to go along with him."

Tony nodded cheerfully, "It was fun though. Papa says that the tenants are an uneducated mob who're not interested in bettering themselves. I'd like him to meet Mr. Milnes and I'd like to start helping our tenants now."

"You're a good boy." Stuart said, "He should be proud of you."

Tony smiled happily.

"And don't forget." Stuart added, "Before you go home, we've got to create a mystery for when we meet in 1925."

Tony seemed even more cheerful and hurried off for a final game of cricket with the monkeys on the lizard planet.

Stuart, in his turn sought out James.

"Once Tony's safely home you can deal with the prisoners you rescued. How's Tiy and Ani?"

"Tiy's hanging on. The Terzons have a range of artificial substances and along with Dr. Tobias they're trying to adapt some bone marrow for human use. Andy not Ani is fine. I chose Memphis because it's also an Egyptian city but he found it hilarious when he discovered who their king is."

"I know, Elvis." Stuart said.

"Most of the prisoners are too confused and disorientated to argue. I've managed to get most home this morning. There's one that doesn't want to go and I can't blame him. He's American, and what was called poor white trash. He worked in the cotton fields besides black workers and they looked down on him because he was white. Sometimes I'm ashamed of my country."

"It doesn't pay to look too closely to any nation's history." Stuart replied, "What are you going to do with him?"

"If you've no objections, I'll give him some gold dust and drop him off in California. If he keeps his head down and just settles somewhere he'll be OK. If he starts talking about what happened to him then he'll be questioned on where he found the gold."

"Is he good looking?" Stuart asked.

"No, why do you ask?"

"I wouldn't want him going to Hollywood and becoming a film star."

"Oh." James exclaimed, "Good point. I don't think he'll make an actor. I was thinking that I could find some information on sound effects. If he got a job as a scene shifter for now, he could find himself in a nice little job. It was your man Phillips who gave me the idea."

"Go for it." Stuart said, "Let's clear up the loose ends then get back to the real problem."

Later that evening Stuart, James and Dave were sitting in the pub chatting

"I didn't think Lord Trey was that bright." Stuart said, "He didn't argue that we came from Mars or at least from outside the biosphere but it didn't seem to register. It was as if he was going along with a story but when it was over he'd go back to the real world. The odd thing so far I'm concerned, they seemed to have an ancient Egyptian feel to them. What's more their social structure seems similar. I wonder if it's a coincidence. I didn't notice it with Talik but he was wrapped up against the weather."

"Yeah, none of them seemed that bright." Dave added.

"Their population was nearly ten thousand just before the war. It's dwindled to less than a thousand in Trey's time." James said, "That biosphere was a remarkable project. It was as if the scientists decided that war was inevitable and began to prepare for it. I'd love to know the full story behind it."

"Lord Trey was a little after Larik and Merrill's time." Stuart said thoughtfully, "I don't know why but I got the feeling he was scared. Maybe he knew that the end was near."

"If you look at the roof beams then you can see the remains of the floodlight system." James said, "There's also a system of vertical pipes above the farmland. There's a series of retractable windows in them and at the bottom there's a diffusing lens that can scatter the sunlight. Now originally the retractable windows could absorb the shorter wavelengths so that they could control the sunlight. It may have been installed as an experiment but it proved very effective.

"Over time, the ultra-violet has degraded the collecting lens and some have been damaged. They've done wonders maintaining the system but they've partly done it by abandoning some areas and scavenging parts."

"OK, they're not very bright, they've lost nearly all their knowledge of technology. It's not important because they can't replicate it even if they had the resources." Stuart said, "We could re-locate them to the beginning of Egypt as just another group settling along the Nile. Maybe they could influence the development of Egyptian culture but it wouldn't matter."

"I'd talk it over with Spock." James said, "See what he thinks."

"How's your own experiment with Egyptian culture doing?" Stuart asked.

"Andy?" James asked, "He understands that he was press-ganged onto a spaceship and he likes being my nephew. He's naturally more outgoing than Demetrius and very intelligent. I don't think that he could settle back home but how could he live here without being an outsider?

"Andy was a farmer's son and at the bottom of the hierarchy but where Demetrius was most respectful speaking to us nobles, Andy was brought up to say what he thought. He's quite happy to call me James and is busily learning to read and write. Being a scribe puts him further up the social scale but I think he's genuinely keen to learn."

"How would he like to visit his parents?" Stuart asked.

"He didn't like being kidnapped." James said, "He'd like some sort of closure. Why?"

"We've built up a lot of data on how time lines fork and blister." Stuart said, "I'd like to try an experiment and visit Andy's people."

"Is that wise?" James asked.

"I think we need to." Stuart replied, "I'd like to go as we are, materialise the portal quite openly and talk freely to the locals. I'd like Brian to operate the portal because he knows what to look out for and I'd like James to come with us in full soldier mode. Anthony too if he feels like it."

"I get it." Dave exclaimed, "That's a big group and we'll attract a lot of attention. We'll see how it affects the time-line but it's got five thousand years to correct itself."

"No, it's only got 500." Stuart said, "Writing in hieroglyphics begins at about Andy's time and then it's King Djoser and his vizier Imhotep who make an impression on world history."

"And you want a successful trip before you tackle the real problem."

"I'm not even sure what the real problem is." Stuart said, "None of the colonies can survive so they can't change our history but if we do help them move then we're going to change history somewhere else. What I'm wondering is if they could actually reinforce history instead."

"I don't get it." Dave said.

"Their community could provide a template for the Egyptian empire. If they're not there the empire will still happen but it'll take more effort to get it right."

"And you want to test the idea." James said, "But we still don't know what Larik and Merrill were really up to. Shouldn't we be focussing on that?"

"We are in a way." Stuart said, "We've got to talk to their superiors and find a way for them to resettle. Early Egypt seems like a possibility so let's check it out."

Early Kingdom

Later that evening, Andy listened to their plans.

"King Narmer has scribes." he said, "I'd like to be able to write in my language as well as yours so I've been looking it up. If you visited my home like that it might be important enough to be written down. Could just James take me home to visit my parents and see what he thinks?"

"It's a good point about writing." Stuart said, "Are you up for it, James?"

"Are you coming along as my slave, again?" James asked Dave.

"No way." Dave exclaimed, "I'm avoiding trips to the past with you unless we can buy a villa and half a dozen slave girls."

"So it's just you and me, son." James said to Andy, "I'll have to remember to call you Ani again."

"No, call me nephew or son." Andy said, "And I'll call you Uncle. My parents might not understand your ways but they'll see you as a soldier and I'll tell them that you are a follower of Djeheuty because he's given you so much wisdom. They'll be flattered that you've included me in your family."

"Anything else?" James asked.

"It'll be far hotter than here." Andy replied, "I'll just wear shorts. You should wear something loose and white."

"You don't want to wear clothes from home, then?" Dave asked.

"I was naked most of the time." Andy replied, "Clothes were for those who could afford them. My parents liked to dress up if they strolled around the village though."

"How come you're so decisive?" Dave asked, "I expected you to be a bit like Demetrius."

"Our laws are in verse." Andy replied, "Yours seem so complicated, but if I put it in your way of speaking then if you know what you're talking about others should listen. If you don't know what you're talking about then shut up. That's what my father taught me."

Andy paused then added, "But I would speak a lot more carefully to one of our soldiers."

James grinned, "Should we be armed?"

"No, there's a grove where we can arrive. It's too close to the village for robbers to hide there. We'll have to make sure none of my friends are playing there, though."

No one saw fit to argue with Andy's planning and that is how they arrived at the village. James wore a light shirt and trousers while Andy was just wearing the shorts, even going barefoot. They both carried backpacks. Visitors were rare enough to arouse considerable excitement and they were soon surrounded by a group of excited youngsters. Although Andy was about fifteen, most of his friends were indeed naked and they stared curiously at the shorts. James tried not staring at the girls though he was sure that a couple were flirting with him.

He tried ignoring the surrounding chatter, contenting himself with looking at the buildings made of baked mud that comprised the village.

Curious villagers followed at a discreet distance. They recognised Ani/Andy and were just as interested as the children in what had happened to him. His mother was simply delighted to see him again, hugging him until Andy exclaimed, "Enough Mother, I'm too old to be breast fed. Give me some air."

James was shocked at the reference to her bare breasts but everyone else including his mother, laughed happily. His father hugged him just as exuberantly. Finally, Andy was able to drag James across to introduce him.

"This is James." he announced, "He's a soldier who's killed many enemies and a follower of Djeheuty so his wisdom is legendary in his own home. He commands that I be known as his nephew. I'm going swimming with my friends."

As he spoke he peeled off his shorts, handing them to James before the whole gang of children ran off towards the River Nile.

"Such rudeness, sir." his father exclaimed, "My father would never have allowed me to behave like that."

"For as long as children are born, fathers will be saying that." James said, "Please call me James."

"I am Bes." Andy's father replied, "I'm called Protector but I couldn't stop my son disappearing these last few months."

"He was taken." James explained, "You couldn't have prevented it."

"And what of you?" Bes responded, "Do you see more than a barrack room servant in him?"

James nodded, "When I rescued him he was ill. He's recovered and I find him to be a highly intelligent young man.”

“Thank you for rescuing him and again for healing him.” Bes said, “Will you stay the night? My wife makes the best beer in the village and the wall around our roof will shield you from prying eyes.”

“Thank you.” James replied, “If Andy returns with me it may not be possible for us to visit again. It'll give him time to be sure what he really wants to do.”

“He wants to spend his time playing with his friends.” Bes said, “It suits me to follow the flow of the River, growing my crops. It'll not suit An-Dee. His brother will be happy here though and my land will be his one day.”

Suddenly Bes' wife cut across them as she yelled, “Bes don't just stand there. Go and borrow a chair. We can't have such an important visitor sitting on the floor.”

Bes looked at James, “And for as long there are men and women, men will jump when a woman speaks.”

“I can sit on the floor.” James said, “Don't go to any trouble on my account.”

Bes grinned, “I know that was kindly meant but my life won't be worth living if she can't entertain a soldier and a priest properly. I can hear her now, 'What will the village think?'”

James was a little uncomfortable that he sat on the only chair in the house as he was handed a bowl of what looked like gruel.

Andy grinned and handed James a spoon that he had brought in his backpack.

“We eat our beer.” he giggled, “Try it. It's like a cold stew.”

Andy's family watched curiously as James tried the beer. It was cold, lumpy but Andy's parents were happy as a delighted smile brightened James face. It was not only tasty but he guessed that it was highly nutritious containing, pulses, beans, lentils, onions, garlic, lettuce and parsley. It was not tart or vinegary so James guessed that there was enough alcohol to prevent it becoming contaminated.

The bread complimented the beer and he found himself enjoying the meal while Bes quietly asked Andy about the strange tool James was using.

“James' people believe that a lot of illness comes from dirt.” Andy explained, “And our hands do all sorts of dirty tasks so it's not a good idea to handle food. Seeing the way he's eating Mum's bread he's not too worried here but it's still a habit to use a spoon.”

“Have you no manners, Ani?” his mother exclaimed, “You do

not comment on a guest's appetite though I'm glad to see it's a healthy one."

"I wasn't being rude." Andy pouted, "I was trying to explain a visitor's ways and that it was a habit and not a religious command."

"Feel free to punish him if he deserves it." Bes said to James, "He always was a cheeky scamp."

James shifted from the chair to sit cross legged on the floor.

"We have another custom. Guests sit beside their hosts in recognition of their kindness though the lowly like Andy should sit further away."

As Bes chuckled and Andy pouted again, his mother asked, "Why An-Dee. Does it have a special meaning?"

"No." James replied, "He can choose either. Andy's just a name from my home and I wanted him to belong."

"Are you taking him away, again?" his mother asked.

"It's his choice." James replied, "I'd welcome him despite his cheek."

Andy reached for his backpack again, then hesitated before turning to James.

"I should have asked first." he said in English, "But I've bought a gift for my parents."

"What is it?" James asked.

Andy opened the backpack to just enough to show James a photograph of himself.

Continuing in English he said, "Stuart showed me how to print it. I said that my mother would love it and he said, 'Yes I expect she would'."

James turned back to Andy's parent, "I'm sorry for our rudeness. Andy should have mentioned this before and it concerns our visit here."

"Please go ahead." Bes said, "I see that it's important."

James reverted to English, "What is important, did Stuart or Brian know that you intended bringing it?"

"I think so. Stuart helped me pack and I'm sure that he saw this as well." Andy replied picking up a camera.

"I might have to take that translator away from you." James growled, "You're learning far too fast. I can't keep up with you."

Andy grinned, "Is it the sort of experiment that you'd like to try while you're here?"

James swung his hand to cuff Andy but the boy ducked still chuckling. His parents seemed a little concerned but were reassured by Andy's cheerfulness.

"Andy should have asked before bringing something but he waited until it was harder for me to say 'no' before asking."

"An-Dee, fetch a stick." Bes said before turning to James, "I'll understand if you don't want him any more but he is going to learn to be more respectful."

James held up his hand.

"No, it's all right." James intervened, "Andy show them what you brought."

It was an ordinary photograph of Andy. At least it was ordinary when it was taken for it showed the boy in T-shirt, jeans and trainers riding a bike. He was obviously enjoying himself for when it was taken, his arms were in the air and his feet were pointing forward, clear of the pedals.

His parents looked at it with some bewilderment.

"Is that some beast he's riding?" his mother asked, "And what is he wearing?"

Andy glanced at James who nodded. He picked up the camera.

"It's not an animal but I had to tame it." Andy laughed, "Watch."

James looked on, surprised at how confidently Andy handled the camera. It was difficult to know what amazed his parents more. There were the magical images moving across the tiny screen, Andy's antics as he mastered the bike, when he confidently pedalled along the track or when he posed for the still photograph.

"Dave is a friend and taught me how to ride." Andy said, "He took those pictures. I'd like to take a picture of you, to take back with me."

Bes glanced at James who nodded. Andy's mother understood the idea of a picture from images on temple walls and there was something else that would never change. She insisted on Bes wearing his best robes, checking his make-up before attending to her own and ensuring that Andy's younger brother washed himself and tidied his hair.

Vanity can be destructive but at that moment it obscured the magic of the camera. It would be five thousand years before such a scene was repeated but Andy found himself taking picture after picture until his mother was satisfied. After each snap everyone gathered around to study it.

They were outside enjoying the cool evening breeze and neighbours gathered around attracted by the flashes. Group shots were taken. One highly honoured neighbour managed to take a picture of Bes' family including Andy and James.

At one point Andy's mother looked around content. Her family had provided an entertainment that would be talked about for years. Neither would it be forgotten that her husband was treated as an equal by such a powerful priest as James.

That night James slept on the roof of the house to escape the oppressive heat. An ordinary visitor might have shared with the rest of the family but they endured the heat of the night inside out of respect for James' position.

It seemed pointless hiding the camera so James spent the next morning taking pictures of village life. Word had spread and the village children all wanted their pictures taken, giggling happily at the resulting scenes on the screen.

“They were a lot less inhibited than 21st century children.” James said when he was home, “And they live closer to nature. Some of those poses were a bit too explicit. I'll have to delete them.”

“Before you do.” Stuart said, “Print them out, bundle them together and send them to Bes via a probe. Their status is going to shoot up in the village and history is going to change. I doubt that we'll be able to detect anything but even if we do it'll be pretty small. It'll be worth it to get data on events.”

“The explicit ones as well.?” James asked.

“The lot.” Stuart said, “Adults were watching while you took the snaps, weren't they? If they just thought them fun and innocent then it's their world.”

For a time, the village became known as the place that the wizard visited. Even King Narmer visited to see the wonderful pictures and like his subjects, hoped that the wizard would return while he was there but he was disappointed.

Gradually over the years, the inks faded, the paper dried, becoming brittle until they crumpled to dust so that the legend of the wizard of magnificent pictures was forgotten. It did not matter for his family knew in their hearts that Ani was alive and well though at first he was in trouble with James.

“Be honest. You did try to manipulate me didn't you?” James asked.

Andy nodded unhappily.

“No one said that I couldn't take the picture.” he replied.

“This time, there's no real harm done,” James said, “but it's going to be difficult to trust you again.”

"Hang on James." Stuart said, "I saw him packing the camera but it didn't register. Let's just put this down to experience. After all it was me who sent those other pictures back. I reckon it shows that we've got some leeway in dealing with the past."

"I am sorry." Andy said, "I just wanted to show my parents that I was safe and well."

"OK, Andy." Stuart said, "I'm glad that you're over your experiences on the ship and I could do with you on our next trip or would you rather stay near Tiy? He hasn't got long now."

"The medicines have failed." Andy said matter of factly.

"Yes." Stuart said, "He's not in pain but the damage was too much."

"And you want me to help the people that did that to him."

"I think that your people believe that there is a harmony to the universe. Not so long ago I was jumping from my body into others. Those jumps caused all sorts of problems but ever since I've had a feeling about what's right and wrong. I think your beliefs describe it better, what's harmonious or not.

"Talik helped. I don't think that these people are all bad so they're worth helping. I also feel that they'll blend in. By the time they've got to grips with being in the open air, discovering that they have neighbours and discovering seasons, they'll realise that they have a lot to learn as well as teach."

"Can you trust these feelings?" James asked.

"As always, I don't know." Stuart replied, "I did think about that alternative world I mentioned, you know, the one struggling after the black death but I could see problems. For one thing the church was still powerful so there would be a conflict. If they settled in the Nile as other settlers arrived they would have to reclaim the land, learn how to hunt and fish. They would need the others and would be sharing in a common goal."

Andy nodded, "I'll help. I can't be with Tiy, can I?"

"It's OK now." Stuart said, "They've flushed all the radioactive material from his body so he won't hurt you but he's very weak. He's asleep most of the time."

"May I visit." Andy asked, "I won't stay but I want to wish him..."

He paused, "Would you say 'bon voyage' through the underworld? I wish I could visit a temple of Anapa. I could pray that he finds Tiy's heart pure and light, and allow him to travel onto Aaru. I could also pray that your feelings are indeed guiding you to create harmony in the world."

"I want to get a feel for the world we would be dropping these people into." Stuart said, "Maybe we could visit a temple first."

"Why not?" James said, "Lunch in the old kingdom and an afternoon stroll along the Nile a thousand years before. It sounds reasonable to me."

"It never sounds reasonable." Stuart chuckled, "It's just that we're always pushing the portal's capabilities and we're never ready for what it can do next but we've got one advantage this time."

The others waited.

"Brian's busily analysing the extended fields we're using." Stuart explained, "He won't come with us but he'll operate the portal and spend his time recording the data."

James frowned.

"I'm supposed to be the one keeping you out of trouble." he said, "Brian trusts me to keep an eye on you."

"We'll have Andy as our guide and you'll be our military escort. I'd like us all to carry tasers and nightsticks."

"Why?" James asked, "I thought the best defence was to run."

"It still is especially if we wear protective vests." Stuart replied, "And with Andy's help we'll still be able to talk our way out of trouble. When James visited Ancient Greece we spent ages surveying the area. There were no bandits or anyone hiding in the rocks and the town was little more than a village. He was bigger than most men of the day and there was something about him. He looked like a soldier. No one was going to take him on because he wore that expensive sword.

"This time there's going to be a lot more interaction. We'll take Andy to some city where he can make his prayers and we can check for anomalies. Then we'll move back a thousand years and start bringing in the Ancients. That's going to push the interaction to a whole new level. We may not be able to land too close to the city or where we want the ancients to settle so I want to be prepared."

"I understand tasers instead of guns." James said, "But why nightsticks?"

"Because they can disable a person without killing them." Stuart replied, "I'm not sure of this Ma'at concept, but it's based on harmony with the universe. Punch ups are hardly harmonious so I'm hoping that the locals will appreciate us dealing with one without anyone being seriously hurt."

"Fighting is not disharmonious." Andy interjected, "It's using it to destroy the harmony that's wrong."

"So we can defend ourselves." James said.

"Yes." Andy agreed, "But stick to beating slaves, farmers and craftsmen. Scribes have too much influence and soldiers may be too good for us."

"Very well." James said, "So the mission to Ma'at's temple is to give Brian more data on time travel and allow Andy to pay his respects.

"I can't see Dave staying behind and Anthony may like one more trip. Richard and Gable might want to come as well. Half a dozen of us should be able to deal with most problems."

Stuart nodded, "I reckon that would be enough in a city. We want to protect ourselves, not start a riot."

"OK." James said, "We've got a purpose and a plan to defend ourselves. How about money?"

"We swap goods." Andy said, "How about taking some chocolate? We could exchange it for beer. I could get grain for Ma'at and it would be given to the poor."

"Good idea." Stuart replied, "That'll really give us some interaction. Afterwards we can see whether a hieroglyph for chocolate appears. Anything else?"

"Don't drink the water." Dave chuckled.

As a final touch, they all carried swords. None of them could use them with any skill but they were a sign that the group was a force to be reckoned with. At Andy's suggestion they wore the protective vests above their clothes so that the vests could be mistaken for armour.

They made a formidable group as they strolled along the track towards the city of Memphis. The irony was not lost on Andy who giggled helplessly at the idea of who might rule the city.

The track they took ran beside the Nile until they encountered a dock and a market. The stalls were laid out on the ground with the stall holders sitting cross legged behind them. James already found the white baked mud familiar but the rest stared curiously at them.

On impulse, Stuart had invited Joe Milnes who cheerfully examined the grain and other produce. They had followed Andy's advice and brought bars of chocolate which they had deep frozen then stored in ice boxes to protect them from the heat.

Joe understood barter and squatted down beside a trader selling the surplus from his farm. The farmer watched curiously as Joe took out a couple of slabs and handed him one. The farmer who took it, nearly dropped it as the cold seeped into his hand and he looked at Joe.

"It'll get soft and melt in this heat." Joe said, "Let's talk before you try it."

Others were watching curiously and as always it was the children who got the closest. Joe smiled contentedly as he took out more bars and allowed them to warm in the tropical sun.

Stuart turned to other matters.

"Can you find the temple you want?" he asked Andy.

"There's one for Anapa." he replied, "I'll ask him to judge Tiy kindly against Ma'at."

"I thought Ma'at was a goddess." Dave said.

"She is all that's harmonious in the universe. She even keeps a balance between the gods." Andy tried to explain though the puzzled looks showed that he had failed.

"OK, it's your world." Stuart said, "Let's see how much grain Joe can get for you to offer. What's he doing now?"

The children were scattering searching for firewood and building a fire. Everyone gasped as he took out a box of matches and struck one, allowing the children to tend the fire until it was well alight before taking out a wok. He poured a little oil into it before his final surprise, packets of oven ready chips.

"I traded chocolate for firewood and now I'll trade it for grain. These are potatoes. I'll trade them for a finger of grain as well. My friend wants an offering when he prays."

Stuart was not sure how much a finger of grain was but he guessed Joe knew what he was doing.

"How did he know all this?" James asked.

"I invited him because he seemed so interested and I lent him a translator." Stuart explained, "I figured he could help to trade for local grain and I guess he's learnt to use it better than I expected."

The pile of grain grew rapidly as the locals tried the novel food. Joe spent his time chatting to his new friends, sharing in the local beer, a thinner but more alcoholic variety that kept the conversation flowing.

James and Anthony accompanied Andy as he sought out the temple of Anapa.

"I don't get all these Egyptian gods." Dave said, "Do you?"

Stuart shook his head, "The translator seems to be telling me that the Ancient Greek name for Anapa is Annubis so for one thing we're used to the Greek versions. The other thing is they don't try to understand the gods. The Greeks and Romans made their gods very human but the Egyptians knew that it was impossible. This probably doesn't help but I think that Andy sees Ma'at as the order in the universe and the goddess of it at the same time."

"You'll like the Egyptians then." Dave laughed, "They make it complicated just like you."

"More to the point, I'm worried about Joe and Anthony knowing about the portals." Richard said, "There's Dr. Tobias as well."

"I'm worried about it too." Stuart said then frowned, "No not worried, unhappy. What worries me is that I feel as if I'm being drawn into something else. I never liked those jumps to parallel worlds and they've unlocked something else. It feels stronger here because we're surrounded by people whose lives centre around the gods and mysticism."

"Surely that's just your imagination." Richard said.

"I hope so." Stuart exclaimed, "Dave complains about me making things complicated but the universe has just kept getting bigger and more complicated ever since we first landed on Terzon."

"So what do these feelings tell you?" Dave asked.

"For one thing we do need a medic." Stuart said, "There's a sense of urgency about that and I'm glad that we've got Dr. Tobias. He's okay as long as he can run his laboratory and sneak into Sylvia's cottage. Sylvia aside, he really does think in terms of the lives he can save and wouldn't do anything to disrupt that."

"You're probably right." Richard conceded, "What about the other two?"

"We have no choice with Anthony but I think that he's more concerned that that everything's right when his child's born." Stuart said, "This is another of those things where we keep having the same conversation. If I'd given more thought to the original landing site then we would never have met the Darringtons and we wouldn't have had to worry about messing up time lines."

"And Joe?" Richard asked.

"That was Freddie again," Stuart said, "but look at him. He's growing that super marrow on Mars for the fête and now I bet he'll have Ancient Egyptian style beer in the home made wine and beer stall. He's like Mum. Neither of them want outsiders disrupting the village but they can both see the world beyond."

"I know what you mean." Dave said, "And I'll tell you something else. He'll talk in front of Bill or us but if Seth Brady comes in he'll clam up. I've got a massive bruise on my ankle where he kicked me. Seth had just come into the bar and Joe was warning me to shut up.”

“Can we drop this conversation.” Stuart asked, “I'm sure we'll have it again soon but I need a break from it.”

“And we are in Ancient Egypt. Let's have a look around.” Dave said, “Can we leave Joe?”

“Don't worry about me.” Joe replied, “Theshen here is telling me how Sobek lets his crocodiles run amok over his fields when the Nile floods. I'm trying to describe how the sky god Deep Depression sends rain and wind to flatten my crops.”

“You're certainly getting into swing of things.” Stuart laughed.

Joe shrugged, “This translator does the work but it's easy enough to follow their pattern of speaking.”

“We're somewhere between King Narmer, which is when Andy comes from, and King Djoser.” Stuart said, “This part of Memphis has been lost for thousands of years or rather it was rebuilt as the Nile shifted its course.”

“Surely Memphis is being excavated.” Dave asked.

“Look around.” Stuart said, “That building looks suspiciously like a town hall with people coming and going like that. What's it made of, clay bricks or baked mud then whitewashed? It looks so much like Andy's parent's house and I don't think anyone expects them to be permanent, this close to the river.”

“Do you reckon we can take some pictures.” Dave asked.

“I don't see why not.” Stuart replied, “Just don't make it obvious.”

Dave took the camera out of his pocket and looked at the screen, stepping back to take in the whole building he collided with a passer-by.

It was a small incident and should have been settled by Dave's simple apology. Unfortunately the passer-by was a drunken soldier who was entering that aggressive phase that drunks sometimes suffer. Friends of his, fellow soldiers stopped, watching them.

“You struck me.” the soldier slurred.

“Yes I'm sorry, mate.” Dave replied, “I was studying that building and didn't see you.”

The soldier stared at Dave trying to take in what Dave had said. The effort was too much.

“I'm not your friend,” his voice still slurred, “You struck me.”

“I'm sorry.” Dave said.

The soldier stared again.

"You struck me."

One of the more sober soldiers stepped forward, "Easy Dedi. He's apologised."

"He struck me." Dedi said once again.

"Walk away, boy." Dedi's friend said to Dave, "We'll take care of him."

As Dave turned to obey, the movement actually penetrated Dedi's brain and triggered a reaction. He drew his sword, swinging it at Dave's neck.

Two things saved Dave's life. Dedi was so drunk that he fumbled with his sword and he was considerably slower than he would normally have been. At the same time, Stuart drew his stun gun and fired in a slick action that would have done credit to Wyatt Earp in the American West.

The result was enough to deflect the blow so that the blade sliced into Dave's shoulder right on the edge of the vest instead of nearly decapitating him. It would still have been a killing blow if the blade had not been stopped by the top of the vest.

Dave collapsed to his knees as shock set in while Dedi fell to the ground, convulsing uncontrollably. The other soldiers reached for their swords but stopped uncertainly as Richard and Gable aimed their own tasers at them.

"Do we continue the fight, or help our friends?" Stuart asked.

Stuart and the others put their stun guns away as the soldiers relaxed and lowered their weapons.

"Your friend is badly wounded." Dedi's friend said, "I'm sorry but I wasn't expecting Dedi to be so stupid."

He looked at Dedi uncertainly, "Is he dying as well?"

"Keep quiet about what you see and they'll both live." Stuart said, "Dad, take a look at Dave. Gable, check Dedi."

The soldier nodded, watching curiously as Stuart took out his mobile phone. Satisfied that he had a signal he phoned Brian.

"We need first aid kits and stretchers urgently." Stuart said, "And patch in Dr. Tobias. I'll need help."

"How did you do that?" Richard asked.

Stuart grinned.

"I thought he'd have a probe hovering around to keep an eye on me." he explained, "He's got software to intercept the signals and simulate a network cell."

"I'm losing touch." Richard said but just then a probe appeared with medical kits.

Stuart grabbed one and listening to Dr. Tobias' instructions applied pads to Dave's shoulder.

At the same time Richard looked at the soldiers and said, "I'm going to give Dedi something to make him relax."

Again the soldier nodded looking warily as Richard gave Dedi an injection.

"OK I need your help." Richard said, "I'm going to roll him on his back. Make sure he doesn't swallow his tongue and can you check his pulse?"

"His life beat, you mean." the soldier said, "It's strong."

Stuart and Richard worked for a time with everyone watching intently. No one noticed when a portal materialised just above head height though the soldiers reached for their swords when equipment seemed to fall out of the sky followed by Dr. Tobias. They relaxed as Stuart glanced up and breathed a deep sigh of relief.

Dr. Tobias quickly checked Dedi before turning to Dave.

"Thank god for Terzon technology." he muttered at one stage, "Do you realise that I couldn't save Dave if I was back home."

Another package dropped beside Stuart with a label addressed to him. When he opened he found a change of clothes and a bar of soap. Glancing down he realised for the first time that he was covered in Dave's blood.

"Is there somewhere where I can wash and change?" he asked.

"The River." a soldier replied, "I'll come with you and watch out for crocodiles."

It was not the answer that Stuart wanted but he was a little happier when two soldiers joined him. He was a little embarrassed as he stripped and everyone around stared at his white skin but when he checked he was surprised to see that less than an hour had passed since the group had split up.

Still with the soldier's escort he headed for the market and in spite of his worry about Dave he could not help bursting out laughing. Joe Milnes was obviously on his own way to getting drunk, oblivious to the dramas elsewhere.

The unmistakable tune of *On Ilkla Mooar baht 'at* wafted towards them and to Stuart's surprise a remarkably harmonious choir backed him with the chorus. Joe was singing in the traditional thick Yorkshire dialect, which even Stuart struggled to understand but it did not matter. For Joe it was a group of farmers celebrating the end of a successful market.

"Hello Stuart lad." Joe greeted him, "Come to join in the fun?"

"No." Stuart replied, "Dave's been wounded and we've completely blown our cover getting medical aid."

Joe was immediately sober. Stuart suspected that he had not drunk that much but like a lot of people who were usually so calm and collected, a little alcohol could allow him to let go completely.

"I didn't know." he said, "I shouldn't have drunk so much."

"Yes you should." Stuart retorted glancing at the soldiers, "You're making sure we leave as friends."

To Stuart's relief, the soldiers nodded in agreement. He turned to them.

"Would one of you show Joe where Dave is and would one of you come with me to find the rest of my friends. They've gone to pray to Anapa."

The soldier grinned.

"They'll be safe there." he chuckled, "The priests spend most of their time talking to the dead. When someone alive is willing to talk to them they'll end up having a banquet if they're not careful."

"I think it's time we left though." Stuart said, "I think we've overstayed our welcome."

"Because of Dedi, you mean. He's going to pick one fight too many and then we'll be taking him to Anapa on a one way journey. Maybe you've given him the warning he'll heed. The priests would be delighted to meet such powerful wizards as you."

Suddenly Stuart was fighting to hold back the tears. Alarmed, the others looked on wondering what was wrong.

"I've just got my best friend killed and we're talking about going off for a cosy little chat." he sobbed.

"Your healer is treating him." one of the soldiers said glancing at Joe, "But you go back to him. We'll find your friends and fetch them."

Joe nodded glad to see Stuart already looking better.

"Come on then." Stuart snapped, hurrying off.

Stuart arrived just in time to see Dave being carried on a stretcher into an alley. Richard hurried over to him.

"He's lost a lot of blood." he said, "It's a deep wound and he'll need surgery to repair the damage but he should be okay."

Stuart trembled as he breathed a sigh of relief.

"It's time to stop." Stuart muttered, "It's too dangerous."

"You might be right but we'll talk about it later," Richard said, "We were incredibly unlucky and it was not your fault."

"Yeah, Dave's death would have been a bit of bad luck. That's all right then."

"I didn't mean that. These men are farmers and had been called up to tackle some pirates in the Nile delta. They were celebrating because it was all settled before they were needed and were on their way home. Dedi had just gone too far."

Stuart nodded, "Where are they taking Dave?"

"Those soldiers were bloody good." Richard said, "They closed that alley off so we could land the portal there. Dave should be on Terzon by now. They're grateful that we didn't just kill Dedi and start a bloodbath. Like I said they just want to go home and they don't want to get on the wrong side of powerful wizards like ourselves."

"And Dave will be all right?" Stuart asked again.

"Dr. Tobias thinks so." Richard said, "We'll know more when we get home."

"If we get home." Stuart said, "We must have disrupted the time line pretty badly."

"Not according to Brian." Richard said, "He reckons that we must have been pretty boring wizards. If we'd raised our arms in prayers and Dave had stood up as if nothing had happened then it may have been talked about. Half an hour stopping the bleeding and Dave still badly injured makes us very feeble. In fact we've lost so much face as wizards that the kids are playing some game trying to find which roof we threw the equipment from. The soldiers know more but they'll keep their word and stay quiet."

Just then Joe, James, Anthony and Andy joined them. As everyone recounted their version of events Dedi staggered over.

"I am sorry." he said, "I have something of Sobek in me. When he's in a good mood then my wife is willing and fertile but she's a day's walk from here. When we're apart, we both let the drink abuse our energy."

"I still don't appreciate you trying to kill my friend." Stuart replied irritably, "Please just go."

Dedi sadly turned to leave but paused.

"You are wizards." he said, "I know that from how you stopped me. You won't put a curse on my family, will you?"

"Draw your sword and hold it at arm's length." Stuart commanded.

Puzzled Dedi obeyed as Stuart drew his own sword raising it above his head and swung it with all his force. He may have just worn it as a recognisable weapon, but hardened steel cut through bronze like butter. The soldiers just stared as half of the blade of Dedi's sword clattered to the ground.

"I was tempted to aim for your wrist." Stuart said, "Your shield won't save you from our blades either so please just go before I forget that I don't like hurting people."

One of his comrades gripped Dedi by the shoulder guiding him away.

"If I was you, I'd have forgotten long ago, so thank you." he said, "Your secrets will remain with us."

As they left Memphis, all Stuart was interested in was finding Dave who was in a Terzon hospital. Dr Tobias greeted him when he arrived.

"He's off the danger list and we expect to be able to completely repair the damage. There's a lot of it so it'll take time. Brian's been here and he's worrying more about what we can tell his parents and Sally."

"Wasn't he at all worried by Dave nearly being killed?" Stuart asked then hesitated, "Sorry that's me still wound up. He was probably panicking until he got the info then moved onto the next problem."

"That's about it. Dave's asleep at the moment. Brian needs you more at the moment."

Dr. Tobias was right. Brian was in his library just staring at the wall when Stuart found him. He barely acknowledged Stuart as he exclaimed, "I'm shutting the whole thing down."

"That's what I said but why?" Stuart asked.

Brian glared at him.

"What sort of bloody stupid question is that?" he shouted, "It could have been you getting stabbed, like that."

"It sounds as if you don't care about Dave." Stuart said quietly, "I'm okay. Dave will be and we've got to do a bit of time travelling so that his parents don't ask too many questions."

"I don't care about that." Brian said, "It's too dangerous. I'm not going to risk losing you."

Stuart stepped forward hugging Brian and holding him tightly.

"Do you remember, I didn't want to take Dave on?" Stuart asked, continuing as Brian nodded, "He was spending more and more time getting drunk in Howkbury. Looking back it was probably because he was so fed up with his life. There were rumours going around our mates that he went to the Railway Inn. That's the place you go to have a fight or deal in drugs."

"So what are you telling me? We've saved Dave so that he can get killed on some distant planet?"

"It's the wrong time to point out that he was wounded on Earth." Stuart smiled, "But you've heard him when he's had a few and he thinks it just us around. He loves what we're doing. Why not ask him what he thinks before you do anything hasty."

They were still holding each other tightly and for a time Brian just stood not moving.

"If I hadn't been working on the portals and you hadn't risked your neck on Baard-Atcha we wouldn't have got together would we? It could have been the happiest time of my life but I'm always worrying about you."

"I know," Stuart said, "but could you just forget about everything we're doing?"

"No." Brian said quietly, "I'd miss Terzon and you'd be bored out of your mind wouldn't you?"

"Except at night, with you," Stuart replied, "but I wonder how quickly we'd start getting on each other's nerves."

"I'll talk to James and Anthony." Brian said, "They've both served in dangerous situations. Let's see what they think."

Stuart nodded.

"Fair enough." he said.

"You get back and see how Dave is." Brian said.

"No I'm staying with you."

"No." Brian said, "I'm going to sit quietly then have an early night and Demetrius can bring me up a nice cup of cocoa."

"Old man." Stuart teased.

"Hmm." Brian retorted, "It's you bloody kids. Your antics put years on me."

Relieved that Brian seemed happier, Stuart headed back to the hospital.

"He's awake." Dr. Tobias said, "We'll be operating again tomorrow so don't tire him out but he won't settle until he's spoken to you, James or someone. Come this way."

To Stuart's surprise, Dave was sitting up in bed, reading though the arm on his wounded side was strapped to hold it immobile. He was attached to a variety of machines one of which appeared to be processing his blood like a dialysis unit and Stuart was not sure whether his shoulder was in plaster or heavily bandaged. To Stuart's inexperienced eyes he was deathly white though. He looked up as Stuart entered.

"Hi Stuart." he said.

"Hi." Stuart replied, "How do you feel? I thought you'd be flat on your back and half asleep."

"That's because I'm being turned into an alien." Dave laughed, before his head drooped as he nearly passed out.

Even as Stuart moved to get help so Dave stirred.

"It's OK." he whispered, "Laughing takes too much energy. Give me a minute."

Stuart waited, still concerned while Dave recovered.

"I've lost so much blood, it could still kill me." he said though very quietly, "They're pumping some artificial concoction through my veins. It's full of oxygen that my organs can use but they can't give me too much, which is why I'm so weak and tired."

"What about blood transfusions?" Stuart asked.

"I'd be overdrawn at the blood bank." Dave said, "And this stuff is carried in a saline solution that fills my veins up so it's sterile. I can't catch anything from it."

"As long as it doesn't really turn you into a bug-eyed monster." Stuart grinned.

"What are you going to tell Sally and my parents?" Dave asked.

"Nothing." Stuart replied, "I'm thinking that we just transport you back to now when you're fit."

"You know that'll cause too many problems. I'd have to stay with Anthony or something otherwise you'd be dealing with two of me."

"One's enough." Stuart chuckled, "It's a thought though. Stay here until you can be discharged then convalesce with the Darringtons. We'd still have to say something to Sally though."

"Sally's used to me being away a few days at a time." Dave said.

Dave lay quietly for a time. A nurse popped in to check and hurried away, apparently satisfied. Dave glanced at the machines.

"My blood sats was dropping a bit but it's OK now." he explained, "I still want to know how you're going to explain it. Mum will be on about compensation and Dad will have the Health & Safety people poring over our operations. I can't even transfer to an Earthside hospital because they'll notify the police."

He paused again, gathering his strength.

"Got it." he said, "Can you patch my mobile through to the regular network from here?"

Stuart nodded.

"Via Australia?" Dave continued.

Stuart nodded again.

"I'll phone them and say I'm in hospital." Dave said, "I'll tell them that it's in Terzon, Austria. Knowing Dad he won't let go until he gets to talk to someone. By the time he realises it's the wrong country and I've convinced him that he must have misheard, I should be able to get home."

"You seem alert enough." Stuart chuckled.

"You know the Terzons." Dave retorted, "They'd let my arms and legs drop off before they risked brain damage. I think that I've been given drugs to stimulate my brain's oxygen absorption."

"So you can't stand up, but you can understand Einstein's Theories of Relativity."

"If you allow Planck's constant to become a variable then it fits in very nicely with our knowledge of dimensions." Dave said quite seriously, "Different parallel universes have slightly different energy levels that stops them getting in phase and merging."

"Right." Stuart said slowly taking in what Dave had just said, "And that's what you're lying here worrying about."

"Partly." Dave said, "I won't be able to go with you for a while so I wondered whether I could work with Brian on his projects until I'm fit."

"So you don't want to quit." Stuart said.

"Hell no." Dave exclaimed before slumping down exhausted again, "Who'd have thought that I'd get slashed by a drunk while doing scientific research. I could have gone to the Railway for that."

Just then Dr. Tobias arrived.

"Talking takes too much energy and oxygen." he said, "You'll have to go now, Stuart."

Stuart agreed, quietly leaving but waiting for Dr. Tobias outside.

"When I first saw the wound, I thought that he'd be dead in an hour." he said, "No matter how hard doctors try, they know in their hearts when it's a lost cause. Lasers let me cauterise the veins and slow the blood loss but it was still a close thing and his blood pressure was dangerously low. He probably would still have died if it wasn't for that artificial blood. Among other things it took the strain off his heart as it tried to supply enough oxygen. He's been given drugs to make him physically sluggish, to prevent rejection of the blood and so on. The aim for now is for him to replenish his own natural blood and reduce the quantity of artificial blood."

"How long will he be in hospital?" Stuart asked, "He's planning some scheme to keep his parents off our backs but we won't be able to keep it up for long."

"On Earth he'd be barely conscious but you saw him. Tomorrow we're operating on his shoulder to repair the damage. Again back home that would be inconceivable so soon. I'd allow a week after the last operation to get him home then up to three months convalescence while his body fully recovers."

"The convalescence will be that long? How come."

"The artificial blood breaks down fairly quickly and is excreted from his body through the normal methods. He'll actually get more tired and weaker for a few days after he gets home. Then as his red blood cells are replenished he'll get stronger again."

"What about his shoulder?" Stuart asked.

"My colleagues here talk in terms of welding severed tissue. It's not that exactly. I think of it in terms of holding the two ends together with scar tissue allowing healthy tissue to knit inside the band of scar material. It's not that exactly, either but it's done on a cellular level and even the flesh is held by these microscopic scar bonds. There shouldn't even be a scar."

"It sounds very high tech." Stuart said.

"It is." Dr. Tobias exclaimed, "The sad thing is, there's no point in developing it on Earth. No hospital could ever afford it."

"And according to Terzon economics no Terzon hospital can afford not to have one." Stuart said.

"Crazy isn't it." Dr. Tobias said, obviously still very passionate.

Stuart suspected that Dr. Tobias was losing interest in his research projects on Earth and was spending more time on Terzon. He was respected there for his abilities as a skilled surgeon. Accidents happen, even on a world as organised as Terzon and often in inaccessible places where it was difficult to provide all the equipment needed. He was recognised for his 'back to basics' skills, able to treat and stabilise a patient on site so that he could be moved.

In one respect, Stuart was relieved to learn of Dr. Tobias's increasing disillusionment with Earth medicine. He was proportionately more inclined to protect his only link with Terzon.

Stuart was also reassured that Dave would recover, deciding to allow him to deal with his parents in his own way and was relaxed enough to call a meeting in Brian's library.

"We got more interaction than we wanted but from a test's

point of view it was extremely useful." he began, "I agree with Dave. He could have met a drunk with a knife in a present day pub. Whatever the age, Earth is the sort of planet that we avoid, it's just too violent. We're only here now because events seem to be set and we've got to let them play out."

Stuart was pleased to see that even Brian nodded though he said, "I agree that we've got to prevent any temporal paradoxes but even Stuart complains that he's in over his head. It's time to stop. You agree, don't you Dick."

Richard was quiet for a moment then shook his head.

"Mavis and I talk about it all the time." Richard replied, "Yes, it's dangerous. Yes, Dave was nearly killed but on the other hand I know three people who have been knocked down by cars that didn't know these lanes. How many people have been killed by farm machinery? Dave's injury is a shock and maybe we should look at our operating procedures and take them more seriously but that's all."

Desperately, Brian turned to Joe for support.

"You're the newest member." he said, "Surely you see how dangerous it is."

"I don't know about other places but it was so much like a normal market day." Joe replied, "We moaned about the gods instead of the government, one fellow tried to palm me off with a scrawny old cow and tried for five bars of chocolate. Here he would have wanted fifty pounds over the market value. But you know, the others had a real go at him for trying to cheat their new friend."

"You make it sound like a trip into Howkbury." Brian complained.

"I don't know about that." Joe chuckled, "I've never seen so many bare breasts in my life. If they were working then the men could be completely naked. I don't suppose Stuart minded the scenery either."

"What puzzles me," James said, "Is why Stuart was so prepared compared to other trips. We had weapons and vests."

"There was something in the back of my mind." Stuart said, "It was a feeling that we were pushing things too far and that we hadn't researched the place enough. I was thinking more of robbers and thieves though."

"Fair enough." James replied, "We did do more checks for that ancient Greek jaunt yet I was still nervous even if the ancient Egyptians do seem more welcoming and friendly."

"That's right." Joe said, "One of the blokes I was talking to was a slave. His master had captured him in some skirmish or other. The master was asking about planting potatoes and it was the slave saying they wouldn't grow there. He wasn't the least bit scared of his master."

"Ma'at." Andy said, "The slave understood the land so he should be listened to."

"So no one else thinks we should stop." Brian asked.

There was silence.

"You might not have any choice." Anthony said, "How are you going to explain Dave's injury?"

"Dave's got his own scheme." Stuart said, "He's going to claim to be in Austria and when they can't find him swear he said Australia. I don't think that his idea will help but we can use his recovery rate. His shoulder will be immobilised for a few days to allow the micro-surgery to knit and then it will be strapped to prevent too much movement for a time. We could get away with saying that he's strained his shoulder. It won't explain his weakness though."

"What do you say, he's caught a bug which is why he fell off the ladder?" Andy suggested.

"And I was beginning to believe that the ancient Egyptians were so honest." Anthony laughed.

"It's balance." Andy replied, "His people will know that he's been injured, which is as it should be, but they needn't know everything. You were happy to let my parents think that you were wizards and they knew that I was going to live in a strange land. They just didn't need to know, how strange."

"Brian?" James asked.

"Maybe Dave will come to his senses. He's not going to risk getting injured again." he muttered more to himself than the group.

"It's not like Brian to be so moody." James said later when he and Andy were alone with Stuart.

"He feels responsible." Stuart explained, "There was the asteroid attack and now this. He's got the idea that if he hadn't built the portal, none of it would have happened."

James nodded, "Dave's injury was bad luck and that can happen to anyone, anywhere. Our planning was sound and we are trying to help people in trouble. One question though. Why don't we go back to just after the war to rescue more people? Are you just worried about time lines?"

"Partly but we have looked at them with probes. They were pretty aggressive and xenophobic, all geared up for their ultimate victory. We're not actually leaving anyone to die, they'll live out their lifespans and have children though there will be fewer and fewer. I just want to choose a time when the colonies are about to fail and we really are saving lives."

"It's a hard decision though." James said.

"I've talked it over with the Terzons." Stuart said, "They convinced me that I should wait until they want to be rescued."

"So how do you plan on doing it?"

Stuart laughed, "The first thing is to wait until Brian's calmed down. He's going to be in full blown headmaster mode when he realises that I've got to visit each colony to invite them. I also want to visit the final arrival site."

"It's only because he worries about you." James said.

"I know." Stuart replied, "Some might find it kinky fun, being a naughty schoolboy reporting to the headmaster. I don't because it means I'm upsetting him and I don't like doing that."

"I'll have a word with him." James said, "He expects me to be the sensible one so maybe he'll listen more."

"Thanks." Stuart replied, "I'll phone Sally and tell her that Dave's got a late night job tonight so he won't be home. She won't like it but she's used to his phone being off when he's working so it'll cover us until tomorrow."

Stuart and Brian wanted the night together so James found himself chatting to Anthony in the pub when Sally arrived.

"How come Dave's working and you're here?" she asked before even greeting James.

"Dave drew the short straw." Anthony replied before James could answer, "Don't worry, we're not slave drivers keeping him at it while we sit back watching. Would you like a drink?"

"Why?" she asked.

Anthony knew of her emotional problems and that he had to be very careful what he said.

"Dave's a friend and a colleague more than an employee so I'm just being sociable." he explained.

"Could I have a small lager please?" she giggled, "Dave doesn't like me drinking when I'm looking after Aidan and Mrs Berridge can't babysit for long."

She was quiet until her drink arrived and she had taken a sip.

"Dave's very secretive." she said, "He never says what he's doing at work. I'd like to know though."

"It's mostly routine and not very interesting." James replied, "He spends a lot of time in front of a computer or clambering up a ladder to replace components"

"Yes but why has he learnt all those languages?" she persisted, "He hated school and was either in detention or bunking off. Now he's so clever."

"Oh it's just Brian and Stuart's influence." James said, "He's got an incentive to study now."

"Stuart was just as bad." she exclaimed, "He might have wanted Brian inside his pants but Dave's not like that. Neither are you."

She paused staring at James, "Or are you, James?"

"They're just responding to Brian's belief that the search for knowledge is more important than anything." James said, "

"Yeah right." Sally retorted, "Do you really expect me to believe that? Brian and Stuart might be weird but Dave should get a proper job and earn more money."

"Unless you're willing to support him while he goes to college or university he's not going to get a better wage than he is now. He earns it by being on call and working odd hours."

"You could pay him more though." Sally persisted, "Then we could get out of this dump."

"You mean Dave stays here and carries on working for us while you go swanning off?" James asked.

Sally paused frowning as she tried to work out just what she did mean.

"I miss Dave." she said eventually, "I wish he could be home all day. Aidan loves him. I'd better go."

"What was all that about?" Anthony asked when they were alone again.

"I don't know." James replied, "Maybe she just saw us as we walked past and decided to have a go at us, it doesn't matter. It's just obvious that we can't tell her anything so how do we deal with Dave's injury."

"We can't just leave him in hospital then bring him back in time when he's recovered." Anthony said, "We'd be dealing with two Daves."

"Stuart would never allow it." James agreed, "It was bad enough dealing with your family."

Anthony laughed, "I understand. Seeing Freddie as a child was a revelation."

Since the hospital on Terzon was three or four hours ahead of Earth, Stuart was able to follow his normal morning routine, arriving just as Dave's surgery was completed. Once again, Dave was awake, still very pale but looking considerably better than the previous day.

"I can't feel my shoulder." he announced, "They'll ease off the local anaesthetic as the nerves settle down but they think everything's going well. They're sending me home tomorrow."

"So soon?" Stuart asked.

"My shoulder's encased in plastic so the wound is immobile. I'll have to rest because I'm still anaemic but I'm producing my own blood okay. They take things like stress and mental well-being far more seriously than we do so they figure that the best place is home. Actually the Terzons reckon that getting back to a regular routine is beneficial so, instead of working with Brian could I monitor the portals while you go exploring with James until I'm fit."

"Brian's all for shutting up shop." Stuart said, "Sally was talking to James last night. She wants you home more. Do you really want to carry on?"

"Too right, I do." Dave exclaimed, almost shouting. He lay back exhausted by the effort, "Don't let's have this conversation again. It was an accident. One thought though. Try visiting parallel Earths where we didn't hook up. How many of those Daves are getting stabbed in the Railway."

"You're joking." Stuart gasped.

"Yep." Dave smiled, "It might tell you something about the universe though."

There was a moment's companionable silence.

"Did you succeed in patching my mobile through?" Dave asked.

Stuart nodded, "All calls will seem as if they originated in Brisbane."

"Ah well, will you cancel that bit, please." Dave said, "I'll phone Sally and say I've got to drive down to London to pick up some parts. Tomorrow I'll phone and tell her I was in an accident and broke my shoulder. I'll say that you're paying for a taxi to bring me home. I only rang when I was discharged from hospital and didn't want a fuss. Then I'll have some real fun and phone my parents."

"Are you sure that you'll be up for it?" Stuart asked.

Dave grimaced, "We'll have to do it right. If Dad's around he'll probably want to pay the fare so he can give the taxi driver the third degree."

"He's not that bad." Stuart said, "I get on with him."

"Yes but you're a partner in the business." Dave said, "That puts you up the scale. He still complains that you're holding me back, though."

"OK we'll do it your way." Stuart agreed.

To Stuart's continuing relief, Dave looked considerably better the following day though still very weak. He was exhausted by the time he had clambered through a portal though everyone was expecting it. They landed in some trees in a cemetery behind the hospital they had chosen and Stuart immediately sat Dave in a wheelchair that they had brought along.

Stuart pushed Dave through the hospital to the front of the hospital where taxis and buses drew up. The taxi driver blinked when he heard the destination but immediately called his office.

"It's £600 pounds." the driver said, "The office wants payment in advance."

Stuart had anticipated such a request and produced his bank card. The driver then cheerfully helped Dave into his seat and Stuart watched them drive off before being picked up in the cemetery.

It might have gone without a hitch if Stuart had not wandered round to greet Dave on his arrival. Dave's parents were waiting outside his cottage choosing not to be under the same roof as Sally. Andy was also there, still feeling guilty that he had asked to visit Memphis so there was a little crowd as the taxi drew up.

They were all a little shocked at his condition though Dave's father recovered first, offering the driver a substantial tip.

"Where did you pick him up?" he asked.

"Charing Cross Hospital." the driver replied, "His friend saw him…"

He tailed off as he spotted Stuart.

"How did you get here?" he asked.

"How do you mean?" Stuart asked.

"You're his mate who paid his fare aren't you?"

Stuart shook his head, "I was working today and I was going to wait in the pub until you arrived. They do teas and coffees as well as food if you'd like a break before heading back."

"Have you got a twin brother or something?" the driver persisted. Stuart could see Dave's father staring suspiciously.

"I'd explain but I want to get to bed." Dave said, "Mum are you going to be civil to Sally or are you going home?"

"Sally can take you upstairs and help you undress." Dave's mother replied, "I'll put the kettle on. If you feel up to it, you can tell us all about it, then."

Tom, Dave's father was torn between listening to David's side of events and questioning the driver. In the circumstances he was just as able to make mistakes and chose to wait with his family. Stuart took the driver for his coffee offering a meal as a tip.

"I wasn't supposed to be in London." Stuart said, "Dave couldn't have coped with all the changes if he came back by train. I caught one and got here just before you and everyone saw me waiting for you."

"Sorry if I landed you in it with your boss," the driver said, "but I'll keep my mouth shut."

"Thanks." Stuart replied, "Enjoy your meal. I'll settle up with Bill later."

Stuart guessed that the taxi driver did not really care one way or the other providing he had a reason for Stuart's unexpected appearance. When Stuart got to Dave's home he found Tom, Dave's father on the phone.

"Yes I do appreciate that there's patient confidentiality but I just need to know how to get a medical report for insurance purposes." he was saying as he glanced at Stuart.

"Thank you for being so helpful." he snapped as put the phone down. From the sarcasm in his tone he was obviously angry at being thwarted.

"Were you in London?" he asked Stuart accusingly.

Stuart disliked lying and he had already lied to the taxi driver but he had no choice.

"I've been around the village all day." he said, "What do you think?"

"Hmm." Tom said, "There's some funny rumours about what you're doing. Why was Dave in London?"

"Look I've come round to see how he is." Stuart said irritably, "Let's focus on that for now."

"Stuart's right, Tom." Brenda, Tom's wife said, "We'll get a solicitor to sort it all out. That way it'll all be fair and above board while we concentrate on Dave getting better."

"Dave wants to see Stuart." Sally said as she came down the stairs.

Brenda stepped towards the stairs but Sally blocked her way.

"I'm to say that this is our house." she said uncertainly, "Will everyone else wait in the living room, please?"

"I really think that he needs his mother." Brenda said confidently assuming that Sally would crumple but she stood her ground.

"Dave says that if you set one foot on these stairs then you'll never come into this house again." she said.

Brenda hesitated, surprised at the confidence in Sally's voice. She shrugged and meekly headed for the living room as Stuart climbed the stairs, entering the bedroom, shocked at how pale and tired Dave looked.

"I heard most of it." Dave said, "I'll deal with Mum and Dad. Will you do something for me though? It's Andy. In his time Ma'at meant learning about the universe to be more in harmony with it. I was going to try to get him up to speed so that he could go to school. Will you get him started?"

"You concentrate on getting well." Stuart said, "Andy will be all right."

"Please." Dave said, "Ever since I showed him how to ride a bike he's come to me if he's had a question and he feels as though it's all his fault. You know how, he took a camera back when he shouldn't have done and he wanted to visit a temple."

Stuart nodded, "Okay. Now what do you want?"

"Peace and quiet but I'm not going to get it." Dave sighed, "Mum's going to try to take over from Sally. You'd better fetch Mum and Dad but will you come back up, please."

"Dad, you are not going to get to the bottom of what happened." Dave said when they were all assembled, "Dr. Tobias is my doctor now and I don't need to see your guy. Mum, Brian and Stuart will pay me full wages and cover any extra expenses. I don't need you to go on about compensation. Sally is my partner. She is going to look after me and this is her house. Is anyone going to argue or can I get some sleep?"

"We'll talk about it tomorrow when you're feeling stronger." Brenda said.

"Mum, Dad, go home." Dave said, "You will not talk about it tomorrow so don't come back."

"You don't mean that." Brenda said, "The pain killers are making you delirious."

"Stuart, show them out." Dave said.

Every time Dave moved an arm or a leg, Stuart could see his face screwing up with the effort yet the Terzon drugs were keeping his mind sharp and alert though he was obviously tiring. He tried ushering Dave's parents from the room. Brenda was about to protest further but Tom took her by the arm and guided her downstairs.

Stuart led them into the living room.

"Dave can be very stubborn." he said, "The more you badger him the more he'll dig his heels in."

"Yes but he's hiding something." Brenda said, "There's something not right. What was he doing in London in the first place?"

"Visiting one of our suppliers." Stuart replied, "Maybe he was sightseeing when he should have been preparing for a meeting. We don't mind because he does take his work very seriously."

"If only he'd been as single minded with his school work." Tom said, "I suppose we do pressure him but what real prospects has he got?"

"I could get a cleaning job while he goes to university." Sally said.

Stuart could see the sneer on Brenda's face as she turned to deal with the interruption but it faded as the significance of Sally's offer sank in.

"You'd do that for him?" she asked quietly.

Sally nodded then plucking up courage added, "He's good to Aidan and me."

"It's time to go." Brenda said, "We'll leave you and Dave in peace. I've got one of those electric stew-pots at home. Would you like me to prepare something and drop it off tomorrow on the way to the office? I know Dave when he's ill. You'll be busy enough looking after two kids tomorrow."

It was as much of a peace offering as Brenda could make and Sally nodded, aware that the tension between them was easing.

No one was in the mood for normal business so Stuart spent a companionable day with Brian in his library, happily fussed over by Demetrius.

"Are you happy here, Demetrius?" Stuart asked at one stage.

"I am now, Master." Demetrius replied, "Writing books is something the great Socrates would do."

"And you don't mind keeping house for us?"

Demetrius laughed, "Instead of sitting in chairs, my masters are reclining on couches at their slave's insistence. I don't feel like a servant."

"I thought you went down to the pub for lunch." Stuart said, "Shouldn't you be going?"

"Not when it's my duty to serve you, Master." Demetrius replied as he left the room.

"Are you still worried about him?" Brian asked.

"No. I suppose I was comparing him to Andy. Their societies were so different. Ma'at seemed to make Egyptian ranks far closer together."

"I think James is finding Andy a bit of a handful." Brian laughed, "He wants to visit Sheffield and Leeds to see the temples as he calls them. The vicar spent a whole day showing him around the village church. It seems Ma'at and Jesus have a lot of similar ideas and the vicar was quite exhausted by it all."

"Yeah and he's got a neat trick." Stuart said, "He tells everyone that his parents are in ancient Egypt. His timing is perfect. He pauses just long enough for them to start wondering then says, 'I'm staying with my Uncle because I need more friends than just archaeologists families'."

"And I suppose both statements are true. It's putting them together that's misleading."

"According to Andy it's what I do." Stuart said, "I suppose we did the right thing bringing them forward."

"I think so." Brian said, "Demetrius brought a lot of Ancient Greece with him and Andy's brought Ma'at. I could almost see Andy adapting his beliefs and entering the church. I wouldn't worry about that."

Village Life

About mid afternoon, Stuart set off to visit Dave. He was surprised to see one of the village boys hanging around outside their cottage.

"Mr. Norton said that Andy was here." the boy said, "I was hoping we could hang out for a bit."

"No school, Zach?" Stuart asked.

"Dentist." Zach replied.

"Come on in." Stuart said, "I don't think Dave or Sally will mind."

Dave looked a lot stronger than the day before though he was settled in a comfortable chair while Aidan and Andy sprawled on the floor surrounded by paper, pencils and crayons. Stuart had a fair idea of what Sally's childhood had been like so wondered what she made of the scene.

In fact, she was blissfully happy. She knew TV's perception of family life and her living room fitted in perfectly with that especially with Dave sitting, looking benignly on. It was so different to the increasing pile of beer cans and the remains of a drug habit that she was so used to seeing at her parent's home. She also understood that she had to do her part and used Stuart's visit as a chance to hurry to the shop.

Puzzled, Zach picked up one of Andy's efforts.

"Those squiggles look like what you see on an Egyptian mummy. How come you can draw them?"

"Life with my parents." Andy said, "I can write them as well as English."

That's true. Stuart thought, *Andy never learnt to read or write in any language.*

"Yeah, you said that they're Egyptologists." Zach said, "Do you know any ancient Egyptian curses?"

"No. That would be against Ma'at." Andy replied, "How about a blessing?"

"What sort of blessing?" Zach asked.

"Beer." Andy replied, "I'm finding recipes for Mr. Milnes."

Zach's face lit up.

"Can I help?" he asked.

With Zach suddenly finding Egyptology very interesting Stuart turned his attention to Dave.

"Andy's been keeping Aidan happy all day." Dave said, "He's a good kid."

"How are you?" Stuart asked.

"Stronger." Dave replied, "Dr. Tobias popped in and scanned it. He reckons everything's bonding as it should. What about you? How are the surveys doing."

Zach looked up.

"Are you exploring another planet?" he said, "Can I come?"

Stuart looked at Dave in despair. Dave just grinned before turning to Zach.

"What's that? An idea for an essay?" he asked.

Zach frowned, "No. It's village business. Dad says, what happens in the village stays in the village. Is Andy an alien?"

"No." Stuart said, "He was born in Memphis."

"Yeah right." Zach exclaimed, "He can write all that Egyptian stuff but he's struggling to write in English. Why can't he use a pencil?"

"There is a secret." Andy said, "But I bet I don't know all yours. Will you help me though. I want to go to school next term, will you help me get ready?"

"If you tell me where you come from." Zach said.

"I'd ask Stuart if you could visit my parents." Andy said, "But transport can be unreliable and we might get stuck there. You'd have to tell your parents something before we went and more people would know."

Zach nodded triumphantly.

"So you are from another planet." he exclaimed.

"No." Andy said, "I was born in a village near Memphis. You're asking the wrong question."

"How do you mean?" Zach asked.

"What I say." Andy said, "If you want the right answer you must ask the right question."

Stuart was impressed. Zach, talking openly about visiting another planet, had shocked him and all he could think of was denying it. Andy was neither confirming nor denying anything but was giving the other boy a problem to solve. Zach might have accepted that he had more to learn before he could go anywhere but the phone rang. It was Dr. Tobias.

"Tiy's near the end." he said, "He's asking for Andy."

Switching languages, Stuart passed the message on. Andy

scrambled up turning to Zach.

"A friend of mine's very ill." he said, "I've got to go to him."

"Would you like me to come with you?" Zach asked, "You know to be your friend."

"That's kind of you," Stuart said, "but you'd have to ask your parents because we won't get back tonight."

"OK." Zach cheerfully replied taking out his phone.

Stuart looked helplessly at Dave who was sporting a smug grin.

"I'm innocent this time." he chuckled.

Almost immediately Zach was thrusting his phone into Stuart's hand.

"Is this journey tied up with your work?" Zach's father asked.

"Yes." Stuart replied hoping that permission would be refused without any further discussion.

"If you can assure me it'll be perfectly safe then OK." Zach's father said, "What really worries me though is your lifestyle. I understand you're in a hurry but you're dragging a fifteen year old boy off, with no night things and presumably he'll be out of contact. If anything improper happens then village business or not I'll call the police. Understood?"

"Yes of course." Stuart replied angrily, "I can…"

"If I didn't trust you then I'd have said no." Zach's father interrupted, "I am his father and I needed to be sure that we understood each other."

"Fair enough." Stuart said, "I'll hand him back."

As they passed his cottage, James joined them and they all hurried to the quarry.

"Are you sure about Zach?" James asked as the boys ran on ahead.

"We're going to have to move." Stuart said, "Even his father seemed to know what we're doing. Brian's going to do his nut."

"So why did you agree to Zach coming?" James asked.

"Damage limitation." Stuart said, "If Brian calms down then he can show Zach his research into stellar gravimetrics. That'll bore him to death and he might lose interest."

"It's certainly a plan." James chuckled, "And as you say Zach already knew. Do you suppose that Andy's said anything?"

"Not deliberately." Stuart replied, "But not many fifteen year olds want to write in Early Kingdom hieroglyphics."

"We've all got careless about security so we're all to blame for this." James said, "I'll deal with Brian. You go and keep Dave company while I wreck what's left of our security."

"Are you sure?" Stuart asked.

"I've more or less adopted Andy so I suppose he is my responsibility. He's dragging me into a little problem that Demetrius has as well" he shrugged, "It's supposed to be difficult being a parent but Andy's something else."

"What's this about Demetrius?" Stuart asked, "He's not said anything to Brian or me."

"He wouldn't." James said, "He'd never disturb you like that. I think that Andy is going to give that professor friend of his a lesson in manners and respect."

Satisfied that there was nothing urgent, Stuart hurried back to Dave's. He was pleased to see Sally and Aidan at the playground in the corner of the village green.

"Sal's got a real thing about a normal family life." Dave said, "And playing in the park is okay on TV so it's okay for Aidan."

"Does she know about our jaunts?" Stuart asked.

"No." Dave replied, "She complains about silly village gossip but 'real', that is TV families, don't travel through space, so we don't."

"Your parents don't know much about it either, do they." Stuart asked.

"I feel a bit sorry for them." Dave confessed, "But it's their own fault because they go on about how they've made something of themselves. None of the local farmers go to her because they reckon she'd side with the tax people and not them. It's the same with Dad. They reckon he's snooping for the authorities if he takes an interest in their farms. We know who bends the rules but he doesn't."

"It's more than bending the rules." Stuart laughed, "I've tried Jack Carter's home made whiskey and I've seen his still. I don't tell the authorities about it because it's village business, he doesn't mention our portal for the same reason."

"I got arrested once or twice when I was drinking at the Railway." Dave said, "I remember giving my address to one custody sergeant. He rolled up his eyes and muttered something about, 'not that place again'."

Stuart laughed, "Maybe we can get away with it here, after all. I've never thought about it before but I don't think that half of the garage's work goes through the books and where does Bill get those cheap cigarettes from? I never see anything but he always keeps his regulars supplied."

"And Dad moans about the price of cigarettes in the shops."

Dave said, "He's just out of the loop completely."

"OK, I'm not so worried about Zach except he's just a kid." Stuart said, "It's a bit much after Tony and Freddie."

"Andy's a bit much after Demetrius." Dave said, "All we need is an ancient Roman and we've got a set."

"OK but what about you?" Stuart said, "How do you feel?"

"I've never realised how much energy it takes to talk." Dave replied, "I'm going to chuck you out soon but I need a piss. Will you help me up and make sure I don't collapse on the floor. Don't worry, I'll be able to stand and do it myself, I'm just a bit wobbly walking."

When Stuart left Dave he was feeling restless so he headed for the pub. Anthony was there waiting for his evening meal.

"I'm glad I've bumped into you." he said, "I'm going home. It's been an amazing experience but I had enough adventure in the army. Thanks to great-grandfather Freddie I've always felt that something would happen, now it has and it's enough. I'm ready to focus on the estate now and that's where I truly belong."

They sat and chatted for a time before Stuart headed home. Brian arrived not long after and Stuart told him of the day's events.

"I think that we should plan on leaving." Brian said, "Most of our gear's on Resolution and we only store a few probes in the bunkers. Even our computers rely on the servers on the space station. As long as we're ready and know what to do if something happens then we can wait and see but we do have to be ready."

"You're pretty calm about it." Stuart said, "I'm more worried than you."

"Oh I'm worried." Brian said, "But this has to be one of the most isolated villages in the country. I don't mean by distance but by terrain and communications. I don't know if there's a prize for the village most often snowed in but we'd be a strong contender. It all helps to create a strong community spirit and we get the benefits of it."

"So you don't mind villagers becoming involved." Stuart asked.

"I'd prefer it if everyone believed our cover story." Brian said, "It's not going to happen so, as long as we can cover our tracks then we may as well go with the flow. More to the point, what are you doing about the Ancients?"

"I don't know." Stuart replied, "I'm still trying to build a picture with probes and it's still all a bit vague. He moans about working in a spacesuit but Dad's having a great time studying their ship. They made far fewer raids than we first thought. I'd guess that biologically mankind has changed very little and they were only interested in making sure that we could interbreed. The Mars colonies may have started out with laboratories working on biological warfare but they didn't have the resources to maintain them. The survivors on Earth don't have the intellect though they do have more resources."

"So why don't you just leave it?" Brian asked.

"Because it's messy." Stuart exclaimed, "The whole thing's been a muddle and I want to be clear that there's no real threat. What I don't want is to spend all my time protecting the time line like we had to with Freddie and Tony. Neither do I want to leave a people to die out when I could help them. Do you realise that I should try to stop them having their nuclear war but if I did then I'd threaten our own existence."

"And you don't like the idea of letting events play out and just rescuing a handful of survivors." Brian said.

"The real problem is I feel that I'm dealing with a series of disjointed problems not connected with each other." Stuart said, "It started off with Demetrius then we had those crazy time loops with Freddie and Tony. OK so Andy isn't really a problem and recceing possible sites to relocate those people is valid but I think I answered the original problem ages ago so why am I carrying on?"

"You need to eliminate any possible threat against us and in return you'll offer them a new home."

"OK," Stuart conceded, "but it feels as if I'm looking at their whole existence from on high. I can swoop down and change their history wherever I feel like it."

"Hello God." Brian chuckled, "Keep to a Terzon like policy. Don't interfere unless they want your help. From what you say about Merrill and Larik their people will choose to take their chances until it's almost too late."

Brian paused, "I am proud of you. Why not start with the Earth colony. Get them established then tell the Mars colonies that their enemy is re-colonising Earth. They won't want to be left behind."

"That sounds too simple." Stuart said.

"It is too simple. For a start you'll have to convince them to abandon their weapons and their space ships."

Stuart nodded.

"I think it's a plan though. All the colonies lead a pretty miserable existence and I've got to allow it to continue."

"You're forgetting one thing." Brian said, "The Martian colonists chose their life style. How can I put it? Let their choice pan out until it's unsustainable then offer to help."

"And in a way Freddie and Tony decided when I should help the Earth colony. I can't change things before their visit."

"No." Brian agreed, "You're bound by temporal laws and you must keep to them."

"I still have this feeling that there's something else and I'm part of their plan." Stuart said, "I don't like it much."

"Could they be asking for help and it's your choice whether you give it?"

"I don't know." Stuart replied, "Let's change the subject. I get fed up with all this uncertainty."

"OK." Brian agreed, "Who's going with you on your jaunts while Dave's laid up?"

"I don't know." Stuart replied, "There was half a dozen of us on that last trip but Dave's stabbing jolted Joe and Anthony. Dave's out of it, of course so that leaves James or Andy and Andy's too young."

"That's what I say about you." Brian chuckled, "And if you took James who would monitor the portal?"

"Yes but Andy's making friends in the village and he wants to go to school to become a scribe as he puts it." Stuart exclaimed, "He can't do that and work for us at the same time."

"That leaves your Dad or Gable." Brian said, "I don't think I could keep up with you in the field."

"Gable would never argue with me." Stuart responded thoughtfully, "Dave kept his eyes open and if he saw something wrong he'd push me back to the portal if he had to. Dad would be the opposite. He's getting the Terzon attitude that we should just study things through a probe."

"And you don't agree?"

"Don't get me wrong. Dave's injury was terrible but we learnt more about their attitudes than a probe survey ever could. I think it's a human thing, events register more if we're involved."

"And ancient Egypt is now too dangerous to take Andy back."

"No." Stuart replied, "The opposite is true. Dedi's friends were as shocked as we were."

"Joe might be entering his Martian marrow and demonstrating Egyptian beers at the village fête but I bet he stays tight lipped about where it all comes from. I've done some research. Zach's dad won't want his tax scam being made public. I could flag his records and warn him if anyone else starts taking an interest, so he'll want to keep everything in the village. Why not take Andy and Zach back to check the settlement sites. Dave might be able to rest better if he's weightless on Resolution so we could give the boys high-resolution cameras and he could monitor them while James runs the portal."

"If they're willing." Stuart said, "And maybe James would like to come with me. Andy could look after Dave while he monitors the portal."

Andy was sobbing quietly when Stuart found them.

"Tiy's with Anapa now." he whispered, "May he find his heart light and pure."

Zach looked puzzled.

"A good person's heart is as light as feather." Stuart explained, "And they're allowed to travel on to Aaru."

"Is that heaven?" Zach asked.

Stuart nodded, "At least something similar."

"His friend seemed all burnt but he wasn't was he?" Zach asked.

"No." Stuart said, "It was radiation poisoning."

"It was fun going to that hospital but it's wrong to think like that it isn't it?" Zach asked, "And Andy got annoyed because I had to keep stopping and looking around but I couldn't take it in."

"Don't knock yourself out about it." Stuart said, "You didn't know Tiy and we should have given you time to get used to it but you were there when Andy needed you. Will you look after Andy though and help him to get used to his new life?"

Zach nodded, "Is the right question 'when does he come from'?"

"And do you know the answer?" Stuart asked.

"Ancient Egypt." Zach replied, "His parents are dead as well so he's lost everyone."

"No, they're not dead." Andy said, "They're a long way away but I could visit them if Stuart agreed."

He raised his hand, looking at Stuart, "I'm not asking. I'm just trying to explain."

"James could take you if you like." Stuart said.

"No." Andy exclaimed, "I've said good bye once. I don't want to do it again and I want to stay here."

"OK." Stuart said, "What do you want to do now?"

Can I take Zach to the Lizard planet and can we stay there tonight, please?"

"As long as James and Zach's father agree then I've no objections."

"Dad's already said I can stay with Andy." Zach replied, "Is it going to be like a camping trip? I could get my gear.”

“Go ahead.” Stuart said, “What about school, tomorrow?”

“It's near the end of term.” Zach said, “If I get the forms could we do something about work experience?”

“Get the forms.” Stuart said, “But I expect you to be at school on time, tomorrow.”

“You sound just like dad.” Zach pouted but he and Andy hurried off.

Of course, Stuart's idea of getting him to school on time was considerably different to Zach's dad. After three days lazing around on the lizard planet Zach felt disorientated as he waited for the bus the next day, courtesy of a little time travel.

“Are you testing him?” Brian asked Stuart as they sat together at breakfast.

“Let's just say that I'm invading his privacy today.” Stuart said, “He's got enough to shoot off his mouth about but if he does, it'll be difficult to prove any of it.”

“So you don't want to take James with you?” Brian asked, “You're seeing if Zach will fit in.”

“If James had retired without meeting us he would have found a job in shop security or something, at least something a lot less demanding than Military Intelligence but something where he could use his skills. Monitoring us and the occasional field trip suits him but he doesn't want field work to be a regular thing.”

“And Zach?” Brian persisted.

“The lizard people like him.” Stuart said, “They remember how those soldiers only thought about hunting and colonisation. All they found in Zach was an intense curiosity. He had a load of questions, which they couldn't answer, because he wanted to hurry off to go swimming or climbing a hill to see what was on the other side.”

“You know.” Brian said, “I think that could be the key. At fifteen he's still forming his ideas of the world. You're showing him a whole new way of looking at it. If the signs are that he'll accept your ways and not reject them then he could become a member of the team.”

“It makes sense.” Stuart said, “I've located a few likely sites and I'm going to spend a few days surveying them. If all goes well then I'll take them with me when I visit.”

It was a week later that they assembled at the quarry. Zach seemed a little uncomfortable wearing just white shorts, t-shirt and flip flops. Andy was bare foot, wearing just shorts while Stuart made do with light coloured shirt, trousers and trainers.

"I still think we should be in army dress or something. What about camouflage or something?" Zach said.

"We've gone through this." Stuart said, "Most people your age will be naked but even with the maximum sun screen you need some protection. If Andy wants to slip his shorts off when we get there, he can because he's used to the sun. He'll also be the most camouflaged because he'll be just like the others."

Zach nodded.

"It just doesn't seem real and I do understand what you've said." he said, ". I'll probably feel better when I get there but we could be talking about some computer game at the moment."

"Don't worry." Stuart smiled, "It doesn't always feel real to me either. Just remember, in this game we're not commandos trying kill as many of the enemy as possible. We're spies trying to blend in."

"At least we won't be shot if we're caught." Zach giggled, "Guns weren't invented then."

"No." Stuart smiled, "I think you'd be impaled. You know, bloody great spikes rammed up your arse."

"Oh!" Zach exclaimed, "They wouldn't really do that, would they?"

"We'll only be visiting farming villages." Stuart said, "I've told you about the colonists we're bringing here, they'll have modern tools to trade in exchange for help to get established."

"What happens if an archaeologist finds them?" Zach asked.

"We'll be in an area that will become Alexandria. There will be subsidence due to earthquakes and anything we do will be buried under the sea or under Greek and Roman remains. Even if some rusty old blade did turn up, it would be difficult to date and we can have the handles made locally."

"And you have to plan all this?" Zach asked.

"I reckon that for every hour we spend exploring a different world we spend at least ten using probes and analysing the results." Stuart replied.

"That doesn't sound like fun." Zach said, "If you learn so much about it, why bother going?"

"Because we need their help." Stuart said.

He paused looking at Zach before continuing slowly and carefully, "I'm going to say something else that sounds unreal. Now that Joe Milnes has brought his marrow back from Mars he's had enough of working with us. If you want a holiday job then I'm sure that he'd take you on especially since he'd have someone to talk to."

"Mr. Milnes has been out with you?" Zach asked, "Who else?"

"No one locally." Stuart replied, "You met the Darringtons though?"

"Everyone thought that they were Brian's cousins or something."

"No, but would you believe that young Tony was born in the 1880's?"

Zach's eyes grew big and round, "Dad laughs when someone says you travel to other planets, but I think he believes it. Do you really do time travel just as easily?"

"You know where we're going." Stuart said, "Why do you find it so difficult to believe."

"And you're going to take me?" Zach asked.

Stuart nodded, "We've got a job for you if you'll do it. Andy wants to go to school and live in the modern world. I want you to study the village we're visiting, particularly how people your age behave then help him to adapt. Will you do that?"

"Sure but he's already got a phone. It won't be that difficult will it."

Zach started to be answered as they approached the village. The path they were travelling along skirted one of the rivers of the Nile delta. Zach was aware of the lush grassland on one side but as he looked on the other side a question sprang into his mind.

"Are those the bulrushes that they hid Moses in?" he asked.

"Not for a couple of thousand years." Stuart chuckled.

"I just wondered," Zach said, "What's the Nile like in our time?"

"I don't know." Stuart replied, "I've never visited."

The grassland gave way to cultivated land as they approached the village. Stuart took in the familiar white baked mud buildings but when he looked at Zach, it was obvious from his flushed, wide-eyed expression that he'd taken in another sight.

As when James visited, it was the children who gathered around first, openly curious about the strangers. Older teens were also in the group and as before most were naked. Zach was desperately trying not stare at the girls about his age.

Stuart smiled to himself. Zach was trying to behave like a seasoned traveller but he had been given a translator and knew that at least a couple of the girls and one boy were happily speculating on his own assets.

"They're too wealthy for you." one called out, "Not unless they want many wives and aren't too choosy."

"Not this trip." Andy called out, "Next time you can all try our poles and we'll marry all those who give us sons."

Zach's blush became even more vivid.

"Shut it, Andy." he snarled in English.

"Your world's so different." Andy replied artlessly, "You should be taking yours out and giving them something to hope for."

"Enough you two." Stuart snapped, "Andy, it's your job to make Zach feel at home, not to tease him."

"Sorry." Andy muttered, "How about going swimming? We'll all be naked then."

"Later." Stuart said, "Give Zach a chance to get used to your world."

They had reached the centre of the village and now the adults were gathering around.

"Welcome strangers." one said, "Are you traders because we don't have much."

Stuart drew the knife he had been wearing, picked up a piece of wood and began whittling. The villagers watched fascinated by the ease with which the blade sliced through the wood.

"I can supply ploughs, knives, anything that farmers need to tend their land." he said, "In exchange I ask you to teach some friends of mine who wish to settle further down stream."

"How many friends?" the man asked suspiciously.

"Many." Stuart relied, "But they know how to draw water from the river and carry it to fields beyond the ones you already have. You'll have more land if you accept them not less."

"Eat with us and tell us more." the man said, "Is your pale brother well?"

"He's taken by the beauty of your girls." Stuart said, "Or maybe your boys."

The man laughed, "We can trade for either but maybe he's still choosing."

Zach was still blushing furiously.

"Stuart, please." he whispered.

"Just relax, Zach." Stuart said, "They're just friendly and are far less inhibited than we are. They wouldn't believe that you haven't seen a naked girl before."

"But I haven't." Zach wailed, "I don't even have an older sister."

"And helping Andy is more than teaching him computer games, isn't it?"

"That's why you brought me along, isn't it?" Zach asked.

"Partly and partly because Andy couldn't stand in for Dave on his own. Do you want to go home?"

"No." Zach replied, "But don't forget it's my first trip."

"Zach has been ill." Stuart said turning back to the villager and his language, "He still needs to rest a lot so he'll stay near me while the others can go off together."

"I'm sorry, Zach." the villager said, "Please come and sit in the shade. Are you hungry? A bowl of my wife's beer will do you good."

He looked around, "There's still plenty of work in the fields, give our guests some peace."

"I didn't expect them to be so friendly." Zach said when he and Stuart were alone.

"We're at the start of a civilisation that lasts for thousands of years. For a lot of the time it was interested in new ideas and believed in a benevolent social order. It's why I'm hoping that they'll accept the Ancients."

"And I'm spoiling it, aren't I?" Zach said sadly.

"No." Stuart said, "Remember Andy won't be able to talk to his new classmates the way those girls were talking to you."

"Andy won't be able to say what he said, either." Zach said, "I get it."

"I said you were convalescing." Stuart said, "Just sit and watch. Enjoy the sights."

Zach grinned.

"It's not like when I went to Tenerife with Mum and Dad, is it. Can I have some money to get some fish and chips, please?"

"Sure, but you'll have to queue for five thousand years though."

If Stuart was satisfied that the day spent in Ancient Egypt had been highly successful he did not realise just how deep an impression the trip had made on Zach until his father phoned a couple of days later.

"It's our next trip to Tenerife." he said, "Zach's learning Spanish and he doesn't want to stay in the hotel. He wants to hire a bike for the holiday and visit places off the tourist routes."

"And that doesn't appeal to you." Stuart said.

"Claire doesn't even have to cook." Zach's father said, "We like to laze around and rest. I suppose Zach's getting to the age where he wants to do his own thing but I'm not happy about him cycling along mountain roads alone in a foreign country."

"So how can I help?" Stuart asked.

Zach's father laughed, "I feel a bit silly worrying about you being gay. It's the least of my problems. Apparently you wouldn't waste your time lying on the beach with a load of other boring Brits. You'd get out, meet the locals and learn about the place. I know we'd lose the booking but could he stay with you while we just take his sister?"

"No." Stuart said, "Zach's not a nuisance or anything like that but we're in the middle of an important project and kids have been a constant headache. We really need to focus now otherwise it's just going to drag on."

"I understand." Zach's father said, "Thanks for your time."

"You've got a couple of weeks before you go." Stuart said, "Why not get him to plan out his itinerary. He could see if there are buses or trains he could use and maybe choose a couple of trips that would interest you. That way, you'll know where he is and what he's doing. If you like you can say it's a training exercise for when he's helping me."

"Thanks I'll do that." Zach's father replied, "I've got a feeling you'll have to approve it though."

There was one sequel for both Zach and Stuart during Zach's holiday. His parents allowed Zach to take the ferry to a neighbouring island. It was a trip that Stuart had suggested and it was already an adventure as he disembarked, happily chatting to a couple of locals who were impressed with such a polite, interesting young holiday maker.

As they went about their different ways Zach stopped and stared at Stuart not sure if he recognised him.

"Do you fancy an extra trip?" Stuart asked.

"Sure." Zach replied trying desperately to be adultly calm about the prospect.

The trip through the portals was straightforward enough but as they stepped out of woods, which hid their arrival, Zach stopped, disorientated.

He was sure that he was standing in the same place where he had got off the ferry but not only was the dock gone, so was the city and every other sign of civilisation.

He glanced across the bay towards three ancient sailing ships. As he watched, sails dropped from yards and the anchors were raised. Zach looked at Stuart, puzzled.

"It's 1492." Stuart said, "Any guesses?"

"Christopher Columbus?" Zach asked and without thinking, grabbed his camera. Suddenly remembering, he glanced at Stuart who nodded.

"You'll have to have a course in image manipulation to show folks how you made them but you'll know that they're genuine." he said.

"Those ships are so small." Zach exclaimed, "I never realised. Kneel down will you, please, I want to steady it on your shoulder while I zoom in."

Moments later he exclaimed, "I'm sure he's just waved to us."

"Who?" Stuart asked innocently.

"Christopher Columbus." Zach forgot that he was supposed to be mature and laid back as he jumped up and down, yelling and waving.

Stuart lay down in the sand, content. Zach and Andy had become firm friends even though Andy sometimes embarrassed Zach by his behaviour. Spending a day watching Columbus sail off was Stuart's way of thanking Zach for his patience. It was also a test. The shots on his camera's memory card were innocuous if Zach was to claim that he had met a Tenerifen interested in CGI effects. However, if Zach tried to claim that he had really travelled back in time then he would be completely frozen out of Stuart's activities as well as being thoroughly humiliated when his 'fraud' was exposed. It was a pleasant break for Stuart because Zach proved to be thoroughly trustworthy and Stuart was happy for him to become Andy's friend.

First Rescue

With Stuart content that one project had been completed, he was now as ready as he would ever be to deal with the Ancients. Stuart used a probe to deposit a portable monitor, complete with built in microphone and camera on Lord Trey's desk just before he was due to arrive. Lord Trey stared at the moving image of Stuart's head and jumped when Stuart greeted him with a cheerful 'Hi'.

"What is this?" Lord Trey asked.

"Put simply it's a CCTV screen adapted for two way conversation." Stuart explained.

"That is not simple." Lord Trey exclaimed, "Why is it here?"

"Would you like to save your people and help others to create a new empire?"

"What with the Kramons? Never."

"Not with just the Kramons." Stuart said, "With others."

"I don't understand."

"No." Stuart agreed, "I don't suppose I'm making myself very clear. Let's start from the beginning. Do you remember me? The last time we met, I told you about the colonies on Mars. You sent me and my er, master outside because we wouldn't help you attack them."

"Yes I remember." Lord Trey replied then paused, "It can't be you. You're alive."

"Yep." Stuart chuckled, "Would you like to know what happened?"

Puzzled, Lord Trey nodded.

"Better still I can show you." Stuart said, "Tell those guards who captured us to take you to the tunnel where they found us."

"Why?"

"To see what we're offering you?"

Bewildered, Lord Trey sat looking at the screen. His role was to organise work rotas and decide how to eke out their dwindling resources. Only one thought penetrated his conscious thought. The strangers were right, the colony was nearly finished and even his rations were scarcely adequate.

He might still have rejected Stuart's offer except for one basic, primeval thought that crept in to dominate his mind. Maybe if conditions were better, his wife would not be barren and he would have a son to continue his line.

"Very well." he said, "I'll see you there."

For Lord Trey seeing the strange round room that Stuart stood in just added to his confusion. An even more bewildering journey, through strange metal tunnels, until he stood in a counterpart of the room he had first entered, did not help. It was the view outside that really startled him. Above was a clear starlit sky that stretched in an infinite dome above him. He might have turned and ran but as ever the shock of being weightless left him relying on Stuart who remained calm and at ease.

"Put this on." Stuart said, handing him a loose Arab like robe and a soft helmet to cover his head.

"The sun will be rising soon." Stuart continued, "Your skin's very pale so it needs to be protected while you acclimatise. Some friends said that they'd be here just after dawn, I'll wait outside for them."

Lord Trey had been in a state of utter confusion since he had first seen the monitor but the mention of sunrise now added terror to his emotions. He watched bewildered and frightened as Stuart stepped through the hatch and leaned unconcernedly against the transparent wall.

It was already brighter and Lord Trey could make out the lush grass and trees as well as seeing the long shadows cast by them. Stuart strolled over to a log and sat fully exposed to the rising sun.

Lord Trey hurriedly donned the clothes that Stuart had given him and prepared to retreat further into the portal yet he remained still. Stuart still sat unconcerned, yet he should already be screaming out his last breaths as sunlight flayed his skin.

Compared to the ordered predictability of the decaying biosphere the scene outside was as alien and as bizarre as anything Lord Trey could have imagined, especially when the group that Stuart was waiting for arrived. Compared to the pale skins that he was used to, they were impossibly brown. The older men wore simple linen kilts wrapped around their waists while the two youngest were completely naked. One, paler than the others showed an even paler area of skin as if used to wearing a kilt or something in the sun.

Stuart glanced across at Lord Trey, beckoning him out, but he hesitated. Proud of himself for not bolting to the safety of the inner portal, it would still take a lot of courage to overcome a lifetime of indoctrination.

In his turn, Stuart was more amused by Zach's dress, or rather lack of it. Zach blushed as he realised that Stuart was looking at him.

"You said I should blend in." he said defensively, "I did a lot of sunbathing on holiday but I wasn't allowed to do it nude. Now Andy's mates are laughing at my tan line."

"The horrors of exploration." Stuart smiled, "Now what about your task last night?"

The spades were a great success." Zach replied, "They all wanted to try them. We talked about chadoufs but wouldn't norias be better."

"Pots on the end of beams were invented about this time and it's when they began irrigation." Stuart said, "Pots on waterwheels won't happen for at least three thousand years."

"So spades and saws will help them get started on irrigation and archaeologists will guess at the technology they used because the steel blades will rust away before any are discovered." Zach rushed his explanation out.

Stuart nodded.

"Oh, I forgot. Dave's awake." Zach added, He's explaining more about irrigation but he's feeling a bit tired so he sent us."

"So my backup team's a couple of kids and an invalid." Stuart grinned, "Once we can coax Trey out of the portal, James can de-materialise it and be ready to rescue us. Ipy do you want to help."

The villager nodded.

"How does a man's skin become so white that the sun burns him?" he asked.

"He lives in a cave, out of the sun so he's not used to it." Stuart explained.

Lord Trey shuddered as Stuart opened the hatch even if it was transparent. He hesitated as Stuart offered his hand then hesitantly took it, allowing himself to be slowly drawn to the hatch. Taking a deep breath he took one more step and found himself standing in direct sunlight for the first time in his life. For him it was the point of no return. He was outside and alive, the thin suit was nowhere enough protection.

Nervously he took the next step and lifted the helmet but Stuart stopped him, grabbing for something in the portal compartment.

"OK." he said, "You need a wide brimmed hat and sunglasses while you acclimatise."

"I should not look like a cripple in front of peasants." Lord Trey retorted, "I must show them who I am."

"You are a refugee from a dying world who needs help." Stuart exclaimed, "Forget the Lord Trey crap or go home."

Trey glared angrily at Stuart and might have argued but he hesitated. More than anything it was Andy and Zach who distracted him. Their colour, their liveliness and barely restrained boisterousness were such a contrast to the sickly children his people were rearing. Again it was his own desire to see his own children grow and thrive that guided him.

"You should not speak to me like that." he replied more to save face than anything but he added, "Is the sun still safe, it seems to be getting brighter and hotter."

"Wear the hat and glasses." Stuart ordered, "Sit in the shade when we get to the village and respect the people who live here because they'll teach you as much as we teach them."

Trey meekly complied, nearly panicking as he turned towards the sun but he was struck by the vividness and range of colours he was seeing. He was aware of the warmth of the sun through his protective clothes but instead of being threatening he felt a sense of rightness, almost that he was on the world of his ancestors.

Stuart found Dave sitting cross legged under the shade of a sycamore tree.

He only wore shorts and the scar from his injury was obvious. Stuart could see just how deep it had been.

"Hi." Dave smiled in greeting, "How are you getting on with my stand ins?"

"It's OK when the natives are friendly." Stuart replied, "It's not the same without you though."

"Dr. Tobias says I'm doing well." Dave said, "I've got most of the use of my arm back and the blood count's okay. I still get tired easily but that's all."

"We can wait until Zach and Andy are back at school then tackle Merrill and Larik's people." Stuart said, "They're likely to be harder to deal with."

"We could still help." Zach said, "We could call it work experience."

"No." Stuart said, "I'm sorry but you're too young. I know you look after Dave but things can go badly wrong."

"And you're worried about people knowing what we're up to." Zach said, "Have you got time to read something. We're supposed to write something about our holiday."

"We're in Ancient Egypt and you want me to read a school report." Stuart exclaimed, "That's one of the reasons I think you're too young. You're not concentrating."

"And maybe you should chill." Dave said, "Look over there. Trey is studying our shovel and Ipy is showing him how well it works. There's enough going on and Zach needs some help. He's doing all this and you expect him and Andy to settle at school next term."

"I'm sorry Zach, what do you want to show me?" Stuart asked.

He took the paper and read.

I've often had to write an essay on what I do in my holidays and often there was not much to tell. This holiday was different as I often felt like an explorer discovering new worlds. While on holiday in Tenerife with my parents I took trips on my own and one day I visited a neighbouring island. I did not think that I was very interested in history but that night I had a dream.

I was back on the island I had visited but there was no town or docks just three ancient ships setting sail. Somehow I knew that I was watching Christopher Columbus set sail but apart from that mysterious piece of knowledge everything else was so real. The Santa Maria seemed tiny compared to the island ferry. I could clearly see the crew on the quarterdeck and I saw Christopher Columbus wave to me. The ships were so close and they travelled so slowly. Once awake I checked and they crossed the Atlantic at less than four miles an hour. They were even slower as they left harbour, it seemed to take forever.

That dream is still as vivid as the rest of my holiday and it doesn't matter that it was not real. It's special because it was an adventure that only I had.

"Was it really that special?" Stuart asked.

Zach nodded, "I know that I've got to keep it all secret but I do understand how different this is."

"If I said that you could work for us part-time and only when I think it's OK what would you say."

"Dave needs us to help him now." Zach replied, "I'm helping Andy with his reading and writing and I'm learning those herioglif things. He's catching up on maths as well. I am trying to help."

"They're pronounced hieroglyphs." Stuart said, "What did your dad say about you staying with us last night?"

"He phoned your dad." Zach replied, "I think yours said something about Dave getting injured but you try to be as careful as possible. Dad said all the usual stuff, I've got to do as I'm told and he's going to tell you to send me home if I cause too much trouble."

The conversation might have dragged on but Trey approached them.

"Those boys are to come back with me." he said, "I want our doctors to examine them."

Stuart frowned but remained silent.

"I ask that they come back with me." he said, "You are Lord here."

"Well it was a good start in being polite but I can't allow the boys to go to your world." Stuart said, "I'm concerned about the higher levels of radiation especially with Andy. How about your doctors visiting here. Maybe some villagers would agree to being examined as well."

Trey stood as he considered the possibilities. He was thinking in terms of sperm count. Did this hot sun damage it? Maybe it would be better if the doctors did examine the villagers.

"All right." Trey said desperately trying to be polite, "Would it be rude to say that I need to be sure that this place is safer than back home."

"No." Stuart replied, "You must be honest and you must look after your people. Make sure that this move is right."

Trey nodded. It was an effort but he had to add something.

"Thank you." he said, "Those shovels. We can make the blades but we have no wood. Ours are all metal."

"Make the blades." Stuart said, "We can sort the handles."

"I thought I was going to kill you. I'm glad I was wrong." Trey said,

"So am I." Stuart chuckled, "Learn their language because you're going to have to teach your people."

"The necklace." Trey said, "Only I can own one. I'll comply."

As Trey hurried off to talk to the villagers Dave looked up and smiled.

"Can you take some more 21st century business?" he asked.

"Go on." Stuart replied.

"I'm going to stay here again tonight and I want to stay in phase so I'll be away from home for the night." Dave said, "Mum and Dad are threatening to come round and 'discuss my options' as they put it. They suddenly like Sally because she wants me to go university as well. I haven't told them that but I've already applied to the Open University to read law."

"Law?" Stuart exclaimed, "How come?"

"Because it's got nothing to do with the portals." Dave

explained, "I'll fail or succeed on my own. If you'll let Zach and Andy be your buddy on the simpler journeys then I'll have plenty of time to study. If I qualify I'd like to take up the cases other lawyers won't."

"And you're still doing it your way." Stuart said.

"What do you think?" Dave asked uncharacteristically nervous.

"You've got my support." Stuart said, "I bet Brian will be all for it or do you want to resign."

"No way." Dave shouted making everyone look then more quietly he continued, "I'll always watch your back, Stuart."

"OK." Stuart said, "There is a problem though."

"What's that?" Dave asked.

"Are ex-slaves allowed to become lawyers. You'll have to check Athenian law in Demetrius' time."

"Fuck off." Dave retorted, "I volunteered so it doesn't count."

"I'm still worried about involving Zach." Stuart said, "He's too young."

"I read that essay." Dave said, "He'll love travelling as much as we do. So will Andy. Joe Milnes is happy because he can say that he's done it but it's not really for him and the same with Anthony. Zach could be one of the gang."

"Until I have to tell his parents that he was eaten by a crocodile and his remains were buried five thousand years ago."

"They're a village family." Dave said, "Get your dad to talk to them."

Stuart nodded.

It was Zach who sidled up to him next with Andy giggling happily not far behind.

"I was helping in the fields." he said, "But they keep touching me. They want me to do stuff."

"While you should be working, do you mean?" Stuart asked.

"No, they want to play with…" he trailed off, blushing furiously as he glanced down his body.

"And you're used to going somewhere private with someone." Stuart said, "But these people don't have much privacy. They also think that sex is a part of life and perfectly normal. All I can say is, remember the time-line and don't get some girl pregnant. Oh and Andy, try to understand Zach's problems. You need to learn our ways just as much as he needs to learn yours."

Andy caught the hint of anger in Stuart's voice and nodded solemnly.

"Zach blushes so easily." Andy said, "And this is my past so

I've got to be careful as well. Supposing we said that we're boyfriends and Sobek makes us very jealous if we play with anyone else."

Zach blushed again.

"It wouldn't be true though, would it?" he said quietly, "I'm not gay."

"I like girls as well." Andy said, "But it would be against Ma'at to split us up."

Suddenly Zach burst out laughing and took Andy's hand.

"I've heard of going where no one has gone before but this is ridiculous." he said, "Come on, lover boy."

Dave was laughing as well.

"Maybe Zach is too young." he said, "What do your feelings tell you?"

"One good thing." Stuart replied, "Trey doesn't want to live in a cave any more. He's allowing Ipy to show him how to plant the crops."

For once, Stuart was happy at how events were unfolding. Towards dusk, when the sun was low Trey had slipped off the protective robe that Stuart had given him and worked in the fields as naked as the others. Even so his shoulders were red and sore when he settled down with the others in the cool of the evening.

"How will I order my people to leave the cave if I burn so quickly?" he asked.

"The robes worked." Stuart said, "You were just a bit eager. Go home tonight and tomorrow we'll fetch you again. See if you can't persuade a dozen or so people to come with you tomorrow. We've got clothes for that number."

"Persuade?" Trey queried then nodded, "I and my people must adapt. They cannot follow blindly if they must learn."

"You're adapting better than I expected." Stuart said, "How come you're willing to surrender your authority so easily."

"I am the last Lord of Traste." he replied, "Unless I can produce a son there will be no more and no one to lead the people. I see life here, I want to live and maybe my wife will prove more fertile here."

"I hope so." Stuart replied, "Let's get you home and tomorrow, Ipy will show you how to build a home for her."

The following day Trey returned with volunteers. Two panicked at the last moment and bolted for the safety of the portal, one was physically sick while the others were obviously scared, looking on in awe as with Trey, stepped confidently out into the sunlight. It took them all morning to get used to their surroundings but then they were willing to trade the local's hospitality for working alongside them in the fields. That night, two men and three women refused to return to the cave. Instead Ipy took them along the rivers edge to an uncultivated area and the following day they were busy building the first hut of a new village.

Dave went home, braced for a row with his family. Sally might like the idea of him studying from home but it would mean that his parents had failed in the second part of their plan. He would still be 'labouring' for Stuart as they put it. He insisted that he was fit for light duties, which he interpreted as sitting in the shade of a tree, finding answers to questions about irrigation. Stuart and Brian examined the data from the portals very carefully and were reassured that there were no anomalies. In fact there was so little turbulence in the time-lines that Stuart wondered whether they really were reinforcing history rather changing it.

Zach and Andy were obviously firm friends. They spent time in the village and Zach gradually introduced Andy to his school friends. The translator was bringing Andy up to date on the core curriculum subjects and, to Stuart's amusement, Zach made him practice using a pen or pencil each day. He was obviously taking his task of looking after Andy very seriously. He was keeping their secrets and although easily embarrassed he did his best to understand Andy's ways so Stuart was less worried about him being involved.

Over the next few weeks it was James who was busiest. He controlled the portals as the inhabitants of the ancient biosphere steadily made the journey to the sunlit paradise of ancient Egypt. By contrast, Stuart found himself with little to do.

He took to joining Demetrius for lunch at the pub then relaxing as Demetrius hurried off to work in his forge.

"He's a clever young man." Bill said one day, "Those Greek lessons of his are so popular. I could believe that he came from ancient Greece, he's so knowledgeable."

"The village could believe a lot of things about us." Stuart replied, "I don't like the gossip about us."

"Don't worry about it, lad." Bill said, "The restaurant's so full of tourists, we've had to extend the lunch session. Demetrius is going to keep a few here shopping at his forge. He's developing some nice lines. You don't think I'm going to kill the golden goose do you?"

"OK, that's you." Stuart said, "What about the rest of the village?"

"Hilda and Janet do their stained glass and now that young Al has teamed up with them, he's getting quite good with his glass blowing. The garage is doing more and more vintage car restorations and I could go on." Bill said, "It's all financed by you and Brian. You need more staff so you've taken young Zach on. Is Dave training him and Andy up while his shoulder mends? I reckon it's better than hiring a couple of know-it-all incomers."

"You don't see Andy as an incomer." Stuart asked.

"He's another stranger like Gable and Demetrius isn't he." Bill said, "He's never been in here alone but Vi from the shop reckons he's more used to haggling than paying. She reckons he's a good lad though if a bit cheeky."

"Going back to Demetrius. Is there a problem with him?"

"You know Demetrius." Bill replied, "He fusses over every detail and that Professor Steadman puts him down. He has to work within Health and Safety and the rest so he does adapt things but a couple of students reckon he knows more than the professor."

If Stuart felt easier with his conversation with Bill, then he was a little concerned when he bumped into Zach's mother as she was coming out of the shop.

"Thank you so much for what you're doing for Zachary." she gushed, "He's a different boy. He's coming up for his exam year and we were worried whether he would settle down. He's talking about university now and is saying that you and Mr. Chapman would sponsor him. You don't let him do anything dangerous though, do you? Dave Hilford was badly injured wasn't he?"

"Yes and I am worried about Zach working for us." Stuart said, "We don't take unnecessary risks but there are some in our line of work."

"My husband spoke to your dad about it." she said, "Apparently Richard was ready for you to shut down completely after Dave's accident but he's calmed down now, hasn't he? How dangerous is it?"

"It's difficult to say." Stuart replied, "What do you know of our work?"

"The rumours say that you visit other planets." she said.

"The rumours make a good cover story." Stuart said, "Dave's accident was the equivalent of coming across a drunk on one. It was the sort of accident we just didn't expect."

"Put like that, I can see what you mean." Zach's mother said, "Zach says that he's Dave's gopher, you know, he runs errands for him and looks after him. How dangerous is that?"

Stuart thought for a moment, "I think the transport we use is safer than if Zach was to cycle to school every day. Tourists don't appreciate how narrow the lanes are around here. He's made himself popular with the people he's working with and they'd try to protect him if there was trouble but it's not completely safe."

"You hear of such terrible accidents in a factory even." she said thoughtfully, "Please look after him. He's threatened to join the army as soon as he's able and to be honest I'd prefer him to be working for you. At least we know where he is."

Stuart felt positively cheerful as he settled down to work. They all tried keeping their body clocks to village time and Stuart was in luck, he could work at his site on the Lizard Planet. He loved the almost constant spring like weather and he could always stop and chat with locals, play some sort of ball game, or swim in the nearby river if he wanted a break. For a time it was in phase with the village and he would be able to spend most of his day there.

While he was content that the Trastes, the survivors from Earth's biosphere would settle down, he wished that he could understand their dramatic change of attitude more. In fact it was Lord Trey who had changed the most. Stuart had watched as he gathered the inhabitants of the biosphere around him and spoke to them.

"Today I stood out in the sun." he announced to astonished gasps, "My shoulder is red because I am not used to it. Tomorrow it will be even redder because I'm going back but soon my skin will stop being white and I will be able to walk around all day feeling it's heat. We all know that this place is dying even if the last Council order forbade you from discussing it but we no longer have to preserve hope. As the last Lord of Traste I order that you look at the truth. We will take part in creating a new civilisation."

He paused, glancing at Stuart before he continued, "The Lords of Traste are natural leaders and will lead in the creation of this new world, but we must remember what our ancestors taught us. We must all look, listen and learn and those around us will know more of our new land than us."

Despite himself, Stuart was impressed. Something of their scientific background had survived and apart from some 'face saving bull', Trey's attitude fitted in with the Egyptian culture that was developing. Stuart doubted that Trey had the mental capacity to become a great leader but again, he realised that he could be wrong. Trey had spoken simply but he had got his people's attention.

Stuart was even more impressed as Trey concluded, "I need twelve of you to accompany me tomorrow even if you spend all day hiding in the shade watching me enjoy the life our ancestors had. The rest will gather the last of our seed ready to carry to the new world. Then they will open as many forges as they can and begin making knives and spades and forks for the farms that we will create."

Some cave dwellers looked unhappy at Trey's instructions. Stuart caught complaints about abandoning crops before they could be gathered.

Stuart wandered between small groups that were talking about Trey's speech. He approached a soldier who had ejected him on his first visit.

"Remember me?" Stuart asked.

The soldier stared at him, frowning, "We sent you outside, a week ago. How did you live?"

"I live near the place that Lord Trey was describing." Stuart replied.

"You want revenge because we turned you into a ghost." the soldier said.

"Could a ghost do this?" Stuart asked, slapping the soldier's face, not hard, just enough so that he could feel it. Before the soldier could react he asked, "Well?"

"I could kill you for that." the soldier exclaimed angrily.

"Can you kill a ghost?" Stuart asked and stood, obviously expecting an answer.

Finally the soldier shook his head.

"I don't want vengeance because you didn't hurt me." Stuart said, "I'm here to help. Will you let me?"

"What about those crops?" the soldier asked, "We're already close to starvation."

"Volunteer for tomorrow." Stuart said, "You'll see."

Stuart was unwilling to stay on ancient Earth for too long so he left as soon as he could, but he left knowing that the Trastians were in a worse position than he had thought. Stuart hoped that they were ready to escape starvation and would follow Trey. Either way, he had done what he could so he increasingly turned his attention to the Mars colonies.

He hesitated because he knew that saving them was a matter of pride. He was respected for rescuing people from certain disaster. True, according to Larik and Merrill, the Kramons intended to colonise his world but he would lose face if he simply abandoned them without giving them a chance. He either had to explain clearly and logically why he left them to their fate or help them. Stuart was human and logic was not enough. His decision had to feel right.

Finally he called his friends together.

"I don't like the Kramons for what they did to Tiy," he began, "and for what they're threatening to do with us. However some of their peasants as they call them were kidnapped and it's possible that others don't agree with their leaders. I want to rescue those who want to be rescued and hope that Larik and Merrill want to stick it out in their caves.

"For once we are interfering in a big way and there's going to be trouble so I want Andy and Zach in school before we start. We'll help anyone who wants a fresh start but it'll be on our terms. Egypt about 3500 BC still seems to be the best place to assimilate them because when the written language appears 500 years later tales of the newcomers will already be lost."

"Can't you change history in another way?" Zach asked, "Supposing my ancestor marries a newcomer instead of their original husband or wife?"

"So far as we can tell, it won't matter." Stuart replied, "It would make a terrific difference if we changed your grandparents but over the centuries your genes are modified by your surroundings. You never know who's going to have affairs, there're all sorts of things. There does seem to be a tendency for different histories to come together so I'm not too worried."

"What about Andy?" Zach persisted.

"Andy's people settled on the other side of the delta. That's 240 kilometres away and this was at a time when people rarely left their villages let alone crossed dangerous waterways."

"It could happen though." Zach said.

"We'll be watching the arrivals to make sure that they're properly assimilated. " Stuart said, "There'll be a few small anomalies but once they settle down then again events can take their course."

"Stuart's right about visitors." Andy said, "Look at how excited we got when you visited. It doesn't happen that often and our world was different. I might get a few extra uncles or aunts but my ancestors would still have ended up fucking each other."

"Andy!" Zach exclaimed, "You can't say that to adults."

"Why not?" Andy asked then grinned, "Sorry I forgot. You pretend that babies appear by magic and no one has sex."

"Zach's got his work cut out assimilating you into our world."

Brian laughed, "But Stuart's right. The arrivals won't suddenly invent the sailing ship and make travel easier. They won't have the tools or the resources to support the builders. I don't see any problems."

"OK. We've got to operate in the time between Larik and Merrill's trip to 1925 and their next trip, presumably to our time." Stuart said, "Stopping that trip will cause anomalies and we have trouble knowing what happened after."

"You mean they'll make the trip as things stand but once we interfere, things won't stand and that causes a paradox or an anomaly." Dave said.

Stuart nodded, "Don't even try to repeat that. The colonies are getting near the end so they might be as reasonable as Trey was."

"So that's when we're going to talk to them." Dave said.

"When I talk to them." Stuart said, "You won't be fit in time."

"So you'll be taking James." Brian said before Dave could protest.

"Yeah, if he wants to come but I'm thinking I should go alone this time." Stuart said and as the others started to protest he added, "Hear me out. The easiest way of handling this is to approach Larik or Merrill. They're going to arrest me and haul me off to their leaders."

"They could just as easily kill you." Richard interrupted.

"That's why I want James at the controls. He can react with a probe faster than any of us. I'll wear a protective vest, James will block their line of fire and distract them and Dave can materialise a portal as close as possible so I can be away before anyone recovers."

"Why don't I just plonk the portal between you." Dave asked.

"If you can do it without squashing anyone then go ahead." Stuart said.

"And I could be standing by in case you're wounded." Richard said.

"Yes and don't forget we've got time travel so you can plan a rescue and still get to me in seconds."

"You know, I still own all this so technically, I'm in charge and could stop you." Brian said, "Explain again why you want to do this."

"The Dambons gave us a mystery." Stuart replied, "OK so we solved the mystery easily enough except that we don't really know what happened to the Martian colonists. And I am concerned for the people they kidnapped."

"Why can't you send them home?" Richard asked.

"Because of the knowledge they've picked up." Stuart replied,

"The further forward in time they come from, the more it could be tied in with contemporary knowledge and technology. If someone demands it then we'll try but we have to protect the time line."

Stuart paused, "Which is why I'm concerned that I got a letter from Freddie the other day."

He paused again, seeing his audience's startled looks.

"It's how it seems." he added, "Or more accurately I've come across a time paradox. You see I found the letter in that box Anthony gave me and I'm sure it wasn't there before yet if I think about it I can find a past when I did."

"That's the one thing you were trying to avoid, isn't it?" Brian asked.

Stuart nodded.

"What does it say?" Zach asked.

"I don't know, the message on the envelope told me to wait until now."

"Very well," James said, "We'll wait here while you go and read it."

Stuart nodded and hurried off. They had been holding their meeting on the Lizard planet so it was easy to disappear into a grove of trees and settle down in the shade.

Dear Stuart,

I'm writing this letter in 1936, a couple of years after coming down from Oxford where I got a first in maths. Unfortunately one or two of my dissertations centred around theoretical concepts in time travel. Don't worry, there was nothing that could be translated into a portal, they focussed on the type of multidimensional universe required to avoid paradoxes. However they were enough to get me invited to expand my theories and take a PHD which I don't think happened before.

Remember I did get some idea of my future just talking to Anthony and I liked the idea of becoming a schoolmaster until the next war but it doesn't seem to be happening now.

I wrote this letter for two reasons. Firstly when I'm dozing, I don't get memories but I have a strong feeling and half remembered dreams that Dave is injured and you need an adult to act as a buddy on your trips. If there's any truth in them then I'm volunteering. I belonged to the university RAFVR squadron so I hope

that I'm a little more disciplined than I was.
My second reason is to mention my alternative memories. Are they important?
I intend spending tomorrow 29th September sitting quietly in the folly my father built. If you would care to visit, I would be glad to see you."
As always, your friend, Freddie.

Stuart sat considering the letter before returning to the others and reading it to them.

"Are you going?" James asked.

"I think I should." Stuart said, "But should I take him up on his offer?"

"At one point we seemed to have ever more helpers." James said, "Then they just vanished. Even Freddie and Tony went home without any drama. I've wondered about it."

"How is that relevant?" Brian asked.

"I don't know if it is." James replied, "I'm not even sure whether this rescue mission is a good idea."

"Luckily Freddie's tomorrow can be my next year so I'm going to sleep on it." Stuart announced, "Tomorrow I'm going to have word with Joe Milnes. Wheat originates from a bit further East from where we're working so someone had to introduce it.

Following his plan, the next day Stuart found himself sitting in a comfortable but old fashioned sitting room. The small television was tucked away in a corner and Joe's wife's sewing basket seemed to take pride of place. However, Stuart could imagine her complaining about the untidy piles of books surrounding Joe's chair.

"How's Dave?" Joe asked as they settled.

"Complaining because he can't come with me and can't play football." Stuart replied, "How about you? It was a pretty traumatic trip for you too."

"Judy's at the church hall this afternoon." Joe said, "I haven't told her anything but she knows something's wrong."

"You don't still feel bad about having a bit of fun, do you?"

"It's all right for you, you're used to it all." Joe said, "I was sitting drinking while Dave nearly got killed. I should have known better."

"It wasn't your fault." Stuart said, "We need a farming expert on this project and you are ideal."

"You need people who are on the ball." Joe said, "Not someone who settles in the pub to chew the fat."

"It's what we do need." Stuart said, "And you were in the market getting us the supplies we needed, not in the pub. You were also getting us friends."

"Same thing." Joe retorted, "I didn't like seeing Dave injured like that."

"No one did." Stuart said, "Even if you'd stayed sober, Dave would still have been wounded. You were making friends with fellow farmers and know more than anyone what's needed to set up a village there. Dedi was the exception and not even his comrades expected him to attack Dave like that. You know Andy, most of the folk we met were as friendly as him."

"I don't know." Joe said, "Whenever we talk about going on holiday, I worry about arranging for the milking and Judy reckons that her committees would all fold up without her so we end up not going. I shouldn't have seen it as a break, should I?"

"You could have one if you don't mind going alone." Stuart said, "You could spend a month somewhere and we'd get you back in time for milking but we do need your help."

"Doing what?" Joe asked.

"Introducing wheat to Egypt and teaching them to make bread and beer."

Joe stared at him, "They already know…"

He paused, remembering where he had been, "You mean we'll be going to an even earlier Egypt. Aren't we going to change history?"

"No. Just anticipate it by a year or so." Stuart replied, "How would you fancy trading new skills for teaching newcomers more traditional ones?"

Joe smiled, "You not such a bad trader yourself, you don't need me."

"Supposing I said, I'd assign Dave to buddy up with you." Stuart said, "You wouldn't be left on your own again and it would give Dave something to do."

"You're a good lad, Stuart." Joe said, "You shouldn't be wasting your time on me. I'll be OK."

"I forget what a jolt to the system our sort of travel can be." Stuart said, "I don't like you being so upset by events because you were just blending in with other farmers."

"I'll think about it." Joe said, "Maybe I'll have a chat with young David first so don't rush me."

Satisfied that Joe was happier Stuart was ready to meet with Freddie though he visited Dave first.

"I've got most of the feeling back." Dave said, "I can lift it higher every day. Dr. Tobias thinks that my recovery's a bit slow though but he's not worried. The main thing is I still get tired easily."

"Does he know why you're slow recovering?" Stuart asked.

"He reckons the artificial blood may have done something. Dave explained, "And Terzon methods are a bit harsh for a human. They saved my life, I'm going to recover but the treatment needs fine tuning for humans."

"Okay." Stuart said, "Joe wants to see you. He feels bad about you being injured while he was enjoying himself. I'd like you to buddy up with him on a couple of trips and help him relax. I'll take Zach and Andy with me to see Freddy."

Stuart paused, "Joe's already got the spare parts he wanted. Since they're already delivered, I'll ask Freddie to order them at the right time."

"My own team." Dave smiled, "I like it."

"I want my old team back." Stuart said, "I still wonder how we got involved with all these kids."

Stuart was surprised to discover that Zach and Andy had gone swimming in the public pool in Howkbury. Cycling was still a novelty for Andy and for once it was Zach who felt at home, guiding Andy through the urban traffic. Again in the pool, it was Zach who felt comfortable wearing shorts while Andy found the briefest of speedos restrictive and uncomfortable. Even a swimming pool where everyone was having fun was an alien world for Andy as he learned what was acceptable and what was not.

They both enjoyed themselves though, and Zach was relieved that Andy remembered that 21st century kids don't have sex. Most 21st century adults would have said that the opposite was true but Zach still blushed at the memories of the relaxed attitudes, Andy's people had.

Both boys were eager to take another trip with Stuart so Freddie was surprised at who Stuart's travelling companions were but he made them all welcome.

"You do look smaller, Stuart." Freddie chuckled, "But it's only been a couple of months for you hasn't it."

"How are you, Freddie?" Stuart said, "I'm supposed to say, 'my how you have grown'. You're older than me now as well, which is weird."

"So I can say, 'and what have you been up to, young man?'" Freddie riposted.

"Oh the usual stuff." Stuart replied, "Dave was attacked by a soldier in ancient Egypt and nearly killed. I'd love to know how you found out about it."

"I don't know but I've got a theory." Freddie replied, "When you returned me and Reggie you spoke to my father who was also my friend Tony."

"Go on." Stuart said.

Well that conversation affected Earth's time-line through your personal time-line, mine, Reggie's and Dad's. It wasn't serious but it did cause minor ripples rather than major anomalies or paradox's. Somehow I took maths more seriously and did better at university. I've studied the two memories I seem to have and seem to remember having to choose between finishing an article I was reading and going for a game of tennis. I chose to read and that's when I started becoming aware of an alternate history."

"I told you about my jumps to alternate worlds." Stuart said, "I didn't like them and time never married up so you could be describing a variation on that."

"Have we changed history much?" Freddie asked.

"No." Stuart replied, "Maybe on your personal level but not for anyone else. Brian's read your papers. He reckons that they were good but harmless. You focussed on the nature of the universe rather than seeking a practical use."

"He liked your papers on cryptology as well." Stuart continued, "It's surprising that the one that was picked up was your one on switching."

"No one's picked up on it yet." Freddie said, "And I'm thinking of a paper on cryptology. I haven't started it yet."

"Whoops." Stuart exclaimed, "I shouldn't have mentioned it."

"My problem is I think in terms of computers." Freddie said, "I learnt about logic gates and the like but they don't mean anything to anyone. I've met an Alan Turing who's also written papers on computing machines, but he doesn't see how to turn my ideas into a practical machine. To be honest, neither do I at the moment."

"It probably does explain how you were sent to Bletchley Park though." Stuart said, "Alan remembered you and your mathematical skills."

"You've heard of him." Freddie exclaimed.

"The work he did during the war was highly secret but in my time he's beginning to be recognised as the father of computing." Stuart said.

"I've heard gossip about him." Freddie said quietly.

"What sort." Stuart asked.

"Nothing that worries me but he and you could get on well together."

"And you can understand better than me what happened when he was arrested."

"Ah." Freddie said, "Poor chap. Now what about my other question, do you need my help?"

"I'd like to but I'm not taking you." Stuart said, "You've proved that nothing is set in stone and I need you to follow the life we expect. I can't risk you being killed."

"Is it that dangerous?" Freddie asked.

"Hopefully no." Stuart replied, "But I can't risk it."

Suddenly Stuart could see the eleven year old boy as Freddie struggled to hide his disappointment.

"I sometimes wish that I had asked you if I could have stayed longer." Freddie said, "It was strange, it took time to realise that I really was on Mars and the whole thing was so overwhelming. I needed time to take it all in. I somehow thought that I could take a break then go back. Stupid, wasn't it?"

"No." Stuart said, "I think you were a little homesick and it must have seemed all wrong that you were getting your dad into trouble."

Freddie nodded, "As I said, it gradually crept up on me that it was real and I just wanted father to be my father and not my younger brother, if you see what I mean. Are you sure that I can't help?"

"I'm worried about the time line," Stuart explained, "but you know that."

"OK. You've just said that whatever gets me to that Bletchley Park is in place and I am married expecting my second child."

"You've been busy." Stuart grinned.

"Let's just say that I got a bit too accepting of the social attitudes I saw in your time. Marrying a village girl because I got her pregnant caused quite a scandal but it's working out very well. I could only say this to you but the sex is fantastic, she allows me my interest in science while I act very 21st century and allow her to indulge her passion for socialism."

"I thought your family was much too capitalist for the Labour party."

"It is. Everything goes quiet if I'm around, but they accept that Emma's the victim of old fashioned conventions so she had to get married. Crazy isn't it."

"It seems to keep everyone happy." Stuart laughed, "And you're claiming that you can't change the time line significantly."

"If I understand things correctly this conversation could make me thoughtful so that I step out in front of the village bus, get run over and killed. On the other hand, not going with you could make me resentful so I join fighter command for the adventure I want. You're risking the time line just by being here, aren't you?"

Stuart nodded.

"Probably." he conceded, "And getting you killed could lose us the next war."

"No it couldn't." Freddie exclaimed, "I'm not that bright. I wouldn't have got a first if I hadn't learnt a bit from you."

"That's selling yourself short." Stuart said, "You might have done better without 21st century data clouding the issue."

"But it does so I'm not likely to contribute much."

"What about Emma if you come with me." Stuart asked.

"Good try. I've travelled through time" Freddie laughed, "I'm terribly unpunctual because I've still got this idea that I can arrive at the right time no matter when I leave."

"Look there's no reason why you shouldn't come back and visit for a time." Stuart conceded.

"Come up to the house." Freddie offered and Stuart nodded.

"Dad will be pleased to see you again. Reggie's squadron is based down on the south coast. We don't see much of him. His dad resigned and opened a taxi firm a year or two ago. Phillips is still butler during the day. During the evening he joins Dad and they're both amateur radio enthusiasts."

"How about Selena?" Stuart asked.

"She prefers her cottage." Freddie smiled, "The village boys are warned to stay away from her, but there's always one digging her garden or servicing her car. She's discreet enough to have very heavy curtains so no one asks what services she offers in return."

"You mentioned it in a letter to me." Stuart laughed, "She sounds happier."

"I'd say that she still misses her fiancé terribly. Everything she does is to forget the pain."

"I'm sorry." Stuart said.

"It's not your fault, it was the bloody war and I'm waiting for the next. That's one way time travel is a curse."

"I've never travelled forward in time." Stuart said, "I'm not sure if I want to."

The conversation petered out as they reached the hall. Stuart recognised Sir Anthony's study and as he glanced around Sir Anthony's face lit up in delighted recognition.

"Stuart, my dear chap." he exclaimed, "How are you? You haven't aged a bit."

He paused, "Of course, you probably haven't. You're still battling Martians I take it."

"It's good to see you again, Sir Anthony." Stuart said, though it's only been a few weeks for me."

"So do you need our help again?"

"Freddie wrote to me, offering his services and I'm trying to persuade him that it's too risky."

"Posted in a tin box, I trust." Sir Anthony laughed, "I hope it wasn't delivered by the post office."

"No. It was by tin box. Delivery the next century guaranteed." Stuart replied.

"I understand your concerns." Sir Anthony said, "And I've often wondered how our family became so involved. Freddie's work is obscure in this time and never fully appreciated or understood so are the risks all that great?"

"Maybe not." Stuart conceded, "I just don't understand it enough."

"This may sound old fashioned to you, but many young men of our class see military service as a duty to their country. Since you have introduced him to the concept allow him to do his duty to his planet."

"Put like that, I can't really refuse."

"You would if you thought the risk was too great." Sir Anthony said, "Again, a member of my class should not say this. I'll be worried about Freddie all the time he's with you though I do understand that a youngster needs an adventure before he settles down. Look after him please."

"There is something that you might do for me." Stuart said, "Order these parts in 1968. They've already been delivered by your great, great-grandson so it's done somehow."

"Leave it with us." Sir Anthony said, "Now tell me, how is Dave and who are these lads?"

"Just a couple of village boys." Stuart chuckled, "You might be interested in Andy's village though."

Andy and Zach became restless as the adults chatted and

wandered into the village. For Zach he could appreciate yet another trip into the past and for once without supervision. For Andy, the clothes, horse and cart, or odd car were not old fashioned and a reminder that they had travelled through time. Instead they were just a variation of his new world. However both boys were fascinated as they explored the countryside beyond the village. They stood on a bridge and watched as an express train roared along the track below, drenching them in steam and soot as it hurtled under the bridge.

"That was a train. It picks up passengers at stations. Why didn't it stop for those." Andy said, pointing to the station on the other side of the bridge.

"It's an express." Zach replied, "Come on. I've never been on a steam train before. Let's take a ride to the next station and back."

"Shouldn't we ask Stuart?" Andy asked.

"What? Scared?" Zach teased but stopped as Andy nodded.

"Let's see what the fare is." Zach said, "We'll wait on the platform near the gate and see how you feel then."

It was evening before two thoroughly excited and, for the time, ill mannered boys burst into Sir Anthony's study describing their day.

"There were so many people running it." Zach exclaimed, "Yet it all seemed so slow and leisurely."

"Slow!" Andy exclaimed, "Those expresses would have frightened Anhur when they galloped past."

"Who is Anhur?" Sir Anthony asked.

"The god of war and hunting." Andy said then without thinking added, "King Narmer is building a new temple for him."

"King Narmer?" Sir Anthony queried again.

"I told you that you'd find Andy's village interesting." Stuart said, "King Narmer is associated with founding the first Egyptian dynasty."

"You can tell me all about it over dinner." Sir Anthony said, "One good thing about entertaining time travellers, they can always make time."

By the end of the school's summer holiday, Dave was almost back to full strength. He spent the day with Trey's people and the neighbouring villages, helping and advising them as they experimented with an irrigation system while beginning his law course. He provided a base for Joe Milnes who was introducing wheat and trying his hand at beer making. However he had to use contemporary resources so he was learning as much as the locals.

Dr. Tobias also visited Trey's new village, monitoring their health.

"Brain function is definitely impaired by their exposure to radiation." he said, "However there's little sign of genetic damage. I'd need to do a study to find out why, but there's evidence on Earth that cells are resistant to low level radiation. Levels in the cave hover around the top end of that level but I think that they've got away with it."

"Rickets is a major problem, they were too scared of sunlight to produce any vitamin D in the skin and their diet was lacking a lot of the vitamins and minerals they needed. I'd say that their health is going to improve dramatically though."

"What about mutations though." Stuart asked, "I know what you said but they were still exposed to radiation."

"There could still be a lot of stillborn children and a good few with birth defects. It's the undamaged ones that will produce their descendants and I expect increasing numbers of children to be born completely healthy."

Satisfied that the Trastes were settling in, Stuart turned his attention to the Martian colonies.

"I think we should aim for settling them near Abydos." Stuart said, "We can get friendly with a village near there, it's 500 kilometres from Trey's people and we'll go about fifty years later."

"Why the time difference?" James asked.

"I'm not sure." Stuart admitted, "But Trey's people are being assimilated faster than I expected. I think it's a combination of feeling safe, knowing that their people have another chance and good old fashioned sunlight. Anyway in a few years time, they'll just be another group of settlers. They might want to spend time checking out other settlements at first but I don't reckon that the second and third generations will see much urgency.

"The Kramons will have Earth's gravity to deal with as well as settling in and, developing their own farming and irrigation systems. When they get around to looking for the Trastes they'll already be more Egyptian than Kramon. Again there won't be much as much urgency and the Trastes will be so well assimilated that they'll be difficult to find. If they arrived at the same time then they'd be more noticeable and be more likely to find each other."

James nodded, "You could be right. It would turn into a race again."

Dave can take Andy and Zach to help establish relations in Egypt, Freddie and I will tackle the Martians. James, are you sure that you don't want to come with us?"

"No," James replied, "Brian and Richard are happier with their regular jobs and I can understand why. I'm happy as the bus driver. I've been thinking about security and this may sound crazy but I think Zach and Andy should have a training programme. The theory is that if they feel part of the team then they'll look out for it more. I could also keep an eye on Andy, I do worry about him."

"It'll also mean that you do the worrying about kids running around all over the universe and time." Stuart said, "Go for it. We can do the bigger stuff while they're at school. Monday morning, I'm visiting Larik and Merrill."

Despite his comments Stuart did not mind Andy and Zach's involvement as much as he thought he would. Andy was a useful guide and Zach's excitement was infectious. Although they were both boisterous they took security seriously and even Zach's mother had the idea that he spent his time playing on computers.

Sally was delighted that Dave spent his afternoons at home studying and happy that Zach and Andy would call in after school and settle down to do their homework around the same table that Dave was working on. Neither did she wonder why Dave and the boys spent Saturdays at the quarry. Sally never guessed that it was so that they could spend a week near Abydos.

Travelling to ancient Egypt could hardly be called routine but Dave was used to checking out possible landing sites and he could greet strangers in a relaxed, affable manner that showed that he was at home with his surroundings. He traded sweets and chocolate for a chance to relax and chat while Andy and Zach often helped in the fields chatting to youngsters around their age.

The villagers accepted them as wizards which explained Dave's studies as he sat in the shade of a tree, willing to pass the time with anyone who wanted to stop and chat. It also explained why they travelled through a metal ring.

Interludes

With Stuart happier with Andy and Zach's involvement, Andy proved to be a useful guide and Zach's excitement was infectious. Although they were both boisterous they took security seriously and even Zach's mother had the idea that he spent his time playing on computers.

Sally was delighted that Dave spent his afternoons at home studying and happy that Zach and Andy would call in after school and settle down to do their homework around the same table that Dave was working on. Neither did she wonder why Dave and the boys spent Saturdays at the quarry. She never guessed that it was so that they could spend a week near Abydos.

Travelling to ancient Egypt could hardly be called routine but Dave was used to checking out possible landing sites and he could greet strangers in a relaxed, affable manner that showed that he was at home with his surroundings. He traded sweets and chocolate for a chance to relax and chat while Andy and Zach often helped in the fields chatting to youngsters around their age.

Although Andy did settle in at school and made rapid progress they did have problems. Sometimes it was little things such as why did Zach become progressively more tanned as summer faded? When he started, Andy was obviously well behind in subjects like maths but he caught up at a phenomenal rate. Zach had been fond of sports and had been average in class. Again his work improved rapidly and he found himself top of the class.

Wisely they left their translators at home but doing homework they amassed massive amounts of data and they had trouble with class discussions where it was impossible to remember the limits to what their knowledge should be.

They attributed school work problems to their Saturday job, supposedly sweeping and cleaning the quarry workshop but being taught how to use the powerful computers installed there. Even so fifteen year olds were not supposed to understand quantum physics and the teaching staff remained concerned.

However, their classmates started seeing them as nerds and not cool which could have upset them but being a little isolated did help them to avoid slipping up.

On their Saturday trips to Abydos a villager, a veteran of minor skirmishes with bandit gangs, taught the village boys including Andy and Zach how to handle a sword and use the bow and arrow. They all took it as seriously as modern boys take sports practice. For Andy it was a reminder of home while Zach felt welcome by being included, and it led to an odd confrontation at home.

Andy and Zach spent a lot of time with Demetrius, Andy in particular had something in common with a fellow 'time immigrant'. However, where Andy threw himself into 21st Century life, Demetrius was more introspective and nervous of the world. He got on with Bill, the pub landlord and Demetrius' forge proved to be a great tourist attraction. Obviously children could not be allowed near molten metal but Demetrius could adapt to the modern world enough to show them how to make latex and silicon moulds for him to cast.

His next feature had been the village well. Children could sit beside it, play and drink from it as they wished or even paddle in it. The modern reality was that water flowed from a tap, they were issued with plastic cups printed with suitable Greek frescos and there was a table of squashes and juices to flavour the water. It proved popular with children a little too old for the Wendy-houses and slides that Bill provided, and those who were a little too young to want to sit with the adults all the time.

Bill placed the 'well' in the middle of the garden arranging the seats around it so that it created a village square effect and parents could keep an eye on their children.

Demetrius also had a stall where he displayed his own wares. It might not have gone any further if Zach and Andy had not been visiting Demetrius when Professor Steadman arrived with a group of students. Now on a Friday afternoon, most people think more of the approaching weekend than work and to his credit Professor Steadman considered the trips a good way of enlivening his last tutorial of the week. Far less to his credit, he found it an opportunity to begin drinking far earlier than he should have done, and an opportunity to belittle another expert: Demetrius.

One afternoon, James was sitting in the garden watching a tutorial while waiting for Andy. He was a little concerned at some of Professor Steadman's remarks but he was not really taking it in.

Andy, Zach and a couple of other boys arrived. James wondered why Andy was carrying some cheap, plastic, toy swords.

"Hi Uncle." Andy greeted him, "I'm glad you could make it. Will you take us through those moves we were shown last week, please?"

James recognised that Andy had not mentioned who or where he had been taught anything so he replied, "I know I was watching but I'm no swordsman. I'm used to a Remington."

"Yeah but you all learn funny stuff as well." one of the newcomers piped up, "I bet you know something."

Brian's going to love that remark. James thought to himself.

"Demetrius will let us handle the swords he makes." the other newcomer said, "But only if we know what we're doing. It'll be just like 'Knights and Combats'."

James recognised the reference to some computer game and grinned to himself. The two new boys were interested in their world, not Andy and Zach's.

Now the translators could pass on messages direct between the speeches of people's brains but it was very imprecise but James kept imagining Zach saying, 'the hacking tree'.

"OK." James said, "Those plastic things are okay for practice but real swords are dangerous. We'll wait until Demetrius takes a break and I'll show you."

He noticed Andy smile and nod.

Breaks were frequent enough as Professor Steadman sought to refill his glass but this time his students were more interested in James as he unlocked one of Demetrius' swords and carried it to a tree stump. It already looked as if it had been half chopped away before James swung at it. James had chopped wood as one of his childhood chores, had played baseball and was an expert marksman. All three skills came together, he hit the stump in just the right place completely separating the top half from the bottom.

"And that shows the weakness of demonstrations like this." Professor Steadman said, "Bronze or even iron from this time would have snapped with such a blow."

"Demetrius." Andy called out in Athenian, "Have you had a metal analysis done?"

"Yes." Demetrius replied, "Brian compared the results with some museum pieces. The composition's very similar."

But his students were only half listening. They played computer games as well and were obediently lining up for a chance to wield a real sword under expert guidance behind the schoolboys.

"Are you going to have a go, Professor Steadman?" Zach asked, again in Athenian.

"Certainly not." Professor Steadman in English, "And wait for university, young man. Learn the language from an expert. That's not how it was spoken."

"Have you ever heard an ancient Greek speak?" Andy asked.

"No." Professor Steadman conceded, wondering what had started Zach giggling uncontrollably.

Professor Steadman had the good sense not to say any more. Although he considered their accent to be naïve and showed their lack of training it still rattled him that schoolboys and Demetrius could speak the language so well. He might have maintained his reputation by disparaging others but it would be difficult to undermine three such confident speakers.

More importantly his students were listening and were beginning to take sides. If the argument got worse, then he might lose his Friday afternoon drinking session and he would have to work to keep his tutorial going. He had learnt a lesson though and from then on, he spoke much more warmly to Demetrius.

Kramon

Meanwhile, Stuart shifted his base back to the outpost. He used probes to track Larik and Merrill's return from their 1925 meeting and watched as they reported their failure to collect any prisoners. Like the Trastes, the Kramon's dress had a decidedly Egyptian flavour though their tunics seemed also to resemble Roman tunics. It was the decoration that had a definite Egyptian flavour. What Stuart noticed more was their leader's sneering contempt as Larik and Merrill reported their failure.

"I don't like them but it's not their fault they stumbled across us." Stuart said, "Merrill didn't deserve that slap. Let's show them the probe."

All the Ancients stared at the probe as it appeared between them.

"Hi, my name's Stuart." he said, "Sorry Merrill, I didn't mean to get you into trouble but these guys should be listening to you, not having tantrums."

By answer, Merrill's superiors drew a stun-gun and aimed it at the probe, which immediately deactivated as an electric charge crackled around the remote end.

Stuart activated another so that it appeared a few seconds later.

"That wasn't very friendly," he said, "and I was going to visit."

The official fired again. This time the two prongs became stuck in the probe's casing but there was no discharge. Instead the Kramon scarcely had time to drop the gun as it heated up and burst into flames. The probe looked the same but it had a highly insulated and sticky casing that carried electric wires. The wires were able to deliver their own massive charge that overloaded the stun-gun.

"Let's try again." Stuart said, "Hi, I'm Stuart, I know Larik and Merrill, but who are you?"

"Guards." the official yelled, then pointing at Larik and Merrill called out just as loudly, "Arrest those two and find a hammer to smash that thing."

Stuart moved the probe upwards until it was about three metres in the air.

"Guards, fetch a ladder as well." he called out.

The official was spluttering, purple with rage unused to being defied. The guards looked on uncertainly and just as uncertainly pointed their guns at Larik and Merrill. Stuart pointed the probe downwards so it was aimed at the guards.

"I've seen your best shot." he said, "Do you want to see mine."

The guards lowered their weapons.

"Listen to me." Stuart commanded, "I can help you resettle on Earth and you'll help an empire to grow so that it lasts for thousands of years. More importantly your children will grow up in the open air."

"We're going to do that but we won't be helping, we'll rule it and you'll serve." the official shouted.

Stuart had been studying Larik, Merrill and the guards while the official had replied. Larik had shifted closer to the official but the guards were looking even more uncertain, glancing at each other. Merrill remained impassive.

"Why don't you visit and see what I'm offering first." Stuart asked.

"I said that you were ignorant." Larik said, "How can we travel to Earth without acclimatising? We'd be crushed by the gravity."

"And you should listen more carefully." Stuart said, "I said visit not stay. You can see how your children could be playing and exploring. Or do you want them to live in a world of dwindling resources?"

"I'll visit," one of the guards said, "But if I don't return or you lie, we'll know."

"You will not go." the official screamed, "You will not defy the Council of Kramon. You will serve us."

"It's up to you." Stuart said, "We'll have transport waiting by your shuttle."

Leaving James to monitor the probe and work the portal, Stuart hurried through the airlock to stand waiting for the guard who hesitated then hurried towards Stuart. The official had met Larik and Merrill just beyond the airlock to the industrial sector and he stared in disbelief as the guard hurried through the hatch. Barely controlling his temper, he grabbed a gun from the other soldier and chased after the guard.

The official fired, stunning the guard so that even in the Martian gravity he crashed to the ground. Stuart watched horror-struck as the official ran towards his victim and grabbed a tool from his belt. Stuart only saw it briefly as it swung through the air. It looked like a cross between a hammer with a narrow head and a hatchet. It struck the guard's neck who twitched, then lay still.

Stuart froze in horror at what was almost a ritual killing. Whatever the tool was, it had dislocated the victim's spine. The official stood up raising the recharged stun-gun to aim it at Stuart who was still standing, shocked by events.

The official might have fired but Merrill had also followed them. Merrill charged into the official sending him flying but keeping his own balance. He kicked the gun clear then ran for the portal.

It was Freddie who grabbed Stuart, hauling him unceremoniously through the hatch, into the safety of the portal. Freddie was still holding Stuart instinctively preventing him from opening the hatch for Merrill but Stuart shook himself free.

"It's OK." he yelled, "He can't go back."

Merrill clambered in and allowed himself to be guided through the portal. He stepped out into the outpost staring in amazement.

"Welcome to about a thousand years in your future." Stuart said.

Merrill nodded then knelt in front of Stuart.

"I can no longer support the Council of Kramon." he said, "I offer my allegiance to you. I only ask that you rescue my family from Calen's vengeance."

"I take it that Calen is the excitable guy outside." Stuart said.

"Yes my lord." Merrill replied.

"Any idea where they might be?" Stuart asked.

"Yes my lord, they're in our personal shuttle with Larik's family."

"OK, we'll send the portal back to ten seconds after we took you and as close to the shuttle as possible. We can use the probe to distract Calen. How does that sound?"

"Thank you my lord."

"And then we're going to have a long talk." Stuart said.

"Yes my lord." Merrill replied, "I have much to answer for but I do not believe that you will harm my children."

The scale of Merrill's mutiny had left Calen confused and uncertain, hesitating to give orders for fear that others would disobey him. His view was obstructed by a strange circular shimmering patch of air, the rear of the portal, so he was unaware of three women, and ten children aged from about five up to nearly twenty hurrying through the portal.

The outpost could accommodate them all but it seemed decidedly crowded when Stuart returned.

"We're going forwards." Stuart said to Merrill heading for the portal again. James caught the order via translator and Merrill found himself in the same cavern but it was deserted and he could see that the fittings were different.

"This is our time." Stuart explained as he sat down, "You can tell by the gravity that we're still on Mars but we can talk quietly."

"Yes my lord." Merrill replied still standing respectfully in front of Stuart.

"If you can still remember that I'm in charge then please sit down and call me Stuart. Oh, and feel free to disagree with me."

"Thank you, My Lord Stuart." Merrill paused, "That's not what you meant, is it? I remember how the village peasants talked to you."

"At least sit down and relax." Stuart smiled, "I'd like to hear your story."

Merrill tried to obey and as he warmed to his tale so he began to succeed, though he was obviously flustered when his lord actually stood up to pour them some drinks. Although Stuart did not usually drink alcohol during the day he thought that a glass or two of Joe's parsnip wine might help Merrill.

Merrill belonged to the scientific class, following on from his father who had helped developed their dimensional warp technologies. Merrill's father had even switched his allegiance to a council member who was interested in inter-stellar exploration.

"So anyone can switch allegiance to another lord." Stuart asked.

"Before the war, it often happened," Merrill replied, "though it helped if your new master was strong enough to protect you from your previous master's vengeance. In my father's case though, his previous master had no interest in science and was glad to get rid of him."

"And this happened before your world was destroyed. How old are you?"

"In your time-scale, I'm about forty." he paused again, "Yes I see. Don't forget that we're time travellers, it'll become clear."

He paused looking nervously at Stuart, "I apologise. I was rude."

"No you weren't. I hate having my long-winded explanations interrupted as well."

Merrill smiled gratefully as he continued, "My father and a group of his colleagues were genuinely interested in developing space travel but the Council of Kramon could only see the military opportunity of destroying Traste. When the Trastes began building their own Mars bases the Council took it as an insult.

"Larik was in charge of scientific research on Mars and I was posted here as a new assistant just before the war began. I could see that Traste would retaliate if we attacked the Trastian colonies, but Larik was actively engaged in deploying the bombs. Calen's ancestor was on the last ship to leave Earth and was the sole survivor of the Council of Kramon. The colonies were relatively small and Calen's ancestor decreed that he should rule alone until the Triumphal Return as he described the re-colonisation of Earth. Larik was charged with planning it. It took time to sink in just how much damage had been done and that the return was many centuries if not millennia away. Larik was ordered to find a solution and he directed his attention to discovering when Earth would become inhabitable again."

Stuart had noticed a degree of contempt in Merrill's voice whenever he mentioned Larik but now the contempt was replaced by respect as Merrill described his efforts to come up with a workable plan.

"You must remember we did not have the resources to do much research. We only had one ship and we needed to stock the colonies as well as work on Larik's project but somehow we managed. He had an amazing knowledge of projects from all around the world."

Merrill laughed, the contempt returning, "It turned out to be his only talent in science, homing in on other people's work and claiming it for his own. He was a good administrator though and after the war his talents were useful. Anyway we ended up with a hotchpotch of dimensional warp equipment and little chance of developing it further."

As Merrill paused to take a sip of wine, Stuart asked, "What about biology and genetic research?"

Merrill laughed again, "A pipe dream. All of Calen's ancestors and Calen himself saw it as a chance to 'improve' the race and make it stronger but we did not have the facilities except for our own sperm. I'll come back to it if I may."

Stuart nodded.

"I think you know the history of the world. What we didn't expect was the deterioration of the atmosphere. All life was damaged by the radiation, even plankton in the sea, certainly other sea life so there was limited oxygen production and the atmosphere became thick with other gases.

"Now few people understood the technology we were using to monitor Earth, and it took time to maintain the equipment with the available resources. Larik and I were ordered to give instructions on the work to be done then jump ahead to check it all. Because the Triumphal Return was our sole reason for existing we were allowed privileges including taking our families along.

As our search went further and further into the future so the demands on our equipment increased and at times we had to spend years looking for parts we needed."

"How did you find that planet you used for time travel?" Stuart asked.

"We didn't, the Trastes did while they attempted true exploration. There were rumours that they were building a great ship to escape to a new world. The council took it as a sign that they were planning to attack us then escape our retaliation but Larik in his usual way acquired their knowledge."

"I'm still not clear on what your plan was." Stuart said.

"Neither am I." Merrill said, "Except that we should look for a way to ensure that we had superiority over any other peoples we may encounter. I'd like to go back a bit and try to explain.

"We jumped forward a couple of thousand years and were shocked at the extent of the atmospheric deterioration I mentioned. Carbon dioxide and sulphur gases from volcanic reactions had built up and there was a distinct smell of methane. It was hot and the whole planet was a desert. There was some basic sea life, it was slow and sluggish and it may have ventured up from the ocean deeps."

"In other words they could resist radiation better and they were protected from the ultra-violet." Stuart said.

"Yes My Lord." Merrill said, "Forgive me but it does come more easily than Stuart. I should have added that there was evidence that this deep sea life had fared better, but of course, we couldn't study anything in the ocean depths.

"As life recovered so the oxygen balance improved but by the time carbon dioxide had been reduced to an acceptable level, the oxygen content was too high. It paved the way for what you call dinosaurs and the oxygen level steadily declined but it brought us perilously close to another life extinction event. We had to be sure that our civilisation could advance enough to destroy a massive asteroid."

Stuart nodded, "I've got the idea. Would you go back again and explain how you worked the way you did, please."

"In our history there had been great sea battles between the

Kramons and the Trastes. I think the leaders of both nations dreamt of similar glorious victories in space so we were expected to make spaceships equipped to fight these battles. Scientists like Larik could see the possibility of a tunnel like the ones you use so that troops could pour through and occupy a city. Larik was ordered to build one up here but it was never used. Ships worked and we did not want to give the Trastes ideas.

"Again it was down to Larik's organising. You may not know this but a ship cannot navigate if it is completely in multi-dimensional space. It needs a reference point in real space. We strapped shuttles to the ship and flew it to that heavy planet. That journey alone took six months but we learnt how to make bigger and bigger jumps across space as well as time and we became confident enough to send more shuttles to the other planet. They were not really suitable for journeys like that so we used the dimensional drill to complete the journey to our world.

"What bothered us was that if the ship or the tunnel failed all would be lost but the ship worked better than expected. The drill also worked well at first but Larik was clumsy materialising it and the damage built up. The biggest strain was on the shuttles even though they used the planet's gravity to jump to and fro in time.

"Now coming back to your earlier question about genetics. We couldn't do much beyond taking blood samples and it amazed us how much of our genetic make up survived even in dinosaurs. When monkeys and apes evolved, the match was even closer. We found likely subjects and tried modifying their DNA to be even closer than ever to ours but our laboratories were near the end of their life. The attempts were crude and inconclusive except a thousand years later we found definite humanoid beings. Whether our experiments were successful or we chose the time well and nature took its course is a matter of debate."

"You mentioned semen." Stuart said.

"Yes. It was a far cruder experiment but we successfully artificially inseminated females some ten thousand years later and the result was healthy off-spring. We're sure that their blood line was stronger than the others. It was all about two million years ago."

"So you think that I should be calling you great-granddad or is it 'multiple greats'-granddad." Stuart said lightly.

"Larik would say yes and have no doubts. Again I think nature could just have easily taken its course."

"And you kept travelling forward." Stuart said, "How many

times?"

"About two hundred times. In my time it took about ten years. Allowing for adjustments in the time shuttles it's nearer twenty.

"But your families only aged ten years."

"Yes… Stuart." Merrill replied, "Parents don't seem to want their children to grow up though even Taren did but so slowly."

"OK why the kidnappings?" Stuart asked.

"We were scared that we would adapt to Mars too much. The intakes provided a benchmark for our young to attain. It also prevented inbreeding."

"I'd like to hear more of your story." Stuart said, "There's a lot to fill in but I've got the gist of it. I don't like the idea of kidnapping but what you did to Tiy was unforgivable."

"The ship is getting old. It won't do many more trips without a major overhaul and there's a hairline crack in a cooling pipe. I'm not sure if we have the facilities to even reach it any more, let alone repair it. I tried saying if we waited until we shut the ship down we could evacuate the air and therefore the radioactive gas and do our maintenance in spacesuits. Larik said that it would delay the Triumphal Return even more."

"It was Cadan, Calan's father who heard us argue about it. He ruled that I had already been warned for being too soft on mere peasants. If I continued to hamper the Return then I'd be taken off the project and my oldest son could become a servant on the ship, followed by my other sons as they grew up."

"How many children do you have?" Stuart asked.

"Five sons and six daughters." Merrill replied proudly, "I have three wives."

"Oh." Stuart said, a little shocked, "Like I said, there's a lot we don't know about you. Did you live on one of the shuttles with Larik's family?"

"Yes My Lord Stuart."

"Just to be clear, the people you kidnapped, interbred with your people and have descendants."

Merrill nodded.

"That solves one problem. I can't send them home." Stuart said, "How many think like you do?"

"Most. Some, like Larik, see the favours they might get for blind obedience but most see the colonies declining while Calan seeks a place where he can rule as emperor."

"And you'd settle for less."

"I liked that village where we first met. There was order but no fear. My children could be happy there."

"I could take you to a place but you'd be the biggest loser because all your technical knowledge would be useless. You'd work in the fields like everyone else."

"But on Earth under the open sky. I'd become your peasant for that."

"No, I think you'd become a village elder guiding your people in a new world."

"I'm only a junior scholar." Merrill gasped in surprise, "I'm no leader."

"Good. Try to be a guide rather than a leader." Stuart said, "Listen to the opinions of others and accept that sometimes you can be wrong."

"Yes my lord." Merrill replied, "I'll lead my people to the land promised by our leaders and see that they all flourish."

"I think you'll be setting a precedent." Stuart chuckled and as Merrill looked on puzzled he continued, "A guy called Moses will do something similar but a couple of thousand years later."

"Yes my lord." Merrill replied, "You're reminding me of something the Council always lacked. Humour. How will you summon your followers?"

"You must learn new ways, Merrill." Stuart said, "I can invite people but I can't summon them. First I need to brief my friends and you need to see the land we're offering."

A little later a small group stood on the bank of the Nile. It was deserted for as far as the eye could see. On the opposite bank however there was a small village of the now familiar mud huts.

Stuart took Andy to one side.

"Merrill had to choose between you and Tiy, and his family." Stuart explained, "It was Larik who treated you so badly."

Andy thought for a moment, "You could be right. I heard them arguing once or twice and Merrill did seem to check on us a lot."

"So will you help him?"

Andy nodded, "I'll help the people who want to make a new life here but not especially for Merrill."

Stuart wanted to talk with James and Dave next.

"Can we create an adjustable gravity environment in one of the caves?" he asked.

"Using generators like they had in the ship you mean?" James asked, "I'd say no. It would put a strain on the rocks. We could use the ship.”

“According to Merrill, it needs a massive refit.”

“It does but we could do it.” James replied, “The Terzons were curious enough to study it and they even gave me a list of faults. They reckon it's been over engineered, you know, using three inch plate when two would do so it's basically sound.”

“And radioactive leaks don't count?”

“Of course they do.” James snapped irritably, “We can do all the repairs using probes. Their power supply is just about exhausted but we could fit a Terzon fusion unit.”

“So we overhaul it, bring it back to Earth and use it to transfer the migrants over. Gradually adjusting the gravity on the journey.”

“And I'm ready to go with you.” Dave said, “I'm over it all now.”

“No, I'd still like Freddie to back me up.” Stuart replied, “It's even more dangerous so I want us both to wear protective vests and, carry stun guns and nightsticks again. Dave you're doing well at Abydos and I'd like you to see it through as your own project. James, I'd like Dad to try to work with Merrill to fix the ship. I don't trust him completely so I'm going to ask Brian and you to monitor them.”

“OK.” James said, “Now getting back to the mundane, I've got to go. I'm collecting Zach's dad and we're going to the school. Zach and Andy are in trouble.”

Seeing the look on Stuart's face he added, “Don't worry, it's fighting. It's nothing to do with this.”

“Dave, Freddie, pub.” Stuart commanded, “I'm forgetting what time I'm in so I'm spending a day getting my bearings. If you can beat me at pool, Dave then I'll agree that you're fit.”

“I could beat you when my arm was in plaster.” Dave riposted.

Distractions

James was also glad of the break. He did not admit it but he sometimes felt thoroughly disorientated. The portals worked quietly and without fuss, which although good in many ways, it did not give the sense of having travelled great distances. The near naked folk in Ancient Egypt gave him more of a sense of being on an alien world than anything else

Acting as a parent or a guardian was a far more novel experience and he was completely out of his depth. His memories of high school dated back to the nineteen fifties America and he simply could not relate to a modern teenager's schooling. Neither was Andy that easy to handle. Where Demetrius still thought himself as a slave and even after a couple of years with Stuart and his team, Gable still thought himself answerable to the village elders, Andy had embraced 21st life with just the odd exception. Where modern teenagers tended to separate their lives from the adults, Andy had no real conception of 'generation gap'.

He had seen a problem between Professor Steadman and Demetrius and had dealt with it himself rather leave it to the adults. He was confident enough to haggle even if he was only buying a bar of chocolate, which irritated shop staff. The village shop could understand, though definitely not approve of, kids shoplifting for a dare and always called the police. They knew Gable, who was notorious for forgetting his money but Andy delayed the other customers.

James had tried to talk to Andy who had replied, "Sorry I keep forgetting. It calls itself a market so I haggle."

"It calls itself a mini-mart." James said, "Some call it a supermarket but they're usually a lot bigger. Just pay up or I stop your allowance."

At least Andy understood the threat and calmed down. James was more relieved than anything that he had got the measure of the boy but for a time he dreaded the boys disappearing off to Howkbury to visit the shops. Now, Andy and Zach were in trouble at school.

"I thought Zach was settling down." his father said when they were in the car, "He's been suspended before for fighting."

Both Zach and Andy looked nervous as they all waited to be

shown into the headmaster's office.

"These four boys were involved in a scrap and it took two teachers to separate them." the headmaster said, "We don't tolerate this sort of behaviour for any reason so I intend to exclude them for the remainder of the term."

"Andy, why don't you tell me what happened." James said.

"It was those two, they were beating up a younger boy." Andy exclaimed, "We were just trying to stop them."

"You could have reported it." James said.

"Yeah right." Zach retorted, "They'd have shoved his head down the toilet before we found a teacher."

"We take a dim view of bullying." the headmaster said, "And you're quite right, Mr. Norton. They should have reported it."

"Excuse us for a moment please." James said reverting to Andy's language.

"Zac, Andy is there anything that you want to tell me." James asked.

"Only that those two pick on the younger ones especially if they have money." Zach said, "They make sure the duty teacher's out-of-the-way then they start. No one stops them because we all get suspended and sometimes the victim runs off so there's no proof and we're the troublemakers."

"That's another thing." the headmaster said, "Staff complain that they talk to each other in that language in class. You should discourage it."

"Zach's picked it up from Andy who was taught it by his parents." James said, "They work on archaeology digs in Egypt."

"So it's a form of Arabic." the headmaster said, "Interesting but you should still discourage it."

"Zach and Andy saw a case of bullying and had to deal with it." James said, "What I'll do is speak to the parents of children who may have been bullied and finance a class action against the school and the relevant parents on their behalf."

There was a deep silence as everyone took in the implications of what he had said.

"You're not getting your kid off and not mine." one of the parents yelled.

"I'm not getting anyone off," James said quietly, "but I expect both Zach and Andy to be dealt with according to the facts and not some blind rule."

The other parent, a mother seemed close to tears

"I can't afford to get involved in this sort of thing, do something, please." she sobbed.

Everyone turned to look at the headmaster.

"Norton is new." he said, "Maybe I could issue him with a warning."

"And Zac?" James asked.

"He's been in trouble before but maybe he was just carried away by events. I'll give the other three a week's suspension."

"It's not good enough." James said, "If there was a case of bullying, they were on the spot and they had to make the decision on how to handle it. The victim kept his money and I don't see that any of them were badly hurt."

"And what about my son?" the father asked belligerently.

"That'll depend on the bullying allegation." James replied.

"It's time he started earning a living anyway." the father said, "The sooner he gets kicked out, the better."

Not long after, James was driving Zach's father and the boys home.

"Thanks for what you did." Zach's father said, "Zach would have been excluded if it hadn't been for you. I'm not sure if I'd have believed Zach as quickly as you believed Andy."

"The other boys never said a word." James said, "I was watching their reactions. They were more annoyed that Andy told on them than wanting to protest their innocence."

"What's that, intelligence training?" Zach's father asked.

"And a bit more." James replied, "Could I have a quiet word with them please?"

"Sure. Take Zach with you and send him home when you're done."

Once home James adopted Brian's trick of having the boys stand in front of him while he sat comfortably. It was formal enough for both boys to look worried, wondering about what sort of trouble they were in.

"I understand Stuart a little better now," James said, "Because I feel that there's unfinished business at the school. The mother seemed completely lost and her son was upset and scared of the other boy. He's a lost cause by the way. He was more worried that he didn't get the kid's money."

"The translator." Zach said, "That was the bit more you meant when you were talking to Dad. But none of that is any of our business is it."

"That's what I mean about understanding Stuart better." James said, "We've made that mother's life a little harder so we should try to make it easier."

"Like Stuart is with all the Ancients." Zach said, "He found them, can give them chances, so he is, even if they don't deserve it."

"We could get more friendly with Billy." Andy said, "Why does everyone laugh at him?"

"His father's a drunk and spends all their money on booze. You saw his clothes. They could be his dad's hand me downs." Zach looked at James, "We should look out for him, shouldn't we?"

James relaxed. Although unhappy at upsetting Billy's mother, other thoughts had whirled around his mind. As a group of time travellers, they had allowed the Ancients to enter their lives and they were going to help. As a pair of schoolboys, Zach and Andy were bringing Billy into their lives and they were going to help. The two boys made an exuberant and forceful duo who could swamp anyone unable to stand up to them. Billy's life was about to change just as dramatically as the Ancients and James was just going to watch, keeping an eye on the boys just as he did with Stuart and Dave.

There was something else on James' mind. Stuart had been badly shaken by not being to help Talik and James felt responsible. Instead of being the cautious one he wanted to do something.

"Would you two like to help me break all the rules of time travel?" he asked.

"How come?" Zach asked.

"OK, I want to bend them and not break them." James said, "Stuart insists on everything staying in sequence and he's quite correct but he doesn't always get it right. I don't think that anyone could."

"What do you want to do?" Andy asked.

"Rescue that guy Talik and his village." James replied, "And get the data on the blocking field."

"How come?" Zach asked again then grinned, "Unfinished business like Billy and his mother and you have a plan."

"Something like that." James agreed, "You both know what happened and I feel bad about it. Stuart's got everything else to worry about so I want to do this myself."

"I'll help." Andy exclaimed and Zach nodded enthusiastically.

"OK, I'll see if Brian will help as well. He'll want to know about their defence shield."

A little later by their time, the residents in Talik's village were distracted by a loud klaxon sounding above the village square. Some peered out, startled to see a strange ring materialise in the middle of the square. They were even more surprised when Zach stepped out of the portal as the klaxon went quiet. Zach put the megaphone he was holding to his mouth.

"There's two hundred people in this village." he said, " The rockets are coming so get them all here now. We'll get you to safety but HURRY."

"Who are you, boy?" someone called out, "What is that thing, a dimensional drill?"

Zach stepped back inside the portal but left the hatch door open.

"I'm the person who's trying to save you and not the guy who'll answer stupid questions. Move it. Get everyone here."

With that, he stepped back through the portal.

"That was well done, Zac." Brian said, "Welcome to the team."

Zach grinned, "I tried to be adult but my voice kept squeaking."

"No, you were fine." Brian said, "And James was right. These communities are so isolated that no one is going to notice that this village suddenly emptied, not even Talik so there's no significant fork or anomaly."

"OK, Uncle James checked with you." Andy said, "And you agreed to help. Won't Stuart be angry with us all?"

"To start with." Brian replied, "But he does check with me when there's likely to be any sort of time paradox so I suppose that I'm still the expert in that field. It'll be a worry off his mind and it'll remind him that I'm in charge. It'll be all right. Are you ready to guide them through?"

Andy nodded, "I'm ready. It'll be like being back on the ship and helping the prisoners. I want to do this though."

Zach had something on his mind.

"Mum worries that working for you could be dangerous." he said, "I can't tell her that I was helping people escape from an incoming nuclear attack, can I?"

Brian was about to warn him that he could not mention anything that they did but Zach could not hide his grin any longer.

"I hope you're taking this seriously, Zac." Brian said, irritably.

"Yes I am." Zach said, "But it does *sound* dangerous doesn't it."

"I suppose it does." Brian said, "There is a risk. Do you want to stop?"

Zach shook his head, "No, and I shouldn't be thinking of school and Billy, should I? It seemed wrong when Andy told on his class mates but it wasn't. He's helped stop kids being bullied and it's what we do isn't it?"

"The villagers are gathering, Zac." James said, "Do you want to stop them being bullied by nuclear bombs?"

Zach grinned and hurried through the portal. Andy followed ready to lead the first villagers through.

"They are young." Brian said, "And it shows at times but they also surprise me with their maturity. It might work out having them on the team."

"We learnt a lot with that trip to Talik." James said, "The portal's stable but there's just that element of danger or uncertainty. Let's see what they can do under a bit of pressure."

Zach was already talking to the villagers.

"We'll collect Talik later." he said, "But it's got to be done just at the right moment. Is everyone else here."

"The village representative is in town." someone replied, "He won't be back for a couple of days… He won't be back at all will he?"

"What about outlying farms?" Zach asked.

"Apart from Talik there aren't any. When the snows come even he comes into the village. The rest of us tend the surrounding fields."

"OK let's have the children through first." Zach said, "Then the women and then the men."

They only had a narrow window to work in. Start too early and a satellite might discover them and turn up the blocking field, leave it too late and villagers would be left behind.

One group of villagers did not join the queue but chose to watch from a distance. They were not hostile but James could sense their anger. Brian asked about them.

"I don't know." James replied, "They all know the news and a portal showing up is certainly different. Do you know the one question we've never asked?"

Brian shook his head, "Go on."

"Have they had an air raid alert?"

"I hate to say it but that's the sort of detail that Stuart would have thought of." Brian said.

"If they've had an alert and warned to stand by for further instructions then that explains why everyone complied so easily."

"And that group over there knows that there's something fishy." Brian contributed glancing at the time.

"We're cutting it too fine." he exclaimed, "Get Zach and Andy back now."

James spoke into the intercom and while Andy was already shepherding arrivals to the back of the cave, Zach had remained in the remote end guiding villagers through.

"Do as you're told, boy." a villager growled, "We can handle things here."

Zach nodded and hurried through to help Andy while, as good as his word, the villager helped his fellow villagers through

It was a near thing for as the last of the villagers climbed into the portal, a vehicle roared into the village square. It reminded James of an armoured car but the driver leapt out yelling, "What are you playing at? Get under cover. Get to your cellars if you've got one."

The driver stopped, stared at the portal and finally understanding ran towards it as did the villagers who had been waiting for him but they were too late for the village disappeared in a blinding light.

The flashes were behind the portal as it faced North. The villager who had been guiding his comrades was blinded, and he felt the reflected heat despite the insulating properties of the outer bulkhead.

Unlike Talik's cabin the buildings were dark wood and absorbed the heat. Some cabins burst into flames while on others the walls smouldered ominously.

Villagers caught in the open screamed as their clothes caught fire and they were instantly blinded. As quickly as he could, James de-activated the portal, blotting out the scene, just as Stuart arrived.

"Having fun?" he asked.

James filled him in on events.

"I was planning something, myself." Stuart said, "Why didn't you disable the satellite and give yourselves more time?"

"We were worried that it might provoke things." Brian replied.

"I was going to use a probe and send false signals." Stuart said, "Even if David thought that I was making it complicated I'd have allowed for the fact that they wouldn't be expecting to step into Martian gravity. Did you?"

"No, I didn't expect it to be that much of a problem." James said.

"Why not?" Stuart asked, "You've seen enough first timers arrive."

"OK, I fouled up again." James snapped irritably, "I guess that I'm less used to this than I thought."

"No you didn't foul up." Stuart said, "You rescued everyone who wanted to be rescued. I feel bad about those caught in the open but if they'd got under cover they would have been in the village hall and that went up like a flare."

"We didn't save that official." Brian said, "I think he wanted to be rescued."

"The village representative." Stuart explained, "You already know that dissenters are exiled to those villages including the rep. He's 'rehabilitating' himself by guiding the village on the correct path. Only he is allowed to leave the village, at least beyond the fields, and then he's only allowed to go to the district office in the city. Talik is the exception.

"He's a highly qualified rocket expert and got into trouble for arguing too vehemently with a noble or a lord or something. He was not so much exiled as advised to go into hiding and he's got a satellite link that allows him to continue working."

"I thought he said that he didn't have any military secrets." James said.

"He probably lied." Stuart replied, "Would you tell strangers about our secret work?"

Stuart paused, "Talik probably knew of the attacks on the Mars colonies and knew what it meant, so he wasn't surprised when James gave the attack warning."

"How do you know all this?" Brian asked.

"Simple." The village representative has an office in the village hall. The hall has a large screen for showing educational/propaganda material and heavily censored news. It's the only communication with the outside world that the rest of the village is allowed."

"Now I've been using the links to look into their databases. I've got the info on the blocking screen, and over the last couple of days I've been allowing more of the news to filter through."

He paused again, "They know of the destruction of the Mars colonies. I assume someone told Talik, and they were told to stand by for an evacuation."

"How were they told?" Brian asked.

"My speech relayed by their announcer with the image manipulated proved to be convincing."

"So they were waiting for us." James said, "I wondered."

"I'd only done bits and pieces to see if I could set the scene," Stuart said, "and to get the data on their blocking screen. Brian will have to look at it but I reckon that we could get round it.

"Now what you two forgot is that events don't have to be hurried at this end. I know it feels that if we've only got ten minutes at their end then we've only got ten here. In fact we could have ten years."

James nodded, "Yes, I can see when you're going off half cocked but I guess I can't see where I'm going wrong."

"Time travel's too crazy." Stuart said, "It does everyone's mind in and we all need someone to help us think straight."

"So you'd begun the groundwork and were planning a rescue. Why didn't you tell us?"

"Why didn't you tell me?" Stuart chuckled, "The village rep realised that someone had tapped into the computer network and went haring off to the district office because the military were already commandeering communications. The villagers congregated in the hall, got my evacuation message then the full uncensored news."

Both James and Brian nodded thoughtfully.

"OK now do you have any thoughts on them." Stuart asked, "Where do we take them?"

"They accepted Zach's instructions and it was an orderly evacuation, I suppose we could ask Trey to look after them."

"Oh, they're willing." Dave grinned, "Stuart still thinks more complicated than you. Five years after Trey arrives they're ready to expand and cultivate more land."

"OK you'd better take over." James shrugged in defeat, "You've planned it all."

"No," Stuart said, "You can read my files, do what you always do and point out the faults then get on with it. Dave and I are going swimming. It's only the Lizard planet so the boys can come too, if you like."

"Good idea." James said then, when they were gone, turned to Brian and added, "I thought that I'd planned this like a military campaign. It's lucky that I wasn't at Gettysburg."

"I complain about Stuart treating the portals like a push-bike but he and Dave can think four dimensionally now. Shall we complete the transfer then see if we can rescue Talik without giving Stuart another excuse to laugh at us?"

Luckily for James and Brian the villagers were too badly shaken by their narrow escape to worry about where they were going. It was as he checked Stuart's notes that he realised that he had to say something. He found a box to stand on.

"OK your comrade who was blinded will be taken to see our

doctor. Now a few of you could see the screen so you know what happened. Once the shock-waves have passed then there's a tornado heading in your general direction. That's because a deep depression sucked in superheated air mixed with radioactive fallout."

He paused, "The only other survivors on Earth are at a biosphere buried underground."

"Will this biosphere succeed?" someone called out.

"No." James answered, "They'll make a go of it for several generations but then it will fail and we'll take the last of them onto another home."

"Then why offer it to us?" another called out.

"Because many would want to defend Traste to the end."

"Look at us." yet another exclaimed, "We haven't done that well under the Lords of Traste. Why should we support it? And you're saying that the dimensional drill can travel through time."

"You can accept that?" James asked.

"They had some funny ways of torturing us. Like Talik, we're all engineers and most of us worked on the drill. Zyron was a farmer who complained about price fixing among the buyers."

"Who's Zyron?" James asked.

"The village representative. He forbade us from talking shop so we had all that accumulated knowledge up here," he tapped his forehead, "But we couldn't use it. We did though and developed theories on the multi-dimensional universe. You appear to be proving us correct."

"OK the place we have in mind is the start of another civilisation. Using iron would be a technological breakthrough. You'll be able to discuss your knowledge but it'll be forgotten when you die."

The villager nodded,

"It's a pity that you couldn't save Talik. He talked of starting a new life but he was as trapped as us."

"Funny you should say that." James grinned, "Would anyone care to help us?"

For James, the strangest part was that he watched the nuclear explosions from a third point of view. He waited until he, Stuart and Dave had hurried off, waited a further five minutes then dematerialised the portal. This time it was a villager who hurried through, to bang on Talik's door.

Talik might not have answered but he hoped that it was Stuart returning. He stared at the villager, then at the portal, nodded in understanding and stepped forward. He glanced at the distant fireballs, only slowly fading and did not even bother closing his door.

247

Final Battle

Stuart's plan was to persuade as many peasants, as Larik called them to leave their colony and resettle near Abydos. Some were original members of the Kramon nation, some the descendants of those who had been kidnapped in the past and a few who been kidnapped and had settled into their new life.

Even if Stuart disliked the methods, he had to concede that by using competition in sport as well as hard work in the fields, the new arrivals had kept the Martian colonists reasonably fit. It would help with their relocation back to Earth.

The real problem would be persuading them to leave. He would have to speak with them in person. The colonists would not trust a disembodied voice over a probe. Merrill could make a start but many would not trust him either. As a time traveller, he appeared briefly, never getting to know anyone closely and he was definitely favoured by the council so many instinctively mistrusted him. Stuart was going to have to visit in person and it would lead to a direct confrontation with Calen.

"I wish I could beam him to a desert island while I talk to the others." Stuart said when he was chatting to Brian that evening, "I'm not looking forwards to this."

"Why not just leave them?" Brian asked, "Maybe they don't want your help."

"For one thing we've changed things by stopping Larik and Merrill." Stuart replied, "The Kramon colonies on Mars are still going to fail yet the Trastes are thriving so I have taken sides and I need to redress the balance."

"And the Trastes haven't changed history?" Brian asked.

"Not so far as we can tell." Stuart replied, "They absorbed so much of the culture that surrounded them that it swamped their own. In Andy's time there're legends of men from the stars who were too sickly to be gods. No one's interested in weaklings so they're well on the way to being forgotten."

"And you think the Kramons will be similarly absorbed."

Stuart thought for a moment, "I think so. Merrill's children are adapting to Earth's gravity faster than even the Terzons expected. It's something psychological, they respond to being in the open air. I don't know how it really works but like ours, their ancestors were natural hunter/gatherers and I guess that they still have that instinct. Not being bounded by cave walls is stimulating that instinct, which in turn is stimulating them physically. The doctors say that should rest more and accept that their bones are weaker but they love swimming.”

“What about crocodiles?” Brian asked.

“They're camping near Lake Moeris away from the Nile.” Stuart explained, “We've gone back a bit and we're keeping the locals happy with a supply of chocolate. Dave checks in on them every day, So does Dr. Tobias and I think he treats the locals as well, though he's not supposed to. Anyway the plan is to transpose the Kramons there in groups, put them through an acclimatisation regime then settle them at the Abydos site.”

“Will it work?” Brian asked.

“We're doing it in stages and there's nothing we haven't done before. Joe is quite happy helping now, he wears a kilt and shows the Trastes basic farming methods and he'll do the same for the Kramons. The only thing he won't do is visit the market.”

“I'm so very proud of you.” Brian said, “I couldn't do what you do and I certainly couldn't stay so calm. How come you never even got annoyed with Trey when he tried to kill you?”

“I've known the Terzons for too long.” Stuart laughed, “Besides it was funny in a way. He was inflicting the worst sort of torture and death he could imagine on me and I didn't care. Wondering why I wasn't scared probably screwed him up more than anything else I could have done.”

“What are your plans?” Brian asked.

“The difference between Trey and Calen is that Trey did not really want to kill me. He wasn't much better off than his people and they did respect him for his efforts. Calen is a bully. He didn't need to kill that guard but he enjoyed it and everyone seemed scared of him. Calen's got his little empire and he's going to keep it.”

He paused, “If anyone wants to follow him then I'm not going to stop them. However I'm going to use a probe to stun him and hold him while I talk to the others. Time travel makes using available space easier, we can take them to the outpost and if there's too many, we can divide them into groups and put them into different time zones. The basic infrastructure we've installed is good for a couple of hundred years so we may as well use it.”

“Will you invite Calen?” Brian asked.

“I don't want to but I have to.” Stuart replied, “He'll have more problems than Trey, though. However, by the time he's adapted to the gravity, learned to live in the open air, and being dependent on the locals' expertise, the political realities will have changed."

"Just don't get yourself killed." Brian said, "We don't go in for the lovey-dovey stuff much but I do love you and I don't think that I could live without you."

"Let's go to bed." Stuart said, "I could sit on your lap but you'd be scared of Demetrius catching us."

The following day, Stuart was outlining his plans to his friends.

"Dave, I'd like you to operate the equipment so that Freddie and James can come with me."

"I am fit." Dave exclaimed angrily, "Don't you trust me any more?"

"I think you scared Stuart more than he let on." James said, "And I think that you should go. Stuart, Dave has much better instincts than I do, I'm trained to kill the enemy, Dave is an explorer like you and respects other people's ways. Freddie's had some firearms training and he remembers your ways from when he was a kid. It'll make a far better team."

Everyone turned to Stuart who grimaced in defeat.

"OK." Stuart said, "Calen's office opens out onto a balcony above the main cave. We can land the portal just outside and James can stun him with a gun mounted on a probe. We rush in from the portal and we should be in charge."

"What about the second colony?" James asked.

"Calen commands the colony with transport facilities so he's in overall control." Stuart explained, "The guy in charge of the second colony should be on the council but Calen's ancestor decreed otherwise. In any case he either agrees with Calen or he loses access to what materials are left in stock."

"If we capture Calen then he will be in control." James said thoughtfully, "I wonder if we can do business with him? We'll have to speak with Merrill."

They found him, sitting quietly watching his children with a group of locals wading through the shallows of the lake holding spears.

"They tire easily of course, My Lord." he said in a reply to a question from Stuart, "But they're doing well. They spend more time in the village than they do with me and want to forget their old ways."

"What can you tell me of the leader of the other colony?" Stuart asked.

"Bastin." Merrill replied, "He'll just see a new supply of young girls and cooperate with you. I don't think he'll live long here though. Taking girls is one thing, abandoning them when they're pregnant will make a lot of fathers angry and he won't have his position to protect him."

"Nice man." Stuart muttered.

"I'd say insecure." Merrill replied, "He should be Calen's equal but he has no real power."

"Fair enough." Stuart said, "I'm off to capture Calen. Have you got a message for him?"

"No, My Lord." Merrill replied, "He proves his authority by doing the opposite to what people want. I could beg him to come here and lead the new colony but it would be a dangerous game."

"I like the sentiment though." Stuart laughed, "I'll bear it in mind."

"And I may continue to sit here until Lord James summons me?" Merrill asked.

"No, you may sit here and enjoy your new home for as long as you like but would you help James if he needs it, please?"

Stuart glanced towards the lake.

"Hey look." he exclaimed, "Your son's caught a fish. He looks so pleased with himself. I'll leave so that he can show you."

Merrill would never be able to lead his people, he simply did not have the drive. Instead he would accept the new reality and get on with his life. If not a leader his quiet acceptance would provide a guide to any who followed him. If his children were eager to forget their narrow, restricted life in the Martian colony then Stuart was content that they would blend in with the inhabitants of Abydos and it boded well for the other colonists.

Stuart felt a lot happier as he gathered his friends together again.

"This is going to be a lot more dangerous than our usual activities." he began, "I can see them drawing their guns and shooting."

"Maybe you should just leave it, son." Richard said, "You've done enough."

"I agree." Brian said, "But it wouldn't be Stuart. He's got to do it if only to stay even handed between the Kramons and the Trastes."

"Why does that matter so much?" Freddie asked.

"You should know us well enough by now." Dave replied.

"Yes of course." Freddie said, "Taking sides is interference.

What would you do if you saw something that you knew to be wrong or even evil?"

"Good question." Stuart replied, "I'd call Calen evil. He killed that soldier without a seconds thought and enjoyed it but he'd been brought up to believe he had that right. A lot of the colonists will agree with him and will follow him. We know that they'll probably die but it must be their choice."

"And choice is the key." Freddie asked, "I understand."

"I'm not sure if the Terzons do." Stuart replied, "They think that even offering the choice is meddling."

"They accept that you only get involved when you're pushed in some way." Brian said, "All I ask is that you're careful."

"Okay we'll arrive as they're raising the lights, their equivalent of dawn. Calen likes to check his office then do his rounds, making that everyone is at work. James, you know what to do."

James materialised the probe just above Calen and fired the stun gun that had been attached. Moments later he materialised the portal in the cave just outside the office allowing Dave and Freddie to charge through and into the office. Calen was handcuffed and propped up against the wall as Stuart sauntered through.

"You can still handle Martian gravity then, Freddie." Stuart grinned.

"You know what they say." Freddie chuckled, "It's like riding a bike. Once you've learnt you never forget."

Stuart picked up a baton, the symbol of a councillor's power that lay on Calen's desk and stepped through the office door. He turned to a startled guard.

"Summon everyone to the assembly area." he commanded.

The guard glanced at the baton, nodded and hurried off while Stuart returned to the office. Calen was conscious and glaring at anyone who glanced his way but he did not speak.

"OK I can take your people to Earth and their children will enjoy a good future. What do you say?"

"I say that you will live for a long time on the end of a rope." Calen spluttered, "If you are from Earth then your necks will fight our gravity and you will struggle beyond all agony."

"Interesting thought." Stuart chuckled, "You were almost poetic. Did you mean that you wish to stay on Mars?"

"No. I intend to lead the Triumphal Return. If you help voluntarily then you will live."

"We'll take him with us." Stuart said, "Let's go."

Stuart led the way leaving Freddie and Dave to support Calen. They all stood on a balcony with the entire population of the colony standing beneath them. If anything Stuart was shocked by how few there were while the colonists were startled and perhaps even angry at the treatment of their leader.

"I'm sorry about the way we're treating Calen." Stuart said, "It's not our way but he would never let me speak to you like this."

He paused, relieved to see everyone was still listening.

"This colony is dying." Stuart continued, "You may survive but your children and your grandchildren will not. I can take you back to Earth where you can flourish. It will not be the Triumphal Return you dream of because you will be one group among many establishing a new civilisation. However you and your descendants will have a future. Those that want to come with me, be ready. There won't be much time when I come for you."

"All of you, back to work." Calen tried yelling. He partly succeeded in that he spoke in a trembling voice without any real power behind it but it was enough for the guards to reach for their weapons. Stuart was surprised and impressed for he had never seen anyone recover from one of their stun guns as quickly as Calen appeared to be doing.

He drew his own gun and aimed it at Calen.

"If I shock him again, I'll probably kill him." Stuart called out, "Just take it easy and no one will get hurt."

One of the guards continued to draw his weapon aiming it, not at Stuart but at Freddie who happened to be in full view. Suddenly two more guards drew their guns but aimed at the first guard. There was an element of farce as the chain of targets developed but it was deadly farce creating a confused situation.

"Lower your weapon Janon." one of the two guards said then turned to Stuart, "Where's Merrill."

"Sitting in the sun watching his son learn to fish." Stuart replied.

"Sitting in the sun." the guard repeated, "Sitting in the sun like our ancestors used to do on Earth? I repeat, where is he?"

"On Earth, in my time." Stuart explained.

"On Earth." the guard repeated, "It is possible for us to return?"

"Providing that you're prepared to start again." Stuart said, "The Trastes and the Kramons will be forgotten but some of your ways will be remembered."

"If you summon Merrill so that we can talk to him then you'll have my loyalty."

"I can ask him." Stuart said, "But I need your loyalty now. Take Janon prisoner and look after Calen. Treat them well, I don't want them hurt. By the way, what's your name?"

"Zagen, my Lord."

"How many guards are there on this base?" Stuart asked.

"Eleven, My Lord." Zagen replied.

"Janon was against me, you two are for me and that guard by the office door seems content to watch. That's seven unaccounted for isn't it."

"Yes My Lord." Zagen replied.

"Please speak if you have something to say." Stuart said, "Argue if you think that I'm wrong but I need help."

"What sort of leader admits to weakness?" Calen spluttered contemptuously.

"The sort that doesn't see help as a weakness." Stuart said, "Zagen and his friend have aligned with me so it's in their best interest to see that I'm not taken."

"My Lord, some will be at their posts overseeing the peasants. There's been a lot of talk about switching allegiance to Lord Bastin so many will just be watching without committing themselves. The rest will be in their quarters ready for the night shift"

"Lord Bastin runs the other base, doesn't he?" Stuart asked, "Will his soldiers be just as divided?"

"Some see him as stronger than Lord Calen." Zagen replied, "A few soldiers have fled through the tunnel to join him."

Two more soldiers arrived to kneel before Stuart.

"My Lord," one began, "Will you talk more of the life you offer. We will not fight for anyone until we hear what you have to say."

"Dave go ask Merrill if he'll join us." Stuart commanded, "Remind him that it is a request but he's got friends who miss him."

"Why is it a request, My Lord." Zagen asked, "Isn't he your vassal."

"He's in a civilisation that will adapt a lot of your ways." Stuart said, "I chose it because they believe in an order to the universe and they actively seek it. It allows people of various ranks to speak much more freely and Merrill may think that returning here even briefly will disturb the order of his new life."

"And you allow that?" Zagen asked, the amazement evident.

"How can he seek order if he's bound to another's thinking?" Stuart asked. It occurred to Stuart that his style of speaking was changing but it seemed to be working.

"In that case, My Lord, allow me to suggest that we retreat. The peasants appear to be arguing and it's becoming very heated."

Stuart glanced over the balcony. As he watched a stone came sailing towards his head. On Earth, Stuart would have described it as a large rock three times larger than anything that could have been thrown but on Mars it was just a stone. It approached considerably slower than on Earth so he had no trouble stepping out-of-the-way. He was tempted to try to catch it but knew that such an attempt would throw him off balance in the low Martian gravity. The rock struck the wall with a resounding crash sending splinters in all directions.

Stuart looked over the balcony again to see a man falling, blood pouring from his head as another stone, apparently the second one to hit him, struck his back. The crowd was jostling around splitting in two halves facing each other.

"Stop." Stuart yelled, then almost immediately "Duck."

One group was dividing itself ready to fight on two fronts, one against Stuart and the other against the second faction and a hail of stones flew towards the balcony. Luckily no one on the balcony was hurt as the missiles smashed uselessly against the wall behind them and Stuart had time to notice that Calen's office wall was undamaged apart from some shallow pits and scratches.

"Zagen," Stuart called out, "They seemed to be aimed at Calen as well as me."

"Yes My Lord." Zagen replied, "I think that Calen's supporters are already dead."

"How come?" Stuart asked, "I mean, how do you know?"

"The ones being attacked seemed to be his most loyal supporters."

"I only saw one guy being attacked." Stuart said, "Then I was diving for cover."

"I know this cave and I'm used to looking out over it, My Lord." Zagen said, "I was also diving for cover but I may have seen more."

"I did see that there were two sides." Stuart said, "How come, if they all hated Calen?"

"It's between you and Lord Bastin, My Lord." Zagen said, "You hold the Staff of Kramon so you succeed Calen but your enemies believe that you are weak like him and so they support Lord

Bastin."

"But they only saw me a few moments ago." Stuart exclaimed.

"After your first visit Calen warned everyone not to go with you if you returned. After he and Larik finished ranting about your treacherous offer, the whole colony knows all about you. Enough heard you through that speaker to know what you're offering. Calen thought it would divide Lord Bastin's supporters but with two choices against him, it was Lord Calen who lost all his support."

"OK but we can't sit behind this barrier discussing politics much longer." Stuart said, "Any ideas."

Almost in reply there was a series of bangs and hisses followed by cries of alarm from below the balcony. The rain of missiles stopped and Stuart risked a peak over the balcony only to see clouds of smoke billowing upwards. Even as he watched the cloud rose above the balcony blotting out the rest of the cave.

Stuart turned to look at Dave and Freddie, just as a portal materialised.

"OK." Stuart yelled, "You can stay and explain which side you're on or you can get out through the portal. Either way, 'MOVE IT!'"

Stuart yelled the last two words as loudly and as sharply as he could. It was Calen who led the way almost dragging Freddie and Dave along with him. The other soldiers followed and in moments the balcony was cleared.

The colonists were not particularly surprised to find themselves in another cave, nor were they disappointed that they were still experiencing Martian gravity.

"OK." Stuart called out, "If any of you want to go back I won't stop you. For those that stay then we'll take you on to Earth. Calen, if you go to Earth then you will not be in charge. Merrill's son is already at home in his new world and he will guide you all."

"I don't think that I shall live long wherever I go." Calen said, "But what of my family?"

"You'll all spend up to a year in a temporary base while you acclimatise to Earth's gravity." Stuart said, "If you can't forget your differences by then I'll settle Calen's followers in a separate community."

Stuart was almost beginning to feel sorry for Calen. He tried to remember how Calen had killed one of his own people in cold blood before threatening him, but he could not link the memory to the tired old man that Calen had become.

"I was taught that the Triumphal Return was all that mattered." Calen said, "No one mattered either, just the Return, then Larik told me that without Merrill he could not repair the spaceship and I knew that it was the end. All our efforts wasted and I knew that I had failed my ancestors. Now I've lost control of the colonies and dishonoured my ancestors even more. Look after my family, please. I must leave the colony."

Stuart looked puzzled, glancing at Zagen who said, "He wishes to exile himself on the planet's surface. As a matter of honour he will walk as far away from the colonies as possible before his air gives out."

"Ah!" Stuart said, "There's plenty that would like to see you dead Calen, and I wouldn't be that sorry but it's not our way. The Kramons and the Trastes were finished the moment they went to war. Neither of you understood just how much damage a nuclear war could do and none of your colonies were sustainable for long enough to return to your Earth."

Calen looked at Stuart, giving an understanding nod.

"My father said that we were just waiting for a miracle," he said, "But as long as the staff is in the hands of the council, Kramon will live. Will you return the staff and let me go."

"You could pass it to Bastin." Stuart said.

"Promise him a harem of young girls and he'll just abandon his people and his heritage." Calen snapped contemptuously, "You are not of the Council of Kramon so give it to me. I wish to guard it and keep it safe. Will you allow me to take it home?"

"Do you mean the site of your capital on Earth?" Stuart asked, Calen nodded

"You'll have supplies for a week and protection from the sun. I'll give you some medicine so that when you're ready you'll just go to sleep."

"I need to bury it as close to the Council Chamber as I can get. It's the heart of the Kramons so we will not die. Do you understand?"

"Yes I do." Stuart said, "You know that I could set up a probe so that you can bury it remotely. You can still live."

"No." Calen said, "You mean well but I must guard it with my life."

"I had to ask." Stuart said, "Zagen, Janon stayed loyal to Calen so I'll ask him to protect Calen's family. Will you help him please?"

"I will protect them as my own, My Lord." Zagen replied, "He wishes to die still protecting Kramon and for that he still has my loyalty."

"Okay the next step is to speak with Lord Bastin." Stuart said, "If he agrees to leave then there's no problem."

"And will he?" Dave asked.

"Do you remember James' briefing?" Stuart asked, "Their history gets very confused after this point and there's the blocking field so we can't visit. I reckon it's anyone's guess what happens."

"Maybe I could perform one last service." Calen said, "Allow me to accompany you, I can order Bastin to listen to you."

Stuart glanced at Zagen who nodded but Stuart replied, "It's a big turn around, Calen."

"Without the support of the prime colony I am nothing and Kramon is gone. You say that the people will live on Earth but will forget Kramon. No, I want them to remember our beloved nation. I will see that they do."

Stuart was developing a grudging admiration for Calen. Given the chance, Stuart had no doubt that Calen would bully, torture or kill to regain control of his people but he was also a realist who could see that now was not the time.

It seemed to Stuart that Calen hated him for forcing him to accept the fact that his world was dying and his planned death had more to do with making himself a martyr. People remember martyrs so he was still attempting to thwart Stuart's plans. Whatever else happened, Calen was going die by the same values that he lived by.

"You should be remembered as the Council of Kramon." Stuart said, "It wouldn't be appropriate to be seen as my servant."

Calen grinned, "A polite way of ignoring my offer. You understand that I would have mentioned my offer to guard the Staff of Kramon."

"Janon and Zagen will see that the people are told." Stuart said.

"Then I'll leave for the city's sunset." Calen said, "I'll only need supplies for the night. I'll take poison before sunrise."

Stuart could still see Calen murdering the soldier and just nodded. He had tried to talk Calen out of going but he knew that he had not been very passionate in his attempt and the truth was, he was glad that Calen was not going with them.

"How do I get to the other colony?" he asked Zagen

"By train, My Lord." Zagen replied.

It was not the answer Stuart was expecting but he remembered the tunnel between the two colonies but he had not thought about how to travel through the full length.

"Why not use the portal?" Dave asked, "We're in our own base why worry about trains."

"I'd forgotten, My Lord." Zagen replied, "I was still thinking that I was at home."

"And I was thinking that arriving by portal causes too much of a stir." Stuart said, "Besides, a ride on a Martian train sounds like fun."

"It's more boring than anything you may have experienced, My Lord." Zagen said, "I suggest you embark at the rail yard."

"Explain." Stuart commanded.

"There's a small cave mid way between the two colonies." Zagen replied, "A number of trains are stored there, though only two are in regular use. If both trains are at one end of the line then a third is despatched to the other. It's all automated but we can activate one at the yard."

"And it's still running." Dave said, "Impressive."

"Remember what James said about the ship." Stuart responded, "It was over engineered. Say what you like about these people but they built things to last."

He paused before speaking to Zagen, "I prefer honesty above all else. How would you describe Lord Bastin?"

"In other words, you don't want me to prove that my old Lords were inferior to my new one." Zagen smiled, "But I truly believe that he is. He gets fat while his peasants go hungry and he's more likely to kill one if he feels slighted. He believes that they're there to serve, especially the girls. He'll kneel and call you 'My Lord' when you face him, then stun you and sever your spine if he sees your back."

"If I said that all the Lords of Kramon demanded absolute obedience, but while Calen is honourable, but vicious, Bastin is just concerned with his own well being," Stuart asked, "What would you say?"

"I would say that you don't understand Calen and he was a better leader than you know." Zagen said, "Bastin should have been arrested for taking so much but it would make a civil war more likely." Zagen thought for a moment, "But yes My Lord, I would agree with most of your assessment and not only because I have to."

"Fair enough." Stuart chuckled, "Will you come with us as far as the rail yard and show us how it works."

"I am a soldier and you are now my lord." Zagen said, "It is my duty to go with you."

"I meant no offence." Stuart replied, "I don't expect you to set yourself against your friends."

Honour was apparently satisfied and Stuart led his group through a portal to the rail yard. He stopped looking at it in amazement and for a moment he was disoriented by what appeared to be tiny trains some distance away. His eyes said that they were further away than they should be but it only lasted until he realised that the rails were nearly three metres apart, almost twice that of the railways back home.

He studied the trains more closely seeing how cylindrical they were then noticing wheels protruding from the roof of the train.

Stuart glanced at the tunnel mouth that seemed barely larger than the trains but he noticed flat rails curving out from the top of the tunnel but leading nowhere.

As the train approached the tunnel so the wheels would touch then roll along the top rails almost pushing the train down onto the track.

"We're about two hundred kilometres from the colony, how long will the journey take?" Stuart asked.

"About twenty minutes, My Lord." Zagen replied.

"Six hundred kilometres an hour?" Stuart exclaimed.

"Faster than that at top speed, My Lord." Zagen replied, "There are airlocks and it takes time to pass through. The rear doors close, the tunnel doors open and the train can then accelerate in a near vacuum. As the train passes through the tunnel what air there is would be squashed up in front of it. Instead it's vented through pipes into the atmosphere and air gets sucked in behind us. You see the ring like ridges around the coaches? At the other end the blow holes stop. Those rings act like seals and the pressure builds up in front of the train to slow it. They're effective at speed but as the train slows enough to enter the airlock you can hear the air whistling past."

"So you've got the minimum of moving parts yet high speed transport." Stuart said, "Impressive, shall we go?"

The inside of the train was simply a long tube. There were seats at either end but otherwise it was cargo space accessed by long doors in the side that swung open. There were no windows except for a narrow windscreen at each end.

Stuart looked over Zagen's shoulder as the train entered the airlock.

"It's a tight fit." Stuart said, "There can't be much air space around us."

"No, and it was designed that way." Zagen replied, "The

pumps could empty the whole airlock if they had to but they scarcely get started before we're ready to go."

So they're underused and last. Stuart thought to himself, *Everything was designed to last.*

The journey itself was boring. The tunnel was pitch black, there was no sense of movement apart from the initial acceleration and Zagen was more interested in a simple manometer, a glass U-tube containing what Stuart assumed was mercury. For most of the journey the levels in the upright parts were the same but then one side began to sink and the other rise.

"We're in the compression zone." Zagen said as he reduced the power, "Good drivers do not wait for the automatic brakes and wear out parts unnecessarily. We let it coast to a stop."

Stuart was still impressed, he had an increasing sense of being pulled forward as the deceleration increased but still he could see nothing in the dark of the tunnel. He started in alarm for suddenly a wall blocked the tunnel but the train was just creeping along and stopped within inches of the wall. It seemed a shame that technology like this was going to be lost though Terzon engineers would want to study it but they would have to wait until the business in hand was done.

He had noticed the whistling of air as something in the background but he was more aware that it had stopped. The airlock door rolled open and the train moved forward, pausing for another door before entering what was obviously a station. Like all trains it juddered as it crossed points then slid into a siding with door height platforms on either side.

He would have looked around but Zagen was becoming nervous and almost dragged him to a flight of stairs to be greeted by a guard at the top.

"This is my Lord Stuart." Zagen said, "He seeks an audience with Lord Bastin."

By reply, the guard drew his gun.

"He is not of the council so he's just a peasant and an imposter." the guard pronounced, "You're all under arrest for treason."

"There's a surprise." Stuart retorted, "And there was me offering to take your family to Earth."

"If you're him then why not arrive by a dimensional drill, a great noble like that would not need a train."

"There are some things that great nobles can never get right."

Stuart snapped, "How to arrive for a quiet chat is one of them."

The guard looked puzzled as Dave sniggered but Zagen suddenly felt proud. He was so close to such a great man that he understood his frustration.

"Whatever you think, Lord Stuart has succeeded Lord Calen in Colony Prime." he said.

Stuart was unhappy about that remark but stayed quiet. Suddenly the guard grinned.

"Either way he should be taken before Lord Bastin. If you give your word that you will follow, I will lead the way."

"Yes, I give it." Stuart said, "I just want a friendly chat."

The guard turned marched off leaving Stuart and his friends to follow. Stuart was already familiar with these caves but it was odd to see them occupied, brightly lit and, apparently thriving. He knew that it was an illusion, because compared to surveys done when the colony was newly established, the plants were smaller, almost stunted and even the guard seemed thin. Stuart would not say that he was malnourished but his weight was bordering on the low side of what was healthy.

They were led through tunnels to a now familiar balcony and into Lord Bastin's office. By contrast to the others that Stuart had seen, including Calen, Bastin was fit, healthy and muscular. He saw Stuart appraising him.

"When I was younger I could defeat any new arrival in athletics." he said proudly, "I confess to obtaining rations to maintain my virility but without me, this colony would fail."

"It's going to anyway." Stuart said, "I'm offering your people the chance of a life back on Earth."

"So I hear." Bastin replied, "Colony Farm is filling with refugees from your offer. It appears to be flawed."

"No, it's not flawed." Stuart replied, "Kramon and Traste will both be forgotten but their people will live and become part of a new civilisation."

"Traste survives despite what it did to Kramon." Bastin exclaimed, "Yet you say it's not flawed."

"Both Traste and Kramon went into terminal decline when you had your war." Dave interrupted, "You know that these colonies aren't viable, they need too much technology that you can't replace."

"The Eternal Ones will never allow Kramon to die." Bastin said, "They will send a miracle to save us."

There was no feeling or passion in his voice and it seemed to

Stuart that Bastin was just reciting a mantra.

"Both Traste and Kramon created this mess." Stuart replied, "And this is your chance to salvage what you can. I don't think Eternal Ones of any description will be too happy with people who are so willing to destroy so much."

"That's blasphemy." Bastin said, "You should be cast out for it."

Again he spoke flatly with no feeling or passion but suddenly he snapped out, "Why should you help us? Are our women so appealing?"

Dave could not help a loud guffaw of laughter and Stuart could not resist a chuckle.

"Is that what's bothering you?" Stuart replied, "There's many a woman at the relocation site who would see you as quite a catch."

"Old women who only go to bed to sleep?" Bastin sneered.

"You'd better not visit my home." Stuart chuckled, "You'd be lucky to escape with your life if you made remarks like that."

"So they have spirit?" Bastin asked, passion finally evident in his voice, "Calen is finished so I would rule and I could choose anyone I want."

"No, you wouldn't rule." Stuart said, "And you'd have to watch out for angry fathers, brothers and husbands."

Bastin's face clouded.

"For a moment, I was forgetting my duty." he said reaching into a drawer. Stuart never saw the stun gun he was drawing but suddenly Bastin collapsed onto the desk.

Dave guessed that James had spotted something via a probe and used it to stun Bastin. He slipped around the desk and picked up the gun.

"I think that we've been here before." he laughed.

Stuart thought for a moment before turning to Zagen.

"That rail yard." he said, "Could we take it over and defend it?"

"Yes My Lord." Zagen replied, "At least, it has its own life support and was designed to double as an emergency shelter."

Stuart drew his stun gun and aimed it the guard who escorted them from the station.

"Sorry about this." he said, "But we'll just tie you up. You'll have a nasty headache when you wake up that's all."

To Stuart's surprise the guard dropped to his knees.

"I offer you my allegiance." he said, "Will my family have a chance?"

"Yes of course." Stuart replied, "What of your loyalty to Bastin?"

"It's always been rumoured that Bastin's loyalty is to the lower parts of his body and now I've heard the proof. If he served Kramon then I would fight you."

"The train we travelled in could take half the colony." Stuart said, "I was wondering how we could defend ourselves while everyone filed through the portal in single file. We could take everyone to the rail yard, close it off then arrange an ordered retreat through the portal."

"I thought you'd have a plan." Dave chuckled, "It's not like you though. It's simple."

"Find other guards who want to leave." Stuart commanded, "Get word to everyone who may be in their quarters. The train leaves in two hours. Zagen, Dave, you're with me. Let's get to the station entrance. If James can hear me, I want a public address system set up so that I can talk to everyone out in the fields now."

"Why not use the one in Bastin's office?" the guard asked, "Because I didn't know about it. James can patch something through."

"My Lord?" Zagen queried, puzzled.

"If there's trouble I want an escape route." Stuart explained, "A portal can only let us through one at a time. The stairs to the station can take up to a dozen abreast and there must be a lift for cargo so we can load a train quicker."

The others nodded in understanding.

Whatever else the colony was, it was a small, tight knit community. Rumours were already circulating and like the other colony, it was dividing itself into factions, either for Bastin or for Stuart.

Flanked by Zagen and the other guard, Dave and Stuart headed for the industrial cave and on to the station. Before they had gone far, groups surrounded them while beyond Stuart could see others congregating, glaring at them angrily.

"Once we're at the station entrance you and your two servants return to the centre cave." the guard said, "Your instructions will be obeyed. Those that want to switch their allegiance to you will have their chance."

"Maybe I should stay." Stuart said.

"With respect, My Lord, you are not Kramon and you don't have the authority of the Council. Allow us to deal with our own affairs."

"You mean, butt out." Stuart chuckled, "I've got friends who'd agree with you but we'll wait in the station."

"No My Lord. As you've said, it'll take time to gather everyone and you can send another train. They can run automatically though guards do take pride in driving them as skilfully and economically as possible."

Stuart had other questions but it was not the time to ask them. Instead he allowed himself to be hustled to the top of the stairs then, taken down and onto the train. Zagen sat at the controls while Stuart and Dave sat a few seats back so they could talk quietly.

"I can't make them out." Dave said, "They're so pompous and don't seem to care who lives or who dies."

"They do but there's a conflict. They seem to have powerful but tightly controlled emotions and they're also intensely practical." Stuart replied, "The emotions especially their pride comes from their history and their practicality comes from their fight to survive since the war."

"So a part of them is saying carry on fighting to the death for Kramon while another part is saying let's go."

"The same applies to the Trastes." Stuart said, "Curiosity is an emotion as well and Trey at least had a degree of that but for both nations the dominant one was pride."

"So they switch allegiance to you because it's practical and then would die for you out of pride." Dave murmured thoughtfully, "And Calen's practical side said that Kramon was finished but his pride demands that he end it with honour."

"I didn't realise the importance of that staff." Stuart said, "I took it from him without any trouble and even if he regained it, I could still retake it whenever I felt like it. He's lost control of it and I think that it showed him how close to the end it all was."

"It was a bit sudden though." Dave said.

"Maybe but I think he was near the end, himself." Stuart said, "He looked exhausted. They all think in terms of protecting their families. Maybe it's part of their pride that they care for them but if it could have saved Kramon, he would have brought the whole cave crashing on their heads, ours as well. Instead, he's going to preserve Kramon in the only way he knows. I can respect him but I don't like him, I can't forget the look on his face when he killed that soldier."

"OK but you can accept killings like that as their way though." Dave said, "What about Bastin?"

"What about him?" Stuart asked, "Some will follow him

simply because he's on the Council of Kramon. Calen's ancestors took over the council's powers but Bastin is some sort of descendent. They'll follow him even though, compared to Trey and Calen, he's got no interest in the colonies, just himself."

"Yet Calen was obviously taking more than his fair share." Dave said.

"It's another reason I dislike him but it could be tradition, an emblem of power or just looking out for his family." Stuart explained, "He took extra, yes but not much, it was still pretty meagre."

"He's just what you like, complicated." Dave laughed.

"Maybe but it's how he was brought up. He's adapted enough to allow his people to live though."

They lapsed into a companionable silence. They had not talked as quietly as they had thought and Zagen had very keen hearing but he was satisfied. His family would live and Kramon would be honoured.

There was a portal already materialised when they arrived at the rail yard.

"Stay here, My Lords." Zagen commanded, "I shall go on to the other colony and fetch your followers from there. You prepare to defend this cave and lead your people to the new land."

"Yes My Lord." Stuart chuckled, "Do you have any more orders?"

Zagen looked briefly worried, then caught Stuart's mood.

"It's my practical side, My Lord." he said, "We need you alive."

Stuart and Dave looked at each other aware that they had been overheard but turned as James hurried through the portal.

"We sent Brian to Terzon." he said, "He's too frantic about you to do much. Richard's supervising Adam and Zach while they operate probes in the two colonies. Gable's working the portal while Freddie's getting ready to receive the refugees. Oh, and Richard's also monitoring Merrill while he works on the ship. The translator's taught me how to take over the subway's controls so once we've got everyone, we can shut it down."

"Will they be able to open it up after we're gone?" Stuart asked.

James nodded, "I think you know that this cave was designed to be a final redoubt if the Trastes had attacked or if there was some natural disaster. The colonies could be blasted wide open and trains would still run beyond the damaged area. All three stations have inspection cars that can travel between stations in about eight hours so they can send teams through to retake control."

"I do admire their engineering." Dave said, "I wonder if it rubs off on the Egyptians and explains why the pyramids lasted so long."

"Who knows." Stuart replied, "You see that train over there, it's almost touching the wall. See if you edge it closer or seal off the gap. Shift the portal so that's between the train and the far wall. If there's any sort of fight then we'll be able to fall back along the corridor we make."

"Instead of finding ourselves surrounded." James said, "It makes sense. It's lucky that the ceilings over those storage sidings are the same height as the tunnels. I suppose it's got something to do with checking the guide wheels"

It did not take long to complete their preparations and then it was just a case of waiting. It did not matter that Stuart was able to pace up and down in steps, two or three metres long. Neither did it matter he was in a cave nearly a kilometre deep, five hundred million years in his past and on Mars. A railway station was a railway station and the sense of waiting for the next train pervaded the atmosphere as it did on any line. The first sign that things were moving was when a train passed through the airlock on its way to Bastin's colony.

Stuart's phone rang. Compared to other equipment they used, cell phone technology was basic and simple. Back on Earth it was also the most discreet way of keeping in contact with everyone scattered through the portal system. It still seemed strange to Stuart, that even if he was in deep space in a spacesuit his mother could call asking if he was coming round for tea but this time it was Andy.

"The train's full and it's on its way." he yelled excitedly, "There's more on the station but it'll have to be quick. Bastin's leading soldiers and some villagers, I mean colonists and they're attacking your guards on the stairs to the station."

It sounded like a scuffle and Zach came on the line.

"I think that Zagen's dead." he said just as excitedly, "There's only half a train full and they only just closed the doors in time."

"OK! Both of you calm down." Stuart said sharply, "I don't like having people killed."

"Sorry." Zach replied, "It's the farmers, they're throwing stones still but the guards are using stunners. I did hear one of ours say 'Leave him, Lord Stuart would not want him killed'."

"Thanks for that, Zac." Stuart said, "Let's hope that Zagen is OK."

"The train's in the tunnel." Zach exclaimed, "And I can see Zagen. There's blood pouring from his head and he's in a group on the platform. They look like prisoners…"

There was a brief pause followed by the sound of the phone being dropped, accompanied by the sound of someone being sick. When the phone was picked up, it was Richard speaking.

"They're hacking the prisoners to death." he said, "It's just a mob and out of control. I'm just checking the rest of the colony. I'll get back to you."

Stuart waited impatiently.

"OK I've got Calen with me." Richard said, "We've looked around and there're bodies everywhere, Calen's family didn't make it. A guy called Droben's taken over and according to Calen he's always claimed to be descended from the Lord High Councillor so Bastin must follow him."

"So it's a three way fight, now." Stuart said.

"No, Droben's got most of the guards behind him so he's got the edge but it's more a case of them all settling old feuds and vendettas. I'm beginning to wonder how Calen held them all together."

"I take it that he feels betrayed by us." Stuart said.

"No, his anger's directed at Droben." Richard replied, "He watched your vassals, that's Zagen and Janon, do their best to protect his family but he says that Droben is in charge now and whoever's left must offer allegiance to him."

"OK." Stuart replied, "If I'm reading the indicators correctly then both trains are arriving at the same time. I've got to go."

He called out to James, "Can you stop a train automatically leaving for Colony Prime?"

"No problem." James replied, "I've set it all for manual departures only."

The cave was filling as the trains emptied. Stuart and Dave guided them to the portal but it was taking time.

"There's another train on the way." Andy called to tell him, "There's a lot of your er, people but they're covered by Bastin's soldiers. I think that they're hostages."

"Hostages are no good if we don't know that they're there." Stuart said, "My bet is that our friends will get off first, then when we step forward to look after them, Bastin's men will attack."

He thought for a moment, "James contact the train anyway. Tell them that we can't clear the station for them so we're going to hold them in the tunnel while we sort things out."

He thought again, "How many armed guards do we have left?"

A guard stepped forward, "I heard what you said, My Lord.

We're all waiting for the civilians to get away."

"OK we've stirred things up too much." Stuart said, "What's Bastin trying to do?"

"To take you and establish himself as a strong member of the Council, My Lord. What else?"

"He really thinks that he can rush through the portal and capture them?" Stuart exclaimed, "I don't think so."

"Put like that then neither do I, My Lord." the guard agreed, "But if he claims this cave as his own then he controls the trains and the food supply to Colony Prime."

"Weapons on stun." Stuart said then paused, "I've heard that before."

He shrugged and continued, "Anyway, we take prisoners alive and once through the portal they'll be treated the same as everyone else. You see how Dave's sending people round that train? Can you make some sort of barricade to defend that end of it. We've done our best to immobilise the doors in the train so they can't just pour through it."

"And you want these people through the portal before you release the other train." the guard said.

Stuart nodded.

"Very well, My Lord." the guard replied, "You've done your part now leave so that we can do ours."

"I keep getting told that." Stuart said, "No one thinks that I'm ready to lead troops into battle."

"Go My Lord," the guard chuckled, "A general's place is at headquarters not in the rearguard."

"He's right of course." James said when Stuart joined him in the railway control room, "You should get to the outpost."

"What about you and Dave?" Stuart asked.

"Dave's at the portal shepherding them through. I'm OK here until they override the airlocks."

"Are you sure?" Stuart asked.

"Go." James snapped.

Stuart hesitated as he saw the crowd. The trains had brought nearly two thousand people, nearly three fifths of the colony and they could only pass through the portal in single file. However he was recognised and someone called out, "Make way for Lord Stuart."

The cries continued as he strode forward, the crowd opening then closing behind him until he reached the portal.

"I've been listening over the translators." Dave said before

Stuart could speak, "Go."

Stuart shrugged in defeat and stepped through to the outpost. To his surprise, Merrill hurried over and knelt before him.

"I did not believe that you could save so many, My Lord." he exclaimed, "I have repaired the ship and it is in orbit. It will not make many more journeys but if it can stay in orbit we can transport people up to it, begin their acclimatisation then send them to Earth by portal."

"Where's Calen?" Stuart asked as Freddy arrived.

"At the council chamber." Freddie replied, "He saw Zagen trying to protect his family and when they were overrun he decided it was time to go. He arrived at midnight, buried the staff and swallowed a tablet."

"You should have sent for me." Stuart exclaimed angrily.

"You had already agreed in principle." Freddie replied, "His last instruction was to obey you while you saved the people."

"And in their turn, the people would remember him and Kramon." Stuart smiled, "He was still fighting for his country so let's hope he finds peace."

Stuart had the sense that his job was done. Others were completing the work he had started and it was in its final stages. He had time and more than anything he needed Brian and headed for Terzon to find him.

"All those people dead because of me." he sobbed hugging Brian tightly.

"No, all those other people saved because of you." Brian said softly, "Calen was worn out trying to holding things together and both Bastin and Droben wanted more power. I did try to sort through all the tiny forks and anomalies and it seems that there was going to be a civil war whatever happened and afterwards the colony would be weakened.

"Even the colonists who are left will be better off for a time. At least you're leaving the infrastructure intact and there's more land per person. They won't leave and they won't let their children leave. That's why they waste their energy on portal technology and reactivating the blocking screen. They won't accept that it's pointless."

Stuart nodded, "I suppose you're right."

"You should go back." Brian said, "I'll come with you if you like but there's a lot of people who need to be reassured by you."

Epilogue

Stuart sat on the bank of the Nile, idly watching the world go past. A jet aircraft droned past high above him and he could hear the quiet pounding of the diesels driving the river traffic along but even the feluccas, the traditional sailing boats seemed modern to him. He still thought in terms of reed boats.

Sometimes coincidences were beyond comprehension and for Stuart, the fact that he was sitting on the site of the Council of Kramon was amazing enough. Somewhere beneath him under half a billion years worth of rock displacement lay the remains of Calen and the staff that Calen wanted to protect. That it should now be under Egypt near Abydos where the Kramons made their home was only part of it.

In the confusion of the escapes from the two colonies, families got separated and events were confused. Most of Calen's family had indeed been killed but his youngest son Sarken had been saved. Guards who had switched to Stuart tried to defend the station while the train filled. There was a certain amount of panic and passengers were trying to shut the doors. Janon and Zagen held one open allowing more onto the train. They suddenly darted out and grabbed a boy and threw him onto the train. It was Sarken, Calen's son.

Droben's men poured down onto the station but they were too late to stop the train. Instead they turned their frustration on those left on the platform

The second train from Bastin's colony was finally allowed to arrive. The train arrived at the centre cave and the prisoners were pushed out. For a moment everything was still and silent until a voice called out.

"We'll take you all if you like but you don't have long to decide."

Realising that their ambush had failed the guards charged out and just stopped looking around for the cave seemed empty.

As they got their bearings, they recognised the barrier at the far side of the cave. Bastin's men may also have been full of blood lust earlier but now reaction had set in and they were at an emotional low unwilling or unable to adapt to an organised opposition. Maybe they just saw a route to Earth.

One of Bastin's guards reacted. He shepherded the hostages towards the barricade and as they reached safety so he followed them.

Still there were no protests as two more guards followed. At first, the remainder just chose to stand and watch.

"It's your last chance." Dave called out again, "Any more for Earth?"

He was surprised when the remainder of the guards dropped their weapons and meekly stepped forward leaving the cave deserted.

Stuart had no idea of what happened to the colony then and, neither did he want to know. Instead he considered the real mystery. Over a couple of generations Sarken's name changed to sound more like Serquet. Serquet meant Scorpion and the first recorded kings of Egypt were known as the Scorpion Kings.

Peter Apps

Peter Apps lives in England, and The Long Way Round was his first novel to be followed by Time Askew and Deja Vu To The Nth. For a complete list, please visit his website at sjtales.co.uk

He was born in 1948 and has lived in Sheerness, Kent for most of his life. The Isle of Sheppey where Sheerness is situated has a long, rich history has always fascinated Peter. History might seem a far cry from Science Fiction but imagining life in a Roman settlement is imagining a world just as alien as a distant planet.

Although he worked in a series of routine jobs he likes to do his own thing when he can. For example, all his computers are Microsoft free zones and prefers to use Linux. He has always had an interest in science, especially Astronomy. Now that planets have been discovered around other suns, he feels that the time is coming when we could discover intelligent life out there.

Other interests include classical music and jazz. He also likes to settle down in the evening watching a good film and enjoying a nice glass of bitter and occasionally visit his local for a chat over a friendly drink.

The author is just a click away by email, peter@sjtales.uk.